ONE MORE CHRISTMAS
AT THE CASTLE

ONE MORE CHRISTMAS AT THE CASTLE

Trisha Ashley

PENGUIN BOOKS

TRANSWORLD PUBLISHERS
Penguin Random House, One Embassy Gardens,
8 Viaduct Gardens, London SW11 7BW
www.penguin.co.uk

Transworld is part of the Penguin Random House group of companies
whose addresses can be found at global.penguinrandomhouse.com

Penguin
Random House
UK

First published in Great Britain in 2021 by Bantam Press
an imprint of Transworld Publishers
Penguin paperback edition published 2022

A CIP catalogue record for this book
is available from the British Library.

ISBN
9781529177008

Typeset in Adobe Garamond by Jouve (UK), Milton Keynes.
Printed and bound in Great Britain by Clays Ltd, Elcograf S.p.A.

The authorized representative in the EEA is Penguin Random House Ireland,
Morrison Chambers, 32 Nassau Street, Dublin D02 YH68.

Penguin Random House is committed to a sustainable future
for our business, our readers and our planet. This book is made
from Forest Stewardship Council® certified paper.

To the Rev. Joanna Yates,
for sharing the true spirit of Christmas!

Character List

Sabine Powys, wealthy widowed owner of Mitras Castle
Asa Powys, Sabine's late husband
Lucy Ripley, companion and a cousin of Sabine's father, Perry Mordue
Nigel Ripley, her older brother, a bachelor antiquarian bookseller
Xan Fellowes, historian and biographer, Sabine's godson
Olive Melling, née Powys, Asa's second cousin
Frank Melling, her husband, a semi-retired cosmetic surgeon
Dominic Melling, their son, a dentist
Nancy Kane, academic turned vicar, now retired
Timothy Makepeace, family solicitor and old friend
Sophie, his divorced granddaughter, now living with him
Maria, housekeeper at Mitras Castle
Andy, Maria's husband, was the gardener at Mitras Castle
Dido Jones, owner of Heavenly Houseparties
Henry, Dido's business partner and friend
Paul and Celia Sedley Jones, Dido's grandparents

Prologue

The Die Is Cast

Mitras Castle
Early November 2018

Winter comes early to the remote uplands of Northumberland, where the remaining grey stones of the plundered Roman Wall cling like a straight, ragged-edged grey ribbon across the irregular landscape, punctuated at intervals by a series of half-excavated forts with adjoining visitor centres.

By October, the sound of curlews calling high above in a clear blue sky, the blowing wildflowers and the contented bleating of sheep are but very distant memories, as are the voices of the hikers and tourists. Many of those visitors thought what a lovely spot this must be to live in and how lucky the local inhabitants were, although they might just have changed their minds if they saw it as it was now, when winter's icy fingers were trying to throttle the life out of it and it seemed improbable that spring would ever manage to pry them loose.

Rowenhead, a few low stone cottages and the remains of a small Roman fort, was hunkered down below the ancient wall, divided from it by a narrow, meandering tarmac road. There was a neat, square lodge and a pair of crumbling, eagle-topped gateposts, guarding the dark maw of a drive that vanished down through woodlands to the hidden splendours of Mitras Castle.

Earlier that day, a small red sports car had emerged from it on to the road and sped off in the direction of Newcastle, like a bright bead sliding along a greased grey string.

Now, under the heavy sky, the car was returning, swooping down through the tunnel of trees and coming to a halt on the sweep of gravel before the tall, battlemented wing that had been grafted on to the original old manor house, like a large baroque chunk of grit adhering to a grey pearl.

The house stood at the head of a deep, narrow, tree-lined valley, looking down across its sweep of lawn on to the sheltered terraces below, through which a stream ran, burbled and fell in a series of small waterfalls and pools. Far below, where it spread into a lake, was the verdigris-patinated domed top of a summerhouse.

Home, thought Sabine Powys, levering herself from the driver's seat, something that had never caused her any difficulty until recently, when her traitorous body had started to betray her.

She was a tall, thin and elderly woman, with a brittle cloud of pale golden hair and a face boldly made up in the style of her youth, with dark arched eyebrows and bright pink lips. She'd never been truly beautiful, but managed to give the impression of it, one that still lingered, along with the ghost of a slightly raffish charm.

Nearly a century ago, a whole colony of small, glossy creatures had been sacrificed to make the long, sleek fur coat she wore, but although she was fond of animals, the fact that it was so old and had also belonged to her beloved mother meant this caused her no qualms.

She was not a very sentimental or over-sensitive woman, although charm could ooze from every pore at the flick of an inner switch and she had always been the life and soul of any party . . . until Asa had died six years ago and most of her life and soul had gone with him.

Maria, looking down at her employer from the first-floor landing window of the tower, turned and scuttled through to the old house and down the stairs to the Garden Hall, where she whipped her coat off a peg and let herself out, closing the door behind her with a click of the lock. Then she hurried off round the back of the house and up the drive, making for her own cottage next to the entrance gates.

Mrs Powys would not be pleased to find her note, informing her she'd left a pan of soup and a lamb casserole ready to be heated up for dinner, with a cold dessert in the fridge.

Usually at times like this, when there was no live-in household help to be had, she stayed to serve the meal before going home, leaving it to Lucy Ripley, that poor excuse of a woman who called Mrs Powys cousin, to clear and stack the dishwasher, then make the coffee. But now that Maria's husband, Andy, had had a stroke, things were different. Her priorities had entirely changed.

She'd explained to Mrs Powys this morning that she wouldn't be able to carry on working her usual hours for the foreseeable future . . . and perhaps ever again. It was, she had told her, in the hands of God.

Then she'd stood listening with downcast dark eyes and in stubborn silence to Mrs Powys's reply, for there was no point in trying to persuade her Lady that her comfort and convenience was no longer Maria's priority or that, once Andy was back at the cottage, she would not be able to resume her usual duties.

The cottage was rent free and she and Andy received generous salaries. Maria was grateful for these and many other perks – like the soft red cashmere coat she was wearing, which Mrs Powys had decided didn't suit her.

But right now, none of that seemed as important as driving to the hospital to sit with her husband for as long as they would let her stay, before returning, late and weary, to an empty house.

And as she drove nervously along the narrow road (Andy had always done most of the driving, the small Citroën his pride and joy), she wondered briefly where Mrs Powys had been today. It wasn't her day to go to the beauty salon in Hexham, her only regular weekly expedition in winter, weather permitting. Maria might have asked Lucy, but as usual, as soon as Mrs Powys had gone out, Lucy had seized the opportunity to retire to her room with a box of chocolates and one of the romantic novels she was addicted to, with a half-naked man on the cover looking as if he'd been oiled ready for spit-roasting. And since Maria didn't hold much opinion of most men, she thought it would serve him right . . . though her own kind, gentle Andy was different. He was the reason she had remained here all these years, long after her parents had fled back to their native Corfu, unable to cope with the bleakness of winter at the Castle.

Maria, hands clenched on the steering wheel, began to murmur a Greek prayer from her childhood that had lain dormant in her memory, until fear pulled it back to the surface, the words familiar and comforting.

Sabine Powys let her coat and silk scarf fall on to a dark, carved chair in the huge entrance hall, and they slithered, snake-like, on to the tiled floor, with its central mosaic depicting Mithras.

She picked up a pile of letters from a side table, her lips

tightening when she noticed the folded sheet on top, with her own name written in Maria's familiar hand.

She carried the post into the sitting room, where she switched on the lights against the darkening afternoon. Feeling chilled to the bone by more than the ice-spikes of the wind outside, she suddenly yearned for the comfort of hot tea and a roaring fire in the grate, despite the clanking but efficient old radiators.

She set a light to the laid fire herself, before reading Maria's note, the contents of which weren't a complete surprise, for she had recognized that stubborn expression on her housekeeper's face that morning.

Andy was no longer in danger and would be allowed home long before Christmas, so things should eventually become easier for Maria . . . which was just as well, because she would need her in the coming months . . . But she would have to try to find live-in help again, too, for Lucy had proved a sore disappointment in that respect.

She was not, she told herself, unreasonable, and if the stroke had left Andy unable to carry out his gardening duties, she would pension him off. She could even install a stairlift in the cottage and perhaps an easily accessible shower room, instead of the antiquated bath . . . That would make things easier for them.

Sabine, having thought about it, determined to put those alterations in train tomorrow.

The fire was now glowing and she began to feel better, a little less of the shakiness caused by anger – mostly with her own rebellious body, which was striking off on a path she had not set for it. After that earlier barrage of tests, she'd guessed what the verdict would be . . . but the progression into pain and debility mapped out for her today, the talk of painkillers and palliative care – no, that she *hadn't* been prepared for. And she wasn't having it.

She liked to be in control of every situation, and now, with new determination, she decided that she *would* damned well stay in control and play her own endgame, not have the consultant's version forced on her.

Going to the door, she shouted impatiently for Lucy, who scuttled in a few minutes later, looking flustered, dishevelled and with a smear of chocolate on one side of her mouth.

She always reminded Sabine of a mouse, with her small face pinched in around a pointed nose, dull brown hair cut into a childish bob and bright, inquisitive dark eyes.

Sabine had never been fond of rodents, with the possible exception of those that formed the fabric of her fur coat.

Lucy's brother, Nigel, who was taller, plumper and more unctuous, was, Sabine thought, more of a glossy water vole – a Mr Ratty.

She really should have smelled a rat when Nigel wrote to her, saying how alone she must feel now and in need of companionship, then hinting that his sister, also alone and out of work, would be glad of a comfortable home. But after all, Sabine thought now, if it was such a good idea, why didn't he have Lucy to live with him in the cottage attached to his antiquarian bookshop in Alnwick?

She must have been mad to have offered Lucy a home in exchange for a little housework and secretarial duties, even if it was almost impossible to get live-in staff any more.

As to companionship, Sabine considered Lucy's intellectual capacity to be on a par with a not-very-bright toddler, and in any case, she was happier dwelling in thoughts of the past now, walking hand in hand with Asa among her happy, sun-filled memories.

'Oh, Cousin Sabine, I'm so sorry that I didn't hear you come in, or I'd—' Lucy began in a twittery, high-pitched voice even before she was through the door, but Sabine cut her short.

'Never mind that, Lucy. Fetch me some hot tea – make sure the kettle is boiling this time – and then you'd better do something about dinner. Here, read Maria's note.'

She thrust the folded paper into Lucy's hand. 'She's bunked off to the hospital to see Andy, but I suppose warming soup and putting a casserole in the oven isn't beyond your capabilities?'

'No, of course not,' Lucy assured her, after scanning the note quickly and then, looking more like a terrified mouse than ever, scurried off towards the kitchen, which was in the Castle's old wing.

Sabine knew it was more than likely she would allow the soup to boil over, and burn the casserole, but she had more important things to think about now, plans to make . . .

She sat down at a small papier mâché desk and slowly the ideas that had been forming at the back of her mind since that first hospital appointment began to come together in her head: she'd hold one final Christmas house party at the Castle, a gathering of the last distant dregs of her family – and of Asa's, too, for she'd include his distant cousins, the Mellings, although they hadn't spoken to her since Asa had died without leaving them anything. In fact, neither he nor Sabine had made a will, feeling somehow that it tempted fate . . .

But now fate had crept up on her and she couldn't afford to put it off any longer – not when it was the fate of her beloved Mitras Castle at stake.

The house party would help her make up her mind on *that* one . . . with the fall-back option of leaving it, suitably endowed, to the National Trust.

Sabine was very wealthy, having inherited both the house

and a fortune from her mother, the last of the Archbold family who had added the battlemented wing early in the nineteenth century. Her father, Perry Mordue, had left what money he had to her younger half-sister, Faye, thinking that made things fair, though Sabine considered it yet another betrayal, like the way he'd married her mother's nurse so soon after her death.

If *Faye* hadn't died so young, she'd have been next in line to inherit – and, by now, Sabine would definitely have taken steps to ensure that didn't happen.

She pushed the idea of Faye away from her; she was out of the reckoning and would be no more than the ghost at the feast.

Some of the guests she'd invite for Christmas would be more welcome than others. Her godson, dear Xan, must be there; she could see another letter from him among her unopened mail. He wanted to write Asa's biography and she had been putting him off, but now she'd give him the answer he wanted . . . on her own terms.

Lucy crept in with a tea tray, laid it at Sabine's elbow and tiptoed out again, as if hoping to go unnoticed, despite the nervous rattling of the crockery. Sabine poured a cup of Earl Grey, added a dash of milk and then unlocked a little drawer at the back of the desk. Taking out the last report she'd received from a private detective she'd hired, she read it through, frowning.

Her half-sister had run away at seventeen – to America, it transpired – but when she was twenty-one, had returned with an illegitimate child in tow, to claim the money their father had left her.

The family solicitor had informed Sabine, of course, and of the child's subsequent adoption by a relative of Faye's mother.

At the time, Sabine had been curious enough to hire a

private investigator to provide her with photos of the boy, but he'd proved to be a small, brown-haired and insignificant child. And since in all the following years he'd never contacted her, she'd assumed he either didn't know about the connection, or didn't care.

But after her diagnosis, Sabine had found herself feeling suddenly curious about what he'd made of his life.

The private detective's report had been a bit of a surprise, not only because that nondescript child had become the curator of a large private art collection in California, but because he, in turn, had fathered an illegitimate child of his own . . . another cuckoo in the nest, it seemed, for his adoptive mother to take on.

There had followed some brief details about the life and career of this second child – now a woman in her thirties – and suddenly, Sabine could see how she might weave this particular thread into her pattern, to provide some extra and entirely secret amusement for herself.

Not only that, but it would solve all the difficulties over Maria and of catering for her Christmas house party in one go.

She'd perhaps left it a little late to arrange, but then, she'd always found that there was no problem that couldn't be fixed if you threw enough money at it.

She sat there, sipping tea and plotting, thinking that it would be fun to direct her cast of characters in the way she wanted, like a vintage murder mystery, where everyone was invited to a remote house and then events unfolded.

Of course, in her plot there would be no body in the library, or anywhere else, for Sabine Powys was not about to leave the building just yet.

She took a large pad of heavy cream writing paper from one of the desk pigeon holes, picked up a pen and began to write.

Christmas at the Castle
Cast of Characters

<u>Sabine Powys</u>, wealthy widowed owner of Mitras Castle

<u>Lucy Ripley</u>, companion and a cousin of Sabine's father, Perry Mordue

<u>Nigel Ripley</u>, her older brother, a bachelor antiquarian bookseller

<u>Xan Fellowes</u>, historian and biographer, Sabine's godson

<u>Olive Melling</u>, née Powys, Asa's second cousin

<u>Frank Melling</u>, her husband, a semi-retired cosmetic surgeon

<u>Dominic Melling</u>, their son, a dentist

Sabine's pen paused here. A dentist didn't sound quite the thing for her cast list, even if he did only take private patients and called himself by some fancy name – 'cosmetic orthodontist', was it?

To leaven the mix, she added the name of her oldest – indeed, only – close friend:

<u>Nancy Kane</u>, academic turned vicar, now retired

She put down her pen and looked over what she'd written. They would be eight for Christmas dinner if everyone accepted her invitation, and she'd be very surprised if they did not.

There might even be another guest or two, for now she came to think of it, she would need to consult her solicitor at some point soon, so why not invite him to join the house party? He and Asa had been old friends, after all. She remembered that his divorced granddaughter had recently gone to live with him, and included her, too. Along with Dominic Melling, she would supply some younger company for Xan.

Timothy Makepeace, family solicitor and old friend
Sophie, his divorced granddaughter, now living with him

She laid down the pen with finality, feeling suddenly tired.

But as Scarlett O'Hara (a heroine she rather admired, except for her obsession with the milky Ashley) said at the end of *Gone with the Wind*, tomorrow was another day.

1

Disconnected

Dido
27 November

I flew across to California to spend my annual pre-Christmas week with my father, though it has to be admitted that he wouldn't have noticed if I hadn't. Dad was both absent-minded and unpaternal to the point of forgetting my existence, unless I actually appeared under his nose, the evidence of his brief lapse from the pursuit of academia some thirty-five years before.

My ex-fiancé, Liam, suggested in his parting letter that the lack of any paternal figure in my life was a big part of my problem . . . though actually, I didn't *have* any problems until that point, when he ran off with Mia, so I'd no idea what he meant by that.

My father, Thomas, was of medium height, stooping and scholarly, with a narrow, beaky face that looked as if it might once have been slammed shut inside a large book, possibly his own, *The Cautious Conservator: An argument against excessive restoration.*

That was hardly a runaway bestseller, but at least the fact

that it was now in its sixth edition showed it was a valuable resource in his own rather rarefied field.

On my arrival, he seemed mildly pleased to see me, once he'd got over the surprise. Luckily, he must have told his employer about my email announcing my arrival date before it went out of his head, because a long, lush limo met me at the airport and whisked me to the mansion where Thomas both lived and worked: he had a small cottage in the grounds. He was in charge of an extensive private art collection, which had its own gallery wing attached to the main house, most of it underground, iceberg fashion.

At night, I often wondered whether I was sleeping over a Matisse, or possibly a cubist Picasso, which might account for my often fractured dreams when I was staying there. I don't think it can have been subterranean surrealism, though, which would have given me proper nightmares.

Dad was also surprised to be reminded that Granny Celia and her friend, Dora, were somewhere in the middle of their latest long cruise, even though I could see a series of bright postcards propped along the mantelpiece, probably put there by one of the housekeeping staff, who came down to the cottage daily, like invisible house elves, while he was at the gallery.

Granny – Celia Sedley Jones – adopted Thomas, the illegitimate son of a distant relative, when he was a small child, and when I came along in my turn she became my guardian: dumping your inconvenient offspring on Celia seemed to have become a family habit. I called her Granny, anyway, my other one, Dad's birth mother, having died not long after depositing her cuckoo in Celia's nest.

My family, or what little of it there was, was not so much dysfunctional as dislocated.

My stay with Dad was as uneventful as usual, but pleasant.

I had a tour of the gallery and saw the latest acquisitions, was invited to dinner twice with the millionaire owner of all those hidden treasures and a young wife I hadn't seen before, also presumably recently acquired.

Other than that, we saw something of Dad's friends from the university, where he was occasionally persuaded to give a lecture, and with whose family he always spent Christmas Day. They collected him – he'd have forgotten what day it was, otherwise.

They had a large family and I'd spent a lot of time with them when I was younger, learning to surf and skateboard, getting a California tan in the process. It was good catching up with them again and hearing the latest news.

In fact, it was a very relaxing break, apart from the long flight home again, which as usual rendered me spaced out with jet lag and rattling with airline peanuts and pretzels. It always took me a day and night to adjust my vision from warmly glorious Californian Technicolor, to monochrome, dark and drippy November in Cheshire.

Still, the thought that Christmas was on the horizon was very consoling because soon Henry and I would be off to provide seasonal cooking, comfort and cheer to one of our regular clients, and too busy working to even notice what the weather outside was doing.

Henry was both my business partner and my best friend – or one of them, since I also had Charlotte, even if I only now saw her very infrequently.

Henry and I, on the other hand, couldn't *miss* seeing each other, since we occupied twin lodges on either side of the gated drive to Cranberry Chase, a bijou Queen Anne des res that belonged to a distant relative of his. His family were cash-strapped, but had a wealth of rich and posh connections.

So there we were: Henry was the Grace and I was the Favour, which is why *he* had the lodge with the large extension on the back and all mod cons, while mine was the original box, though with the outside loo and coalhouse now knocked through into a tiny bathroom. It had the kind of shower cubicle you need to stand in with your elbows clamped to your sides, feeling as if at any moment you might be sucked up a force-beam to a starship, starkers and slippery as an eel with soap.

Henry had filled my fridge with fresh food and drink before my return, but then left me alone to recover. But as usual, by the next morning I was more or less back in my right mind and ready for action.

This was just as well, because as I was finishing my second round of buttered toast and Marmite, he sent me a text:

Disaster, darling! Come quickly – I'll put the coffee on!

I wasn't unduly worried by this, because he's such a drama queen – it's his way of making life exciting and squeezing the last drop of enjoyment out of everything.

We run our business, Heavenly Houseparties, from the huge kitchen extension at the back of his lodge, where there's plenty of room to spread out the paperwork on the pine table and stick up the charts of our bookings – *and* our projected absences, during which we both had other fish to fry – so I texted back that I was on my way and headed over.

Henry kissed me on both cheeks rather distractedly and exclaimed, in a voice of sepulchral doom: 'You have come!'

Then he led the way into the kitchen, where he handed me a large mug of coffee.

'Though given the bad news, it ought to be a stiff gin and

tonic!' he said, in more natural tones, but since he wasn't looking desperately worried, I assumed the problem wasn't life or death.

Henry had curling, rose-gold hair, pink cheeks and round, bright blue eyes, so he looked like a Botticelli cherub with attitude . . . until you noticed the short, square, muscular, rugby-playing physique. His curls were currently dishevelled from having agitated fingers raked through them, but he stopped now after suddenly catching sight of himself in the mirror and asked if I thought it was a good look.

'No, people will simply think you've forgotten to brush your hair,' I said, taking a gulp of good coffee. 'And I couldn't have drunk alcohol anyway, because I'll have to drive over to Granny's house in a bit, to make sure Mrs Frant has watered the succulents this week. It's a pity Granny couldn't take them on the cruise with her, because she does fret about them.'

Henry abandoned the mirror and plumped down opposite me. 'Don't you want to know what the bad news is?'

'You haven't had a single date from that upmarket dating site you paid so much money to join, while I've been away?' I guessed.

'No, it isn't that . . . though actually, I haven't had a single bite yet, you're quite right,' he said. 'But this is *business* bad: Lady B has done a Grinch and cancelled Christmas!'

'What, Lady Bugle has cancelled her booking?' I exclaimed, astounded, because we'd catered for her Christmas house parties for four years running.

'Tootled her tin trumpet and toddled off,' agreed Henry. 'I thought she was as good as money in the bank.'

You certainly *needed* a lot of money to afford the services of Heavenly Houseparties – 'complete, carefree house party catering: from a weekend to a month' – and especially the Christmas bookings, which came at a premium.

'Why?' I demanded. 'I mean, it's nearly the end of November, a bit late in the day for her to cancel, or for *us* to find another gig.'

'Family illness, apparently. You can't really argue with that, and she said she wasn't expecting her deposit back.'

I sighed. 'It must be serious then, because even though she's *loaded*, she always expects her money's worth out of us, and more, doesn't she?'

We did work very hard for our money, though: we cooked, served, tidied, made beds and generally took the stress out of house parties (Henry even did a very grand butler, if the host was out to impress), but it's surprising how many of our clients seemed to expect us to do all the cleaning and provide twenty-four-hour room service, too.

'She only told me yesterday, so I suppose I'd better change our availability on the website,' Henry said. 'I could try contacting people who enquired about a Christmas booking and were turned away, I suppose. There was that woman quite recently who was very pressing and didn't want to take no for an answer.'

'They've probably all made alternative arrangements by now,' I said rather gloomily. Our Christmas booking is so lucrative we don't have to take another one till Easter.

'It gets even worse, Dido,' Henry said. 'If I'm not away working, Mummy will force me to join the annual family gathering instead, and apart from feeling I'd rather be shut into a small walled town rife with bubonic plague, I simply can't afford all those presents.'

'I suppose that's the drawback with having so many richer relatives,' I said, and of course, *we'd* be much richer if we worked for most of the year, and not just a few selected weeks of it. But we preferred to earn just enough to keep us during our precious time off, when Henry worked on his increasingly popular blog and I wrote my recipe and reminiscence books.

It was a way of life that had worked well for us both for ten years now.

'Well, Granny Celia and Dora will still be away and I've just seen Dad, so if we don't get a booking I won't have anywhere else to go.'

'You could come to the gathering of the clan with me,' suggested Henry.

I shuddered, remembering the year I'd tried that, before the business took off. 'No, thank you. I'm still traumatized by the experience of dancing the Gay Gordons with your cousin Hector.'

'He's very *hearty*,' he agreed, which was one way of putting it.

'We could simply both stay at home over Christmas and pretend we're away,' I pointed out, and he brightened slightly.

'Of course, Mummy would find out eventually, but by then it would be too late. We could overindulge in the eating and drinking, play Scrabble and watch old films back-to-back.'

If those were the Interests he'd listed on that dating site, it wasn't really surprising he hadn't had any takers . . . though it sounded fun to me.

'There we are then, we have a contingency plan if we don't get a last-minute booking,' I said. 'We could make up some of the shortfall by taking a spring half-term post, as well as our usual Easter booking next year.'

I got up and stretched – economy aeroplane seats are cramped and not designed for any known human form, especially one six foot tall in her bare flippers, and my spine was still kinked into knots.

'I'd better leave you to it, Henry, and get over to Great

Mumming to make sure Granny's succulents still *are* succulent. I'll see you later.'

I grew up in Great Mumming, a pleasant small market town in West Lancashire, set where the fertile farmlands start to rise towards the moors. Granny's cottage was right on the edge of it and built from mellow old bricks. The central part dated back to the early 1800s, though it had seen a lot of changes since then.

When Granny and her husband, Paul, had bought it, soon after their marriage, it had been in need of total renovation and they'd worked hard to turn it into a happy family home, completed by the adoption of my father.

I'm very sure that Granny hadn't been expecting to have to start all over again with a newborn – me – when she was widowed and in her late fifties. It was lucky that she and her best friend, Dora, also a widow, had by then decided to pool their resources and share the cottage – and, as it turned out, the childcare.

Mrs Frant, Granny's long-term cleaner, lived in one of a nearby row of terraced houses and kept an eye on the cottage when Granny and Dora were away. Once Dora, who was younger than Granny, had retired from teaching, they could indulge their shared passion for travelling outside the school holidays, so nowadays they seemed to be away more often than they were at home. Luckily they were both well enough off to globetrot – or globecruise – to their hearts' content.

Mrs Frant had a major fear of burglars learning about their habits, so popped in and out of the cottage several times a day, opening the curtains in the morning, drawing them at night and making sure the switches that caused random lights to go on and off, like a mini version of the Blackpool Illuminations, were still working. She religiously reset the burglar alarm after every visit, too, not just at night.

She refused to let the man who came to do the garden into the house, which was why she was in charge of the row of huge, tree-like succulents in the conservatory, though unfortunately, she didn't have green fingers.

As soon as I'd got there and turned off the alarm, I checked on them, but they looked fine to me, and the heating was kept on a low setting, so they never got too cold.

Everything in the cottage was dusted and polished immaculately, the air smelling of lavender, beeswax and, indefinably, *home*: I might always have felt like a giant and inconvenient cuckoo in the nest, but there had been a place for me there.

The mahogany wall clock ticked, the old floorboards creaked and sighed, and, apart from the pile of post on a small gateleg table in the hall, you would have thought the owners had just stepped out for a walk, rather than being afloat on a far-flung ocean, cocktail of the day in hand.

I noticed one of the kitchen taps had begun to drip, so I changed the old-fashioned rubber washer before it became any worse – I'm nothing if not practical – then went through the post, tossing the junk in the recycling bin and putting anything else in the bureau. Granny and Dora preferred not to be bothered while on their travels, unless it was something really urgent. There was nothing else to do, so I'd put my coat back on and headed for the door when, with perfect timing, Mrs Frant arrived and insisted on setting the burglar alarm for me, as if I'd never done it before.

As we walked down the path, I told her our Christmas booking had fallen through so I might be able to come over occasionally if we didn't manage to get another one, and she said it made no difference to her, she'd be keeping an eye on the place as usual, Christmas or no Christmas, but to let her know.

'I will, and I'll be here again next week anyway, whatever happens,' I promised. I had her Christmas present from Granny Celia and Dora to leave in the cottage, along with one from me, and all our cards.

We stood at the gate for a few minutes while Mrs Frant filled me in on the local gossip, then she toddled off home, her grey curls bobbing and her long tweedy cape flapping, looking just like Margaret Rutherford in a Miss Marple film.

Henry's predilection for old movies had permanently warped my subconscious.

Time was getting on and I suddenly decided to treat myself to lunch at the café in the town square before going home. I'd only just parked and got out, when I spotted Liam, my loathly ex-fiancé, pushing a monstrous baby buggy along the street, in which were the twins, side by side, and a toddler seated above and behind them – followed by a very pregnant Mia. She had to walk behind, because the ginormous buggy took up most of the pavement. I knew they had an older child, too, presumably at school.

The noise from two screaming infants and a toddler who was having a tantrum was clearly audible even after I'd flung myself back in the car and closed the door. Liam and Mia both looked harassed, but I knew from previous inadvertent encounters that, on sight of me, those expressions would immediately switch to a strange mix of defiant guilt and smug domestic bliss. If fecundity was an Olympic sport, they'd both be wearing gold medals.

This was extremely irritating, for although their double betrayal – Mia had been a friend – had hurt at the time, it seemed now as if it had happened to someone else. I was only avoiding them because it was annoying they thought I still cared, or envied them.

I bent my head down as if I'd dropped my keys on the floor, then as soon as the wailing receded, I sat up again. I'd gone right off the idea of lunch now and was just about to start the car and head home, when my phone burst into that mad xylophone thing that I'm always meaning to change. It was Henry.

'You'll never believe this, Dido, but not ten minutes after I changed our Christmas availability on the website, we had a new booking. Haven't you always *yearned* to spend December in a castle in Northumberland?'

'Frankly, *no*. It's bleak as hell up there in winter,' I told him, shivering, but he was too jubilant to listen.

'Come home, darling, all is forgiven!' he said, then rang off.

Sabine

I spent a satisfactory morning, securing the services of Heavenly Houseparties and discussing the arrangements with a young man who, of course, had no idea that I'd bought off his former client, Lady Bugle!

After that, it was necessary to put Lucy in the picture about both my illness and my plans, even if not the *entire* picture, but a rather washy watercolour version.

After lunch, I explained that I'd recently seen a hospital consultant and knew that I wasn't long for this world, a saccharine euphemism I despised, but which I knew would resonate with her.

I allowed her to run the full gamut of her emotions, from blank incomprehension, via shocked surprise, to lachrymose sympathy, but once she'd reached the stage of emitting faint moans and wringing her thin hands, like an actress in a cut-price *Macbeth* production, I finally snapped.

'Oh, never mind all that, Lucy! I hate fuss.'

'But it's so dreadful!' Lucy wailed. 'What are you going to *do*?'

'Well, *die*, obviously, though not just yet,' I said tartly. 'First, I need to put my affairs in order and make a will, once I've decided what will best secure the future of Mitras Castle. And to that end,' I continued, 'I've decided to hold one last Christmas house party and invite all the family . . . or what's left of it. I want to look them over, before I finally make up my mind.'

Lucy gazed at me, her mouth half open, and then surprised me by blurting out: 'But Nigel and I are your *only* relatives, aren't we? I mean, we're your father's cousins!'

'Second cousins,' I agreed.

'Nigel says that if Faye was still alive, or had married and had children, things would be different . . .' Lucy began revealingly, then tailed off, for the name of my half-sister is not usually uttered aloud in this house.

'That's immaterial, because she didn't,' I snapped, reflecting that Lucy wasn't quite as stupid as she looked, and also that it sounded as if she and her brother had already been anticipating their eventual inheritance.

'In any case, the question of who inherits as my nearest relative only applies if I die without making a will, and I've no intention of doing so.'

'No, Cousin Sabine,' she agreed meekly. 'But there *aren't* any other close relatives, are there?'

'No. When I came to think about it, I realized the direct line had dwindled almost entirely away. But of course, there's Olive Melling, Asa's second cousin.'

'But . . . Cousin Sabine! Surely you'd prefer Mitras Castle to descend in your own family, rather than your late husband's?'

'Since you and Nigel are related to my father, a Mordue, rather than from my mother, whose family built the Castle, that doesn't really seem to make much difference,' I said. 'The Mellings have a son, too, and I do want to ensure there will be some continuity of ownership in the Castle's future.'

Of course, I had no real idea of leaving the Castle to the Mellings, but Lucy rose to the bait beautifully.

'Nigel might still get married,' she said quickly.

'As far as I can see, he's wedded to his old books and his amateur theatricals,' I said. 'But I'll have him over, and the Mellings, and I'm sure seeing them all again will help me come to a decision. I'm inviting a couple more people to leaven the mix too. Xan, for instance.'

'Xan?' Lucy echoed blankly.

'Xan Fellowes, my godson – you've met him here at past Christmas parties. He was Asa's godson, as well as mine, and he was very fond of him.'

'But of course I remember him, because he's so *very* handsome, just like my idea of a romantic hero!' she simpered.

I shot her a scornful look; she's more than old enough to distinguish real life from that found between the pages of the novels she reads.

'I've already invited Xan to spend the month of December with us, because he's going to write a biography of Asa and needs access to his papers, but the rest of them can just come for Christmas – and you can write the invitations, Lucy.'

I grinned, a little maliciously, I fear. 'Even the Mellings will come, if I make it sound like an offer they can't refuse!'

She blinked and then began to count on her fingers. 'It will be quite a small party, then, Cousin Sabine? Me and Nigel, the three Mellings, Xan . . .'

'Plus my dear old friend Nancy and also, I hope, my solicitor, Timothy Makepeace, and possibly his granddaughter.'

Lucy began to count all over again. 'I think that makes . . . ten, including yourself? But do you think Maria will be able to cope with a houseful of guests?'

'Of course not, but I've already thought of that and engaged a couple who will live in and take care of the cooking and housekeeping over December. It will mean that Maria can take some time off when Andy returns home, and then she'll be able to come back to work refreshed in the New Year.'

'You've found some live-in staff?' Lucy exclaimed, surprised.

'I have, though only temporary. And I'm sure, Lucy, that *you* will step up to the mark and help make things run smoothly behind the scenes. Another pair of hands, however inept, is always useful.'

'You know I'd work my fingers to the bone for you,' Lucy assured me earnestly, but I reflected that there was so little flesh on them that that wouldn't take very long.

2

Accommodations

I stopped at the supermarket and then returned to my lodge, still feeling somewhat ruffled and also hollow, so I assuaged the howling wolves of hunger before heading over to Henry's to hear all about our new Christmas booking.

I must still have looked a little less than my usual serene and sunny self, because once we were in the kitchen, he asked: 'Are you cross with me for accepting this new Christmas booking without consulting you first, darling?'

He'd automatically switched on the coffee machine and popped in my favourite pod. His glass teapot was on the table, full of some pale green fluid with drowned flowers floating in it, but I'm not a fan of any kind of tea, including those made from random berries, herbs and spices.

'No, of course I'm not!' I assured him. 'We need the booking and we were lucky to get one at all at this late date.'

'Well, something's up, Dido,' he said, putting a mug in front of me. 'What is it, O Queen of Carthage?'

I smiled at this old joke and said wryly, 'You know me too well, Henry, although I'm not *upset*, just a bit . . . unsettled, because I saw Liam, Mia and the youngest children in Great Mumming.'

'Oh, right!' he said, light dawning. 'And did they give you pitying looks, before treating you to a demonstration of marital bliss and Happy Families?'

'No, because luckily I saw them before they spotted me. I'd just got out of the car in the market square, so I dived straight back in and hid until they were past. Mia is pregnant again.'

'My God!' he said with feeling. 'Haven't they heard of television and box sets?'

I ignored that. 'They had the twins and the toddler in one enormous kind of two-tier baby buggy that took up the entire width of the pavement, so everyone else got pushed off.'

'People must have thought the circus had come to town,' said Henry.

'It certainly *sounded* like it, because the twins were howling like banshees and the toddler was throwing a roaring tantrum. And I don't think it can be good for a child to turn that shade of dark puce,' I added.

He grinned engagingly. 'Only think, if Liam hadn't suddenly dumped you and taken off with Mia, all that family bliss could have been yours.'

'I know, that was the thought that really unsettled me.'

I shuddered, then took a reviving draught of coffee. 'When Liam and I used to talk about our future lives together, we agreed we only wanted one, or perhaps two, children.'

'These childhood sweetheart things rarely work out long term, Dido. Too claustrophobic.'

'We did spend a lot of time apart after junior school, though, because he went to the local grammar and I went to a small boarding school,' I pointed out. 'After that, I only saw him in the school holidays . . . when I wasn't staying with Charlotte's family, or in California with Dad. Still, since Liam and I were best friends too, when we met up, it was as though we'd never been apart.'

Except, I suddenly remembered, the summer when I'd turned sixteen when, while staying with Charlotte and her family near Hexham, I'd developed a major adolescent crush on a friend of her brother's . . .

It was over by the time I'd got back to Great Mumming but I'd still felt guilty when I saw Liam again, though also safe and secure: I knew where I was with Liam.

Henry waved this aside with an airy hand. 'But it was never *exciting*, was it? Don't tell me friendship didn't just drift into a relationship, because I wouldn't believe you.'

Since that was exactly how it had been, I said nothing.

'It's only surprising you didn't split up when you went to university, but by the time we all graduated and set off for our road trip, I could see you were drifting apart, even if *you* couldn't. And then, in Avignon, up popped Mia in the middle, a sleek, spoilt little seal, ready to pounce.'

'I suppose we'd sunk into a boring, comfortable rut, but although I knew she'd always fancied him I still didn't see it coming.'

In our second and third years at university, Liam and I had shared a house rented by Mia's rich father, with Henry and his boyfriend, Kieran. We'd all become friends, so that after we graduated, it had seemed like a good idea to travel around Europe together for the summer, all crammed into Henry's battered old Ford estate car. And it *had* been fun, right up until we reached Avignon, which proved to be a bridge too far.

Early one evening, Henry, Kieran and I had gone out to buy food and wine and then, as usual, stopped at a small café for a drink on the way home. But when we got back to our digs, the birds had flown, leaving only a brief note of explanation.

'At the time, you said if it was a film you'd call it: *Abandoned in Avignon: an epic story of love and betrayal*,' I reminded him.

'It wasn't a lucky place for either of us, after Kieran decided to stay on and move in with that waiter,' Henry said sadly. Then he brightened. 'Never mind, we still managed to have some good times after that, didn't we?'

'We certainly did,' I agreed, remembering our slow, meandering journey down to the South of France, detouring to look at anything that sounded interesting.

'And stepping in at the last moment to cater for that big house party at Uncle Rafe's villa in Antibes, after all the staff walked out, gave us the idea for Heavenly Houseparties,' Henry reminded me.

'I still can't figure out how you came to be distantly related to a prince!'

He shrugged. 'Foreign princes are two a penny. They pop up in lots of family trees.'

They were unlikely to pop up in mine, even if I'd been able to fill in the gaps and trace it back far enough. I'd never really been interested, though I had sometimes wondered where I'd got my height and fairness from.

'It was so kind of your uncle Rafe to let us use his name and title to promote our website. I mean, being recommended by a *prince* looks so impressive, it's no wonder our business took off, even at the prices we charge,' I said, thinking warmly of Henry's uncle, who resembled a small, jolly frog attired in full nautical gear, as interpreted by an expensive and exclusive couturier.

'Yes, the only thing we both lack now is True Lurrrve,' Henry said. 'I expected both our Mr Rights to put in an appearance long before this, but it's simply never happened. I've no idea why, since we're both *gorgeous*.'

'Speak for yourself,' I said, because although I'm tall, blonde and leggy, my eyes are an odd shade of duck-egg blue, rather than Henry's limpid cerulean, and also, I have the kind of long, straight nose that only looks good on a Greek statue.

'Maybe in the New Year you'll find someone nice on that new dating site,' I suggested encouragingly. 'I've given up on them. The men I've met so far have all been at least twenty years older than their photographs and a foot shorter than me.'

I'd always specified in my dating profile that I was looking for someone over six foot tall. Ever since I was a student I'd usually worn my hair plaited around my head like a crown, which added another inch or two. It was such an old-fashioned style that I thought it looked pleasantly bizarre, especially when teamed with T-shirt and jeans, or a short shift dress and leggings.

'It's the challenge they can't resist,' Henry said vaguely, pouring out the last of the green liquid from his glass teapot. Then he looked up and said, more briskly, 'I suppose we'd better get back to business – and aren't you *dying* to hear all about our new client?'

'Go on: tell me all,' I said encouragingly, reaching out for Henry's biscuit barrel and finding it full of home-baked madeleines. 'All I know is, it's a castle in Northumberland, so I may have to stock up on Uggs and thermal underwear.'

'I've found out a bit more since Mrs Powys – that's our client – rang me first thing and booked us. She said she was just checking in case of late availability. She certainly picked the right moment!'

'Serendipity,' I agreed. 'Have you sent her the standard contract?'

'Yes, I emailed it to her. We discussed the details of the

booking in general terms on the phone, but she said I could email for any further information I needed and her cousin, Lucy Ripley, would reply on her behalf – which she already has and she's OK'd the contract.'

'That was fast!'

'There isn't a lot of time to arrange things in,' Henry pointed out. 'Besides, Mrs Powys came across as quite a forceful character.'

I wasn't entirely sure I liked the sound of the persistent and forceful Mrs Powys . . .

'I don't suppose you'll have time to go up and check the place out, so a contact will be useful,' I said, because normally with a new client Henry would pay an advance visit to see what the kitchen arrangements were like, and inspect the staff accommodation, which was frequently something our employers overlooked. Perhaps they assumed we just slept hanging from the rafters, like bats, for a few brief hours between duties. It also gave him an opportunity to settle the finer details of what, exactly, they needed – or expected – from us. The rules of engagement, as it were.

'No, there certainly won't be time to visit first, and it's a very long drive,' he agreed. 'This time I'll find out everything we need by email. I've already discovered quite a bit of background information about the venue, too: Mitras Castle *isn't* a real castle, it's just called that. And it's near the Roman Wall.'

'Have you been googling it?'

'Of course! But there isn't a huge amount of information to be had, because it's a private residence.'

He flipped open his laptop and turned it to show me a view of an old stone manor house on to which had been grafted a battlemented wing, like a giant turret, set against a dark backdrop of trees.

I frowned over it. 'It looks *vaguely* familiar. I know the area quite well because when I used to stay with Charlotte's family near Hexham in the school hols, we often visited the Roman Wall, but I can't have been to Mitras Castle if it's never open to the public.'

'Rowenhead Roman Fort is right next to it, though, so you might have glimpsed it from there,' he suggested, and I agreed that that was probably it.

'We visited the remains of a lot of forts; they're dotted right along the wall.'

'The Rowenhead one is run by a trust, but the land belongs to the family at Mitras Castle,' he said.

'Who *are* the family, other than this Mrs Powys?'

'Mrs *Sabine* Powys, and she's an elderly widow with no children.'

'Did she tell you that, or was it more internet snooping?'

'Internet *research*,' he said with dignity. 'And very interesting it was, too.'

He moved round to sit next to me, the laptop between us.

'When I googled her name, a whole load of stuff came up about her and her husband, Asa Powys. Apparently, they were pioneers of marine archaeology way back in the late fifties, early sixties. They made several hugely popular TV documentary series.'

'Just a little before our time,' I pointed out, though I was interested.

'It certainly was, but there are some clips of them on YouTube.'

His fingers moved on the keys and then he turned on the sound.

A deep voice intoned portentously: 'Together with their photographer, Tommy Fellowes, and the trusty crew of the good ship *Artemis*, Asa and Sabine Powys once more set sail to explore the lost underwater civilizations that lie concealed beneath the azure waters of the Aegean Sea.'

The film showed a tall couple, presumably Asa and Sabine, standing in the prow of a boat, gazing out to sea. Even captured in this old footage, they looked vibrantly glowing and alive. The man was dressed only in shorts, showing a well-muscled torso, and his arm was around his wife, who was laughing. A breeze was blowing their blond hair back from their tanned faces.

There was some underwater footage, too, where they were exploring a fallen statue of huge proportions, almost concealed by the sand, while fish flicked past, disinterestedly.

'I didn't know they had scuba gear back then,' I said.

'I think they called them aqualungs at the time, Dido. I found an obituary for Asa Powys with loads of info. He was a lot older than she was, but he only died a few years ago. I'll email you the links to the interesting stuff later, if you like?'

'OK,' I agreed. 'But although it's fascinating to know that our client has had an interesting past, I'm more concerned right now with the present and the details of our booking – like, when do we start and how long is it for?'

'Well, that's the thing,' Henry said, slightly shiftily. 'She's booked us for four weeks, from December the third.'

I stared at him for a moment, then exclaimed, 'But that's less than a week away! She's not holding a Christmas house party for a *month*, is she?'

While we often had longer bookings during the summer holidays, Christmas ones were usually confined to a week, at most.

A thought struck me: 'She knows she'll be charged the Christmas rate for the entire month, doesn't she?'

'Yes, I made that clear on the phone, before I accepted the

booking and she didn't quibble about it at all,' he assured me. 'She said her health was declining and she wanted to hold one last family gathering, with most of the guests arriving only a few days before Christmas.'

'How many guests?' I demanded.

'She thought a maximum of ten for Christmas dinner, including the household, which is usually just herself and this cousin.'

'That doesn't sound too bad. But why on earth does she want us so early, when it's only going to be the two of them in the house?'

'One guest will already be there when we arrive. He's a biographer, writing the life of Asa Powys.'

'That's still only three people. How does she usually manage?'

'She told me she had a daily cook/housekeeper, but due to illness in her family she can't work her usual hours at the moment. It doesn't sound as if she'd be up to cooking for a large house party anyway.'

'Did she tell you that on the phone?'

'No, I gleaned most of that from the emails in answer to mine from this cousin, Lucy. There's a weekly cleaning and laundry service too, so they're not going to expect us to do all the housework.'

'Just as well!' I said. 'I suppose if she wants to pay through the nose for us to look after just the three of them, that's up to her and we'll have lots of time to settle in before the other guests arrive and the festivities commence.'

I do enjoy organizing a good Christmas party and making sure everyone has a wonderful time, and good food plays a large part in that. There would be no damp, limp sprouts, dried-out turkey or instant gravy coming out of *my* kitchen. Henry, too, is adept at making sure there's enough alcohol flowing to oil the wheels of conversation and jollity, without derailing it.

'It's going to be chilly up there, so I hope the Castle has good central heating,' Henry said. 'I forgot to ask about that!'

'So do I! Do you remember when we did that Christmas gig in the Highlands and the heating didn't get as far as the kitchen or servants' quarters?'

'We'd better pack the down duvets and our thermals, just in case,' he suggested. 'And we'll have to get a move on, if we're going to be ready in time.'

'We certainly will. There's such a lot to do first and then the van to pack.'

We liked to be prepared for any eventuality . . . or emergency.

'I expect we'll have loads of time off before the rest of the guests arrive,' Henry said optimistically, considering how much Mrs Powys would be paying for our services, 'but we can chill, watch films and relax before we run ourselves ragged providing the Christmas cheer. And if it's going to be really cold up there, I'll put my snowboard in, just in case.'

'I think that's a bit *too* optimistic, Henry. It sounds to me as if Mrs Powys is the sort of woman who wants her money's worth, like Lady Bugle, and will keep trying to add jobs to our workload, or sneakily tell the cleaning service not to come and expect us to do all that, too.'

These were all things that had happened more than once in the past.

'Or she'll expect us to look after the children as well,' I continued, 'like that ghastly couple in Hampshire a few years back.'

'I like children, but I couldn't eat a *whole* one,' said Henry absently, smoothing the sleeves of his pale blue cashmere jumper over the cuffs of his Tattersall-check shirt. His sartorial style varies wildly between Hooray Henry and rather grungy teenage snowboarder. This seems to fascinate the followers of his very popular blog, Rudge the Roamer.

The tea cosy was lying within reach so I threw it at him, but he caught it and jammed it over his curls. Since it was knitted in the form of a giant strawberry, it looked very odd indeed.

Sabine

I kept Lucy busy, replying to emails from Heavenly House-parties and sending out the invitations.

The final missive I dictated to her was to Xan, by which time she was looking a little harassed: although she had spent her working life as a secretary, competence in anything seemed to be beyond her.

Dear Xan,

Much though I enjoy your letters, the recent delay in receiving your last one, due to the tardiness of the postal service (which would be faster if they used carrier pigeons), means that I have decided to utilize Lucy's skills to email you for, as you know, since I cannot touch-type, I find it tiresome. Still, the fact that Lucy has any useful accomplishment never ceases to amaze me.

Lucy ceased pecking at the keyboard and said, with a weak smile, 'You will have your little joke, Cousin Sabine!'

'New paragraph,' I said, ignoring this.

I am delighted that you are prepared to fall in with my suggestion that you take up residence here for the month of December, which should give you sufficient time to go through Asa's papers and collect enough material for his biography. As you know, I have found myself unable to look at them myself – indeed, I have barely entered Asa's study since the terrible day he died, and keep it locked except when Maria goes in to air and dust it. I use the library now as my own study.

But I am sure Asa would be happy that you were the one to use it again and also to write an account of his life and works, because he was so very fond of you, as am I.

I paused again and waited for Lucy to catch up.

Still, now that I know my own days are numbered, it is time to throw open the door on to the past and enjoy reliving those wonderful early years in Greece. I expect your grandfather, Tommy, told you many stories of our underwater exploits in the Aegean: it was all a great adventure. You will dispel the ghosts and do justice to Asa's life and work. I also hope that you can assist me to decide what to do with Asa's papers – which his old university would quite like to have – and the many valuable artefacts in his collection.

I could see Lucy mouthing the word 'artefacts' as she typed and I hoped she knew how to spell it.

'Artefacts? Are those the treasures you found when you were diving?' Lucy asked eagerly, looking up. 'I'd love to see them!'

I couldn't imagine what Lucy thought was in the locked

room – some kind of Tutankhamen's treasure trove, perhaps, with added barnacles?

'We weren't plundering gold bullion from old shipwrecks, like the early so-called marine archaeologists,' I said patiently. 'Asa was passionate about discovering lost towns and sea defences: signs of civilizations that had been drowned centuries before. It was the people who lived at that time he was interested in.'

'Oh,' said Lucy, sounding disappointed.

'You've already seen some of the larger artefacts, Lucy, because they're on the pedestals around the Great Hall – the amphora in a niche and some of Asa's collection of early diving helmets.'

There were other, smaller things in the locked study, many of them dating from our later, land-based years on Corfu, when we devoted ourselves to exploring and charting what turned out to be a surprisingly extensive temple complex.

Asa had always found the everyday domestic objects of the past more interesting than any gold or jewels. The spindles for spinning yarn, the millstones, worn with use, a broken toy or musical instrument – these were the finds that made the past come alive for him. *And* for me, for I had always caught fire at his enthusiasms and shared them, from the moment our eyes had met across a crowded room in Oxford, just after I had taken my final exams . . .

I blinked and came back to the present. At first after his death, it had hurt to even think of Asa, though now I found myself increasingly retreating into those heady, wonderful days. Once Xan arrived, I would positively revel in reminiscing to a sympathetic listener, though I must always be careful what I disclosed. Nothing must be allowed to tarnish the image of the glowing, golden couple we had been.

I must have been silent for some minutes, for Lucy now

gave a small, affected cough, and asked timidly: 'Would you like me to add anything more, Cousin Sabine?'

'New paragraph,' I snapped, and she resumed her position, poised like a pianist over the keyboard.

Your arrival on 3 December will happily coincide with that of the couple from an agency, whom I am employing for a month to cook and housekeep, since Maria's husband, though ready to come home from the hospital after his stroke, seems set to occupy most of her time. Her cooking was never up to much and Lucy can't even boil an egg without burning the pan dry . . .

Lucy made a small protesting noise, but continued to hammer doggedly on.

So, since I have invited a small party of guests for Christmas, mostly family connections, I thought it would be a good idea to employ some extra help. You will at least be assured of decent food during your stay with us, which I hope you will also consider as a holiday.

I silently pondered for a moment, then decided that I'd said everything I needed to.

'Final paragraph,' I announced.

Do pass on my regards to your parents. I miss the warmth of Corfu, but always felt that Christmas should be cold and, preferably, snowy. I look forward to seeing you very soon.

Your affectionate godmother,
Sabine

'I hadn't realized before how fond you were of him,' Lucy said, straightening and flexing her thin, twig-like fingers.

'Why should you?' I said. 'I may have shut myself off from most visitors for the last few years, but not from Xan. Besides, he has remained a frequent and interesting correspondent. Goodness knows, the one thing lacking round here is intellectual conversation.'

Lucy blinked; this dart seemed to have passed right over her head. It's a pity she so often brings out the worst in me. I'm sure when my friend Nancy arrives she will take me to task for it.

'Shall I send the email off now, Cousin Sabine?'

'I don't know what else you imagine I want you to do with it,' I said with a sigh, and when it had vanished, to be resurrected miles away by some magical process I couldn't fathom, added: 'I'm going for a walk in the garden and then I'll lie down for a little while. Unless Maria puts in an appearance, I'll expect you with tea in the sitting room later.'

'Of course, Cousin Sabine,' she murmured, but even before I closed the library door behind me, I could hear the click of her fingers tapping the keys again and was sure she was letting her brother, Nigel, know about both my illness and my plans – and that their anticipated inheritance was not quite the sure thing they had thought it.

As I put on my fur coat and tied a silk scarf around my head, I reflected that if this really was a vintage Christmas murder mystery, then I would be the prime candidate for the victim!

3

Due North

Only a few days later, following a flurry of emails between Henry and Lucy Ripley, who on no evidence whatsoever, he insisted on calling the Poor Relation, we climbed into our dark green Heavenly Houseparties van and pointed the bonnet due north.

It was crammed to the gunnels with everything we might possibly need, including some items you might not have thought of, had you not had our past experiences to make you think a very long way outside the box.

As always, I'd packed my favourite kitchen utensils and equipment, because you just never knew what you were going to find – or not find – in someone else's kitchen.

We also carried a basic stock of baking and cooking ingredients – spices, dried yeast, baking powder . . . tinned goods that could be jazzed up to make a meal in an emergency. Mitras Castle was not only in a remote spot, but far enough north to make winter driving conditions potentially hazardous, so we might well not be able to pop out to the shops for anything we'd run out of.

One of the first things I'd do when we'd settled in was make an inventory of what was in the store cupboards and freezer and what extras needed to be ordered in for the Christmas house party. I had some handy checklists I'd drawn up over the years. A successful house party is all in the planning and organization really, and in accommodating yourself to the usual household routine.

Henry's contribution to the cooking utensils was mostly confined to his madeleine baking trays and the rest of the equipment he would need for the production of tasty hors d'oeuvres, little cakes and biscuits, which were his speciality, while I did most of the rest of the cooking. We had our own roles and made a good team.

Even though Mrs Powys had expressed no desire to have her guests greeted with pomp and circumstance, Henry had packed his very natty butler's outfit, just in case, which made him look like an escapee from a Bertie Wooster novel. Also the things he considered vital to his existence: his glass teapot and a large supply of weird teabags, his down duvet and pillow, a supply of old films and a DVD player, for you never knew if the staff sitting room – if one even existed – would have one, let alone a Sky subscription . . . Unfortunately there was no guarantee of a fast internet connection, either.

He'd put his favourite snowboard in, too, though as I'd already pointed out, even if there was snow over Christmas, breaking his leg snowboarding in unfamiliar terrain would probably not go down well with our employer.

My personal comforts were a small coffee machine and a supply of pods to go in it, my Kindle, well stocked, and a box of real books too – plus a box of copies of my own new book, which had arrived while I was away in the States: *A Tiny Taste of Andalusia.*

By the time we'd added our suitcases and warm outdoor

clothing, boots and wellies, found a space for the box marked 'Instant Christmas' (for us, with a pop-up tree, crackers and decorations), there was little room left.

I squeezed in my toolbox and other household emergency equipment – people expect Henry to be the handyman, but he's almost entirely useless, even with a sink plunger, let alone coping with bigger plumbing or any other catastrophes – and then, right near the rear door, two folding snow shovels that we hoped we wouldn't need.

'Where's the picnic hamper?' Henry asked as he speeded up to join the M6.

'On the floor, next to my feet. Soup, tea, coffee, sandwiches, crisps and a packet of those mini chocolate swiss rolls you like,' I said. I'd assembled our travelling feast while he went to fill up the van with petrol and set the satnav with the Mitras Castle postcode.

'When can we stop for lunch?' he said greedily.

'Not until we're well north of the Blackpool turn,' I told him severely. 'We've barely started and you've not long since had breakfast.'

'That seems like hours ago,' he complained, then added suddenly: 'Did you remember your laptop and phone?'

'Of course – and my charger. We checked every single thing off the list, remember?'

'I know, but we *always* forget something.'

'True, but it's usually something we don't *know* we're going to need, like that house where we couldn't find a single corkscrew.'

'That was weird, considering they had a cellar full of wine. They must have pulled the corks out with their teeth,' he said. 'Where's the nearest shopping centre, if we need something urgently?'

'I don't know if there's a village with a shop anywhere near, but the road past Mitras Castle goes to Carlisle one way and Newcastle the other. The nearest town will be Hexham, I expect, which I know quite well, of course, because of Charlotte's family living nearby. I've told her we're coming up, and she and the children are spending Christmas with her parents, so if the weather's OK we might manage to meet up.'

Charlotte was now divorced and she and her two little girls lived in Barnard Castle, where she had a small shop specializing in tapestry and cross-stitch supplies.

'Fat chance if she doesn't come up before the guests arrive, because we'll be too busy.'

'I know and she's posting my present directly to the Castle, just in case,' I agreed. 'I've already sent hers – a tiny painting I bought in California.'

In fact, I was giving everyone a small picture this year, which I'd bought from a pavement artist. They were no great works of art, but colourful and fun. Henry's was of a surfboard leaning against a palm tree and was packed away in my suitcase.

'I ordered the usual amphora of strawberry jam from Fortnum and Mason to be delivered to Mummy,' Henry said. 'I think she must bathe in the stuff. And some of their hideously expensive crystallized fruits, too. She won't take them to the family gathering, though; she'll hoard them for when she gets home again.'

'Duty done, then,' I said. 'I expect Granny and Dora will bring us both back some souvenirs of their travels.'

'Where are they now?' he asked.

'I've entirely forgotten, and their postcards usually arrive weeks after they've moved on to the next place,' I said. 'I have the cruise ship details for emergencies, though. They're back some time in February.'

'Didn't you say you knew the area round Hexham pretty

well, from spending school summer holidays with Charlotte's family?' Henry said.

'Yes, we often went into Hexham. Charlie's family were happy she had someone her own age to keep her company and there were ponies, a tennis court and even a small, freezing open-air swimming pool.'

'They must be loaded!'

'Pretty well off. The house was a former rectory – one of those vast Victorian ones, though they'd installed all the mod cons. Charlie has an older brother, Gerry, but he didn't take a lot of notice of us,' I added and then, as I did whenever I remembered the events of my last visit there, when I was sixteen, went hot all over.

'Bit like my school hols, parked with one lot of rellies or another, while Mummy freeloaded on friends in Amalfi.'

'It was quite fun and we were both pony mad – it was only just starting to wear off a bit at sixteen. And my stays there meant Dora and Granny could go off on a cruise, or an extensive European train trip, unfettered and free.'

I frowned, looking back. 'Things weren't quite the same that last summer holiday, though, especially after Charlie's mum lost a valuable old family ring. She was totally distraught about it.'

Even though I'd been so engrossed in my crush on the friend Charlie's brother had staying with them, I remembered that, and the way the house had been turned upside down looking for it.

'Did it turn up?' asked Henry.

'No, though she said she was sure she left it by the basin in the downstairs cloakroom when she washed her hands . . . and sometimes I even thought she suspected *I'd* taken it, for she looked at me so strangely once or twice and her manner changed.'

'Surely not? I expect you just imagined that.'

'I don't know. But anyway, that was the last time I stayed with them, because the two summers after that, Charlotte and I were allowed to fly out to California on our own for the summer. We spent most of our days with the family of Dad's university friends, sometimes at their beach cabin. That was fun – we learned to surf and waterski.'

'I learned to waterski on a freezing cold Scottish loch,' said Henry. 'You pick it up fast when you don't want to fall in.'

'I can imagine,' I said. 'You can see why I said that Liam and I didn't see much of each other once he'd gone to the local grammar and I was at boarding school, then off with Charlie for weeks in summer. But with Liam, it was just like we'd never been apart once I got back to Great Mumming.'

Except, perhaps, after that last summer at Charlie's . . . But then, the guilt had soon worn off and his familiar affection had been balm to my soul.

'You and I were living through similar kinds of experience, really: our families were fond of us, but not so fond they didn't take every opportunity of parking us elsewhere in the school holidays,' I said, though of course Henry's was the posher version, with a big public school paid for by an uncle, while mine was a small Quaker affair, funded by Dad and my birth mother, who had become a research chemist for a big pharmaceutical firm in Switzerland and took a remote but punctilious interest in my progress.

'Then we met up in the first days at uni,' Henry said reminiscently, 'and a whole new friendship was forged.'

'Several of them,' I said. 'We turned into a fairly tight group once we moved into that house together, didn't we? But only *our* friendship has stood the test of time.'

'I suppose Mia and Liam's has too, in its way, since they're still together,' he pointed out.

'And all of us were studying English and secretly convinced we were going to be the next great British novelists,' I said wryly.

'Not Kieran – he thought he was a poet. And I think Liam only took the same degree to be with you. He went back to living and working on his parents' farm fast enough when he got home with Mia, didn't he?'

'True, but he writes a nature notes column that's syndicated in local newspapers . . . and he wrote a coffee-table book, too, about rambles round the area.'

'I know, he sent me a copy. It's propping up the corner of that wonky bookcase in my hall.'

'Mia's still writing the Great Novel, but she always says the children must come first and I'd understand if I had any,' I said.

'Cow,' Henry commented amiably. '*I'm* still writing, even if I did change direction.'

'You're all over the internet; you've turned into a complete media tart,' I told him.

'I'm an increasingly successful vlogger,' Henry said, with dignity, then grinned. 'But yes, I am all over it and it's getting quite lucrative now.'

Henry started blogging about his travel experiences soon after we finally got back from our extended globetrotting, and it had just grown from there. He liked to explore and talk about unusual things he'd done on his travels, but basically I think he simply liked talking to himself on camera. Between our catering gigs he would fly off to explore new places, and occasionally I would go with him.

As for me, I'd come home with several fat notebooks containing recipes and notes. Then, when I started to turn them into books, I was lucky enough to find a small publisher who issued one little fat hardback in a retro cover every Christmas. There were eight now, and they were modestly popular.

'I've still got *my* great novel in a drawer,' confessed Henry.

'Me too,' I said, grinning. 'I get it out occasionally and tinker with it.'

'Pretend novelists,' said Henry. 'But real life is much more fun. It's a pity I can't blog about our house party assignments, but the clients would sue me.'

'Yes, and then no one else would hire us,' I pointed out. 'But I was thinking last night, Henry, that you probably make enough from your blog to survive without the business now, and maybe, after ten years, we should both be thinking about hanging up our wooden spoons and butler's outfit and doing something else?'

'You know, I had started to wonder the same thing,' Henry admitted. 'I enjoy Heavenly Houseparties, but we never meant to go on doing it for ever, did we? Let's have a think about it over Christmas, shall we?'

'Good idea. I know I'd still need some more income coming in, but there are always jobs for good cooks.'

The sky, which had been a clear if icy blue in Cheshire, seemed to have grown steadily more leaden as we drove endlessly on up the motorway, singing along to old Christmas pop songs to get us in the appropriate festive frame of mind.

I took over the wheel after the lunch stop, while Henry, who was unfamiliar with this part of the country, looked out of the window and occasionally asked Brian Blessed, who was the chosen voice of his satnav, and who had been remarkably silent for what seemed like hours, if we were nearly there yet.

'There's nothing for him to say for ages,' I told him patiently. 'We just drive north until we hit Carlisle, then turn right and drive along the road that runs more or less parallel with the Roman Wall, until we get to Rowenhead.'

Brian woke up in time to direct us off the motorway and

along a rather narrow, bleakly scenic road. At Henry's request, I stopped to let him get out to admire a bit of the crumbling Wall on the skyline, but he was soon back in the van, shivering.

'It's a different climate up here!'

'So was Scotland when we did that booking there one winter, so you should have expected it.'

'I'm prepared for it . . . or I will be when I've unpacked,' he said. 'It was just a bit of a shock to the system.'

We carried on, though Brian suddenly threw some kind of hissy fit and attempted to tell us our destination was in an empty field.

We ignored him, but he'd been *almost* right, for a sign for 'Rowenhead Roman Fort and Visitor Centre' soon appeared and then a small cluster of stone cottages.

'The entrance is to the right here, somewhere,' Henry said, and I slowed down.

Luckily, there was no other traffic in either direction. In fact, there was no sign of life, other than some smoke issuing from a couple of the cottage chimneys and an escaped hen high-stepping through the yard in front of a small barn-like building.

'The Poor Relation said we couldn't miss the entrance to the drive, because it's flanked by stone pillars with eagles on top . . .'

'I see it,' I said, 'though they look more like vultures from this angle, don't they?'

'I think they'd look like vultures from any angle,' Henry said, eyeing them critically as I turned the van between them and found myself at the top of a dark woodland tunnel, heading steeply downwards.

Henry reached over and unplugged the satnav, so that Brian, who was now trying to tell us to do a U-turn and go back to the field he favoured as our destination, spluttered into silence.

'Pity he got it wrong this time,' I said. 'I always like it when he bellows: "Congratulations! You've arrived at your destination!"'

'But we haven't yet,' Henry said. 'And this drive must be difficult when the weather's bad.'

'The trees are so closed in overhead, it probably never gets really icy or snowy,' I pointed out.

The day was slowly darkening now and I'd put the headlights on to see where the drive was going, but then light literally appeared at the end of the tunnel.

And all at once, just as I was feeling like I was trapped in some giant helter-skelter, we shot out on to a sweep of gravel, where I slowed to a stop.

We were on a sort of plateau overlooking the valley, with a lawn to our left and, to our right, the imposing, battlemented tower we'd seen on the internet, though it looked infinitely more impressive, and perhaps even a little forbidding, with the dark backdrop of trees and the lowering sky.

But the tower had been grafted on to an older and mellower manor house, which wore the appearance of a surprised mother standing next to a suddenly enormous teenage son.

'It's quite something, isn't it?' Henry said. 'The tower is an early Victorian monstrosity, but it sort of works.'

'Where do we go?' I asked.

'Round the far corner of the old part of the house, to the tradesmen's entrance, darling, where someone will be waiting to greet us. The Poor Relation, possibly.'

'You'd better stop calling her that, or you'll do it to her face,' I warned him, as I rounded the corner and drew to a halt in front of a large, old studded door.

It was as if we'd gone back a few centuries, with a stretch of lichen-spotted grey paving instead of the gravel, though that continued on after it to some outbuildings at the back.

Across from the house was a small knot garden, probably for herbs, reached by a stone slab bridge over a stream.

When I turned the engine off I could hear rooks making uncouth noises in the trees.

'Honey, we're home,' I said . . . and oddly, I had felt a sudden affinity with the house the moment I'd pulled up outside this older, mellower part of it.

'And here's the welcoming party,' Henry said somewhat optimistically, as the studded oak door under its carved lintel slowly opened to reveal a small woman with dark hair streaked with grey, beetle-black eyes and a belligerent expression.

Her arms were crossed over her bosom and if she wasn't holding a rolling pin and demanding to know what time of night we called this, she looked as if she might do at any moment.

'That's not exactly how I pictured the Poor Relation,' Henry said thoughtfully.

4

Welcome Party

Of course, she *wasn't* the Poor Relation at all. I'd been prepared to bet that Cousin Lucy would not be wearing an old-fashioned cotton wrap-around floral pinafore over a black dress with a full skirt. This ensemble was teamed with purple Crocs.

'You are the temporary help?' she asked in a deep, slightly accented voice as we approached, huddled shivering into our anoraks. The question seemed a bit redundant, since most people don't drive around in dark green vans with 'Heavenly Houseparties' painted in large gold lettering up the side.

'*You* are Mr and Mrs Rudge?' she added, looking doubtfully first at me and then Henry, whose rose-gold curls were being blown about by a savagely icy wind. His cheeks were as pink as any cherub's and his bright blue eyes round and innocent.

'Not exactly. This is Henry Rudge, but I'm Dido Jones,' I said, with my best professional smile and holding out my hand. 'We're business partners, not a married couple.'

She looked at my outstretched hand as if uncertain what to do with it, then barely touched my fingertips before dropping it.

'I am Maria . . . Maria Stuart.' She stepped back reluctantly to let us into a flagged hall. It was surprisingly warm, which boded well for the rest of the house.

So this, I thought, was the cook/housekeeper with the convalescing husband we'd been told about, and whose duties we'd come to take over temporarily, but if she was pleased about that, she was hiding it well. Still, she might just be naturally dour.

'Pleased to meet you, Maria,' said Henry as he passed her, and his beaming smile and plummy accent seemed to take her aback even more than our appearance. We never do seem to be quite what people expect.

'I hope we're not putting you to any trouble,' Henry said. 'I thought the person I'd been emailing, Lucy Ripley, was to meet us.'

'The Lady's godson arrived early, so Lucy took the coffee through to the sitting room after lunch. I was to wait and show you the kitchen quarters and where you are to sleep. Then later this afternoon, the Lady will see you when she rings for tea.'

'The Lady?' I questioned. There had been no mention of any titles in those emails that had been bouncing into Henry's inbox and passed on to me.

'Mrs Powys. You will wipe your feet well,' she added ferociously, before leading the way down a passage to her left, past several closed doors and then through a swinging, green baize-lined one into a big, bright kitchen.

I caught Henry's eye and he winked at me. Permanent staff were sometimes inclined to be territorial, so our arrival would often be met with resentment, however much the extra help was needed, but if this was the case with Maria, Henry would soon soften her up and have her eating out of his hand.

It was possible, however, that she wasn't resentful at all and her belligerent expression was her usual one, the effect enhanced by thick, straight, dark eyebrows that almost met in the middle.

'What a lovely kitchen, and so warm, too!' enthused Henry, removing his coat and draping it over one of the wheelback chairs around a big, dark pine table. 'We've had *such* a long, cold journey – perhaps we could have a hot drink, before you show us round?'

'I only show you the servants' wing, where you will spend most time,' she replied, which put *us* in our place. 'Lucy, she will show you the rest of the house later.'

'Super,' said Henry in his usual sunny way, and she frowned at him, which was not a good idea, since the eyebrows joined into one dark, hairy caterpillar.

I thought she must be impervious to his charm, but then her expression softened slightly and she turned and began filling the kettle.

'You want tea?'

'Coffee, perhaps, if it isn't any trouble? Dido doesn't drink tea and I prefer the herbal kind,' Henry said.

'I do not like the tea either,' said Maria. 'But I make it very well, the way my husband likes it – dark and strong. *Mashed*,' she expanded, with emphasis, as if this was a mysterious extra rite.

Henry shuddered. 'It sounds wonderful – but another time, perhaps.'

She spooned a generous amount of ground coffee into the largest cafetière I'd ever seen, filled it with boiling water and then set it on the table, along with three mugs advertising Rowenhead Roman Fort, a sugar bowl and a carton of milk from the fridge.

She also, slightly ominously, fetched two fat ring binders and one of those concertina filing boxes and placed them to one side, before sitting down and pressing down the plunger of the cafetière with the air of one detonating a block of flats.

Henry, who has a sweet tooth, added three teaspoons of

sugar and a dash of milk to his coffee when she passed it to him, then began the process of winning her round. It's almost impossible to resist him when he sets out to do this and soon she had unloosened to the point where she was chatting to him as if he was an old friend and ally.

I don't know how he does it, but I didn't interrupt the process, instead sipping my coffee while looking around the kitchen. It was a charming mix of the old, like the glazed wall cupboards full of copper pans and pottery and glass moulds, which I longed to examine, and the new. All the mod cons were there: a very modern double oven and hob was built into a new range of worktops, and there were cupboards along one wall, as well as a dishwasher and a huge fridge.

I brought my attention back to the conversation in time to hear Henry saying, 'I believe you've worked here for many years, Maria?'

'Nearly forty,' she agreed, 'which makes everything very difficult now.' She heaved a great sigh. 'From a child, I knew Mrs Powys and her husband, who was a very learned and famous man. Asa Powys, you will have heard of him?'

She seemed to take this for granted, for she went on: 'My parents looked after them in Corfu, where they had a villa. But often they would visit here, for it is the Lady's family home and she loves it. Once, at Christmas time, my parents and I came back with them because there was some difficulty with the staff at the Castle . . .' She tailed off and shivered reminiscently. 'That winter was *very* bad!'

'That must have been quite a change from Corfu,' Henry said.

'My parents found it too cold – they never came here again. But I met my Andy, who was the gardener, and stayed. After that, I worked in the Castle, but of course, there was always a cook/housekeeper in charge. But since the last one, Mrs Hill, retired six years ago, after Mr Powys died, the Lady has had trouble finding anyone who will stay very long and I have had to take over the cooking and running of the house.'

'That's quite a lot for one person to manage, and especially now,' I said sympathetically. 'We were so sorry to hear of your husband's illness.'

'He is older than me, but very strong and active, so it was unexpected, yes. A stroke. Now he has had the physiotherapy and he is making a good recovery. Once I have him home again, all will be well. But . . . he must retire now.'

She turned to Henry. 'You will have to do Andy's work around the house instead: bring in the logs and see to the fires in the sitting and dining rooms.'

'That's all right. I can do all that,' Henry assured her. 'We're here to take over all the work of the house, while you concentrate on getting your husband back to full strength. Mrs Powys told me as much in the emails she had her cousin send to me.'

'That Lucy!' Maria made a noise that expressed a mixture of emotions, all of them disparaging. I noted that she referred to her employer as 'Mrs Powys or 'the Lady,' but the Poor Relation by her Christian name.

'She is *some* kind of cousin of the Lady's father, that is all. She has been here now almost a year, but sending emails is the only useful thing she has done!'

She expounded on this, which seemed to be a sore subject. 'She is supposed to see to breakfast and then make the beds, but those she leaves for me to do when I come in at about ten. I tidy up and put into the dishwasher the dinner dishes she has carried into the kitchen the night before, then prepare the lunch before I go back to my cottage for a while. Before Andy was ill, he would go back to the Castle with me later to see to the fires, and I would cook and serve the dinner before I went home again. It was Lucy's job to make the coffee and clear the table afterwards. But now in the afternoons, I go straight to the hospital instead.'

'That was a busy schedule,' I said. 'You can't have had much time to yourself.'

She shrugged. 'The work had to be done but it was not hard when it was just the Lady here alone. Mrs Powys had begun trying again to find live-in help, but then, she found you instead, though I understand for a month only?'

'That's right, we leave on New Year's Day,' Henry agreed.

'But you might want to stay,' she suggested. 'The Lady is generous and will appreciate good service.'

'I'm afraid we don't stay anywhere for longer than a month, at the most. It suits us to work short contracts,' I explained. 'But while we're here, we'll take all the housekeeping and cooking off your shoulders, so you can concentrate on your husband's health.'

'Yes, don't you worry about a thing,' Henry told her. 'And if there are any household emergencies, like dripping taps and blocked loos, then Dido's ace at sorting them out.'

She looked at me doubtfully, as if wondering if he was joking.

'Henry's a dab hand with the ironing board, if you do all the laundry in house,' I said, which *really* seemed to throw her.

'A laundress comes in with the cleaners on a Wednesday morning and sees to most of it,' Maria said. 'I try and do some in between.'

'Lucy told us about the cleaning service – that's great,' I said.

'They clean right through and are very thorough. Also, they change the bedlinen.'

We'd finished our coffee by then and Maria looked at

her watch and said she had better show us round the servants'
wing now.

'Everything else you will need to know is in there.' She indicated the ring binders and the concertina file. 'The Lady likes
everything organized and to run smoothly, and the old housekeeper, Mrs Hill, she was the same, so they make these. The
purple one has the instructions for all the household appli-
ances, as well as the boiler,' she told Henry, as if he might
understand these things better than me, being a man. 'And by
the way, the oil tank is in the outbuilding next to the wood
store, because of the cold, but it is filled up in summer.'

'That's one less thing to worry about, then,' said Henry.

Maria continued: 'This blue file has everything you might
want to know about the running of the house and the days
for the collection of the recycling, and for supermarket
deliveries . . .'

I'd pulled the blue one over and was now flicking through it.
It was a complete compendium of the day-to-day running of
the Castle, down to every tiny detail! I'd never seen anything
quite like it before, but it would make taking over very easy for
us. I shoved it across to Henry and saw his eyebrows rise as he
looked at it.

'In this other file are the extra lists with boxes to tick for
ordering from the supermarket – usually I do that once a week
on the computer in the library – and menu plans and so on.'

'This is all amazingly thorough,' I said.

'It was necessary to keep it up to date, because so many staff
have come and gone in the last few years,' Maria explained.
'You will find in the purple file the phone numbers for the
plumber, electrician and others you might need to call, too.
The doctor's number is on the corkboard by the door over
there.'

'I'm sure everything we need will be at our fingertips,' Henry assured her.

'I hope you will manage, because tomorrow afternoon my husband comes home,' Maria said. 'The Lady has already had a stairlift and shower put in the cottage, to make it easier for him.'

'That was kind,' Henry said.

'It was, but also she thinks it will mean I can work my old hours from the New Year, once he is settled,' she said practically. 'But we are not young, and now we think we would like to retire. But that is difficult now that the Lady has told me she is very ill, though she does not look it.'

'She gave *us* to understand that she's seriously ill, too. That's why she wanted to hold this last family party over Christmas,' Henry agreed.

'If she has not long to live, then I will find it hard to leave her without help.'

'That puts you in a very difficult situation,' I said sympathetically, realizing what a conflict of loyalties she must be feeling. 'But it will be easier to make up your mind after Christmas, when you've had some rest and can get things into perspective.'

Maria nodded slowly. 'Yes, that is what my daughter says. She and her husband are both doctors and they live in York,' she added with a note of pride.

'There we are, then – you take her advice,' Henry said comfortably. 'Now, I expect you want to show us where we're sleeping and then we'd better bring in our stuff.'

'You are right – time passes. But I am not going to the hospital today, since Andy is home tomorrow, so I do not need to rush away.'

She gave us a brief, whistle-stop tour of the laundry room, a big larder, scullery and various other rooms of indeterminate purpose, though one contained two big freezers and another a store of cut logs.

Then she marched us back through the kitchen and threw open another door.

'This was the Servants' Hall, but is now the staff sitting room.'

It was large, with a stone fireplace containing a log-effect electric stove, though since there were radiators here, too, it was warm enough already.

There were shabby chintz-covered chairs and a sofa, probably cast-offs from the main part of the house. The floor was covered in coconut matting, on which lay a few worn rugs.

'Cosy,' I said politely, which I am sure it would be with the curtains drawn and the log-effect fire glowing. Henry was examining the TV, which was not huge, but looked fairly modern and there was a DVD player, too.

The rest of the furnishings consisted of a huge dark sideboard, a table and a large bookcase, empty apart from a few dog-eared paperbacks on the bottom shelf, presumably left by some of the transient staff.

A narrow, winding staircase went up from one corner and Maria said, 'This is the old backstairs for the servants and we go up. Your bedrooms are above.'

A corridor ran off from the top of the twisty little staircase and Maria showed me into a large, pleasant bedroom with a rose-patterned pink carpet and embossed wallpaper in a design of gilded baskets of flowers. The double bed had brass knobs.

'Lovely,' I said, hoping I wouldn't overdose on conflicting flower patterns, but it was at least clean and warm.

'I only make one bed up, because I think you are a married couple,' she said. 'But all the bedrooms are kept aired and dusted, so it is just a matter of making up the bed in the next room.'

'We can do that later, if you show us the linen cupboard,' I said.

'Here it is,' she said, opening a door opposite on to heaps of linen and the smell of lavender. 'And this next to it, the bathroom.'

That was old-fashioned but adequate, fluffy towels already hanging over the rail.

'Lovely,' I said, and we passed more bedrooms before the passage was blocked by a green-baize-lined door, like the one to the kitchen.

Beyond it, the passage continued, though more lushly carpeted.

'That leads to the family part of the house, but we go down these stairs now, into the Garden Hall, where you came in.'

There was a cloakroom off the hall, which was large and also used for arranging flowers, with a shelf for vases and a table.

'And next to it, the door to the wine cellar and the boiler room, but you can look at those later,' she said, and then led the way back into the bright, warm kitchen again.

'That all seems fine,' said Henry. 'We can settle in and study all your helpful files later, when we've seen Mrs Powys, but I'm sure we'll manage perfectly well.'

'I will come in in the morning to make sure all is well, but then I go home to wait for the ambulance bringing my husband and to cook his favourite dinner.'

'What is his favourite dinner?' I asked curiously, wondering if it was traditional meat and two veg, or some Greek speciality she had converted him to.

'Haggis with neeps and tatties,' she said. 'He is Scottish, and his late mother, she taught me to make the traditional food.'

She glanced at the wall clock. 'It is not yet time for me to take the tea through and for the Lady to see you, so you could bring in your things?'

'Good idea, and I'd like to tidy up a bit before I see her, too,' I said.

The light was going and Maria said she would show Henry the outbuildings in the morning.

'Yes, that can wait,' Henry agreed. 'Come on, Dido, let's bring in the stuff. We can pile it in the corner of that vast sitting room and sort it out later.'

Maria looked up at a row of servants' bells, which I hadn't previously noticed.

'The Lady knows I am still here, so she may ring for her tea. But now her godson has arrived, she may forget. He is to stay till after Christmas, to make notes for the book he will write about Mr Powys, who was a very famous and clever man, so they will be talking, talking . . .'

We donned our Arctic gear and emptied the contents of the van first into the Garden Hall, and then onwards to the staff sitting room.

Last out of the van was the snowboard, which Maria eyed dubiously.

'You bring your surfboards at this time of year, and so far from the sea?'

'Snowboard,' Henry explained.

She opened a large cupboard under the hall stairs. 'You put in here with the skis and skates and golf clubs,' she said firmly.

We stripped off our outdoor clothing, faces glowing from the cold after even such a short exposure to the elements, and then left Maria assembling the tea tray, while we took our suitcases and went to freshen up, ready to meet our formidable-sounding employer.

When we came back to the kitchen, the tea tray was groaning under the weight of the pot, crockery and a small cafetière of coffee, plus a plate of that sticky Greek delicacy, baklava.

'You could do with a tea trolley—' Henry began, when a bell suddenly jangled on the board over the door, making us jump.

'You had both better come with me. She is impatient.'

Henry insisted on carrying the heavy tray for Maria and she led the way through a door on the other side of the Garden Hall and through what must have been the original manor house, not letting us linger, but announcing the purpose of the rooms we passed, like a house agent.

'Morning room, dining room, Mr Powys's old study, which is kept locked . . . the summer sitting room and the library.'

Through the open door of the latter, I saw a hard drive and monitor sitting incongruously on an antique leather-topped desk, a printer next to it on a small table.

'Did you say you could get broadband here, then?' Henry asked.

'Yes, but not fast.'

'I didn't really think I'd be streaming films in the evenings,' Henry muttered to me.

'You'll be too exhausted after lugging firewood about, anyway,' I whispered back, as Maria passed through an archway. 'You might even have to chop it.'

The stone archway, an example of Victorian Gothic Revival, marked the transition from the oldest part of the house to the huge, square hall of the battlemented tower. It had a tiled floor with an inset circular mosaic in the middle.

'Wow!' I said, but we barely had a chance to take in its magnificence, before Maria was chivvying us across it, practically snapping at our heels like a sheepdog, and into a warm, well-lit sitting room on the other side.

Maria took the tray from Henry and placed it on a large coffee table.

'Here are the new staff, Mrs Powys. I thought you would want to see them now.'

There were three people in the room: a small, mousy-looking woman, who I was sure was Cousin Lucy; a tall, thin, elderly and imposing-looking lady standing by the window, who Maria was addressing; and a dark-haired man seated by the fire, who turned his head to reveal an improbably handsome face with high cheekbones, a straight nose, beautifully moulded lips and dreamy, lilac-grey eyes fringed with long black lashes.

It was a heart-stopping face – and mine did just that. For, despite the almost twenty years that had elapsed since I last saw him, there was no mistaking who it was.

Xan Fellowes.

5

The Scarlet Tide

I stared at him, transfixed, feeling a tide of scarlet wash over me like wildfire and then vanish as quickly, leaving me ice cold.

Just in that instant, I saw him as the tall, willowy, dreamy and devastatingly handsome youth of nineteen, who had stolen my heart during that long-ago summer . . . and then that image was replaced by Xan as he was now: older, but no less attractive.

My momentary reaction had, I hoped, gone unnoticed. Certainly Xan hadn't yet looked at me, for his strangely beautiful light eyes were gazing at Henry, with a puzzled expression.

'I know you, don't I?' he said. 'But where from?'

'School. I'm Henry Rudge and I was two years below you at Rugby.'

'That's it!' Xan got up, dislodging a small brown-and-white spaniel from his lap and shook hands, like Victorian explorers meeting unexpectedly in the jungle, though I don't suppose they would have followed it up with hearty thumps on each other's backs.

'Yo, dude!' Henry said, and they both grinned, though I have no idea why. Henry can be *so* eighties, sometimes.

Anyway, their exchange gave me a chance to get a grip on

myself and turn to greet my employer – only to discover that she was gazing at me with a very strange expression on *her* face. I'm familiar with the one of someone who has ordered a donkey and been sent a giraffe, because I get that all the time – but there somehow seemed to be a little more to it this time.

'How do you do, Mrs Powys?' I said politely, giving her the smile that Henry always says makes me look like Pallas Athene on a bad day. 'I'm Dido Jones and this is Henry Rudge.'

'I'm very well . . .' she murmured absently, her pale blue eyes still wide – and then she seemed to come back to herself and her attention suddenly switched to Henry.

Recalled to duty by my mention of his name, he bestowed on her one of his most engaging smiles and said he was very pleased to meet her.

'You were at school with Xan?' she asked in her clear, clipped voice. 'And you're a Rudge? One of the Shropshire Rudges?'

'The merest tiny twig on the outermost branch. I was only at Rugby because one of my uncles paid the fees,' Henry said, cheerfully. 'I'm the poor relation, earning an honest crust as a house fairy – and I hope Dido and I can lift all the cares of the household from your shoulders, leaving you free to enjoy a truly heavenly Christmas.'

This was said in his usual effulgent fashion and I could see Mrs Powys didn't know quite how to take him.

Out of the corner of my eye, I could see Xan grinning again, though Lucy Ripley was sitting with her mouth slightly open and her small, beady dark eyes glazed over. It made her look half-witted, but was probably just her default expression.

'I sincerely hope so,' Mrs Powys said crisply, recovering herself, 'since that is what I am paying you a fortune for. Now, you obviously know Mr Fellowes, who is staying here until the New Year—'

'I refuse to be Mr Fellowes – just call me Xan, both of you,' he said, and his eyes met mine for the first time, though he showed no sign of recognition, or even, come to that, interest.

Mrs Powys looked a little disapproving at this informality, but introduced us to Miss Ripley and said we might as well address *her* as Lucy, since even Maria did so.

'Of course, there's so little formality these days and I'm sure I'm quite happy for you to do so and—'

'Yes, Lucy,' said Mrs Powys, ruthlessly cutting across her. I got the feeling that if she hadn't, Lucy would have rambled on disjointedly for hours.

There was no suggestion that we call Mrs Powys by her Christian name and I hadn't really expected that.

Maria had unloaded the contents of the tea tray on to the low table and went out with some used coffee cups. Lucy poured tea into two cups, but Xan helped himself to the coffee. Perhaps, like me, he wasn't a tea drinker.

Mrs Powys had seated herself on a buttoned velvet sofa and now contemplated us coolly.

'Of course, there won't actually be much work for you to do before the rest of the house party arrive nearer Christmas, though you will also have to assume my gardener's usual winter tasks of seeing to the open fires and bringing in logs.'

'Maria's going to pop in tomorrow morning to show me where the logs are kept and anything else she hadn't time for today,' Henry said. 'It's no problem.'

'I'm glad to hear it! And *I* will see you both in the library tomorrow at nine thirty, to discuss your duties in more detail, once I've opened up my late husband's study for Xan to work in.'

'Of course,' I said, and inadvertently catching Xan's eye again, bestowed a cool, indifferent look on him. It seemed to take him aback slightly; I don't suppose it's the usual reaction he gets from women.

There still wasn't the faintest sign of recognition, though, which was a great relief. But then, I suppose that wasn't really surprising, considering how much I'd changed since I was sixteen.

'I know Maria will have shown you the staff quarters, but Lucy will take you round the rest of the house in a moment,' said Mrs Powys. 'Lucy usually brings my breakfast tray up at eight, but it will be much better if you take that over from tomorrow morning, Dido.'

'Certainly,' I said.

'Once I've carried the tray up, I take mine into the breakfast room,' Lucy said.

She gave a slight simper in Xan's direction. 'Perhaps tomorrow, we can breakfast together, Xan?'

His eyes took on a slightly wary expression and he made the kind of noise that could be interpreted in any way the listener wished, but really meant: *Not if I can help it!*

'I'm not used to being waited on,' he said. 'I normally get my own breakfast – and Plum's.'

The little dog looked up eagerly at the sound of his name, or possibly the mention of the word 'breakfast'.

'Nonsense!' exclaimed Mrs Powys. 'That's what Dido and Henry are here for, after all, to cook and housekeep, Xan. And when you used to stay with us while Mrs Hill was still here we would all sit down to a cooked breakfast together.'

'Yes, we're happy to cook whatever you fancy for breakfast, Xan,' Henry told him. 'Just tell us what you'd like when you come down and we'll bring it through to the morning room for you.'

'OK,' Xan said. 'I'll have to give Plum his breakfast in the kitchen anyway, once he's been out, so I can tell you then.'

'I hope Maria will take a complete break until the New Year, after she's called in tomorrow morning,' Mrs Powys said. 'Andy must be settled back into the cottage and she can devote herself to him over Christmas.'

I remembered Maria telling us about the new shower room and stairlift Mrs Powys had had installed in the cottage to make things easier for Andy and reflected that my employer clearly had a kinder heart than her cool, incisive manner led you to think.

'We'll make sure she doesn't lift a finger while we are here,' Henry promised.

'We can discuss everything else tomorrow, including the arrangements for Christmas,' Mrs Powys said. 'Maria has always done her best but, even without Andy's illness, she wouldn't have been up to catering for a house party.'

'We've had years of experience,' Henry assured her. 'It'll all go swimmingly, you'll see.'

'For the fees you charge, I would expect no less!'

'No, indeed,' echoed Lucy sycophantically. I'd almost forgotten she was there while we were talking, but now I noticed she was holding a plate covered in crumbs.

'Right, Lucy,' Mrs Powys said briskly. 'If you've finished your tea, you can give Dido and Henry a tour of the house.'

'Of course, Cousin Sabine,' Lucy said, though not without a longing glance at the somewhat depleted plate of sticky baklava.

'I wish you wouldn't keep calling me that, Lucy! You were my father's cousin, not mine, and it just makes me feel as if I've strayed into a Daphne du Maurier novel.'

'I don't really see myself in the Mrs Danvers role,' I said

without thinking, and I saw the corners of Xan's mouth twitch upwards as he poured himself a second cup of coffee.

'Cousin Sabine is how I've always thought of you, so I keep forgetting,' apologized Lucy, getting to her feet and dropping a fat, old-fashioned handbag as she did so, which burst open, spilling out a far from old-fashioned phone, a Mars bar and a paperback novel with a half-naked man on the front cover.

Plum went to sniff interestedly at the chocolate, but Lucy hastily shovelled everything back in again, babbling disjointedly in a voice that wavered up and down like a cracked flute.

'Come along, then,' she said finally, leading the way out, her handbag now looped over her arm in the manner of the Queen.

Mrs Powys called after her: 'Oh, Lucy, you needn't come back till dinner. I want to have a cosy chat with my godson before I go up to change.'

It was a dismissal for all of us and I noticed a slight pink tinge in Lucy's cheeks, as if she resented it.

Henry and I had no objection to being treated as staff – why should we, when we were? – but Lucy's position was clearly a little more ambiguous.

In some more casual households where we'd worked, the lines of interaction were blurred, but here, I was sure, Mrs Powys would like us to keep to our place and we'd do that . . . though Xan being an old friend of Henry's might cause a few difficulties.

The tower was actually rectangular rather than square, as it had looked from the front, stretching back quite a long way. Lucy began her tour in the hall – called the Great Hall, naturally – where I noticed for the first time that what I'd taken to be statues on the plinths around the room, were actually antique diving helmets.

'The mosaic in the middle of the floor is a perfect replica of the Roman one they found at the nearby fort,' Lucy informed us as she skirted round the edge of it. 'The original was moved to a folly in the garden in Victorian times. It depicts Mithras.'

'Why is he wearing a pixie hat?' I asked.

'Mithras was usually shown emerging from a rock and wearing a Phrygian cap,' Henry explained. 'Mitras is another form of Mithras, so I expect that's where the Castle got its name from.'

'How clever of you to know that!' Lucy said admiringly. 'The furniture is all Victorian Gothic – such dark wood, I always think – and there's a small downstairs cloakroom.'

She turned to me and said with emphasis, '*Dark blue* towels in there, always.'

'I'll remember,' I said gravely, though I was sure it would all be in those very detailed files in the kitchen.

A door at the back of the hall led to a billiard room and we went through it into a formal drawing room, all straw-coloured satin and gilded mirrors, but with a large-screen TV in one corner.

'The double doors to the sitting room can be thrown open to make one large space for entertaining,' she said, lowering her voice, before adding slightly acidly, 'but we'll go back through the billiard room, so we don't disturb Mrs Powys's important talk with Xan.'

The wide staircase rose from one side of the hall and as we climbed it she said, 'There are three further floors, as you will see. Cousin Sabine has a suite on this first one so there's only one further bedroom and a small bathroom.'

We were allowed the briefest glimpses inside the rooms, as if we wouldn't soon be very well acquainted with them after bed making and bathroom tidying, though at least I now knew where to bring Mrs Powys's breakfast in the morning – at 8 a.m. precisely!

The Castle had all been well modernized, with more bathrooms than you generally found in old houses of this kind, not to mention having linen and cleaning cupboards on every floor, too. All the bedroom doors had porcelain name plaques with a flower theme going on – the Bluebell Room, the Daffodil Room and so on. Mrs Powys's was Rose.

When I mentioned this, Lucy said, 'Cousin Sabine's mother had them made. She was a keen gardener. I never knew her, of course, because she died when Sabine was a child, but she was the last of the Archbold family, the original owners of the Castle . . .'

She trailed off as we reached the top floor and she allowed us a peep into her own large bedroom, which also contained a sofa and TV.

'Of course, I've helped Cousin Sabine in the house as much as I could since I came to live here – a little light dusting and arranging the flowers, that kind of thing – but my own health is really quite delicate, so it will be a relief for me to hand over those duties to you during the next few weeks.'

For that, I thought, read: 'Now you're here, I'm not going to lift a finger, if I can possibly help it.'

Henry and I exchanged glances: this was pretty much what we expected and, indeed, preferred.

'My cousin will tell you which rooms to make ready for our guests later.'

Lucy indicated a small flight of wooden stairs, more like a ladder. 'There's no attic, of course, because of the flat roof. You can go up those steps and get out on to that in fine weather, but I dislike heights intensely so I never have.'

'I'd like to see the view from there,' Henry said. He'd probably like to try abseiling down the tower from it, too. I was only glad he hadn't packed his climbing gear as well as the snowboard.

'There's just the old part of the house to show you now,' she said. 'We go back down to the first floor.'

We did, and through another of the pointed Gothic archways, this one opposite the door of Mrs Powys's bedroom.

Lucy seemed to be flagging and merely gestured at the closed doors along the passage.

'More bedrooms – and this one on the right was the old schoolroom, but apparently Xan always slept there when he visited the Castle as a child and has continued to prefer doing so.'

There were no porcelain plaques on the doors in this wing, but if there had been, a thistle would have been most suitable for Xan's, since my conscience had been prickling ever since I'd seen him.

We'd now arrived at the top of the wide stairs down to the Garden Hall again, with the baize door blocking the passage ahead.

'There,' she said, 'I expect you know where you are, now?'

'Yes, through there to the staff bedrooms and the backstairs,' I said, 'or down to the Garden Hall.'

'Thank you, Lucy – we can find our way now,' Henry said, with one of his charming smiles and she simpered a little. Xan might soon have a rival for her interest.

She looked coyly at Henry again, smiled and then turned and made her way back along the landing and through the archway to the tower.

We found Maria in the kitchen, hand-washing delicate porcelain coffee cups, and she looked round as we came in.

'You have now seen all the rest of the house?'

76

'Most of it, so I'm sure we won't have any trouble finding our way about,' I said.

'It is not one of your great stately homes,' she agreed. 'You cannot get lost.'

'I suppose we should take our suitcases upstairs and change now,' I suggested. 'Then we can help you with dinner.'

'It is at seven tonight, so there is plenty of time – and also, I have made the lamb casserole, it just needs to be heated up.'

'That's easy, then,' I said. 'Seven was the usual time, when they had live-in staff before, wasn't it?'

'That is so. It was only six when I had all to do and needed to get home to my husband. Lunch is always at one, also in the dining room.'

'What, even when there were only two of them?'

'Even when it was just the Lady. And in winter, always the fire must be lit.'

'We'll help you lay the table tonight and then we'll know where everything is,' I suggested.

'What are you serving before the casserole?' asked Henry curiously.

'The Lady has her own way of doing things and she likes the starter to be some small savoury nibbles, as she calls them, served in the sitting room: a few canapés, or toast triangles with pâté, that kind of thing.'

'Good idea,' approved Henry. 'What are they to be tonight?'

'Open finger sandwiches of buttered brown bread with smoked salmon. I will see to those now, while you unpack.'

I noticed for the first time that there were two stainless-steel dog bowls on the floor in a corner, one filled with water, which I assumed were for Plum. Maria saw where I was looking and exclaimed: 'I had forgotten! The Lady asked me earlier to put down a bowl of water for the little dog in the Garden Hall too.

Always this was done when the Lady's old spaniel was alive and the bowls are still in the storeroom next door.'

'I can do that now,' offered Henry, and she took him off to show him where the bowls and a plastic watering can he could use to fill them were kept.

I left them to it and ferried my suitcase and bags upstairs from the staff sitting room. But before I unpacked, I thought I'd get the linen out of the cupboard for Henry's bed, since it seemed unfair that I had got the one already made up.

The pale blue duvet cover, sheet and pillowcases smelled rather deliciously of lavender. I'd just taken them into his bedroom and removed the dustcover from the bed, when Henry arrived, hefting his heavy holdall and his duvet.

'There you are! I thought you'd fallen into a dog bowl and drowned,' I said. 'Come and help me to make your bed up.'

But Henry unburdened himself of his luggage and then said firmly, 'I will, once you've told me why you looked so appalled when you spotted Xan in the sitting room!'

'Oh God,' I blurted, horrified, sinking down on to the mattress: 'Do you think anyone else noticed?'

6

Well Served

'I don't think so. *I* only did because I happened to be looking in your direction and it just flashed across your face for an instant. It was very Lady of Shalott.'

'Lady of Shalott?' I echoed blankly.

'You know: "'The curse is come upon me!' cried The Lady of Shalott." Sort of transfixed by horror and dread.'

'As long as no one saw,' I said. 'Xan didn't, because he'd immediately recognized you and was trying to remember where from. And Mrs Powys was standing by the window, so she couldn't see my face until I turned to speak to her. And then *she* looked at me really strangely,' I added thoughtfully. 'But I think it was just the usual surprise, really. We never seem to be quite what new clients are expecting.'

'We're wandering from the point, Dido,' Henry said firmly. 'I want to know why you looked at poor Xan like that. I know he's totally gorgeous, but it certainly wasn't a total love-at-first-sight thing. Come clean and tell all to Uncle Henry. You'll feel *so* much better for it.'

He was probably right, so I capitulated. 'OK then. I have

met him before, but it was years ago and I've changed so much since then that he didn't seem to recognize me, thank God!'

'No, he certainly didn't seem to know you at all, did he? Though I wouldn't have thought you were that forgettable.'

'It was when I was sixteen – and he'd probably *want* to forget me. It was that last summer holiday I spent with Charlotte's family. Xan was a friend of her older brother, Gerry, and staying there for the first two weeks of the holiday, before they both flew out to stay with Xan's parents in Greece.'

I paused, as a wave of shame swept over me, then continued: 'At sixteen, I was a scrawny, horse-mad teenager with a ponytail and a brace. I wasn't even all that tall, because I was a late developer and had a growth spurt during the following year.'

After that, I'd *really* felt I didn't fit in anywhere. The height, the bright golden hair, the straight Greek nose – they all made me stick out like a sore thumb. And like in that scene in *Alice in Wonderland*, I'd suddenly been too big for Granny's old, low-beamed cottage.

'I expect you were still cute, though,' Henry said kindly.

'I've never been cute and I certainly don't think Xan thought so at the time! He seemed so grown up, though he was only a couple of years older than me and Charlotte.'

'I think I vaguely remember Gerry from school, but he and Xan were not only older than me, they were in the geeky set whereas I was sporty. In fact, I only really remember Xan because he was so good-looking and he walked off with all the history and literary prizes.'

'Well, you can imagine what happened when Charlotte and I set eyes on him. One look and we were straight into a major crush. We spent the next fortnight following him around and making a total nuisance of ourselves – especially me.'

'We all go through embarrassing phases, and since you *were* so much younger he probably thought of you as children and hardly noticed. A couple of years makes a big difference at that age.'

'I made such a nuisance of myself, he could hardly have helped noticing,' I said gloomily. 'He and Gerry were more interested in hanging out with a couple of the local girls their own age. Xan seemed very smitten with one of them . . .'

Sophie, she'd been called, and at the time she'd struck me as very sophisticated, with her perfect make-up, fashionable clothes and sleek, dark hair.

'I was horribly jealous of her,' I admitted. 'I think it made me even worse. My behaviour was toe-curlingly embarrassing, in retrospect. Xan and Gerry avoided us as much as possible and I expect they were glad when it was time to fly out to Greece.'

They'd had to change their tickets and fly out a day early, because Xan's grandmother had been taken ill.

'You know, I don't suppose you were half as silly as you think you were,' Henry said comfortingly. 'I don't expect he's given you another thought. I think you're safe.'

'I expect you're right,' I said. 'My unusual name might have given the game away, but luckily Charlie's always called me Di, so her family did the same.'

I began to feel more relaxed about the situation – in fact, I hadn't realized quite how wound up about it I'd been until now – but it was so long ago, what did any of it matter now?

'Xan isn't to know that you went into your chrysalis as a scraggy, uncouth teenager and came out as a more-than-life-size Pallas Athene,' Henry said. 'You should be safe – unless you fall for him all over again, of course.'

'That's *not* going to happen,' I told him firmly. 'Even my crush wore off practically the minute he and Gerry left, and after that, Charlotte and I were back to the ponies, the pool and the tennis court.'

'And, presumably, back to faithful childhood sweetheart Liam in Great Mumming?'

'Yes, but he didn't know anything about it, of course.

'I'll just have to be careful not to say anything that might remind him he's met me in the past. I don't expect I'll have much to do with him anyway – *you're* the front-of-house man until we get busier, and also the old school chum.'

'I hope we get a chance to have a catch-up at some point,' he said, 'though Mrs Powys was clearly putting us in our place as the help, wasn't she? Not that we need it – we never encroach because we're here to work and are paid a fortune for it.'

'And we like being busy and making everyone comfortable and happy,' I said. 'It's why we're such a success!'

'Mrs Powys is very impressive, isn't she?' Henry said.

'Yes, she has presence and she's nearly as tall as me. She doesn't look ill, does she?'

'I don't know. She's thin to the point of being gaunt,' he said. 'And since she told me when we were arranging the booking that her health was deteriorating and she wanted to hold one last Christmas party, like they had in the old days, she must be.'

'Then if that's what she wants, that's what she'll have,' I said. 'Come on, I'll help you make your bed and then we can unpack, and meet back downstairs in half an hour.'

Back in my bedroom, I plugged in my own good reading lamp on the bedside table and then unpacked. My clothes, hung in one corner of the vast mahogany wardrobe, looked as if they were trying to hide and I only used the top two drawers of the matching dressing table.

Tidying my hair in front of an old, clouded mirror, I saw that it softened my coldly classical features in a very flattering way and wished I looked like that all the time.

'Mirror, mirror, on the wall, who is the fairest Dido of them all?' I asked, as I rammed a couple of hairclips into the ends of my plaits to hold them more firmly. Then I went down to find Henry arranging his DVD collection on one of the empty bookcase shelves.

We'd both changed into our working clothes – we'd long ago decided on black cotton trousers, or jeans, teamed with a white or black T-shirt. Over these we wore loose buttoned tunic jackets, black for Henry and white for me. It was all very practical, as was our footwear. I'd fallen into the habit of always wearing moccasin shoes, being on my feet all the time – suede in the house and leather out. I even had fringed moccasin boots.

Henry favoured dark trainers, unless he was in his butler role. It was all a bit of a contrast to when he was in Mutant Teenage Snowboarder mode.

'Come on,' I said, 'let's go and help Maria. We can make this room look like home later.'

But Maria seemed to have everything under control in the kitchen without us. Indeed, with that fat file of instruction and information, it would be hard not to be organized.

She told us we'd just missed Xan, who had come in to feed his little dog, which was a shame . . . not.

We both accompanied her to the dining room when she went to lay the table, so we could see where everything was kept. We had a better look at the morning room on the way and she point out the hotplates, the toaster, Tupperware containers of cereals and the breakfast china.

'And the table extends, when there are more guests,' she added. 'The dining table also, as I will show you.'

The dining room was large and dark, but in a sumptuous kind of way, with damson velvet curtains and candlestick-style wall lights above polished wooden panelling.

Maria put a match to the fire laid in the grate, before opening the various cupboards around the room to show us the everyday table linen, and the special occasion stuff, including Christmas tablecloths, runners and napkins.

There was a splendid Minton dinner service gleaming softly behind glazed doors and an array of silver cutlery, alongside the good stainless steel. I suspected all the good stuff would only come out for Christmas dinner and it would take Henry and me till Boxing Day to hand-wash and polish everything.

There was more china and porcelain in the cupboards, which I longed to explore, but that would have to wait.

Maria and Henry covered the polished wood of the table in white damask and laid it for dinner. Or rather, Henry laid it and Maria watched him critically. She wasn't going to catch him out, though; he was brought up to know these things.

I wandered round the room, looking at the hotplates on a side table and one of those heated hostess trolleys that were in vogue years ago. There was an array of flat-bottomed decanters and a soda syphon standing on top of a huge sideboard, and when I peeped inside the doors underneath I found an extensive collection of liqueurs and mixers. The tall cupboard next to it was full of glasses, the expensive cut-glass kind.

'There's a drinks cupboard in the sitting room, too,' Maria told me, seeing what I was doing. 'With the sherry for Lucy, and whisky – the Lady likes whisky in the evening. The cocktail shakers are there, too, but no one drinks the cocktails now.'

'I expect the guests will, though, if some of them are young?' I suggested. 'Henry, you'd better check we have all the ingredients for the popular ones.'

'Yeah, and on the gin and vodka situation too,' he agreed.

I went over to the window and drew back the heavy, plushy

drapes, but outside it was too dark to see anything, though you could hear the icy wind whistling round the house.

'There must be a lovely view from here during the day, right down the valley,' I said.

'Across the valley,' corrected Maria. 'The terraced gardens you only see when you get to the edge of the lawn and look down. But it is sheltered and the Lady grows all kinds of flowers and plants there.'

'Mrs Powys is a keen gardener?' I asked.

'Yes, like her mother before her. Especially she likes the Winter Garden on the middle terrace, where flowers bloom even now: it is like a miracle.'

'I must see that. You wouldn't think anything would flower this far north in winter,' I agreed.

Henry was looking over the dining table with satisfaction. 'There, that looks lovely – and now I know where everything we need is.'

He's always quick to grasp and remember these things.

'When there is no other staff, I do not use the silver cutlery that must be polished – there is no time. You saw the old diving helmets in the Great Hall?'

'The copper and brass ones? Yes, you could hardly miss them!' I said.

'The cleaning service dusts them. The Lady is very particular and would like me to polish them, but as I tell her, I am just one person and cannot do everything.'

'I'm amazed at all the work you have been doing single-handed,' Henry told her admiringly.

Maria shrugged. 'I have done my best. Now, there is nothing more to do in here. Henry, you come with me to the cellar, to fetch a bottle of red wine. You will see the boiler there, too, but rarely does it need attention.'

'Of course,' he agreed, and they went off back towards the servants' wing. I followed more slowly, past the doors of the library and the locked study that had been Asa Powys's, which were at the back of the house.

'It's an Aladdin's cave of alcohol down there,' Henry said, reappearing in the kitchen with a bottle of wine.

'They used to entertain a lot. Mr Powys loved to have a house full of guests and he especially enjoyed Christmas – and the Lady, too. She told me once she had happy memories of Christmas when she was a little girl and her mother was alive.'

Perhaps a combination of those long-ago Christmases and the more recent ones with her husband was what Mrs Powys yearned for now.

Maria added, 'She said that one year her present was a Shetland pony and she came down to find it standing in the hall, wearing a ribbon, though they had put down matting to protect the tiles. They are quite mad, the English gentry.'

'I know, it's the sort of thing some of my relatives would do, too,' Henry agreed. 'My great-aunt Pamela once rode her hunter up the main staircase and along the gallery for a bet, but it wasn't too keen on coming back down again.'

Maria looked unsure if he was joking or not, then decided he was and smiled at him.

'They kept on the Christmas parties until Mr Powys died, even though less and less friends were left . . . but the young ones came, like Xan, and the few relatives remaining. But after Mr Powys died, there were no parties, no Christmas. The Lady shut up the house and went to stay with her friend Mrs Kane in Oxford. But now, the friend will come here. She is very nice, Mrs Kane, though I find it odd that she was a vicar.'

'Oh, really?' I said, thinking that she probably still *was* a vicar, unless she was unfrocked or whatever they called it, which seemed unlikely.

'Before that, she lectured at the university – she is very clever,' Maria said. 'She and the Lady went to Oxford together.'

'I look forward to meeting the learned Reverend Mrs Kane,' Henry said.

Maria had switched on the oven and now put the large casserole in the middle.

'There – and I have peeled sprouts to go with it. I cook them in the microwave just before I serve dinner. They take only minutes.'

I suppressed a shudder.

'The starter is ready, in the fridge. I told you the Lady likes that to be served in the sitting room?' She glanced at the clock. 'I take them through now.'

'I'll carry the tray,' Henry offered and they went out together. I wondered how I could tactfully suggest I take charge of the sprouts, before they were microwaved to mush.

Henry and Maria came back chatting amicably. He can twist practically anyone round his finger and he genuinely finds people interesting. I bet he had already got her to promise to write down her baklava recipe for him.

That reminded me about dessert, but she showed me a huge jar of pears in Calvados – from Fortnum and Mason, no less – chilling in the fridge. These were to be served with thick cream.

'We switched on the hotplate in the dining room on the way back,' Henry told me, 'so there isn't really much more to do than dish up and serve, then clear away, Dido. I've been trying to persuade Maria to go home and leave it all to us now.'

'Oh, yes, do! You must be exhausted!'

'You've been here all day and I know you said you usually

went home once you'd put the dessert on the table,' Henry said to her. 'I'm positive that Dido and I can manage perfectly well now. Why not go home?'

'It makes sense because you're going to have a busy day tomorrow,' I pointed out.

'I suppose I could do that . . .' she said. 'It has been a very long day and I still have things to do at home.'

She looked at me doubtfully. 'You understand about breakfast?'

'Yes, I set the table in the morning room for two, and take up Mrs Powys's tray at exactly eight. It'll be fine.'

'I come back in the morning about ten, just to show you where is the oil tank.'

'Fine, we'll see you then,' Henry said, and with a lot more last-minute instructions, she finally went home.

'At last we're alone together, darling,' Henry said, gazing soulfully at me.

'Don't be an idiot,' I said, putting the sprouts in a pan and setting it on the stove.

'Don't you want to microwave those into green gloop?' he suggested with a grin.

'Not in *my* kitchen. They go out *al dente* or not at all. See if you can find any cooking sherry, or *any* dry sherry; I suspect the casserole will need a little last-minute jazzing up.'

'OK, and I'll open that bottle of red and take it into the dining room with the water carafe.'

While I finished off the main course, Henry went in and out with the warm bread rolls and butter, then the casserole dish and the vegetables.

Then, when all was ready, he beat the big brass gong on the table in the passage outside the dining room.

I divided the big jar of pears in Calvados between three little glass dishes and put them in the fridge, with a jug of cream, ready to go.

Henry reported that everyone was tucking in and he'd taken the opportunity to fetch the used glasses and hors d'oeuvre dishes from the sitting room.

'All tidy and the cushions plumped up, ready for when they take their coffee there,' he said. 'All according to those exhaustive instructions!'

'Handy, though,' I said. 'Because of them, we know all the little details, such as Mrs Powys liking the cheeseboard on the table with the dessert, and the coffee served in the sitting room.'

'Yes, and she'll ring when they leave the dining room, so we can clear.'

I laid out the coffee tray and when the bell finally jangled, Henry took it through, while I went to lay the table in the morning room for two, ready for breakfast.

The dishwasher was soon glugging away in the kitchen and Henry began hand-washing the delicate things. I foraged for bacon in the freezer; Henry is partial to a cooked breakfast, even if no one else fancied it.

'I'll make some *petits fours* to go with their after-dinner coffee tomorrow,' Henry said, putting the last wine glass in the rack and then drying his hands.

'I don't think they'll starve without them,' I told him.

'I know, but the coffee tray looked sort of naked without any little nibbles.'

'I could do with a bit of a nibble now,' I said. 'Let's finish off the leftovers.'

'There we are – duty done,' said Henry, a little while later, when he'd come back from putting the guard over the fire in the dining room. 'I don't know about you, but I'm shattered.'

'It's been one hell of a long day,' I agreed, 'and we didn't expect to start work tonight.'

We'd eaten up the remains of the casserole and finished off the pears in the jar – there were two, so they obviously had our names on them – but now we divested ourselves of our tunics and retired to the staff sitting room with hot cocoa and the huge tin of chocolate biscuits we'd brought with us. Henry put on the DVD of *White Christmas*, but just for background noise, really. I'd brought the fat household ring binder with me for bedtime reading. I wanted to compare Mrs Hill's Christmas shopping list with mine and also look at the old Christmas menus, which were helpfully still filed there.

'So, it starts,' Henry said. 'And Mrs Powys will give us the once-over in the library at half past nine tomorrow – a bit like seeing the headmistress when you've been naughty.'

'I think we'd better *not* be naughty, but I expect she only wants to discuss the house party and the Christmas menus, that kind of thing.'

'I'm guessing traditional turkey and all the trimmings,' he said. 'Oh, and while I remember, Xan says he'll come down to the kitchen for his breakfast, when he's taken Plum out.'

I sat up straight again and stared at him. 'I've laid two places in the morning room for him and Lucy. I don't want him in my kitchen, under my feet! In fact, in the circumstances, I'd prefer to see him as little as possible, just in case something stirs his memory and he recognizes me.'

'Well, you tell him to get out of your kitchen tomorrow, then,' he said comfortably, and I threw a fat cushion at him.

When Henry switched to watching an old horror film, *Night of the Lepus* – and personally, I can't find rabbits scary, even if they have been made to look huge and have fake blood smeared all over their faces – I left him to it and went up to bed.

I finished the last of the unpacking and got into my warm, comfortable bed, but tired though I was, I found it very hard to go to sleep.

Xan's face seemed to be imprinted on the inside of my eyelids – the younger version I'd had such an insane crush on.

It would be hideously embarrassing if he suddenly realized who I was! If it had only been the crush, it wouldn't be so bad . . . but no, my conscience still squirmed whenever I thought back to that time and what I had done . . .

Sabine

I confess I was momentarily startled when I set eyes on the couple from Heavenly Houseparties, for neither was quite what I envisaged. The woman – Dido – was so unexpectedly tall and fair that, with her Grecian nose and hair coiled up in that old-fashioned style, she'd reminded me strongly of the caryatids I'd seen holding up temple porticos! She certainly didn't resemble that photograph of her father in the least.

Her voice was almost accentless, apart from a slight Lancashire inflection in the flattened vowels. Henry, on the other hand, had both looked and sounded more like one of my guests – but then, he had been at Rugby with Xan and, even if he said he was a poor relation, was very well-connected. I thought this might make things awkward for my plans, but he made himself very unobtrusive at dinner and didn't encroach in any way, while the young woman remained out of sight in the kitchen.

How lovely it will be to have Xan here for a whole month. He's already quite at home at the Castle, of course, having stayed here so often since he was a boy. Asa and I have always been so fond of him that he is the perfect person to write Asa's biography . . . and though I expect old Tommy, his grandfather and once our expedition photographer, told him lots of stories from the old days, I'm sure I can rely on Xan's discretion.

Perhaps Asa talked to Tommy about those things we never discussed together. What old secrets might he have let slip?

During our chat this afternoon, Xan suggested he write the book more as a joint biography, but I said no, I would have been nothing without Asa and my role had been to help him in every way: he was a great man and I was lucky to be his friend, lover, assistant and, in those early years, his diving partner.

Oh, those wonderful times beneath the translucent azure seas of the Aegean . . . The silky feel of the water, the bubbles rising towards the light . . . the strange, different world of the sea bed.

The diagnosis of my illness seems to have already stirred the silt of my memory, releasing all kinds of scenes from the past, not only of my life with Asa, but also my early childhood, when Mummy was alive and life seemed quite perfect.

And now that Xan is here, I'll be reliving the past with him, for he means to record some of my memories.

Those will soon be all that remains of me, for I certainly won't see out most of next year. I'll know when the right moment has come, and I intend bowing out with a bang, and not after a drawn-out whimpering half-life.

I don't sleep well now, but it's cosy here in my little boudoir, as Mummy always called the small sitting room off the master bedroom, now mine. I have a radio for company, and a funny little mother-of-pearl desk with a good lock against prying fingers, where I have moved the information and photographs the private investigator obtained for me. A large, silver-framed photograph of Asa smiles at me from the top of it.

I heard Xan's footsteps earlier going through into the old wing, where his bedroom is, with the scampering sound of dear little Plum's paws. I miss having a dog about the place, but felt I could not take on another once Asa's old spaniel had died not long after he did.

Xan took Plum out for his last walk before bedtime, which reminded me of how I used to stand under the stars in the dark with poor old Fudge, waiting for him to remember why we were out there. The old dog had felt like the last living link connecting me to Asa.

My thoughts turned to Nancy, who has been my stalwart friend right from our first undergraduate days at Oxford. With her clear vision and ruthless honesty, she's not always a comfortable person to have around; I call her the voice of my conscience. It would be hard to keep my plans from her and she could well put a spanner in my works. But then, so be it. Let events unfold with just a little nudge from me, or from Fate, from time to time!

7

Invasions

Early next morning, Henry and I were up and swinging into action with the ease of long practice.

After a mug of good, strong coffee, Henry went off to unbolt doors, draw curtains and generally tidy up downstairs, while I emptied the dishwasher and put everything away.

He came back with a tray of used glasses. 'My fine detective instincts tell me that last night Xan and Mrs Powys drank whisky, while Lucy does indeed prefer a disgustingly sweet sherry.'

'It sounds like it's bought specially for her. I can't imagine Mrs Powys drinking that stuff . . . and I must remember to put a bottle of cooking sherry on the shopping list, because that bottle you fetched from the dining room last night to jazz up the casserole is too good for the purpose, really,' I said. 'It doesn't seem to have been a staple of the old housekeeper's lists, though it *does* appear on one for additional items to be ordered for Christmas, under "sherry for trifle" along with "dark rum for Christmas cake".'

'We're well past Stir-up Sunday, so if Mrs Powys wants a Christmas cake and a pudding, you'll have to make your quick versions, Dido. Actually, I prefer those.'

'I expect we'll find out exactly what she wants later, when we see her.'

'Well, must get on,' Henry said. 'Fires to do next. Luckily, I think there are enough logs in the baskets for today, and I noticed kindling and old newspapers in that room off the passage where the old dog bowls were stored. There's a big, empty log basket in there too, but perhaps I can fill that up later, when Maria has shown us the outbuildings.'

'I'd better come with you when she does, so I know where everything is, too,' I said. 'I won't be chopping any logs, though I'm sure you can hardly wait to get your hands on the axe.'

'You know me only too well, darling,' he said and went off to find the ash can.

Time was passing and, after glancing at the clock, I began to assemble Mrs Powys's breakfast on the tray I'd already laid with an embroidered cloth and chintzy flowered plate, cup and saucer. She only had toast, according to Maria's note: two rounds, almost, but not quite, burnt. I added butter in a small dish, a tiny jar of set honey, a small glass of orange juice, some milk in a tiny jug and a large cup of freshly brewed coffee.

Lucy came into the kitchen just as I picked the laden tray up.

'Oh, good, it's all ready!' she fluted breathily, as if I'd managed to perform some esoteric rite single-handedly. 'Cousin Sabine is *such* a stickler for time and I'm often late because I've burned the first lot of toast – so difficult to get it right – and—'

'I'm afraid *I* will be late if I don't take this upstairs now,' I said, edging past her, though I softened the words with a slight smile. 'Why not go through into the morning room and I'll bring your breakfast when I come down, if you tell me what you'd like. I've already put bread, butter and milk out.'

'Oh, not to worry – I only have toast and I can pop that in

the toaster myself. So just a pot of tea for me. Unless Xan – Mr Fellowes – is down and wants coffee.'

'I expect he takes his dog out first thing,' I suggested, then headed out through the swinging baize door to the Garden Hall and up the stairs.

I tapped at Mrs Powys's door – the Rose Room – and balancing one end of the tray on my hip with the ease of long practice, turned the porcelain knob and went in.

The brocade curtains, which, like the walls, were a soft and unusual fondant pinkish-lilac colour, had already been pulled back and Sabine Powys was sitting up in bed, propped against a great bank of pillows.

I have *no* idea how people sleep on embroidered pillows without waking up next morning with the pattern embossed into their faces, and the French knots must feel like *hell*.

But Mrs Powys's face was only imprinted with the marks of time. Without the bright mask of make-up she'd worn the previous night, her skin had a marked pallor and there were pale violet shadows under her eyes.

There was a netting of fine lines, too, so she looked very much her age this morning, but her huge pale blue eyes were diamond bright, emphasized by surprisingly dark eyelashes. She must have them dyed, I thought inconsequentially, while wishing her a cheerful good morning and laying the tray over her knees – it was the sort with handy little fold-down legs.

She surveyed her breakfast without comment, so it must have passed muster, then said, 'Now that fool of a woman isn't cooking it, I'd like a lightly boiled egg with my toast tomorrow.'

'Certainly,' I agreed.

'What are you usually called?' she asked abruptly. 'Di, perhaps? Dido is such a ridiculous name!'

'I'm never called Di,' I said firmly. Only Charlotte had ever called me that.

I didn't think Sabine was that great a choice, either – I mean, those Sabine women didn't exactly sound a laugh-a-minute – but I said politely, 'I know it's unusual, but my father liked it. You need something fairly distinctive to go with Jones.'

She made no further comment, so I asked if I could get her anything else. 'I could still boil you an egg now and make fresh toast, if you fancy it?'

'No, tomorrow will do. I'm just grateful not to have my coffee slopped all over the tray and burnt, scraped toast, which is all that Lucy can usually manage. And half the time, she forgets and makes me instant coffee, without even letting the kettle come to the boil.'

'I think she must be a little absent-minded,' I suggested. 'This is dark Italian ground coffee, made in a cafetière – that's what Maria said you preferred. She wrote everything down for me in great detail.'

'I'm sure she's told Lucy what I like repeatedly, too, though since there's nothing in Lucy's head to impede it, it will have gone in one ear and out of the other,' she said, then I suddenly noticed she was looking at me with an indefinable expression on her face, just as she had the night before, when we had first met.

But it vanished so quickly I thought I must have imagined it and she said, dismissively, 'Well, I'll see you and Henry in the library at half past nine and we can discuss your duties and all the arrangements for the house party, then.'

'Yes, Mrs Powys,' I agreed and, taking my cue, went out.

There was no sign of the Poor Relation when I got back to the kitchen, but instead, Xan was there, sitting at the table with a mug of coffee, watching Henry grilling bacon.

The small brown-and-white spaniel was also watching Henry,

with rapt attention in his slightly bulging eyes, and barely spared me a glance.

Xan was speaking to Henry in the deep, soft and mellow voice that I remembered so well.

'Ignore Plum, he's already wolfed down all of his own breakfast, but he's so greedy.'

The small, stainless-steel dog bowl in the corner was certainly shining as if it had had an extensive tongue-polishing and a pool of water was spreading out from the bowl next to it. I suspected Plum, with his slightly undershot jaw, was a messy eater and drinker.

'Good morning,' Xan said, half-turning and automatically giving me the wary half-smile of a man whose every word and expression was likely to be misinterpreted by the opposite sex. He hadn't quite perfected that in his previous incarnation as a dreamy youth, though I did remember the occasional startled look of a stag at bay, when Charlotte and I had cornered him.

'Good morning,' I replied coolly, not answering the smile.

'We're having bacon rolls and there's enough for you, too, Dido,' Henry said, flipping the rashers over with a pair of tongs. 'Xan's joining us. He doesn't fancy a tête-à-tête in the morning room with Cousin Lucy, but luckily she'd just taken her pot of tea through before he got here.'

'I hope you don't mind my invading your kitchen like this,' Xan remarked, stepping up the wattage of the smile a little. 'Henry said you wouldn't.'

'Not at all,' I said politely, meaning, of course, the opposite, and the smile faded.

'I'd better check Lucy's got everything she wants, before I have mine,' I added.

'Except Xan – he came down the servants' stairs to try and avoid running into her,' said Henry, grinning.

'I had the run of the place when I stayed here as a boy, so I know my way around,' explained Xan. 'Asa and Sabine were my godparents – and my father's before me – because my grandfather, Tommy Fellowes, was Asa's best friend, as well as the photographer on all the early underwater documentaries.'

'We've seen some clips from those on YouTube,' I said, interested despite myself.

'Xan and I've had a quick catch-up,' said Henry. 'I've told him that we knew all about the marine archaeology stuff, because we googled Sabine Powys. Xan's going to write a biography of Asa. He's been trying to get Sabine to agree to it for ages.'

'I wanted to make it a joint biography, but Sabine wouldn't hear of it. She'll come into it a lot, though, because they worked on everything together, even if she does always cast herself as Asa's assistant.'

'She did tell me when we were discussing the booking that someone would be staying all of December, to collect material for a biography,' Henry said. 'I just hadn't expected it would be you.'

Nor me! I thought. If I'd only known, I might have tried to get Henry to turn the booking down. But at least there still wasn't even a flicker of recognition in Xan's eyes when he looked at me, so if I didn't say anything to jog his memory, it should all stay hunky-dory . . . sort of.

Henry was now putting the bacon into rolls and I suddenly remembered I'd been going to go to the morning room to check that Lucy had everything she needed: duty first, even before bacon rolls.

But I found her sitting at the table, toast crumbs on a plate, squeezing out a final cup of tea from the pot. She declined a fresh pot, hot water, or anything else.

'I'm sure Xan intended to join me for breakfast, but perhaps he overslept,' she fluted like a mournful bird, looking disgruntled. 'I don't suppose you've seen him?'

I had a moment's temptation, but then realized that if I shopped him, *she* was quite likely to come and infest my kitchen, too, so I lied through my teeth.

'I'm afraid not, but I expect he'll come down soon. There's no rush, is there? He probably had an even longer drive yesterday than we did.'

'Perhaps, but surely he must have had to take his dear little doggy out first thing?'

'I didn't hear anything,' I said truthfully. 'Well, I'd better get back to the kitchen, if there's nothing more you want, because Maria's calling in later, in case there's anything she's forgotten to tell us about.'

'Oh, good, though you can always call on me if any difficulties arise.'

'That's very kind of you,' I said, though actually, asking Plum for advice would probably prove more useful. You only had to take one glance at Lucy to get her dithering and ineffectual measure. But still, she seemed well meaning and entirely harmless, so I didn't expect she'd give us any trouble.

'We want to take the cares off *your* shoulders too, over Christmas,' I said gravely.

Lucy sighed long-sufferingly. 'I'll still have to fetch the newspapers from the shop in Wallstone, the nearest village, after breakfast – they simply won't deliver any more. And Cousin Sabine wants fresh flowers, because I forgot to top up the water in the vases yesterday, though they perked up again once I'd realized. But no . . . such a long drive, just for flowers.'

She sighed again in a martyred way and drifted out of the room, and I put everything together on a tray and took it back to the kitchen.

Xan and Henry had almost finished their rolls, but Henry fetched mine from the hotplate where it was keeping warm and poured me a cup of coffee.

'Eat it, before I do – I'm still hungry,' he said. 'What took you so long?'

'Lucy was wittering on. She was disappointed not to see you at breakfast, Mr Fellowes.'

'Xan,' he corrected.

'But she's going out shortly to fetch the newspapers and buy flowers, so you're safe for a while.'

'I should be safe most of the time, once Sabine opens up Asa's study and lets me loose in there,' he said. 'I'll be working, so Sabine won't let her disturb me. I'm looking forward to it, and to recording Sabine as she fleshes out the past for me, though Grandpa did tell me some stories about that time . . .'

A cloud suddenly seemed to cross his face, but vanished as quickly, and he began feeding his bacon rinds to Plum, who was now sitting at his feet, looking hopeful.

But when no more were forthcoming from his master, Plum switched his attention and his melting dark gaze to me.

'He's very cute,' I said, immediately losing both my heart and my bacon rinds. 'He looks just like one of those little spaniels in portraits of Cavaliers and their ladies, though he isn't a Cavalier spaniel at all, is he?'

'No, but he is a direct descendant of those little dogs in old portraits. His breed is simply called King Charles, without the Cavalier bit – they're smaller, with a domed head and broad nose,' Xan explained. 'They usually have a bit of an undershot jaw, like Plum, too.'

I gave Plum my last bit of rind and then stroked his silky head. Looking up, my eyes met Xan's strangely light, lilac-grey ones and saw his straight, dark brows drawn together in a slightly puzzled way.

'You know, I keep having the feeling we've met before, though I'm sure if we had I'd remember you!'

My heart stopped and restarted again with a thud. I'd been so sure he wouldn't realize who I was that for a moment I couldn't speak, but then I said quickly, 'I don't think so, because I'd probably remember you, too.'

'There's only one Dido walking around looking like an escaped Greek caryatid,' Henry said with a grin. 'So there's no way you could forget her!'

I'd *kill* him for that remark later.

'I'm sure you're right,' Xan said, also grinning, though I couldn't see what was so amusing. Lots of people have Greek noses . . . especially Greeks.

I glanced at the clock and got up.

'I'd better clear up, because Maria's popping in about ten and I don't want her to find her kitchen already looking a mess.'

Xan took the hint and got up, too – I'd forgotten how tall he was, though still as willowy as ever.

'Sabine's going to ceremonially hand me the key of Asa's study at nine and then induct me into the mysteries within,' he said. 'I've just got time to give Plum another quick run first.'

'Mrs Powys is going to have a busy morning,' said Henry, 'since she's seeing us at half past nine. I keep thinking of Cluedo for some reason – you know: "Mrs Powys, in the library, with an axe".'

'Not an axe, unless it's an antique double-headed bronze one,' Xan said seriously. 'And since she wants you to cater for a large Christmas house party, I don't think she would finish you off till the New Year.'

'Yes, she mentioned to us when making the booking that she was in failing health and wanted a last party at the Castle,' Henry said.

Xan frowned. 'She told me that too, though I can't really see any sign of it. It's worrying, because I'm very fond of her.'

'Well, we're going to give her exactly the kind of Christmas she wants. It's our forte, really,' Henry said modestly. 'It will all go with a swing!'

'Since she seems to have invited all her remaining, though not very exciting, relatives, good luck with that one!' Xan said, and headed out towards the Garden Hall, Plum scampering at his heels.

'Looks like I might have been wrong about him forgetting you, Dido, and it might all suddenly come back to him,' Henry said, sounding amused. 'Perhaps you ought to brace yourself and tell him now, get it over with? You might find it quite cathartic.'

Henry had something there, but it would only release all the embarrassment and guilt if I confessed all, which I wasn't about to. 'I don't think I really need to, because I'm sure he only had the vaguest suspicion he'd seen me before,' I said optimistically.

'Well, if he does, you'll simply have to pretend it was so long ago, you'd entirely forgotten him, improbable as it might seem,' he suggested.

'Or if he suddenly remembers me as that pestilential child who made his life a misery for a fortnight, he might pretend *he* doesn't remember me either, while avoiding me like the plague, in case I make a nuisance of myself all over again,' I said.

'He's so handsome, you still might.'

'I'm much more likely to fall for Plum – he's *gorgeous*!'

'Xan's not just a handsome face, he's really nice, too, once you get to know him. Everyone liked him at school, even if he was a bit of a swot.'

'For such a good-looking man, he doesn't seem at all up himself,' I admitted grudgingly. 'But since he isn't married, perhaps he's gay?'

Henry shook his head. 'Definitely not, but he might be glad to hang out with me a bit when I'm off duty, if the other guests all turn out to be elderly.'

'I expect we'll find out who's been invited shortly, when Mrs Powys has given Xan the run of her husband's old study. While she's doing that, let's pop up to make the beds and bring down Mrs Powys's tray,' I said. 'At least there are only three beds to make at the moment.'

We whipped round upstairs in no time.

Normally, we'd have taken an hour or two off after that, before it was time to start lunch, although the first day was usually one spent getting a handle on the normal routine of the house, checking supplies and the ordering system and that kind of thing. Thanks to the uber-organized system with the files, however, that was a doddle.

Henry was finishing the last of a pot of strangely pink tea when he looked up at the clock. 'Time to go.'

I put a notebook and pen into my tunic pocket and got up.

'Come on then,' I said. 'Mrs Powys, in the library, with a double-headed axe, it is!'

Sabine

When Dido brought my breakfast, it suddenly struck me how like an Archbold she was – so tall and fair. Or she would have been if her eyes were blue, instead of that odd duck-egg shade.

But of course, there wasn't a drop of Archbold blood in her veins – only much-diluted Mordue, from my father. He had been thin and brown-haired . . . and now I came to think of it, in the recent photograph, Dido's father had had a slight resemblance to him.

Dido probably got her looks from her birth mother and I thought I'd get Mr Jarrold, the private detective I'd been using, to investigate her a little, just out of curiosity.

Dido's manner is very cool and reserved, but I'm certain that she has no idea of our connection, so I can hug the secret to myself for as long as I wish, to reveal or not, as I choose.

Probably not.

When I got up, I opened the desk in my boudoir and looked again at the recent photo of Faye's son – and the resemblance to my father was indeed there, in the brown hair and the slightly beaky nose, set in a narrow face.

I had so loved Daddy, until he married that woman, and so soon after Mummy died that later I'd realized they must have been having an affair all along.

And even though Mummy had left her fortune and the Castle to me, my father received an income from the estate during his life and he and the Usurper continued to live here . . . and Faye, when she came along.

Their presence had put me off coming home during my university years and after, even though I loved the Castle so. But then, not long after I'd married Asa, Daddy and the Usurper had been killed in a car crash on the way back from a race meeting and my half-sister, Faye, who was then fourteen and at boarding school, was left to the guardianship of the family solicitor and a relative of her mother's.

And after that, Asa and I were free to divide our time between Mitras Castle and our villa on Corfu.

Happy days!

As to Faye, after that terrible summer when Asa was taken ill while diving, her name was never mentioned between us. It was as if she'd never really existed, except as a bad dream, pushed away into the darkest corners of our minds.

8

Brown Study

The door from the passage into Asa Powys's study, which was opposite the dining room, was slightly ajar when we passed it on the way to the library and I caught the sound of Xan's voice, though not what he was saying.

The library was empty and I looked around curiously. We'd had a glimpse of the room yesterday, of course, with its computer and printer looking incongruous among the antique furniture, dark wood bookshelves and richly patterned rugs.

Now I saw that it was a bigger room than I had realized, with squashy-looking sofas and armchairs, upholstered in delft-blue linen, arranged around an old carved stone fireplace. Any walls not covered in bookshelves were panelled in dark brown wood.

We didn't have much time to take it in, though, because a door in the wall that adjoined Asa's study suddenly swung open and Mrs Powys came in. I had a brief glimpse of Xan standing by a large filing cabinet, Plum at his feet, before she shut it behind her.

'Ah, *there* you are,' she said, as if we were late, which we weren't, then invited us to take the two chairs opposite the sofa, where she sat down with a business-like air, holding a clipboard notebook, as well as a sheaf of papers she'd collected from the desk.

This morning she was dressed in upmarket country casuals, which would have looked frumpy on anyone less slim and elegant: a lavender twinset in silk-fine cashmere, teamed with a heather-mix tweed skirt, well fitted and coming below the knee, revealing slender, but still shapely legs and ankles. On her feet were thin glacé leather house shoes.

From long experience, I recognized that the necklace and earrings she wore were genuine, and hideously expensive, matched South Sea pearls of great size.

Her bouffant hair looked like a precious bird's nest lacquered in pale gold, and since I'd seen her when I'd taken up her breakfast tray, she had put on a mask of make-up: her eyebrows were thin dark arcs, her pale blue eyes ringed in dark liner and her lips generously painted a deep rose.

Of course, her brittle, thin, age-spotted hands were a bit of a giveaway, though even there your eye was first drawn to the huge solitaire diamond ring that sat above a gold wedding band.

Come to think of it, her appearance was all about distraction: smoke and mirrors. I don't think she'd ever been truly beautiful even when young, but simply projected the impression of it.

By now I suspected that doing her face and hair every morning was so automatic, she did it without even thinking about it, even when there had only been Maria here to see it.

By the time she looked up from her notes, we'd assumed our professional expressions: Henry's was polite, slightly eager and deferential, with only a trace of the impertinent cherub about it, while mine, Henry has often told me, looks like someone started to blow life into a marble statue, but soon ran out of puff.

Mrs Powys didn't waste any time in attending to the large clipboard and a pen and getting down to business, ticking things off as she went. We already knew from those extensive kitchen files that she was a great one for organization. But then so was I, so that should make things very much easier than in more chaotic households.

She ran us briskly through what she expected of us regarding the normal day-to-day running of the house, which was as agreed, and then she said, 'Henry, you told me when I made the booking that you didn't take a day or half-day off during your assignments?'

'No, but instead we snatch an hour or two mid-morning and after lunch, if possible. Then, in the evening, we've usually finished for the day by nine.'

'That sounds perfectly reasonable,' she said, adding yet another tick to her list and moved on to the next thing.

'I like to keep the Castle cosy – what is the point of being rich and cold? Besides, it would be a false economy if all the pipes froze up.'

'Very true,' I agreed, 'and old houses can quickly get damp, too – they need to be kept warm and aired. The boiler is quite new and reliable and the oil tank is well filled.'

'Maria's going to show us where that is this morning,' Henry told her, 'and I can relight the boiler in the cellar, if need be, too.'

'Good.'

She unclipped the first page and started on the second.

'I like to have open fires in the dining room and sitting room in winter. A forestry management service looks after the trees on the estate and provides us with a supply of logs, ready to chop for firewood.'

'Maria's going to show us where those are stored too,' I said.

The pen made another brisk upward sweep, after which she

made sure we understood the arrangements with the cleaning service, who would be coming in the morning, Wednesdays being their day.

'A team of them go right through the house very thoroughly, including changing the beds. One of them spends all morning in the laundry room, washing and ironing – there's one of those rotary ironing machines there, for large items like towels and bedding. Any dry-cleaning is hung on a special rail and will be brought back the following week.'

'It's such a luxury to have a separate laundry room and someone to do the bulk of it, though I can keep up with any other laundry during the rest of the week,' I said.

'And *I'm* a dab hand at pressing delicate things,' Henry said, with one of his delightful smiles, and Mrs Powys's lips twitched, so that for a moment I thought she was about to break into an answering smile.

'Magic Mops will be carrying out an extra deep clean next week, before we put up the tree and decorations.'

She looked up. 'By the way, I'm always out on Wednesdays. I go into Hexham to have my hair done and lunch out. Lucy also takes herself off to some church bunfight in Wallstone. Xan will be working in the study all day, I expect, but the cleaners won't go in there without permission.'

'Just Xan for lunch tomorrow, then,' I said, making my own note of it.

'If he's hard at work, he might prefer a tray of sandwiches and coffee in the library,' Henry suggested. 'I'll ask him, Dido.'

'Now, as to the everyday catering,' continued Mrs Powys, as if neither of us had spoken, 'we've always kept the freezers, store cupboards and larder well stocked, in case we're snowed in, which happens occasionally, or the roads are so icy its dangerous to attempt to drive anywhere. There's probably quite a lot in the freezer that needs using up. I don't think Maria has ever plumbed the depths.'

'I'm going to do a complete stocktake later today,' I assured her.

'You will see from the file that I order quite a lot from Fortnum and Mason – preserves, bottled fruits and pâté, for instance. I usually do that myself. I can use the computer perfectly competently, I simply prefer to dictate most of my emails to Lucy, which at least gives her some purpose in life. Unlike me, she can touch-type, since she used to be a secretary, but she's not very competent at that, either.'

Poor old Lucy! I was starting to feel sorry for her, though it did sound as if she had involved herself in the affairs of the local village and, I hoped, made some friends there.

'Maria puts in the weekly supermarket order, using this computer, so you can do the same. I expect she's told you about the staff credit card, which is kept in the desk drawer?'

I nodded, thinking this was a very trusting way of going on!

'I have an online account with one of the big supermarkets in Hexham and a wine merchant. You will also find a good delicatessen in Corbridge, and there's a general shop in Wallstone, which is about four miles away. That's where Lucy collects our newspapers from, though they will deliver groceries, if you order a large amount at astronomical prices. You can walk there quite easily, using the path from the bottom of the estate, but of course, it's all uphill coming back.'

She paused again, then added, reminiscently: 'My Scottish nanny was a great walker and on most fine days she would lead me down to the village on my Shetland pony . . .'

Then she came back from the past and gave an unexpected, rather gamine, three-cornered smile that suddenly made her look much more attractive. 'Since Lucy is a church hen and attends all the services and various meetings in Wallstone any-way, she can always bring back anything you suddenly need.'

'I can do all the online ordering,' Henry said, 'and I have the van, so I can also pick up any fresh supplies we need between deliveries. That's no problem.'

Mrs Powys's pen made another brisk tick and she moved on to what I hoped was the final page on her clipboard!

'I usually put in an extra big Fortnum and Mason order before Christmas. We must discuss it, Dido.'

This seemed extravagant, but it was her house and whatever she wanted was fine by me.

'Certainly, Mrs Powys. Could you tell me whether you usu-ally order a Christmas cake and pudding from them, or if you would like me to make them? I'm happy to do so, if that's what you would like, and I have an excellent quick Christmas cake recipe.'

'Yes, do make them and I'll cross those off the list. It's only since Mrs Hill left that I've had to buy them. The cake decor-ations, the round pudding mould and the set of silver charms must still be stored somewhere . . . Mrs Hill used to wrap the charms in tinfoil before stirring them into the pudding, so we found them easily.'

'Yes, I do that, too. I wouldn't want one of the guests chok-ing on a charm!'

'That would definitely not be lucky,' Henry agreed cheerfully.

'As for the daily menus, I leave that entirely to you, Dido. I expect you have a larger repertoire than Maria's. She's good with lamb and rice, or stuffed vine leaves, but one tires of lamb. And she does tend to serve up tinned soup, rice pudding and fruit, unless I'm firm with her.'

'I'd already noticed there were quite a lot of tins in the

larder. Though that's no bad thing if we get cut off,' I said, then asked her if there were any particular dishes she was partial to.

'My appetite is smaller now, but I do find myself thinking of all the lovely meals Mrs Hill made for us – kedgeree, risotto, beef Wellington, salmon en croûte . . . souffles, good, spicy curry . . . Then all the traditional dishes, like roast chicken, or beef and Yorkshire pudding, sausages with mustard mash, cottage pie . . . steak and chips. Asa used to *love* steak and chips!'

'Most men seem to – I do myself,' Henry said.

'Mrs Hill made her own soup, too: mulligatawny, vichyssoise, pea and ham . . . and her raised pork pies and curry puffs were wonderful.'

I thought Mrs Hill sounded pretty wonderful, too! I'd been scribbling away and when I'd caught up, I said, 'I'll look for the curry puff recipe. That sounds interesting and not something I've made before.'

'They might make nice starters,' Henry suggested. 'My department!'

'What about desserts? Are there any you particularly favour, Mrs Powys?'

'I like *good* rice pudding, not tinned . . .'

'I have an excellent Anglo-Indian recipe with cardamom pods and cream.'

'Sticky ginger pudding and custard, fresh fruit salad, crème caramel . . . treacle tart,' she reeled off. 'Maria's baklava is delicious, but she usually only makes it on high days and holidays. We had it for tea yesterday only because Xan is a favourite and she knows he likes it.'

'I do have my own recipe for that – we spent some time in Greece – but I'd like to compare mine with Maria's.'

'She's promised to write it down for me and bring it with her today, so you can,' Henry told me.

'The usual routine of meals will continue up till Christmas. Breakfast is always at eight in the morning room – any guests arriving after nine will find it cleared away. Then lunch in the dining room at one – just something simple, like soup, salad, sandwiches, fruit, cheese – variations on that. Sometimes Welsh rarebit, or eggs Benedict, for a change.'

'Yes, that's all clear,' I assured her. 'And tea in the sitting room at four fifteen?'

'Indeed, and you will need to remember that Xan is a coffee drinker. When Lucy is in charge of making the afternoon tea, I'm lucky if I get a limp digestive biscuit with it.'

'Oh, I can do much better than that,' Henry assured her. 'I make *the* most delicious little sweet or savoury scones, and my madeleines are to *die* for!'

'That would certainly be a sweet way to go,' Mrs Powys said drily.

'I was wondering,' said Henry, 'why you don't have a tea trolley – so much easier than that heavy tray Maria used yesterday.'

She blinked at him and frowned. 'There is one, but Maria doesn't like it, for some reason. I expect it's somewhere about if you look for it.'

'Oh, good – I will,' he said. 'Probably stashed away in one of those little rooms off the kitchen passage.'

'I dare say,' she said disinterestedly. 'Now, you already know all about dinner in the dining room at seven, and that I like some form of starter served in the sitting room first: canapés of some kind, savoury nibbles. I found that the easiest option when we lived on Corfu and now I prefer it.'

'Much simpler,' Henry agreed.

'You will find yourselves with more to do once the guests start to arrive and, of course, the arrangements for meal times will change over Christmas itself.'

'Naturally,' I agreed.

She passed me a sheet of paper. 'Here's a list of my guests, who are mostly relatives, like Lucy. There's her elder brother, Nigel, who has an antiquarian bookshop in Alnwick. I'm afraid you'll find him rather wearing – I certainly do. He adores Christmas and tends to try and be the life and soul of the party.'

Henry and I exchanged glances: we knew that type of old.

'Then there's Asa's cousin Olive Melling, her husband, Frank, and their son, Dominic. Then Timothy Makepeace, who is both an old family friend and my solicitor,' she continued. 'He is bringing his granddaughter, who has been living with him since her divorce. She and Dominic will provide some company for Xan.'

She seemed to be mentally counting up. Then she said, 'Of course! My friend, Mrs Nancy Kane, will also be here, but she's arriving earlier than the rest.'

'Including yourself and Lucy, that will make ten for Christmas?'

'Indeed. You'll see that I've written down which room the guests are to have next to their names, but Mrs Kane always has the bedroom on my floor.'

'Bluebell,' I said, remembering the name plaque.

'Her favourite flower,' said Mrs Powys unexpectedly. 'Now, I expect most of the guests will arrive on Friday the twenty-first, but if the forecast is bad, some may wish to come earlier. Mrs Kane, though, I'm expecting on the thirteenth, and I hope she will stay till the New Year.'

There was the ghost of that youthful gamine grin again. 'I

imagine I'll have had enough of the rest of my guests by Boxing Day, so I hope they'll take themselves off the day after. That old saying about visitors being like fish – they stink after three days – is only too true.'

'I sincerely hope the weather makes that possible, then,' Henry said, his face straight.

'Yes, indeed, and I'm trusting that you two can ensure that if we *are* cooped up here together for longer, they don't kill each other in the manner of a country house crime novel.'

I was getting to recognize her deadpan, dry sense of humour now and accorded this a smile.

'Making house parties go with a swing is our strength,' Henry assured her, with one of his beaming and, I sometimes think, slightly *unhinged* smiles. 'You can trust us.'

'I should hope so, at the prices you charge! As I mentioned to you, my health is in decline and that prompted me to throw what will be my last house party at the Castle. But I don't want that to cast a damper over things. I want it to be a *fun* Christmas.'

'We understand,' Henry said, 'and we were very sorry to hear of your ill health.'

Not that she *looked* ill, apart from being very thin, and her light blue eyes were so *very* alive.

'Thank you, but there's nothing to be done about it, so there's no point in dwelling on it,' she said briskly. 'After I'd had the diagnosis, I decided I wanted one final, traditional, old-fashioned Christmas, like the ones I remember from my childhood. Of course, we had Christmas parties when Asa was alive, but those were bigger and more riotous occasions. Great fun in their way, though – he had such an outgoing personality and was so gregarious that he just drew people to him like a magnet.'

Her expression was suddenly tragic and I hastened to say,

'We're quite used to organizing traditional Christmas parties and it will be exactly as you want it. If there are any particular family traditions you want incorporated, you need only mention them.'

'It's partly atmosphere, I suppose . . .' she said slowly. 'Christmases at the Castle when Mummy was still alive were quite magical and bound up with the scent of the fir tree in the Great Hall and evergreen swags down the staircase . . . and the aroma of spicy potpourri and Christmas baking.'

'Yes, I know what you mean,' I agreed, writing down 'florist's wire' in my notebook. Creating greenery swags would be Henry's task; I was useless at that kind of thing.

Mrs Powys was still reminiscing. 'Present opening was immediately after breakfast, in the sitting room, then dinner on Christmas Day was always at two in the afternoon. After that, we'd play charades, or board games . . . or if there was snow, go tobogganing down the slope below the Roman fort.'

I could see Henry prick up his ears at this.

'The terraced gardens below the house are sheltered, but they open out at the bottom and the lake there often freezes over, so you can skate on it.'

'Great,' Henry murmured, and I expected he was storing away the location of the steep field, possibly suitable for snowboarding, if he got the chance.

It all sounded lovely anyway, and I found myself hoping for a white Christmas, even if it did cut us off for a while.

Granny and Dora had made a token effort at Christmas when I was very small, but after that we would spend it at a small, country house hotel near Bath. It had been quite fun and there were usually a few other children, and a Santa and activities laid on, but I'd learned since that there was so much more to it, especially the lovely, warm spirit of the season. I think that's why I love endlessly creating that kind of Christmas for others and it's lucky Henry enjoys it, too.

'I suppose I'll have to buy everyone presents, since I'm sure they'll bring me some expensive and entirely useless bits of tat,' Mrs Powys said. 'I'll have to think about that one, though Nancy is easy. I always get her Penhaligon's Bluebell perfume.'

'I could look at the guest list and come up with some suggestions, if you like?' Henry offered, and she agreed.

'You might find something suitable on the Fortnum and Mason website,' she said. 'By the way, I usually order our crackers from there, too.'

'Oh, but Marwood's crackers are the best!' I said. 'The factory is close to where I was brought up, and you can see them making them – and the contents are a lot more original and exciting than other kinds.'

'I can't say I've ever found *anything* exciting in a cracker,' Mrs Powys said. 'But do go ahead and order a couple of dozen of whichever seems most suitable.'

'They do several varieties. I'll check them out,' I promised.

'I think that's about it for now,' she said, looking suddenly tired. 'I expect Nancy – Mrs Kane – will be in and out of the kitchen, making herself endless cups of tea, but she won't get in your way.'

'Of course, that's no problem,' I said, and it occurred to me that a retired vicar seemed an unlikely friend for Sabine Powys to have, so I looked forward to meeting her. Perhaps she would be the one to inject some of the real meaning of Christmas into the proceedings, too?

Mrs Powys gathered her clipboard and papers together and rose to her feet, and we got up, too.

'Let me know if there are any difficulties,' she said, the tone of her voice making it clear that she wasn't expecting any. 'And when Maria arrives, tell her to bring me a cup of coffee to the sitting room. I want a word with her before she takes her break until after the New Year.'

'I'll do that,' Henry agreed. 'She may have already arrived.'

'Thank you,' she said dismissively, the audience evidently at an end, and we escaped into the passage, where Plum had nosed his way out of the study and appeared to be waiting for us, our royal escort back to the kitchen.

9

Up the Garden Path

The baize-lined door to the kitchen was propped open with a flat, green glass doorstop that reminded me of a jellyfish and Maria was sitting at the table, dunking gingernuts into a mug of coffee. Plum made a beeline for her and sat by her feet, gazing hopefully up at her.

'Are you back again?' she said, breaking off a bit of biscuit for him. 'He's only just been in here with Xan – *he* wanted coffee, but he's taken it back to the study with him.'

She looked at me over the rim of her mug. 'He was already here when I arrived and he was using that coffee machine, which must be yours?'

'It is, but it's OK, I'll simply add a couple of boxes of pods to the next supermarket order,' I said. 'By the way, Mrs Powys said she'd like you to take her some coffee to the sitting room, Maria, because she wants to see you before you take Christmas off. And since she likes milk in her coffee, why don't we try her with one of the *café au lait* pods?'

'We can try and I will blame you if she does not like it,' she agreed, and when it was ready took it through, returning five minutes later, looking inscrutable.

'She didn't spit it out in disgust, then?' Henry said with a grin, stirring the murky pink contents of his glass teapot with a spoon, so that a hibiscus flower swirled around like a sea creature.

Maria looked at it in a fascinated kind of way, then said, 'No, she liked it! She told me it reminded her of the breakfast coffee they serve at cafés in France. But I would not try her with whatever you have in that teapot, Henry!'

'Henry's herbal teas are an acquired taste and most sane people don't want to acquire it,' I said.

'Some of them are very good for your health,' Henry protested. 'Anyway, you *like* my Yogi liquorice tea!'

'I can keep it down,' I admitted. 'I wouldn't go further than that.'

Maria refused to try Henry's hell-brew and my offer to make her another cup of coffee, and said, sitting down: 'The Lady says she thinks you will cope very well with everything and I am not to worry over Christmas, but relax and rest until the New Year. And she gave me my Christmas bonus, so I did not like to say that it was all now getting too much for me and I wished to retire.'

'It's difficult,' Henry said sympathetically, 'but you'll have to do what's best for you and your husband.'

Maria brightened. 'Andy will be coming home by ambulance after lunch, and I have been up since the early hours to make everything clean and nice for him. And tonight he will have his favourite dinner of haggis with neeps and tatties, followed by Bramley apple tart and custard.'

'Lovely,' said Henry kindly, though he'd once said he found the sight of a haggis almost as gross as a black pudding, and I can't say *I* much fancied either, myself.

'Last night, I went up and down in the new stairlift the Lady had put in, to make sure it was safe.'

'I think they're generally pretty reliable,' said Henry. 'If ever you have any kind of problem, day or night, do ring my mobile and I'll be straight up there.'

'You can have my number, too,' I said.

'Thank you both, that is a relief to me, because there is no one nearby to help me if anything happens. There is only old Ken in one of the cottages. He is a shepherd on a farm nearby, but the rheumatism is bad in his hands now. And the other two cottages are holiday homes and no one comes near them till spring.'

'It is fairly remote here, isn't it?' I said. 'It must be totally different in summer, with all the tourists and hikers.'

Henry had finished his tea and was now trying to poke the hibiscus flower out of the spout of the teapot, where it had wedged itself like a shy octopus.

Plum, having cadged one more bit of biscuit from me, had vanished, presumably back to his master in the study.

'Time is getting on and I'm sure you need to get back home soon,' I said to Maria. 'Come on, you'd better show us the outbuilding now.'

So we donned our outdoor gear in the Garden Hall and stepped out into a bright, frosty morning.

'This tub by the door is full of grit for the paving, if it should be slippery,' Maria informed us. 'And also, you do not want to fall off the slab bridge into the stream, if you are going across it to the herb garden for a bit of rosemary, or a bay leaf.'

'Absolutely not,' agreed Henry. 'Just as well there's only this area of stone paving and the bridge and then we're back on to gravel again.'

He led the way towards the back of the servants' wing, where he'd parked the van the previous day when we'd finished unloading. I hadn't gone with him then, so I was surprised by how extensive the outbuildings were.

The largest had possibly once been a coach house and now sheltered a red sports car with the hood up, a small white hatchback and an ancient-looking Ford estate. Around it were grouped several other stone buildings and Maria unlocked one side of a pair of large double doors and pulled it open, revealing an ancient and battered Land Rover and a sit-on mower.

'Andy mostly used the Land Rover. There is a track around the woodland just wide enough to take it. And sometimes, in bad weather, he could drive down to the village in it when nothing much else was able to use the road.'

'I've driven a lot of old Land Rovers,' Henry said, 'so I could do that if necessary.'

'The logs are stored in the other half of this building,' Maria said, 'as you see.'

There were stacks of logs, piled high around the walls and a large axe leaned against a chopping block made from a hefty slice of tree. There was a sawhorse and a small heap of kindling, too, and the air smelled pleasantly of sawdust.

'Ah, a mighty chopper – just what I yearned for,' said Henry, and I gave him a quelling look.

'The seasoned wood is all on this left-hand wall, to be used first,' Maria said. 'There's quite a lot of firewood cut ready to be taken into the house.'

'I noticed that huge empty log basket in one of the little rooms off the kitchen passage,' Henry said. 'I'll fill it up later. And I'll have a go at chopping some more in a bit. It should be good exercise.'

We closed the double doors and went to look in on a huge and very unexciting oil tank.

'Kept indoors because of the bad weather up here,' Maria explained. 'And also, thieves visit remote places to steal the oil, so the tank and the door are kept locked, as you see.'

The rest of the buildings seemed to be unused, though a large, open-fronted barn would make good extra garage space when the guests arrived.

The gravelled drive clearly did a complete circuit of the house and we walked along it a little way, where we could see into a paved courtyard, enclosed by the U-shape made by the tower and the servants' wing. It had a central fountain, surrounded by box-hedged beds with small topiary trees in their centres.

'Mr Powys's study looks out on the courtyard and fountain. Sometimes, when it was hot, he would open the French doors and sit on the stone bench by the fountain,' Maria said reminiscently, and we looked towards the study, as if somehow expecting the ghost of its old master to appear there.

Instead, as if on cue, a tall, willowy and unmistakable figure was standing there, looking out. Xan, spotting us, waved, before turning back into the room.

Maria consulted her watch. 'I will leave you now and go home this way. It is quicker than going right round the front of the house again.'

'Good idea – and I think I've just got time for a little walk before I start lunch,' I said. 'I could do with some fresh air and stretching my legs.'

'There are many paths through the woods,' Maria said. 'Then, if you take the one up the hill on the other side of the herb garden, there is a private gate to the Roman site. It has a visitor centre, but of course, that is closed in winter. At the other side of it, by the entrance gate, there is an old cottage, where Simon, who looks after the fort, lives. He is a nice man, a widower, but was badly injured in the car crash that killed his wife. It was before he came here, though he is still quite young.'

'How sad,' I said.

'What does he do when the site is closed?' Henry asked.

'He lectures one day a week at the university in Carlisle and also, from spring to the end of summer, he organizes digs for the students at the fort. I think, too, he is writing a book. Everyone, it seems, is writing a book.'

'*I'm* not,' said Henry. 'I just blog. But Dido writes a book of recipes and reminiscences every year.'

Maria looked at me curiously. 'You have more than one string to your bow, then, as they say?'

'We both have – that's why we only take a few Heavenly Houseparties bookings a year.'

Maria checked her watch again and, with an exclamation, said, as if we'd been holding her captive, 'I *must* go!' She trod briskly off along the drive.

Henry said he was going back to the house, with the intention of changing into old jeans and sweatshirt and having a go at chopping logs, even though we hadn't yet run out.

I thought this occupation would soon pall and reminded him to fill the log basket in the house when he'd finished pretending to be a lumberjack.

By then, the morning was vanishing fast and I decided I only had time to briefly explore the terraced gardens at the front of the Castle.

A path in front of the house led across the half-circle of lawn to the low balustrade that edged it, where I paused by the top of a flight of steps, to admire the view.

The steeply terraced garden fell away below me, and the

rushing stream that ran past the herb garden, before vanishing underground, reappeared in a cascade to one side of the steps.

As I began to explore, I discovered that it had been artfully channelled into a series of small waterfalls and spreading pools.

The path I took meandered steadily downwards, but never far from the stream, where sometimes the rocky walls came in close, and at others moved outwards, to enclose a wider space, with lawns, shrubs and flowerbeds.

It all looked very natural, even though I was sure a lot of work had gone into creating this enchanted valley.

Shrubs climbed up the retaining walls and spread their branches through the pergolas and trellised arches. The stone heads of strange beasts spouted water and, at one point, the path ran through a short stone tunnel, pierced with lancet windows and framed in ferns.

All was quiet, except for birdsong, and as I made my way ever downwards, I felt as if I had strayed into another, enchanted world.

At every turn was evidence of loving care. Presumably Andy's main purpose in life was to tend this little hidden Eden . . . or it had been.

I emerged from a short, clipped holly walk and suddenly found myself on a more open terrace, though the rocky walls still encircled it, protecting the plants within from the worst of the weather. The water pooled here, with a little bridge to take you across to the other side. I knew at once that this must be the Winter Garden Maria had mentioned, for it was full of flowers – so *many* flowers for this far north and in December!

I loved gardens, but I only knew enough to recognize a few of the plants and shrubs there. Many blossomed in bold shades of yellow: winter daffodils, with their goblet-shaped cups of waxy petals, jasmine . . . and aconites, wearing ruffs of green leaves.

But it wasn't *all* yellow, for there were clumps of purple heather, too, and witch hazel in shades of red and orange.

I stood in the middle of the bridge for ages, drinking it all in, before I tore myself away and took the path on the other side of the stream and down to the remaining levels, until a final flight of steps brought me out at the very bottom of the valley, by a small lake.

It was bordered by sloping lawns, with a little temple-style folly raised a short way above.

I huddled into my anorak, because it was more open to the elements here, the trees pushed back into a dark circle, and the temperature seemed to drop even further as the icy wind whipped strands from my braided crown of hair – lese-majesty – and blew them round my face.

Pulling my hood up, I headed for the temple, which was actually not that small, now I was close to it. The copper dome was patinated with verdigris and there were classically simple marble pillars at either side of the open entrance. I went up the steps to find inside a low barrier enclosing the Roman mosaic Lucy had mentioned.

The interior was lit by high windows and a mirror had been attached to the ceiling, presumably to reflect Mithras in all his glory.

The mosaic was circular, like the replica in the Great Hall, but of course, not perfect, for many of the tesserae were faded or broken. It was an amazing survival, all the same.

I walked all the way around it, but didn't sit on either of the two inviting benches because I really needed to get back to the house again. I'd let myself be seduced by the gardens into going much further than I'd intended.

It was gloomy in the temple and when I went out and down the steps, the bright wintry sunshine made me blink.

Reflections of ice-blue sky and scudding white clouds sped across the surface of the lake and all was peaceful; even the birds seemed quiet now, as if waiting for something.

And then, quite suddenly, I was startled by the sharp crack of a twig trodden underfoot and, looking round, saw Xan emerging from the nearby trees, looking, in his long dark coat and rainbow-striped scarf, like the hero of an updated Jane Austen adaptation. One lock of his black hair, tousled by the breeze, even fell romantically over his brow, as if a make-up girl had just darted out and tweaked it there.

His light, strangely coloured eyes were abstracted and he seemed deep in thought as he came to a halt, looking out at the lake.

I was just wondering if I could very slowly edge back into the nearby path without him seeing me when Plum plodded out of the trees, his tongue lolling from one corner of his mouth, and immediately spotted me.

'Woof!' he said amiably, and waved his muddy flag of a tail.

10

Thin Ice

Xan seemed to be coming back from a long distance away. Perhaps, after a morning spent sifting through Asa's papers, he had been mentally swimming in the azure Aegean Sea, in search of drowned civilizations? But as his eyes slowly focused on me, amusement dawned in their lilac-grey depths.

'Hello,' he said, before adding, as if he couldn't help himself, 'That's a coat of many colours!'

I squinted down at my anorak, every quilted diamond a different, jewel-bright colour. 'I got it in California, though I have to say, it didn't look quite so bright at the time. But it's very warm, that's the main thing. And *you've* some need to talk. Your scarf is one long neon rainbow!'

Too late, I remembered that this was not only the godson of my employer I was talking to, but someone I'd really meant to avoid.

He didn't seem to mind, though, he just said mildly, 'I like a bit of colour. The scarf is knitted silk. Sabine gave it to me last Christmas, when she was staying with her friend, Nancy, near Oxford. She's done that the last few years, since Asa died, but this time Nancy is coming here instead.'

I was glad to have my hood up, but he was wearing a long black, rather military-style overcoat and his head was bare. An icy breeze was running ghost fingers through his black hair.

'You should wear a hat,' I told him. 'It's so cold down here by the lake that your ears might freeze solid and fall off.'

'It's usually in my pocket, but I must have left it somewhere,' he said apologetically and I realized I was now bossing him about the same way I did with Henry's dippy friends.

'I expect it didn't feel so cold in the trees. I found it quite mild coming down the terraces, until I came out here.'

'It's always like that. The ground opens out so much that it's more exposed, I suppose . . .' he said, then felt his ears gingerly with both hands. 'I don't *think* my ears have gone brittle.'

Plum sat down on the toes of my moccasin boots, which was obviously warmer than the ground and I bent down and stroked his silky little domed head. He looked appealingly up at me.

'The poor little thing looks *so* exhausted!'

'He always looks tired. In a minute he'll demand I carry him up to the house, but I thought we could both do with a bit of air and exercise before lunch and I expect you felt the same way.'

'Yes, but I really *must* be getting back now, or there won't be any lunch! I've been out longer than I meant to.'

And nor, despite my resolve, had I kept the distance between Xan and myself that I'd intended to . . .

He didn't seem to have taken in what I said, for he was once more gazing out at the lake.

'In summer, you can swim here – there's a small changing hut behind the temple,' he said. 'But in winter, it often freezes over hard enough to skate on. Sabine used to be an ace skater!'

'Really?' I said, fascinated by this unexpected insight into my employer, despite my urge to get away.

'There's a whole collection of skates in the cupboard under the stairs in the Garden Hall, from strap-on Victorian ones to the modern boot type. I think the Castle family down the generations must all have skated on the lake.'

'It's quite big, so it's hard to imagine it freezing solid.'

'You'd be surprised: the weather now is amazingly mild for this time of the year, but it can be changeable, so you need to keep your eye on the weather reports for the possibility of ice and snow.'

'Mrs Powys did mention that to us, because of having enough supplies in. But Henry would *love* some snow! He's brought one of his snowboards with him, just in case.'

'Oh? I've never tried that, or surfing. I suspect you get on better if you have a lower centre of gravity than I have, like Henry.'

'Yes, that's what he says, too: being short and muscular is good. I *can* surf, because I learned while out in California, staying with my dad, but I'm not very good.'

'The field below the fort runs downwards steeply for quite a way, then plateaus out at the bottom, so Henry could probably stop before he hit the dry-stone wall,' Xan suggested.

'I think someone else mentioned that field, but I'll tell him,' I said. 'Being Henry, he'd probably just bounce off the wall, while recording the whole thing on the little camera he straps to his head, for his blog, or vlog, or whatever he calls it.'

Xan was looking amused again. 'I must check it out! What's it called?'

'Rudge the Roamer,' I told him.

'I remember Henry being sporty at school – rugby and all the team things I hated. I was always a swotty geek.'

'I suppose you were, really,' I said absently, and then realized he was looking at me strangely and added, quickly, 'I mean, that's more or less what Henry said about you.'

'Oh, right. No, I'm definitely not sporty, though I like walking Plum – or *carrying* Plum – and swimming, when I get the chance, and visiting historic sites. But that's about it.'

'Me too, though I love visiting gardens. And I did try skiing once, when we were catering for a winter house party in an Austrian chalet, but I just kept landing on my back, unable to get up again, like a dying insect. Of course, Henry was in his element and spent all his free time snowboarding down horrendous mountain slopes. I couldn't bear to watch him, but I do think it's time he gave up extreme sports now.'

'Since he's two years younger than me, I suppose the poor old thing must be all of thirty-five now,' he said gravely, though a smile lurked in his eyes. 'I wonder how I came to forget to bring my bath chair with me . . .'

'Well, you know what I mean,' I protested. 'You don't bounce the same way when you get older.'

I cast a look at the lake and shivered. 'It's hard to imagine that it's ever warm enough to swim in there! And really, I prefer the water I'm swimming in to be clear enough so I can see what's sharing it with me.'

'You'd love the beach near my parents' house on Corfu, then,' he said. 'It was my grandparents', originally. My grandfather, Tommy, married and settled on Corfu and my parents have kept it on as a holiday home. They both work at the university in Athens.'

'Since you spent a lot of time here when you were younger, Mitras Castle must feel like a home from home, too?' I suggested.

'It does and I'm very fond of it. After I'd got a scholarship to Rugby – which was a bit of a shock after living at home in Athens and going to the International School – I spent the half-terms and a week or two of the summer holidays here with

Asa and Sabine, which was always fun. Asa could make even going to the village shop an exciting expedition.'

'Henry's a bit like that. He's a cheerful, glass-half-full person and likes to wring the last bit of enjoyment out of everything – like chopping logs, which he was doing when I came out . . .'

I suddenly checked my watch. 'Look at the time! I really must get back. I wanted to make some soup to go with the cheese omelettes and I'll just have time if I don't hang about.'

Without ceremony, I headed straight for the steps, but Xan soon caught up and fell in beside me, Plum under his arm.

'Henry told us he was a house elf,' he reminded me. 'So perhaps you're the kitchen elf and do the cooking, while he's the front-of-house elf, as it were?'

'Pretty much, unless we're really busy with a house full of guests. I do most of the cooking, though Henry makes the canapés, nibbles, scones and biscuits, because he enjoys it.'

I kept up a fast pace as we crossed the bridge over the stream in the Winter Garden and went on up the path that led us through the stone tunnel, where we had to go in single file. Or one and a bit file, in Xan's case.

'We have our main roles,' I continued, once we'd emerged through the ferns at the other end, 'but we can both multitask when necessary. And we both adore organizing successful house parties, making sure everyone, including our employers, has a lovely, relaxed time. Creating delicious food is my main contribution to that.'

We went up the remaining terraces so quickly that I felt quite warm and out of breath by the time we arrived at the top of the final flight of steps. As I paused to catch my breath, a small white hatchback shot out of the dark maw of the drive and came to a halt on the gravel in front of the porticoed front door.

'That's got to be Lucy coming back!' Xan said, sounding

alarmed. 'I'll dodge down the steps and cut round through the woods. You haven't seen me.'

'Coward,' I called after his retreating form. Really, I would have to get a grip on my tongue and stop being so familiar!

I assumed my polite, professional expression and followed the path across the lawn to the car, where luckily, Lucy had been too busy extricating herself to spot Xan. As I neared, she managed to untangle a woolly scarf that had wrapped itself around the gear stick and then went round to open the boot.

'Can I help you carry anything in?' I asked as she began to haul out a bundle of newspapers and magazines, a couple of large paper carrier bags, one oozing ominously from a corner, and a lot of flowers.

'Oh, it's you, Dido! Yes, if you don't mind, that would be such a help!' she said gratefully. 'Perhaps you could take the flowers round to the Garden Hall. We use the cloakroom off it to do the floral arrangements in – you know where that is?'

'Yes, I noticed the vases on the shelf above a little worktop.'

I relieved her of the flowers, which were bundled in thick, striped paper.

'They will have to stand in buckets of water until I have time to arrange them,' she fluted, tightening her grasp on a sliding armful of papers. She clutched them to her more firmly and took hold of the handles of the carrier bags.

'Henry can arrange them for you, if you prefer?' I offered. 'He does it very well.'

'Really? That would be excellent, because I'm quite exhausted! And I simply *must* dash in with the papers, because usually they're on the table in the hall long before this and I expect Sabine has been looking for *The Times*.'

She paused to draw breath, but showed no signs of moving.

'Well, I must go and start on lunch,' I said firmly, and escaped round the side of the house. Behind me I'd heard the sound of a lot of papers and magazines cascading on to gravel and some high-pitched twittering, but I didn't look back.

I deposited the flowers in buckets of water – they were not a terribly inspiring selection, though there were a dozen elegantly tall and straight-stemmed roses, probably flown in at huge expense from some far country – and went to inform Henry that he had an extra task to perform. On the way, I nearly fell over Plum, who was sitting in the doorway, watching me.

'Hello!' I said, and he got up, wagging his tail, and followed me through the swinging baize door, which always reminded me of a vertical billiard table.

There was no sign of Xan, so perhaps he'd gone straight back to the study to do some more work before lunch.

I could hear Henry, though. He was singing the Monty Python 'Lumberjack Song' from the direction of the staff sitting room.

When I put my head round the door, I found him arranging our board games on the bookshelf beneath his DVD collection, and he'd already unpacked our tins of chocolates, biscuits and savoury snacks, ready for late-night film watching.

'This is starting to look more homely already,' I said. 'I'm just going to put some soup on for lunch – it had better be French onion, that's quick – and cheese omelettes to follow. Then, once that's sorted, I'm going to take an inventory of food and drink and make some lists. It's time to get organized.'

'Yes, I thought I might look into the booze supplies later,' he agreed.

I told him about the flowers and he said, 'Oh, good! I've been dying to do something with the dismal floral arrangements! I'll go and work my magic on them before I lay the table for lunch.'

He went off, still humming the 'Lumberjack Song' and I soon had the soup simmering.

When Henry beat the gong and then took out the soup, I grated cheese for the omelettes – I make wonderfully fluffy omelettes, if I say it myself – and soon he was returning with the empty plates and some compliments.

'They're down to the cheeseboard and fruit. Mrs Powys says she'll ring when she wants coffee, and she and Xan want theirs in the study, because he's going to record the first session of her memories for the biography.'

'That's quick! He doesn't hang about.'

'Mrs Powys also told me she hadn't had proper onion soup for years and Xan said your omelettes are amazing.'

'Huh!' I said, but I was pleased, all the same.

'You're a sweet-and-sour dish in yourself,' Henry said with a grin, giving me a quick hug, and began to load the dirty crockery into the dishwasher.

So the first lunch had been a success, but we still had four weeks' worth to go.

11

Plum Pudding

Once lunch was out of the way and the coffee taken through, I began my big stocktaking session, throwing open all the kitchen cupboard doors, examining the contents of the huge fridge, the two freezers and the large larder.

It certainly needed reorganizing, for so many things were out of date and would need replacing. Maria had clearly tended to use whatever was nearest to hand, which was of course the most recently bought, but since the last live-in help had departed some time ago, she'd had to cope with everything single-handed, so I couldn't really blame her.

Soon there was a steadily growing pile of things to throw out on one end of the long kitchen table and many ticks on my shopping list.

The big upright freezer was not too bad – Maria must use that the most – but the chest one was another matter and I removed several anonymous items from the bottom of it, along with some with dates from so long ago that they would have entirely lost both taste and texture.

'I'll sort all this lot out,' Henry offered as I dumped another load of rejects on the kitchen table, then made to return to the larder.

He was polishing up a sturdy vintage tea trolley he'd found in one of the rooms off the passage, and the wood and brass now gleamed.

'I just need to oil the wheels on this and it's ready for action.'

'I can't imagine why Maria didn't use it,' I said. 'Can you recycle the packaging from the stuff I'm throwing out and bin the rest?'

'I'll do that. According to the notice board, it's refuse collection day on Fridays. It doesn't say we have to take it up to the gate, so I assume they come down for it.'

'I hope so – and thanks, Henry.'

'No problemo,' he said, squirting oil into the trolley wheels and then wiping them clean with a bit of kitchen towel. 'The booze list won't take so long.'

There were a lot of tins of expensive soup in the larder and one shelf looked like a minor branch of Fortnum and Mason, with enough tins and jars of preserves, pickles, jam, honey, fruit and pâté to keep the inhabitants of the Castle going for at least a year. I rearranged everything into correct date order – luckily none of these had run out – and made a memo to tell Mrs Powys she needn't order any more, though I supposed she might buy her Christmas ham from them? I made another note about that, and also to ask about ordering the turkey.

I took my lists back to the kitchen to work on and found that Henry had already disposed of the discards and was about to go and see if the coast was clear in the sitting room so he could have a good look at the contents of the drinks cabinet in there.

He returned with a log basket full of jars and bottles.

'I went through the drinks in the dining-room cupboard,

too,' he explained. 'They were both so full of bottles of out-of-date and half-used liqueurs, and jars of things like olives, maraschino cherries and lemon slices that I had to fetch this basket to carry them all in! I don't think anyone has drunk anything but sherry and whisky for years, other than a little wine with dinner, perhaps.'

He dumped the basket on the floor and vanished down to the wine cellar, to see what was there.

Xan wandered in, Plum at his heels, but I was absorbed in compiling my shopping lists and barely looked up.

'Just going to make some coffee,' he said. 'I don't want to disturb you.'

'You won't,' I said absently, comparing Mrs Hill's list of supplies with my own and amalgamating them into one long one, adding some ingredients for Christmas baking that I needed urgently, not all of which Mrs Hill seemed to have considered necessary . . .

When I looked up again, Xan had gone, but Henry had reappeared, cobwebs in his red-gold curls.

'I don't think the cleaning service get as far as the wine cellar,' he observed. 'Do you want a cup of coffee? I'm going to make a pot of mint tea and then we can compare notes.'

When we did, I added cooking sherry and brandy to his list, along with a bottle of dark rum for the Christmas cake and he put a few things on mine, like jars of olives, cocktail sticks and small paper napkins.

Finally we sat back, satisfied we'd listed pretty much everything we'd need till the New Year – apart from fresh stuff, of course.

We do this mammoth shop as soon as we start a new assignment, which makes catering so much easier.

'I suppose we need to run our lists past Mrs Powys?' I said.

'She probably isn't expecting this week's order to be the size of a small novel. Then you can put the order in, Henry.'

'The sooner the better, if we're going to get a delivery this week,' agreed Henry.

'You'd better check with Mrs Powys whether she wants champagne ordering. It is nice to serve it at Christmas and Boxing Day dinners, but it's up to her.'

'I can't wait to decorate the house for Christmas, can you?' he said enthusiastically. 'It's the best part . . . which reminds me, have you written down that we need florist's wire and ribbon for those evergreen garlands Mrs Powys mentioned?'

I pulled out another, shorter list. 'Yes, they're on here, along with the crackers and a couple more odds and ends. I don't know if there's a local stockist for Marwood's crackers.'

He pulled out his phone and checked. 'There's a store in Hexham that has them.'

'That's handy. You could probably pick up everything else on this list, too, if you had a little trip there, maybe tomorrow? The cleaners will be in all morning and Mrs Powys and Lucy, out.'

'I can do that. When is Charlotte coming up to stay with her family?'

'She sent me a text to say she was coming up for the day with the twins when school breaks up for Christmas, to leave them with her parents, but then she has to get back to the shop. I expect by the time she does come up again to stay, I'll be too busy to meet her.'

'We could take a wild dogleg through Barnard Castle and call in on our way back,' he suggested.

'It's a thought,' I agreed. I made another cup of coffee and he joined me, this time.

'I wonder where we're to get the Christmas tree?' pondered Henry.

'Another thing we'll have to ask Mrs Powys about.' I put that on my to-do list.

'Well,' said Henry, 'I think I'll just bake a few cheese straws for afternoon tea . . . and perhaps a few little savoury tarts for tonight's starter.'

I looked at the clock. 'Good idea, and I'll make a proper start on my menu plans, now I know what we have in stock and what to order – and, most importantly, what Mrs Powys would most like to eat!'

A little while later, perhaps attracted by the smell of baking, the baize door suddenly swung open and a small, furry shape somersaulted backwards into the kitchen.

'Plum has his own way of getting through that swinging door – I saw him do it earlier,' Henry said, looking up. 'He sits against it and then slowly leans backwards till it opens.'

'The somersault is fairly spectacular,' I said, leaning down to give him a tiny piece of the cheese straw I'd sneaked off the cooking rack. 'Who's a little Christmas pudding, then?'

'He is, and Xan says he's not to have too many treats because he's getting too fat.'

'It's nearly time for tea, so he might have got out of the study when Xan went to join Mrs Powys in the sitting room?' I suggested. 'I'd better get it ready.'

'You do that, but if he isn't joining them for tea, I can take his into the study on my way back,' Henry agreed. 'He won't want to miss out on my warm cheese straws!'

Dinner was a simple but delicious dish of chicken in white wine, served with baked potatoes and caramelized carrots – nothing could be easier. It was followed by baked apples, stuffed with dried fruit, sugar and treacle.

'I've lit the dining-room fire,' Henry said, returning after taking the starter through, 'and switched the hotplate on in there, so it's all set for dinner. Xan was in the sitting room and he'd put more wood on the fire, but if he gets too generous with the logs, I'll tell him to go and chop some!'

'You can't tell the guests to chop wood,' I said. 'You're only a minion and don't you forget it!'

He grinned. 'I know my place, and if I didn't I expect Mrs Powys would be perfectly capable of putting me in it!'

But it seemed that she was prepared to blur the lines a little where Henry was concerned, for much later that evening, after she and Lucy had gone up to bed, he went off to play billiards with Xan. Royal permission had been granted . . .

It could be my imagination, but I'd already got the impression that Mrs Powys seemed to like Henry rather more than me, though I expect that was because they both came from the same sort of background.

Tired but satisfied with my day's work, I retired to our sitting room, put on some Christmas music, and started unpacking our mini pop-up tree and some decorations.

You'd think my head would have been full of lists, menus and recipes when I finally went to bed, but instead, when I closed my eyes, it was Xan's dreamy and abstracted poet's face that I saw, just the way he'd looked that afternoon, by the lake.

No longer blinded by an adolescent crush into endowing him with the attributes of a romantic hero, I saw him for what he was: a nice, friendly man with scholarly tastes and no yearnings to be Lancelot to anyone's Guinevere.

Sabine

These days, although I sleep little, I always retire to my rooms by ten, feeling quite exhausted. The pangs of pain and aching in my bones increase too, harbingers of what is to come, but I'm hoarding the painkillers they obviously mean to dole out in meagre amounts.

It has been an emotionally draining day, opening up Asa's study to Xan, seeming also to open a floodgate to memories of the past, both the good ones and the ones I've tried hardest to forget. Whether this will prove a good thing or not, I don't know – but it was never possible to shut Pandora's box again once it had been opened.

I gave Xan Asa's bunch of keys to the doors, the desk, the low cupboards and filing cabinets, along with the free run of whatever he might find in there.

Of course, I had my own desk, computer and printer moved into the library very soon after Asa died. That way, it was easier to pretend Asa was just next door, sitting in his big leather office chair. So, though Maria regularly dusted and aired the room, it was almost six years since I'd last entered it.

When I unlocked the doors for Xan this morning, it was as

if Asa had just strolled out a few minutes ago. That's what almost stopped my heart. Xan pulled back the drapes to let in the light, which was symbolic, I suppose, of what he was about to do, and looked around the room in amazement.

'It's as if Asa had just gone out for a few minutes,' he said, echoing my own thoughts. 'Even his computer is still sitting there on his desk!'

'Yes . . .' I said on a sigh. 'It hasn't been touched since Asa died. You're going to have quite a task.'

There were books, papers, artefacts, magazines and journals crammed on the shelves and piled on every surface, coloured maps and charts pinned to the walls, and a framed photograph of the two of us, young, bronzed and carefree in the bright Greek sunshine, expecting the bright golden bubble of our happiness to surround us for ever.

I resolutely turned away from the photograph and told Xan that I entirely trusted his discretion on what he might find, and which material he would use in the biography. I said I knew that his grandfather, Tommy, would have told him many stories about his early days with Asa, too.

They'd been inseparable friends from school, so perhaps he and Asa were together now, having a riotous time in heaven, which has many houses, at least one of which should be full of cheerful, argumentative academics.

Xan assured me that I need have no worries and, in any case, could read the book before he sent it in to his publishers, if I wished.

I thought I'd probably be long gone by then, but suggested that as he wrote, he could ask himself: 'Would Sabine like this to be included?' and he grinned.

He'd earlier told me he had already researched Asa's child-hood onwards – I am sure he would have written the biography with or without my co-operation – and made notes about his later career and achievements. The framework was there, but the man, Asa himself, was not and must be brought to life within its pages.

'I have no idea if the computer still works but the password is "amphorae",' I said. 'He printed out all his emails and replies and I filed them away for him. I doubt there's much of interest left on it.'

'I'll check and let you know,' he said, and looked around. 'I think I'll set up my laptop and printer and unpack my recording gear. Perhaps you'll give me a short session after lunch?' he suggested. 'Just a little background about your life up to the point where you met Asa.'

I agreed and then, hearing the voices of Henry and Dido in the library, where they awaited my instructions, went through and closed the adjoining door behind me.

Lunch was simple but good, served by the boy – he seems a boy to me – Henry. Dido so far has effaced herself, other than bringing my breakfast and receiving my orders this morning, but I am conscious of her presence in the house in a way I wasn't expecting.

After lunch, Xan and I took our coffee in the study, where he had placed two chairs opposite each other across the coffee table in front of the fireplace, his recording equipment between us. He told me to think of it as a pleasant chat about my childhood at the Castle and the years until I went up to Oxford University.

I have to say that I quickly forgot he was holding a microphone and told him all about my early childhood at the Castle, when my mother was alive – ponies, dogs, skating and tobogganing in winter – and the wonderful warm memories of the

Christmases we had. The Castle was my mother's family home and she ran the estate and the household with perfect ease. My father had a share in a London antique shop and often went to country house sales and auctions, in search of suitable items to send down to it. These trips, and going to race meetings, were interests Mummy shared.

'It was a magical, wonderful childhood and we were so happy . . . until Mummy suddenly became ill, when I was seven. Eventually a nurse came to live in and look after her. And although I'd thought Mummy and Daddy were devoted to each other, not three months after she died, he married this nurse, Barbara Jones. Babs, she called herself. And things were never the same again.'

'That must have been very difficult for you, while you were still grieving for your mother,' Xan said softly.

'It was – I think I hated Daddy almost as much as her – and I was sent off to boarding school when I turned eight. Not that I wanted to be at home, for although Mummy had left the Castle and her estate to me, my father had an income derived from it and could continue living there. I'm sure Mummy never expected him to marry again,' I added. 'My home felt tainted when the *Usurper* – that's what I called her – took over. Then she had my half-sister, Faye, and they both doted on her . . .'

I paused, feeling again the turmoil of anger, bitterness and jealousy that had filled me then, before shrugging off the past: 'She was so much younger than me that I barely knew her and, in any case, I spent as much of the school holidays as possible away, staying with the family of friends, or on school trips abroad. I became interested in history and archaeology and was accepted by Oxford University.'

I looked up, only then remembering that this was all being

recorded. 'I've been running on a bit, but I really don't want any of that in the book!'

'It's all right, I'll just briefly skate over the years till you arrived at uni. I already knew a little about your past from Tommy – that your father had remarried and you had a half-sister. But your life before then sounded very happy.'

'It was, and I'd like some of the family Christmas traditions I remember from that time to be incorporated in this one, even though I know you can never go back and recapture the magic.'

I'd experienced such a mixture of emotions while I was talking that I felt quite drained and yet restless afterwards, so I went down to seek the solace of the Winter Garden – and to see what flowers were out. Mummy planted it. She was an avid collector of plants and shrubs that could be coaxed into winter flowering in this sheltered spot on the middle terrace. Andy has tended it well all these years too, but now there will need to be a new gardener . . . But that, and the Castle's future, will be in the hands of someone else and I need to ensure that it all goes on after *I* do not.

The National Trust would certainly do that, but impersonally. Would there be anyone to love and feel a connection with the house and garden?

I rested until dinner, which was, I have to say, excellently cooked and served.

Then later, when I was about to retire to bed at my usual time, accompanied by Lucy, who always goes up with me – even though I suspect she then spends hours reading romantic novels and consuming chocolates – she showed a tendency to linger.

I'd noticed she was being very silly over Xan and I hope she's not going to make a nuisance of herself. I was firm with her, though, and said that we old fogeys always retired early and I hoped he could amuse himself. *That* firmly reminded Lucy that she was almost old enough to be his mother.

He said of course he could and, if I had no objection, he'd see if Henry would like a game of billiards.

I couldn't really say no to this – Henry must have long since finished his duties for the day. And I suppose I don't really mind Henry, who is from an excellent family, keeping Xan company until my other guests arrive.

Dido, though, would be another kettle of fish entirely.

12

Stone Cold

I awoke very early next morning and lay there for a while feeling, after everything I'd done the day before, empowered, energetic and in control.

I had the running of the household – especially the catering – at my fingertips . . . or at least, I would have, once Henry had ordered in the supplies.

After that, I could produce all the delicious meals Mrs Powys yearned for *and* begin to stock up the freezer with batches of soup, quiches, pies, flans, stock and casseroles, ready for the arrival of the house party. There were several things I could make and freeze in advance for Christmas dinner, too, from cranberry sauce and stuffing, to pigs in blankets.

Preparation in advance is the key to easy Christmas catering and can be scaled up or down, according to the numbers.

Today being Wednesday, the cleaners would be in from nine till one, and since Henry was going into Hexham, and Lucy and Mrs Powys would be out till the afternoon, there would only be lunch to get for Xan.

It was no wonder I'd woken up in a good mood!

When I'd dressed and drawn back my curtains, there was

still a lingering, bright, late star in the dark indigo sky. I loved stars, though I couldn't tell which was which and my knowledge of nebulas was nebulous.

Henry came down soon after me, looking disarmingly like a sleepy cherub, and shared my coffee, though not the toast and marmalade.

'Xan's joining me for a cooked breakfast again,' he told me, 'though I expect once this friend of Mrs Powys's arrives, he'll feel he should join her and Lucy in the morning room.'

I lightly boiled an egg for Mrs Powys and, on my way through the Garden Hall with it, noticed that Plum's lead was missing from the hook by the door, so presumably Xan had already gone out with him.

This morning when I tapped on my employer's door and went in, the curtains were still closed and the bedside lamp was casting a warm pool of light across the bed, where Mrs Powys was sitting propped up against her banked pillows, reading a small book.

The dark shadows under her eyes looked positively inky this morning.

She laid the book face down on the duvet. It was the writings of Dame Julian of Norwich, which I recognized because it was a favourite of Granny's and she often quoted from it, especially the strangely comforting line: '. . . all shall be well and all shall be well and all manner of thing shall be well.'

I hadn't had Mrs Powys down as religious, but then, her best friend *was* a vicar, or retired vicar, if vicars ever really retire.

'Good morning, Mrs Powys,' I said, laying the tray across her knees. 'I hope you slept well?'

She looked at me with those clear, pale blue eyes that were so startling in her lined face, as if the young Sabine was in there, looking out, and said, 'At my age, one is just grateful to sleep at all. Perhaps in old age, the body ceases to need sleep to repair itself.'

'It's a theory,' I agreed, then pulled a copy of the very long shopping list from my pocket and said that I thought she might like to look over it, before Henry put in the order. 'It is very extensive, but apart from fresh fruit and vegetables and so on, there should be almost everything we need until the New Year.'

'You can give it to me, but I'll leave all that to you. It is what you're here for, after all.'

'Certainly, Mrs Powys. There are one or two other things I wanted to query with you, though, and also to tell you there are enough preserves, pickles and pâté in the larder to see you well into next year, so you won't need to order any more from Fortnum and Mason.'

'Really? I've simply continued putting in an order from habit.'

'I don't know if you usually order your ham from them, or perhaps Harrods, or would like me to source one?'

'It is already on order. When all the guests are here, I'd like sliced ham on the breakfast table, as well as a full cooked breakfast.'

'Of course, I'll see that there is.'

'Asa always liked a good slice or two of ham with his eggs in the morning . . .' she murmured. Then, after a moment, her eyes sharpened again and she said, 'I'll probably come down to breakfast once Nancy has arrived. It was having Lucy incessantly twittering at me that made me stop in the first place.'

Mrs Powys had poured her coffee and picked up the butter knife.

'Anything further?' she enquired coldly.

'Can I order a turkey, or do you usually source it somewhere in particular?'

'You can order it,' she said.

'If you've no objection I'll get a very large one, so I can freeze leftovers for future meals and make a lot of good stock for the freezer, too.'

'As you wish. What are we having for dinner tonight?'

I wasn't expecting that, and looked up from stuffing my notebook back in my tunic pocket.

'You mentioned steak and chips, and I found some very nice steaks in the freezer yesterday, while I was stocktaking. And I thought a chocolate mousse to follow?'

'I'm sure Xan will enjoy a good steak. I don't think he remembers to eat properly when he's at home,' she said.

'He can make up for that while he's here, Mrs Powys,' I said, preparing to leave. 'Henry would like a word with you about getting in the wines and spirits. He's been checking the supplies too and made his own list of what he thinks we'll need.'

'I can spare him a few minutes in the library before I go out. I'll ring when I'm ready,' she said, which sounded like we were back to Cluedo: Mrs Powys, in the library, with a double-headed Minoan axe.

'I'll tell him,' I said, and left her to her boiled egg.

Back in the kitchen, Plum was wolfing down food as if he'd been starved for a month, and Xan and Henry were tucking into eggs and bacon. They smelled delicious, but when Henry offered to share his, I refused.

'If I eat that kind of thing every day, I can feel my arteries starting to fur up.'

Xan grinned and Plum, who had polished his bowl with such keenness that it had skidded right across the floor, came to say hello to me, before seating himself hopefully next to his master.

'Is Lucy down?' I asked.

'In the morning room. I made her a pot of tea and took it through. Luckily, she came down while Xan was out with Plum,' Henry replied. 'But she's bound to catch him eating his breakfast in here one of these mornings.'

'Not if I can help it,' Xan said. 'She told me yesterday that I looked just like the heroes in her favourite novels. I said I wasn't hero material, just a sheep in wolf's clothing.'

That surprised a laugh out of me. 'A geek in wolf's clothing,' I amended, and he grinned.

I suddenly had the uncomfortable thought that when I was sixteen, I'd been just as silly as Lucy over him, without really knowing what he was like at all, though I suppose at that age I had more excuse.

I looked up and caught Xan's eye and he said, 'Sabine told her not to be silly last night, when she was trying to flirt with me like a Victorian debutante. She did everything except rap my knuckles with a fan and say she knew I was very wicked.'

'How embarrassing!' I said.

'It did dampen her down a bit, though when Sabine got up to go to bed just before ten, Lucy offered to stay and keep me company. Sabine told her to leave me in peace, though, and Lucy looked mortified.'

'Poor thing! But perhaps she'll come to her senses now,' I suggested.

'I'm not sure she has any sense to come to,' Henry said. 'But she seems entirely harmless and means well.'

'Damned with faint praise,' Xan said. 'I do feel a *bit* sorry for her, because from what Sabine has told me, she hasn't had much of a life. She worked as a secretary and was her boss's mistress for years, but when he died, she was left with nothing and out of a job. Sabine offering her a home and allowance came just at the right moment.'

'That is a bit sad,' I said. 'And I don't think it's really working out between her and Mrs Powys, is it? Lucy's just the kind of person to rub her up the wrong way.'

'She certainly does, and Sabine isn't one to suffer fools gladly. Or incompetence, which is probably Lucy's middle name,' said Xan.

I remembered to tell Henry that Mrs Powys would discuss the booze ordering with him when she came down. 'She'll ring the library bell when she's ready.'

'OK,' he said, polishing off the last bit of his bacon. 'Then I'll go into Hexham.'

'The cleaners will be in shortly,' I said, glancing at the clock. 'Everyone will be out to lunch today except you, Xan, and I expect you'll be holed up in the study?'

'Yes, they won't disturb me there. I want to open all the cupboards and drawers and try and make a rough list of what's there.'

'You sound like Dido – she's the queen of lists. I think she has lists of lists,' Henry said.

'There's nothing wrong with being organized,' I said with dignity, and then went to see if Lucy wanted anything more.

I found her just leaving and asked if she was going to fetch the newspapers.

'There looks to have been a hard frost, so those little roads might be still slippery,' I said. 'I could ask Henry to go and fetch them instead?'

'So kind!' she twittered. 'But I always go to the village on Wednesdays anyway, just not quite this early.'

'Well, do take care,' I said. 'If the weather gets too bad,

Henry can fetch the papers in that old Land Rover, which will be much safer.'

'Oh, really?' she said, brightening. 'I'm sure I shouldn't be so timid, but in winter I would prefer to wait till later in the mornings when the roads have thawed, or the local farmers have gritted them. I'm very much involved in village activities, you know.'

I had a mental image of her doing yoga on a village green, or polishing the church brasses. The latter was, I thought, more likely.

'There's a little local history museum with a lending library, staffed by volunteers, and I like to take a turn once a week. But the person who usually opens up today is ill, so the vicar asked me *specially* . . .'

This had clearly been an offer she couldn't refuse.

'So you see, I have to get there early. Then later on, I'll be lunching with the vicar and his wife, before the Knit and Stitch club. I'll be back in time for tea.'

I hoped this riot of dissipation didn't exhaust her.

She suddenly looked at her watch, squawked and rushed out. Then ten minutes later, looking out of the kitchen window, I saw the small white hatchback creep past, Lucy hunched over the wheel.

Henry had gone to speak to Mrs Powys – with or without the two-headed axe – and Xan had already retreated with Plum to the study.

I'd just taken a small packet of smoked salmon out of the freezer, intending to make Xan three kinds of finger sandwiches for his lunch – and then extra for afternoon tea – when a large white minibus pulled up and disgorged the cleaning team. Rather like the A-Team, but without all the jewellery and attitude.

I went to open the door and introduce myself, and then they swung into action with practised ease, while a cheerful young woman called Fran, who had a round face and bright pink hair, vanished into the laundry room.

Henry came out of the staff sitting room, dressed like a teenage surfboarder and shrugging into a disreputable padded jacket.

'Mrs Powys suggested I go to the wine merchant she has the account with in Corbridge first, and talk to them – they'll deliver. Then I'll carry on to Hexham and buy those crackers and anything else on your odds and ends list I can find.'

'Great – thanks, Henry,' I agreed, fetching it. 'If they have a selection of crackers and you can't decide, text me.'

'OK, see you later!'

I went to find one of the cleaners and said there was no point in stripping mine and Henry's beds this week, because we'd only been in them five minutes, but someone carried all the other bedding and towels through to the laundry room soon after. I looked in and found both the washing machines whirring and Fran feeding clean towels through a rotary iron-ing device.

She looked up and smiled, but turned down my offer of tea or coffee. 'We all bring flasks and cold drinks with us,' she said, as another fluffy towel emerged from the machine.

'I've seen those irons in other big houses. They look really quick and handy,' I said.

'Yes, they're great for all the big things – sheets, towels, tablecloths – but if you need anything else ironing, leave it on the second rail near the door.'

'It's all so well organized!'

'Many hands make light work,' she said. 'Though it's just me in here doing the laundry, because I enjoy it.'

I left her in the warm and slightly steamy room, and went back to the kitchen where, since the cleaners still seemed to be in the tower, I gave the fridge a good clean out, which I'd been dying to do.

But when the Magic Mops contingent showed signs of approaching the servants' wing, I thought it was time to make myself scarce. I'd go for a walk, leaving Xan in charge.

I took a cup of coffee with me and found him sitting in the big office chair, looking rather despairingly at all the open cupboards, which seemed to be crammed with papers, journals and files.

'How's it going?' I asked.

'Slowly. The drawers in the filing cabinet are in order because Sabine used to keep that tidy, but the rest of it is just chaos. I could really do with something like a pasting table to lay things out on, but I don't suppose there's such a thing in the Castle.'

'Probably not, but Henry's in Hexham this morning, so I could text him and tell him to get one? They're very cheap and they fold, so it won't be any trouble.'

'Please do that,' he said, brightening. 'It'll really help.'

I told him I was going out for about an hour. 'I wouldn't like to simply leave the house with the cleaners in, somehow, but if you're here I'm sure Mrs Powys won't mind.'

He looked slightly alarmed. 'I don't know anything about the cleaning!'

'You don't need to. I doubt if they'll want to ask you about anything; they just sort of piled in and got on with it.'

'OK,' he said. 'Plum doesn't seem to want to go out again for a walk, or I'd ask you to take him with you.'

Plum, in fact, was curled up on a small sofa and hadn't even raised his head when I went in, though he'd thumped his tail a couple of times. Now he sighed and closed his eyes again.

'The word "walk" usually has most dogs going berserk,' I observed. 'I'll bring you some lunch when I get back.'

'I'm perfectly capable of making myself a sandwich,' he objected.

'Don't be daft – you do *your* job and I'll do *mine*.'

I saw him grinning as I closed the door.

It still looked bitterly cold out there and I changed into warm clothes and got kitted up in my padded anorak of many colours before setting off.

Frost still furred everything that the weak sun hadn't yet touched. I crossed the stone slab bridge over the stream and cut through the herb garden to the path Maria had said led to the Roman fort.

It was quite a climb up through the trees and the path was crossed at one point by the track that circled the estate. I'd have liked Plum's company this morning, but not if I had had to carry him most of the way . . .

I let myself through a wicket gate into a huge field and found it was distinctly parky up there on the open hillside. The site was large and I could see the hummocks and exposed stones where old buildings and walls must lie.

With an icy wind tugging at my hair, I walked over to the nearest information board, and looked down into a deep trench, lined and paved with worked stone. To my surprise, there was also the crouched figure of a man with his back to me, who seemed to be examining the wall of the trench.

I made a startled noise and he turned his head and looked up at me, seeming equally surprised to see me standing there.

He was perhaps in his thirties, but his face was etched with lines of old pain and scarred badly up one side, from jawline to cheekbone. It made his mouth twist a little when he smiled, as he did now, though it was still surprisingly sweet.

'Hello! Where did you spring from?' he asked.

13

A Little Grimm

He got to his feet slowly and moved in an ungainly way to where the wall of the trench was lower and he could step up on to the turf.

He limped towards me, saying, cheerfully, 'Well, that was a silly question, wasn't it? Since the main gates are locked, you must have come from the Castle.'

'That's right,' I said, answering his smile and shaking the hand he held out to me. 'My business partner and I run Heavenly Houseparties and we're working at the Castle. I'm Dido Jones,' I added.

'And I'm Simon Cardew. I'm the Director of Archaeology for the site and I keep an eye on things in winter.'

'Oh, yes, Maria told us about you!' I said, remembering. 'You live in a cottage nearby, don't you?'

He nodded. 'It's on the other side of the site, but you can't see it from here because of the visitor centre.'

By now, I was also recalling Maria mentioning that he'd been badly hurt in the car crash in which his wife had been killed, which explained the scar and the limp, and close to, he did give the impression of one prematurely aged by pain and sorrow, with streaks of grey in his brown hair, which was brushed straight back from a bony and interesting face. He would never have been handsome, like Xan, but he must have been very arresting before the accident. He had soft, sad brown eyes and was perhaps two or three inches shorter than me. I felt like letting down my coronet of hair to equal things up a bit, but by then the wind was really getting up and, having blown down my hood, was now tugging at my hair like invisible hands, so it would soon come down on its own.

'Sorry if I startled you, but I was checking something out in that trench. I walk around the whole site every day,' he explained. 'Occasionally local teenagers get in, though there's nothing very exciting to do here except tear down the notice boards.'

'I suppose you get moronic vandals everywhere,' I said. 'But surely it's too cold up here now to lure them away from their computer games?'

'Probably, but I like to do the rounds every morning anyway. And when I got to this trench the sun came out briefly and was slanting into it, and I thought I saw markings on one of the stones.'

'Was it anything interesting?'

'I'm not sure yet, but I think it's a name. Probably a very bored Roman soldier carved the equivalent of "Septimus was here".'

His face twisted into that engaging, lop-sided smile. 'But you've chosen a bitterly cold day to look at the ruins.'

'I needed a walk and some fresh air, though I wasn't expecting it to be quite *this* fresh up here!'

He looked at me curiously. 'Did you say you ran . . . heavenly house parties?'

'Yes, with my friend Henry Rudge. We take over the

housekeeping and catering for our clients on a temporary basis – anything from a week to a month. Our customers can relax knowing everything is being taken care of. Mrs Powys has booked us until the New Year.'

'Really? I knew from Maria that she's been having trouble finding live-in staff since the old housekeeper left, though that was just before my time,' he said.

With wordless accord we had turned and were making our way in the direction of the visitor centre – and also into the teeth of the wind, though at least, I thought, it would be at my back on the way home.

Two hairpins slid coldly down my back and my plaits fell down. I pulled up my hood and stuffed them inside.

Simon pointed out one or two interesting features of the fort as we walked, though the wind tended to make his words come in short, disjointed snatches.

The visitor centre, a low modern building, was completely shuttered up for the winter and looked vandal-proof to me.

'There are seasonal staff, who run the actual site and the visitor centre,' Simon explained. 'I'm just in charge of the Roman remains and, since I live here, I keep an eye on things when it's closed. I also lecture part-time at the university in Carlisle, and every year I organize a long dig on the site and excavate a bit more of it, with the help of students and local volunteers. The whole site is run by a trust, headed by Mrs Powys.'

'Since it's on her land, I suppose that figures,' I said. 'I've seen the Roman mosaic in that little temple folly in the Castle grounds.'

'Yes, that was moved there when it was discovered in Victorian times. One of the Castle family fancied himself as an archaeologist, though apart from that act of vandalism he didn't cause too much damage. At the time, archaeologists didn't so much excavate carefully as dig holes, searching for some kind of treasure.'

'Well, they found it – that's mosaic's lovely,' I said. 'It's just a pity they removed it. Have you seen the very good copy in the Great Hall?'

'I have. Mrs Powys asks me up there occasionally for dinner. The house always seems to have had a connection to Mithras even before they found the mosaic, though – perhaps something to do with a carved stone near where the mosaic was eventually found. We're sure there was a temple to Mithras there.'

'It's all fascinating,' I said, though it would have been more so if I hadn't been about to freeze to death.

'I think it was a more important site than it was first thought. I'm working on a book about what we've found here, which also connects the fort to the others along the Wall.'

His face clouded. 'I and the rest of the trust have been trying to persuade Mrs Powys to bring the mosaic back to the site, but she won't hear of it. It would be a great draw. We could display it in a wing of the visitor centre, made to look like the interior of the original temple of Mithras.'

'Like the museum in Bath?' I suggested. 'I've seen those, and with the lighting and video effects, you really do feel you've stepped back into Roman times.'

'That's it, though on a much smaller scale, of course.'

As we rounded the corner of the visitor centre, which seemed to be a stubby star shape, he added, 'It's totally different here in the summer – a constant stream of cars arriving and people all over the place. The visitor centre has a museum displaying some of the less valuable finds and there's a small café, too. These places have to make their money as best they can in a short season.'

'I wish the café was open right now. I could do with a hot coffee to thaw me out!'

'Well, come into my cottage and I'll make you one,' he offered, and I looked up and for the first time clocked the strange little house standing right by a huge pair of wrought-iron gates.

'But it looks just like a gingerbread cottage from Grimms' fairy tales!' I exclaimed, for it was small and made of mellow brick, with strange, barley-sugar twisted chimneys and a gabled roof that seemed to be pulled down over its upper windows, like a strange hat.

'I know, it is a bit twee, isn't it?' Simon agreed. 'I've got used to it, though it's rather dark and poky inside and the mod cons were the latest thing in about 1930. But it came with the job and it's handy for work,' he ended. 'Now, what about that coffee?'

'It's tempting, but perhaps another time? I really ought to get back to the Castle. The weekly cleaning service is going through the place like a dose of salts and when I left Xan – Xan Fellowes – in charge, I promised I'd be back in an hour. He might need to take his dog out soon.'

'I've met Xan a couple of times, though it's a while since I've seen him,' Simon said. 'I was summoned to dinner the last time he was up here. I think I was the entertainment.'

'With Xan being a historian, I expect you have a lot in common.'

'True, and we did have an interesting discussion on an aspect of my book,' he said.

'He's staying at the Castle till New Year too, to gather ma-terial for a biography of Asa Powys. And there are several more guests coming for Christmas.'

'I don't remember anyone other than Xan staying at the

Castle since I've been here, but then, Asa Powys had only just died and there was only Mrs Powys here.'

'You must have been very young when you got this job?'

'Twenty-eight . . . but I didn't *feel* very young,' he said, a sad look crossing his face. 'Still, I was glad of the cottage and the small salary and I eke it out with my bit of lecturing and the occasional magazine or journal article.'

Then he smiled. 'I'd better let you go before you get frost-bite,' he joked. 'But do call in any time for a coffee. I have the keys to the visitor centre too, so I could always show you the museum.'

'Thank you, I'd love to. And you might see my partner, Henry, wandering about, sussing out the sloping field below the fort for snowboarding!' I warned.

'Really? Well, it's pretty steep, but I suppose it would be doable, if we get some snow. And we usually do . . .'

'It seems cold enough now,' I said, and after saying goodbye, retraced my steps.

The wind blew me back across the field, but as soon as I was through the wicket gate and in the shelter of the trees, I immediately felt much warmer. It still took a big mug of hot chocolate to thaw me out all the way through.

Apart from the faint sound of pop music from the direction of the laundry room, there was no sign of the cleaners, other than the shiny surfaces all round me.

I changed into my working tunic and trousers and then made three kinds of finger sandwiches – smoked salmon, cheese with finely grated onion, and egg mayonnaise. I put some on a plate for Xan's lunch and then covered the rest with damp kitchen towel under clingfilm and put them in the fridge ready for tea.

I made some coffee and then carried Xan's tray to the study.

As I turned the handle of the door I could see, through the pointed Gothic arch at the end of the passage, a thin young man dusting one of the diving helmets in the Great Hall.

'Hi, Rapunzel,' Xan said, looking up as I came in and it was only then I realized I'd forgotten to put my hair up again and it was still in two long, schoolgirl braids down my back.

'It was windy out,' I explained. 'I went to look at the Roman fort and it's a wonder I didn't blow away, too.'

'It is exposed up there,' he agreed.

'I met the archaeologist in charge of the site, Simon Cardew,' I told him.

'Did you? I'd forgotten about Simon. I must suggest to Sabine she invites him for dinner.'

'He seemed very nice and he was interesting about the ruins, though it wasn't a day for hanging about listening.'

I looked around at the study curiously. 'How are you doing?' I asked, though the answer was evident from the chaos of papers spilling from one open cupboard and a few miscellaneous stacks on the floor. 'I found a text on my phone from Henry when I got back and he's got you a pasting table. He should be home soon.'

'Thank goodness for that!' Xan ruffled up his black hair so that it stood on end, and sighed. 'Apart from the filing cabinets, which Sabine organized, every single cupboard and drawer is crammed to bursting point.'

'So I see,' I said, looking at the cupboard spilling its contents on to the floor.

'That one just sort of exploded in a paper avalanche when I unlocked it.' He sighed again. 'I'll have my lunch and then I'd better take Plum for a quick walk, whether he wants to go or not.'

Plum, who was now snoring, didn't look as if he'd moved from the sofa since I last saw him.

166

'I could give you a hand when Henry gets back. I'll have time before I need to get tea ready,' I offered. 'We can at least get the stuff off the floor and on to the pasting table, ready to sort.'

'Would you? That would be a real help, though won't you want to have a walk, or rest or something, instead? I don't want to take up your free time.'

'I've had more than enough fresh air and exercise for one day and I'm not at all tired. Besides,' I added, 'I love organizing things! It's why I'm so good at my job.'

'If it's your idea of fun, then I accept,' he said gravely.

'I'll be back as soon as Henry returns then,' I said. A thought struck me: 'You don't think Mrs Powys will mind if I help you?'

'I don't see why she should. You aren't going to read any private papers, just help me transfer everything on to the table for sorting.'

'That's true,' I said. 'And I'll dust and clean the cupboards and shelves when they're empty.'

'I'm hoping Sabine will give me another half-hour of her time after tea, so I can record some more of her memories. Whatever she says, she's integral to the biography. At the moment, I'm fleshing out her life before she met Asa, and although I knew her mother died before she was eight, I hadn't really thought about how much that must have affected her.'

'She did tell me and Henry that she wanted to try and recapture the kind of Christmas she had as a child, when her mother was alive . . . so no pressure there,' I said. 'But we'll do our best to instil a bit of magic into the proceedings.'

'I'm hoping to hear about her Oxford student days next, and her first meeting with Asa, just after she'd taken her final exams. She got a First and had already set her sights on a career in archaeology. Once she married Asa, she became just as fascinated by marine archaeology as he was and they were . . . like twin souls, Grandpa used to say.'

I remembered that YouTube clip of the glowing, golden couple standing in the prow of a boat, vibrantly alive and with a future full of promise, and knew what he meant. They'd *belonged* together.

14

Cleaned Out

The first thing I did when I left him was go and put my hair up again, feeling a lot more dignified and professional once I'd done so.

Henry came in soon after the cleaners had driven off and, although he'd had lunch in a café, still wolfed down the spare sandwich I'd made for him, just in case.

While I was making coffee, he said he'd fetch things in.

'Then I had better move the van round to the back again. There isn't much to carry in – the wine merchant's delivering the bulk of the order on Friday.'

There still seemed to be several boxes containing bottles, though, including, I was glad to see, my dry cooking sherry, brandy and dark rum.

The rest of the shopping was mostly things from my list: small, good quality Christmas paper napkins for drinks and nibbles, two dozen Marwood's Magical Crackers and an assortment of other odds and ends.

'That's board wax, you don't want that,' he said, removing a box with a picture of a snowboard on it from my hand. 'I got this great beanie hat, too, and took a selfie by some old tower.'

'It looks like a green squid has landed on your head and is waving its tentacles in the air.'

'Yeah, it's supposed to. When that goes on the vlog, everyone will want one.'

'I hope you didn't pay a lot for it!'

'Six squid,' he said happily, and went out again, this time reappearing empty-handed, though I'd heard him moving the van.

'I took the pasting tables straight to the study – I got two of them, because they were dirt cheap – but Xan wasn't there.'

'He said he was going to take Plum out. Then I'm going to help him in the study,' I amended. 'I'll have about an hour till I need to get tea ready.'

Henry raised an eyebrow at me, though the effect was somewhat lost, since he was wearing the squid hat.

'So much for avoiding him, in case he realizes you were the teenager monster from hell.'

'If it hasn't clicked by now, it isn't going to,' I said with dignity. 'So long as I don't let slip anything that would jog his memory, of course . . .'

'Famous last words, O Queen of Carthage,' he said. 'What exactly are you going to help him with?'

'Just moving things from the cupboards and shelves on to the pasting tables for him to sort more easily. Everything is so crammed in, he can't tell what's there, and not only is he looking for material for the biography, but Mrs Powys has asked him to put aside any papers that should go to Mr Powys's old university's archive.'

'Sooner him than me,' he said. 'Maria sent me a text to say she'd already pre-booked the supermarket delivery slot for tomorrow, by the way, so I'd better go and add everything we need to that before I do anything else.'

I handed him the shopping list and he said, 'It might take me a while, but after that, this little elf is going to light the sitting-room fire and then restock the drinks in there before anyone gets home. And on the way back, I'm going to collect all those gorgeous copper and brass diving helmets from the Great Hall and put them in that little boot room, ready for a good polish.'

'Well, I'm dying to clean out those cupboards and shelves in the study, so we each have our own idea of fun,' I said. 'But I don't think you'll get all that done before you take tea through!'

'No, I'll probably be polishing after that – and I still have all the joy of reorganizing the cellar, too, before the wine merchant's delivery on Friday.'

He went off with the shopping list and I could hear him talking to Xan in the Garden Hall, before the baize door stopped swinging and cut them off.

I exchanged my white tunic for a big, wrap-around pinafore, because I suspected it would be a dusty job, and after collecting some cleaning materials, went through to the study.

Plum, who had lingered in the hall to lap water from the bowl there, creating a small tsunami across the tiled floor, pattered after me.

Xan had put up the two pasting tables and arranged them next to each other down the middle of the long room, with a walkway between. They were not things of beauty, being of the usual hardboard and rough wood construction, with metal rods to hold them steady when unfolded. There were a few empty cardboard boxes underneath.

'Henry's going to save you the empty wine boxes,' I said. 'He thought they'd come in useful.'

'They will, and I suspect we'll need a large one marked "Rubbish",' he said, looking up. He'd clearly just dumped an armful of what looked like a mixture of manuscripts, magazines and loose papers on one end of a table and the upper layer was trying to slide off.

'These are from the cupboard by the French window. I couldn't get everything back into that one once I'd opened the door anyway, so it seemed as good a place to start as any.'

'I expect they're all just as crammed full,' I said. 'You need a Cunning Plan.'

'I suppose I do,' he admitted. 'I hadn't anticipated the scale of the problem!'

'Well, I'm here to fetch, carry and clean, while you're the one who has to look through everything, so I'll empty each cupboard on to the first pasting table and then you rough-sort it all on to the second. You know – journals, newspapers, manuscripts, bundles of whatever they are . . .'

'Emails, I think,' he said looking down. 'According to Sabine, Asa printed out all his emails and pinned copies of his answers to them. He even did carbons of his replies to hand-written letters.'

'That would generate quite a bit of paper on its own,' I said, and then, since he was still looking down at the first heap in rather a lost way, I added firmly, 'You make a start on that pile, while I'm getting the rest out of the cupboard. If you toss any journals and magazines straight into one of the boxes under the table I could sort those out, because they're not personal.'

'OK, bossy boots,' he said mildly, and began pulling out glossy periodicals and lobbing them into the nearest box.

When the first cupboard was empty I gave it a good clean, before cautiously opening the doors to the next.

The usual miscellany slid out on to the carpet, but right at the back were piled a few small and slightly crushed cardboard boxes, which rattled when I pulled them out.

I lifted the lid and peeped inside one. 'These might be archaeological finds, Xan. There are labels, though they're very faded.'

He had a look and said, 'You're right – these are all pottery – mostly Samian ware, I think. We'll put them at the end of the second table to go through later.'

It was quicker for me to empty the cupboards than it was for Xan to go through everything, of course, so he hadn't made a huge amount of progress by the time I'd finished cleaning the second cupboard.

'There we are – I've made a start,' I said, getting to my feet. 'But I'll have to leave you to it now, because time's getting on—'

I broke off as the door to the library swung open and, for a minute, I expected to see Henry, come to see where I'd got to.

Instead, framed in the doorway stood Mrs Powys, still in a long coat of glossy brown fur, though she had thrown it open.

She didn't see me at first, but said to Xan: 'I just came to tell you I was home again and see how you were getting on. Where did those tables come from? I don't think—'

She broke off suddenly, spotting me standing on the far side of the room, still brandishing the feather duster like the Cleaning Fairy's wand, and stared.

'Dido? What are *you* doing here?' she demanded.

'Henry got me these pasting tables in Hexham earlier and Dido's kindly been helping me empty the contents of the first cupboards on to them,' Xan explained, before I could say anything.

'Indeed?' Her bright, light blue eyes examined me coldly. 'I assumed you would realize, Xan, that I preferred that only you were privy to Asa's papers and certainly *not* the staff.'

I'm not sure Xan had ever seen her in a cold rage, because he blinked in a surprised kind of way, before saying, soothingly,

'Of course, Sabine – that goes without saying! Dido's simply been doing the donkey work, to speed things up.'

'Yes, just carrying and cleaning, that's all,' I agreed. 'Anything else was none of my business. But I'm sorry I didn't ask you first if that was all right, Mrs Powys.'

'Or me,' Xan said ruefully. 'But I can see now that I've been insensitive and I'm very sorry.'

She turned those glacial blue eyes on him instead, which was a relief. 'I suppose, if that is all she has been doing, and not prying, it doesn't matter . . . but it was a shock to see her here.'

Then she looked back at me. 'I'm sure you meant well, but surely you have other things you should be doing? I didn't hire you and Henry at huge expense to do this kind of thing.'

'No, but it was my free time.'

'It may have been, but isn't it almost time for tea?' she said coldly.

'Not quite, but I was about to go and wash and change before getting it ready,' I agreed calmly. I've had much more volatile employers than Mrs Powys in the past, sometimes flying into a rage because Henry and I refused to do all kinds of extra things we hadn't bargained for. It was certainly a change to have an employer who was angry because I'd voluntarily done extra work!

I lowered my feathery wand, which I realized I was still brandishing aloft, and turned for the door. Plum got up to follow me; he'd probably picked up on the icy atmosphere.

'Thank you for your help, Dido,' said Xan quietly, before I closed the door to the passage.

I felt dusty, dishevelled and distinctly disgruntled as I reached the servants' wing. There was no sign of Henry and I went straight to wash and tidy up. Plum waited for me in the kitchen, sitting by his empty bowl as if expecting it to magically fill up with his favourite food.

I could hear Henry singing something operatic when I returned and tracked him down to the boot room.

He looked up and smiled. 'I've ordered everything on your list, so that'll be here in the morning. And I'm about to make a start on cleaning the diving helmets.'

'So I see,' I said, looking at the row of them on the bench.

'Lucy's been back a while and I heard Mrs Powys's car when I went to fetch the second lot of helmets.'

'I know Mrs Powys is back, because she came into the study while I was helping Xan.'

He looked at me more closely 'What's up?' he asked. There's no hiding anything from him; he knows me too well.

I described how angry she'd been to find me helping Xan. 'And I mean, we'd already agreed I was just doing the fetching and carrying and cleaning, and had nothing to do with the actual sorting out.'

'Since the room's been shut up since her husband died and she's only just opened it to Xan, I suppose she feels touchy about it, and you *are* a stranger, after all,' he said.

'Yes, we realized that too late, and that Xan should have asked her if she minded before we started. I have apologized and I hope she's accepted that I wasn't doing it out of sheer nosiness! But I expect that's the end of my helping Xan, which is a pity, because we were getting on well and I'd already cleaned out the first two cupboards.'

I sighed. 'Oh, well, I'd better go and make tea.'

'I'll get ready now to take it through. I didn't want to start polishing until afterwards because of the smell of Brasso. I'll probably need a quick shower later to get rid of it, but at least all these will be gleaming by then.'

'Polishing brass and copper isn't something we're contracted to do,' I said, 'but I shouldn't think Mrs Powys is going to complain about your extracurricular activities!'

After taking tea through, Henry reported that things seemed amicable enough in the sitting room and he'd heard Mrs Powys tell Xan that she wasn't too tired to record another short session with him as soon as she had finished tea.

Then he added, 'Lucy appears to have stopped trying to flirt with Xan, which is good . . . except that she seems to be turning her attention to *me*.'

'Oh, no!' I said, bursting out laughing. 'Though, of course, you're just as good-looking as Xan in your own way.'

'Thank you, darling,' he said drily. 'Poor old Xan will be relieved, I'm sure, but I hope she isn't going to try and dog my footsteps like she did his.'

'Poor old Xan nothing!' I exclaimed indignantly. 'He's only two years older than we are!'

Henry raised one eyebrow in an irritating way. 'Oooh, touchy! Are we falling for Xan all over again, then?'

He ducked the kitchen glove I threw at him and went to lay the dining-room table, before he began lovingly polishing the helmets.

Of course, I hadn't fallen for Xan all over again. It was just that, now I was getting to know him better, I really *liked* him . . . in a purely friendly way.

When Xan came into the kitchen to feed Plum, though, that didn't stop me going slightly pink. Henry is such an idiot!

I hoped Xan didn't notice anything and think I was turning into a Lucy, but no, he was opening a tub of gourmet doggy dinner, while apologizing for the scene in the study.

'When I explained things properly to Sabine and that you'd

already asked me if I was sure she wouldn't mind your helping me, she said she'd overreacted.'

'I only realized later how she must have felt. I'm sorry if I upset her,' I said. 'I'll leave you to it, now. Pity, because I do enjoy creating order from chaos!'

'No, it's OK now. She says if you want to spend your spare time cleaning out cupboards and hefting stacks of dusty archaeological journals about, she has no objection.'

'Really?' I said, surprised. 'Great! And I'm saving any more strong cardboard cartons that arrive because you're going to need them.'

'I brought a few small ones with me, for any papers I needed to take back, but I hadn't quite grasped the scale of the problem.'

Plum had licked his bowl so vigorously it had skated across the kitchen floor and under the table, where I was now finely grating dark chocolate into a small bowl.

'Sabine's lying down and I'm going to walk over to Simon's cottage with Plum, to deliver an invitation to dinner on Friday. I mentioned to Sabine at tea that you had met him. Do you want to come?'

'I haven't time. I'm about to make individual pots of chocolate mousse for tonight's dessert and then start on dinner.'

'Which is?' he asked interestedly.

'Steak and chips – one of the meals Mrs Powys said she missed. She was sure you would enjoy it, too, because her theory is that all men do.'

'She's right about this one, because I do. Thin French fries or thick ones?'

'Which do you think she would prefer?'

'I remember Mrs Hill making wavy ones with one of those crinkly cutters,' he offered.

'I think I've seen that chip cutter in one of the drawers. Thick, crinkly chips it is, then.'

'I haven't had home-made chips for years,' he said.

'Well, you'll be getting them tonight. Properly cooked, too – my chips are fat and fluffy inside and golden and crispy on the outside.'

'I like the way you have no false modesty about your cooking.'

'If you do something *really* well, there isn't any point in pretending otherwise, is there? I expect your biographies are very good and you don't mind telling people that?'

'I'm brilliant,' he said modestly. 'Though, actually, I don't generally go about telling everyone so.'

He got off the end of the table.

'And by the way, you looked a lot less forbidding with your hair down,' he said with a grin, and went out with Plum.

I gazed at the swinging door. *Forbidding*?

I grated the rest of the dark chocolate so fiercely that it nearly included my fingertips.

Sabine

When I so unexpectedly found Dido in the study with Xan, I felt a mixture of shock and an icy rage sweep over me: that she and Xan should be working there together, as Asa and I had once done . . .

It felt as if they were replacing us: Dido, tall, dusty, but looking happier than I'd seen her before; Xan, his handsome face serious as he looked up from a bundle of letters.

Knowing that Dido was also Faye's granddaughter – insinuating her presence into that sacred space – only stoked my fury the more.

I could see Xan was shocked by my reaction, but at first I barely took in his explanations and apology, though later, when I had calmed down, I did.

I know him so well that I must accept his assurances that Dido wouldn't dream of prying into what didn't concern her.

After all, she has no idea of any connection between us – indeed, since Faye was small, slight and chestnut-haired, I sometimes briefly forget it myself – or that I brought her here for my own amusement.

Xan was so contrite that in the end I said that she could continue to help, but still . . . I do not like it.

After tea, I recorded another little session with Xan and, although the study had already taken on a slightly alien air, with the long tables in the middle and papers everywhere, once I began to talk about my undergraduate days at Oxford, I soon lost myself in memories.

I'd been such a bitter, angry young woman, very serious and focused on a career in archaeology, which would take me far away from my beloved home, now tainted by the presence of my father's second wife and the ghastly spoilt moppet that was Faye.

But I found I enjoyed life in Oxford, especially since in my very first term I made friends with Nancy, an unlikely attraction of opposites: she was small and wiry, with flyaway, light brown hair, and blue-grey eyes that always saw the best in people, even me. Her warmth thawed out my frozen heart.

I liked Nancy's boyfriend, Stephen, who was destined to be a vicar, but I didn't want to be side-tracked from my ambitions by any man.

Then, just after our final exams, one of the dons had thrown an end-of-term party, which Nancy and Stephen had persuaded me to attend . . . and there, the centre of attention, was old-student-turned-minor-celebrity Asa Powys, who had just given a talk on his recent archaeological discoveries beneath the Aegean Sea.

At that time, marine archaeology wasn't really something I'd given much thought to . . .

So there I stood, drink in hand and slightly bored, taller than most of the men and certainly all the women.

But Asa, the centre of a lively group on the other side of the room, was head and shoulders taller than anyone there. He was tanned and his thick mane of hair bleached almost white by the sun, and though he was a generation older than most of the students, he was so alive that I had the impression the air crackled around him.

He seemed to feel my gaze, for he turned his head and our eyes met – and held.

I've always truly believed that in that moment, our souls joined, so that nothing that ever happened afterwards could tear us apart.

15

Waxing and Waning

Next morning when I carried up her breakfast tray, I found Mrs Powys in bed, as usual, though not reading. Instead, she was leaning back against her pillows, crinkle-crepe eyelids closed. They snapped open at my entrance, the eyes behind them as clear, bright and alive as usual while the rest of her remained still.

I've never liked old-fashioned dolls for this very reason. Give me teddy bears every time.

Of course, Mrs Powys *was* alive, it was just disconcerting that her youthful eyes made it look as if a young Sabine Powys was trapped inside an old body – which I suppose she was.

It threw me off balance for a moment, anyway, though I don't suppose it showed on my face. According to Henry, not a lot *does* unless I'm with friends.

I think I'm like a swan – serene on the surface and paddling like mad underneath.

'Good morning, Mrs Powys,' I said, laying the tray across her knees, then I stepped back and launched into my prepared apology for yesterday's offence. I still felt bad about it, even though Xan had assured me it was all ironed out now. I didn't feel ironed: my conscience was still wrinkly.

'Mrs Powys, I'd like to offer you an apology for my thoughtless and insensitive behaviour yesterday. I should have obtained your permission before helping Xan. I don't know what I was thinking of!'

She stared hard at me for a long moment, then said, coolly, 'It was a shock to find you there, but once Xan had explained your very minor role in the proceedings, I realized I'd over-reacted. You may continue, if you wish, so long as it doesn't impinge on any of the duties I'm paying you for.'

'Of course not – my work always comes first,' I assured her. 'And . . . may I also sort out the journals and periodicals into title and date order, too? There are rather a lot of them.'

'I see no reason why not, if you really want to spend your free time in that way.'

'I'm looking forward to cleaning the bookshelves, too, once I've finished with the cupboards,' I said eagerly. 'Maria only seems to have had time to dust along the tops.'

She now looked faintly amused. 'If that's your idea of fun, go ahead. But as I said, not at the expense of neglecting the duties you're actually hired to perform.'

'Certainly not,' I said. 'In fact, I hope to make a start on the Christmas cake today, once the supermarket delivery has arrived.'

'Good – the sooner the better, I would have thought.'

'I have a good recipe for a quick version. You steep the fruit in alcohol for a few days before making it,' I explained.

She made no comment on this but said, buttering her toast, 'Henry seems determined to add to his workload, too. He asked me yesterday evening if he could fetch the newspapers every day, instead of Lucy. I assume,' she added, 'that since the floral arrangements around the house have suddenly improved a hundredfold, either you or Henry must be responsible.'

'Henry – one of his many talents,' I said.

'Indeed?' she said, and then turned her attention fully on her breakfast, which I took as my dismissal.

In fact, I'd opened the door when her voice stopped me in my tracks.

'And dinner tonight is . . . ?'

'One of the main courses you mentioned was Mrs Hill's giant Yorkshire puddings, filled with sausages, onion gravy and mashed potatoes, so I thought I'd cook that tonight.'

It was hardly cordon bleu, but good home cooking of a traditional kind seemed to be what she was yearning for. Comfort food, I supposed, in the face of her illness.

'And perhaps roast chicken with all the trimmings for dinner tomorrow, when you have a guest. With apple pie to follow.'

'Very good,' she said, and this time it really *was* a dismissal.

In the kitchen, Xan and Plum were watching Henry grilling bacon, though Plum was the only one drooling.

'Do you know if Lucy is in the morning room yet?' I asked.

'Yes, I made her tea and took it in,' Henry said. 'You were ages upstairs.'

'I wanted to apologize personally to Mrs Powys for intruding into her husband's study without permission yesterday, but now you've explained, Xan, she does seem OK with it.'

'I told you so,' he said, but smiled warmly at me. 'It was nice of you to apologize, though. We're going to record another session at half past nine. We've covered her childhood and undergraduate years to the point where she met Asa, so today will be the first of her memories of their life together in Greece. I hope she won't find talking about it too upsetting.'

'I expect it'll be poignant, but also good to remember the happy times,' I suggested.

'I hope so,' he said. 'After the recording session, I think I'll start going through those bundles of handwritten letters from the second cupboard we emptied yesterday. All the elastic bands that held them together seem to have shrivelled over the years, though, and look more like desiccated worms.'

'Yes, I kept picking up bits of brittle rubber when I was cleaning. Plum tried to eat one, but it would probably simply go straight through his system without touching the sides, anyway.'

I paused. 'Since Mrs Powys is OK now with my helping you, Xan, I could give you an hour after lunch? I'll be a bit busier today, once the order arrives, but I can manage that.'

'Yes, that would be great, if you're sure you don't mind giving up your spare time again.'

'She's dying to clean and organize the whole room now, so you'd probably have to keep the door locked to prevent her,' said Henry.

'I'm sure Xan will prefer to work in a clean, tidy room,' I said with dignity.

'I asked Mrs Powys if I could do the daily paper run to the village instead of Lucy, and she agreed,' Henry said.

'Oh, yes – she did mention that,' I said.

'Lucy's a nervous driver and the weather is supposed to be turning colder tomorrow, so the sooner I take over, the better,' he said. 'Anyway, Maria said Andy's fretting because the Land Rover isn't being used. He thinks the battery might go dead, or something seize up permanently.'

'When did Maria say that?' I asked.

'When I rang her to see if she wanted me to get her any shopping yesterday, when I was going into Hexham.'

'That was kind of you, Henry, and to suggest taking over the newspaper pickup for Lucy, too,' Xan said, looking slightly guilty. 'I'd never thought of offering to do either.'

'Why should you? You're here to do your own work and this is more ours,' Henry said cheerfully. 'But I'd better be careful not to be *too* kind to Lucy, because I'm sure now she's switched her affections to me instead of you, Xan.'

As if on cue, Lucy's mousy brown head appeared around the edge of the baize door, her beady dark eyes homing in on Henry as if Xan and I weren't there.

'I've finished breakfast now, Henry, and I'm off to the village, but it's such a relief to know I won't have to do the early run again after today!' Then her eyes finally fell on Xan. 'Oh – good morning, Xan! I didn't see you there.'

Since he was sitting right next to Henry, it was obvious his star had now waned. *I* didn't seem to register at all.

'I could fetch the papers for you today, if you'd rather?' Henry offered kindly.

'Oh, so lovely of you!' she twittered. 'But it doesn't look too bad out there at the moment, does it? And I don't need to make a second trip to the village today unless I feel like taking a little run down later to see my friend Daphne. She runs the village committee and the church flower group, as well as the folk museum and library.'

The head vanished and the sound of her feet pattered off down the passage. I'd swear she was the reincarnation of a small rodent . . . possibly one of the ones making up Mrs Powys's fur coat.

'Yes, you're definitely the favourite now, Henry,' Xan said, grinning.

'Oh, well, if she gets too much, I'll just tell her I'm gay and then she'll probably switch back to you,' he threatened.

'*Are* you gay?' asked Xan with mild interest.

'Is the Pope Catholic?' replied Henry, with one of his seraphic smiles. 'You should see me dance the Gay Gordons!'

'I have,' I reminded him, 'but I think you lack the insane exuberance of your cousin Hector.'

'You're only saying that because Hector asked you to marry him.'

'That was hardly flattering, since he only asked me because he saw an endless vista of his favourite steamed sponge puddings and custard,' I said. 'I blame public schools for this passion for stodgy puds. You know you'd eat jam roly-poly until it came out of your ears, if you got the chance, Henry.'

'You might have something there,' Xan said. 'If I'm dining out anywhere serving sponge pudding and custard, I always order it. What's *your* favourite pudding, Dido?'

'Believe it or not, it's a ripe mango. Best eaten in private, standing over a sink and with your sleeves rolled up.'

'Spare ribs are a bit like that, too,' said Henry. 'You can't *really* indulge in them with full gluttony unless you go completely caveman.'

Then he grinned wickedly at me and said, confidentially to Xan, 'I'll let you into Dido's secret vice – she has a passion for Jaffa Cakes.'

'My vice doesn't seem to be a secret any more,' I said, and went to clear the morning-room table.

Miss Mouse – or possibly Miss Mink – had scattered crumbs all over it.

16

Soft Centred

I passed Xan in the doorway when I got back, as he left for the study, carrying another mug of coffee and accompanied by Plum.

Henry, declining my offer of help with his round of morning tasks, soon followed.

He'd already cleared up after himself and Xan, but I tidied the kitchen, lifted a couple of things out of the freezer and then prepped some vegetables, ready to make soup for lunch.

Checking the time, I decided I could fit in a walk before the supermarket delivery arrived, which would take me ages to put away.

I dressed warmly, which was just as well, because when I went out my breath hung in the air like white ectoplasm and I could feel the ghostly brushing of snowflakes against my cheek. I didn't think the snow would amount to much today, though, because the sky didn't have that pinkish-grey leaden look that so often precedes it.

I went down the steps from the front lawn and then walked fairly briskly along the paths that descended the terraces, intending to spend a few minutes in the Winter Garden on my way back.

I chose the top of the final flight of stone steps that led down to the lake and temple as my turning point, but paused there for a moment, looking out across the water.

Today the surface was rippling, as if stirred by a giant, invisible hand, and it was the same dull, cold-porridge grey of the sky.

I leaned against a stone pillar and all kinds of random thoughts chased themselves through my mind . . . How much I was growing to like Xan, for instance, now I knew him a little better. In fact, from the day we first talked, down by the lake, I'd kept forgetting he wasn't just one of Henry's friends.

My sixteen-year-old self had simply cast him as a romantic hero without knowing the least thing about him. It was so lucky he hadn't remembered me.

This assignment was proving a little tricky anyway, without that complication, what with Xan knowing Henry and being so friendly, which I'm sure our employer wouldn't like in the least.

Mrs Powys was a bit scary, but very much a product of her age and background, though with a slight bohemian edge that was presumably due to her years in Greece.

I suspected she was turning into the autocrat her mother had probably been – but now she was so ill, it was natural that she should long for the comfort of the Christmases of her childhood, and Henry and I would do our best to give her what she wanted.

Of course, quite a lot would depend on what the guests were like, and I only had the bare bones of the list she'd given us, to go on.

I shivered, suddenly realizing how cold I was and began to retrace my steps up towards the house, my thoughts now turning more cheerfully to the Christmas baking to come: the cake and pudding, the first batches of mince pies. I loved the seasonal smell of spices and the heady aroma of dried fruit soaking in rum!

I was just wondering if I'd ordered enough marzipan to make stollen, too, when I emerged from a clipped holly arch into the Winter Garden and found Mrs Powys standing in the middle of it, looking lost in thought.

Her hands were thrust into the pockets of her long fur coat and the shawl collar pulled up high around her neck.

I always imagined I could see the ghosts of the creatures killed to make fur coats circling them, but this one was obviously an antique, perhaps her mother's, and, if the ghosts of the mink were still hanging around it, they had faded to invisibility.

I'd stopped when I first spotted her and would have gone back to find another way had her eyes, below her Russian-style hat, not suddenly focused on me.

'Excuse me – I didn't mean to disturb you,' I said quickly. 'I've been getting some air before the supermarket delivery arrives and this part of the garden, with all these amazing winter-flowering shrubs and plants, is irresistible.'

'My mother created the Winter Garden. She loved to find plants that would bloom in the middle of winter, supposedly the dead time, especially so far north. She said this terrace was a magical place, because it was so protected.'

'It does somehow feel much warmer in this part of the garden,' I agreed.

'I recorded some memories of my early childhood for Xan, and it brought my mother back to me so clearly. This spot was very special to her.'

She was almost talking to herself and I hovered uncertainly, not knowing whether to go or stay.

'I'm not surprised, because it feels somehow other-worldly,

as if I'd strayed into *A Midsummer Night's Dream*,' I said tentatively.

She looked at me more intently. '*You* feel that, too?'

'I should think everyone lucky enough to see the Winter Garden at this time of year must feel the same.'

'Perhaps . . . but I didn't expect it of *you*,' she said, rather bafflingly.

A silence fell, apart from the warbling of a few birds. Then, from way above, came the sound of car wheels on gravel.

'Lucy must be back again, with the papers,' she said. 'She'll be happy tomorrow when Henry relieves her of yet another duty, though I expect she'll still spend a lot of time in Wallstone.'

'She does seem very involved in the village activities,' I agreed.

'Yes, her friend Daphne appears to organize most of what goes on in Wallstone. I've met her and she's almost as silly as Lucy.'

I thought that would be difficult, but didn't say so.

'The Land Rover needs using, though, and Henry will also need it to fetch the Christmas tree for the Great Hall.'

'Where does that come from?' I asked.

'The estate. There's a small plantation of fir trees beyond the lake. He may cut a smaller one for the staff sitting room, too, if you wish.'

She turned away towards a small wooden bridge that spanned the stream where it narrowed, and I took the opportunity to slip away. It was more than time I got back.

As I came up the final flight of steps that brought me out on to the lawn in front of the house, I noticed for the first time that the small shrubs in a bed at one side were grouped around a much larger fir tree – and I suddenly imagined how it would look at night, if it was covered in fairy lights . . . which would be so easy with big outdoor solar ones.

I was still thinking about this when I ran into Maria, who was emerging from the door of the Garden Hall.

'Hello!' I said. 'Were you looking for me?'

'It is all right, I find Henry instead. I bring more baklava for Xan, because I made a batch for Andy, but not enough for that greedy Lucy. Henry says he will slip it to Xan when he is having coffee in the study.'

'I'm sure he'll enjoy that,' I said. 'How is Andy doing?'

I'd texted to enquire, of course, but hadn't actually seen her since the morning after we arrived.

'Better for being home, he says, and he is doing all the exercises the physiotherapist told him to do.'

'That's good, Maria. But why don't you come back and have some coffee with me?' I suggested.

But she declined, saying she wanted to get home again, though before she went I asked her if they ever put lights on the ornamental fir tree at the front of the house. She looked at me as if I was mad and said no, they only decorated the tree indoors.

Suddenly I was determined that this year it would be lit up – a little surprise for my employer.

Since leeks and potatoes were now pretty much the only vegetables in the house till the delivery arrived, that was the kind of soup I made for lunch and then debated over whether to make *croque-monsieur* or *croque-madame* as the second course. *Madame*, I decided.

Henry took Xan his coffee and the baklava, and said he'd found him still sifting the material from the first cupboards and it looked like a very strange jumble sale in there with the varied contents spread along the tables.

I told him about my conversations with Mrs Powys in the garden, and how she seemed to keep forgetting I was there.

He was, predictably, delighted with the idea of an expedition in the Land Rover down a steep and probably very rough track through the woods, to chop down a Christmas tree or two.

'You'll have to come and help – maybe Xan too,' he said. 'We need a *really* big one for the Great Hall!'

I'd definitely be going with him, but mainly to ensure he didn't hurt himself with the axe, or pick some ludicrously giant conifer. I wouldn't put a giant redwood past him.

'We don't need to do that till later next week, once the cleaners have been in again,' I said, then added, 'It was rather sad when Mrs Powys told me she'd been thinking about her mother a lot, since starting recording her memories for Xan, and the wonderful Christmases they had when she was a child.'

'We're going to incorporate all the traditions she can remember into this one, so it's really special,' Henry said. 'It's a pity she never had any children, isn't it? There might have been grandchildren now, to share the magic with.'

'I thought that, too, and I did wonder who would inherit the Castle.'

'I think the only relatives left on her side are Lucy and her brother, Nigel, because the Mellings are related to her husband,' Henry said.

'How do you know?'

'Well, from what Mrs Powys said about her guests and then, from Lucy, too. If you listen to the babble carefully enough, you can pick out the odd nugget of information.'

'I think I'd be more likely to go into a coma of boredom,' I said, then shrugged. 'Oh, well, it's none of our business anyway.'

'True,' he said, and went to lay the table for lunch, before saying he was going to fetch more firewood.

'There's still lots cut, but I might chop some more tomorrow, because the weather forecast says it'll probably snow.'

'It was trying to snow a bit when I went out, but we don't want too much of it if it does, just a pretty sprinkling,' I said. 'It can snow heavily once the rest of the houseguests have arrived!'

It took me ages to put the huge supermarket delivery away, but once I had, I felt as happy as a squirrel with a huge hoard of nuts.

The fridge and freezers were groaning, and one of the small rooms off the corridor was stacked with all the bulky household items, like kitchen and loo rolls.

I ticked off the last things from the order: dried fruit and citrus peel, glacé cherries, flour, treacle, golden syrup, jars and jars of mincemeat, packets of gelatine and fruit jelly, trifle sponges, and my favourite quick cheats: frozen puff pastry and Yorkshire puddings – large ones, the size of soup bowls, and the small, traditional ones. Both these things are time-consuming to make and the frozen versions are just as good. I confess, I do pretend I made them myself and hide the packets well down in the kitchen bin, though.

The soup for lunch was gently simmering as I got out the scales and a giant mixing bowl, blue inside and biscuit-coloured out, into which went the mixed fruit and citrus peel for the Christmas cake, which would be a substantial one.

Then I poured a generous amount of dark rum over it, gave it a good stir, placed a plate over the top and finally stowed it away on a nice cold shelf in the larder.

It's best left for at least three days to soak up the rum, before making the cake, stirring it every day and adding a little more alcohol if necessary. I think it tastes even nicer than Christmas cake made the traditional way, but the amount of treacle I add later is probably the clincher . . .

I still had the giant Christmas pudding to make, but I'd already discovered the football-sized metal mould for it in one of the cupboards.

Henry took the soup tureen through and then beat the gong for lunch, while I made the *croque-madames* in the French way.

At least now the supplies had arrived, there was a better choice on the cheeseboard, as well as a replenished fruit bowl: the jewel-bright satsumas looked festive in themselves.

Later, when we'd cleared lunch, Henry said he was going to make a few little savoury scones for tea and some vol-au-vents for tonight's starter while I was indulging my passion for cleanliness and order in the study with Xan.

I took him a handful of large elastic bands I'd found in a drawer.

'Just what I need!' he said gratefully. 'Now I've sorted a lot of them out, I don't want them mixed up again.'

'You've really done a lot since yesterday,' I said admiringly. 'The first table's almost clear.'

'I've put some of the material back in the first cupboards, but at least everything's now labelled and tagged, so I know what's what.'

'Let's see what's in the next one along, then,' I said, going over to open the doors, but cautiously, in case everything sprang out like the previous ones.

But this time everything was so tightly packed, it was more of an excavation, layer by careful layer. Right at the bottom were some strange, flat canisters.

'Old cine film,' Xan said, looking at the faded labels. 'Copies of ones in Grandpa's collection, which I've got now. Oddly enough, I've brought one with me, along with the old screen and projector, because I don't think Sabine's seen it.'

'Oh, a film show!' I said. 'You'll have to lock the door to keep Henry out!'

'I don't think it's going to be that exciting: just film of parties and picnics and maybe an archaeological site or two.'

He looked down at one of the teetering stacks of papers I'd dumped on the table and said, 'I suspect Asa's old college won't want to treasure several years' worth of his Inland Revenue correspondence!'

I left him after an hour, and when I'd washed the dust off and changed, laid the tea trolley.

The kitchen smelled deliciously of Henry's baking, the fruits of which were cooling on wire racks that covered half the table.

He buttered a warm scone for me and then watched as I assembled the Christmas pudding ingredients, wrapping the silver charms individually in foil. They went into the mixture last.

'Bags me the bachelor's button,' Henry said.

'You'll be lucky to get any of this one,' I told him, but we both took turns to stir the pudding, while making a wish.

Mine was that Henry would finally find Mr Right and live happily ever after.

I have no idea what he wished for, but his expression was unusually serious.

For that night's main course, I dished up the sausages, mash and peas straight into the giant Yorkshire puddings and poured on a little onion gravy, before Henry took them through.

'Mrs Powys said the Yorkshire puddings were just the way Mrs Hill used to make them, and Xan said they were wonderful,' he reported back later, with a grin.

'Only Lucy seemed to have trouble eating all of hers, though she still managed to get through the apple crumble and custard all right. But, of course, she'd finished off the last of my vol-au-vents before dinner,' he said complacently. 'They were too delish to resist.'

Mrs Powys rang the bell when they moved back to the sitting room and were ready for coffee.

'No rest for the wicked!' Henry said.

'I'll put our dinner out and we'll have it before we clear up,' I suggested.

'Good,' he said, hefting the heavy coffee tray with ease, 'because my inner man is feeling famished!'

When our work was done, I had a long, relaxing shower, though I found it distracting having to stand in the big, claw-footed bath to do so, because I felt it might scuttle off with me at any minute.

I went back downstairs with my hair loose to dry and wearing comfortable velvet joggers and a sweatshirt.

Henry was just on his way out to play billiards again with Xan, who had suggested I join them this time. Somehow, though, I didn't think that Mrs Powys would have endorsed this suggestion.

'And anyway, I simply want to put my feet up and chill in front of a cheesy Christmas film,' I said.

'But we always watch those together,' Henry protested indignantly.

'It doesn't matter if you miss one, does it? I mean, we've watched them all several times before anyway! I thought I'd start the annual Christmas film festival with *Elf*.'

'Ooh, you know that's my favourite!' he said, but I told him we could watch it again another night.

He still looked disgruntled and I'd barely settled down on the sofa in front of the TV, with a big tin of chocolates next to me, when the door opened and he and Xan came in, Plum at their heels.

'Xan said *he'd* rather watch *Elf*, too,' Henry announced. 'I told him you wouldn't mind, Dido.'

'No, not unless he eats all my favourite chocolates,' I said, removing the one I was about to unwrap from Plum's questing nose.

Looking up, I caught a strange expression in Xan's lilac-grey eyes . . . but so fleeting that I wasn't sure if I'd imagined it.

'I only like soft centres, Rapunzel,' he said gravely, then picked up Plum and sat down with him on his knee, at the other end of the sofa.

Sabine

'So, off we go again,' Xan had said, smiling at me across the coffee table in the study, as we started the next recording session. 'We stopped yesterday just as you and Asa had met at that party in Oxford after your finals.'

'Yes . . .' I said, looking back across the years to that wonderful moment. 'The moment our eyes met, we were instantly drawn together and spent the rest of the evening walking around Oxford and talking. It was . . . magical.'

'You'd been intending to make your career in archaeology, so you must have had a lot in common?'

'Oh, yes, though Asa was a few years older and already making a name for himself as a pioneer in marine archaeology, an aspect of the subject I'd never really considered before. Of course I knew of his book on the subject and had seen the first short TV documentary he made with his best friend, your grandfather, Tommy.'

'I know he and Asa had been best friends from school,' Xan said. 'But Tommy's interests lay in photography, so he found filming underwater an exciting challenge at that time.'

'He and Asa made a good team,' I said. 'Their interests

complemented each other and they both settled on Corfu. At that time, there were a lot of artists and writers living there and it was quite bohemian.'

'I think they flocked there to escape the post-war austerity,' Xan suggested. 'It sounded like they had a lot of fun – parties and picnics and generally having a good time!'

'It seemed a totally different world to me, and it *was* huge fun. Asa was very gregarious, so the house was always full of people. Of course, Asa was serious about his work – that always came first. Up till then, marine archaeology had mostly meant finding sunken ships and searching for treasure, but for Asa, the *real* treasure lay in tracing the remains of old civilizations that had vanished below the sea, usually because of some seismic disturbance, and I caught fire at his enthusiasm.'

'I'm not surprised. He could make anything sound fascinating, let alone his own pet subject!'

'That's because he was interested in everything – *and* everyone. He was so charismatic, wasn't he?' I said. 'After our first meeting, we spent every possible minute of the next few days together – and we married in a registry office just before he was due to fly back to Greece.'

'That was a whirlwind romance!'

'Having found each other, we just couldn't bear to be apart. The only guests at the wedding were Nancy, and her fiancé, Stephen. After the wedding, we drove here, to Mitras Castle, to break the news to my father. I'd come into my inheritance at twenty-one, of course, but under the terms of Mummy's will, he had the right to live here and received an income from the estate.'

'And your stepmother and half-sister, too, of course,' Xan said.

'I'm sure Mummy never envisaged that Father would marry again, or she would have arranged things differently,' I said.

'Your father must have been very surprised at your sudden marriage?'

'Of course, but he could have no objection to Asa who, apart from his career, came from a wealthy background,' I said. 'Asa completely understood the situation: that although I loved my home, it was tainted for me by the presence of my stepmother. Faye was at boarding school when we visited so he didn't meet her at that time.'

I paused a moment, thinking back.

'We didn't even stay the night. I just packed up what I wanted to take to Greece with me and two days later we were in Corfu!'

'Quite a change,' Xan commented, smiling.

'Oh, I loved it from the first moment! And Asa's villa on Corfu became my second home. Tommy had a house nearby and he'd recently married your grandmother, Rose. We all immediately became good friends. By the oddest of coincidences, I discovered Rose's maiden name had been Archbold and we managed to trace a distant link to a branch of my mother's side of the family.'

'It's strange how these coincidences happen,' Xan agreed. 'I know quite a bit from Tommy about the social life out there at the time, though of course, by the time I came along Corfu was more about tourists than artists and writers, but still lovely.'

'Asa and I were very fond of your father – I still am, of course – and of you, too.'

'You and Asa have always felt like family,' Xan said, smiling at me.

'You *are* family, even if very distantly related, through Rose,' I pointed out.

'I think that's so diluted, it's the merest trace of a connection,' he said. 'And we seem to have wandered off course a bit, haven't we? You'd just arrived on the island and begun to settle in.'

'Everything was so new, different and exciting. It was the start of the most wonderful period of my life!'

A kaleidoscope of happy, sunlit images sparkled in my mind and I must have fallen quiet for a while, because Xan said, softly: 'Sabine? I think that's a good point to end on today, don't you?'

17

Lightly Frosted

There was a very Christmas-card sprinkling of snow when I looked out next morning, though the sky was still dark indigo with a sequin spatter of stars.

Henry had told me he'd be out early to fetch the papers, but I wasn't worried because he'd checked over the old Land Rover the previous day and also found some chains for the wheels, if the roads got really bad. I didn't think he'd need them today, though; the snow looked no more than a decorative powdering.

He came back soon after I'd made the first pot of coffee, with snowflakes starring his red-gold curls and his cheeks pink from the cold, so he looked even more cherubic than usual.

He took the bundle of papers and a couple of upmarket magazines through to the Great Hall, where they were always laid out on a round table under one of the front windows.

'I think *Horse and Hound* must be a nostalgia trip for Mrs Powys,' he said, returning and gratefully accepting his mug of coffee. 'Perhaps her mother rode to hounds?'

'Maybe, though it's all drag hunting now, isn't it? They don't kill anything. What was the other glossy magazine?'

'*Country House Living.* There was an article on creating

Christmas garlands and swags from garden gleanings, which looked good. Their idea of a garden seemed to be on the same scale as the grounds here. I might borrow the mag when I make the ones for the Great Hall.'

'I'm sure there must be holly and ivy, and there's a big bay tree in the herb garden, too. What with those and a few fir tree clippings you should have plenty to work with,' I agreed.

'Xan was just going out with Plum when I got back, but I don't think he'll hang about out there this morning, so he'll probably be in for breakfast shortly,' Henry said. 'Bacon rolls again, I think – do you want one, too?'

'OK,' I agreed, succumbing to temptation. 'What's Wall-stone like?'

'It's a fairly substantial village. There's an old church, a pub and a tea room, as well as the shop. I think in the tourist season they get quite a lot of visitors to the local history museum and to look at the big Roman stone in the middle of the Green. It's supposed to be that two-headed god, Janus, but it was still dark, so I'll have a look another time.'

'Were the roads OK?'

'No problem. There was already a tractor and gritter out. The sky's clear, too, so I doubt there'll be any more snow for a while, anyway.'

He sounded regretful. He was probably hoping for enough to try a little snowboarding down the field below the Roman site.

'If the weather turns *really* rough, I can always collect the papers later in the day. Mrs Powys won't expect me to kill myself, just so she can read *The Times* in the mornings.'

'No, I don't think that's one of the things we offer along with our other services,' I agreed.

Henry took the bread, butter and milk through to the breakfast room while I got Mrs Powys's tray ready and took it up, passing Xan on the way. He was in one of the small rooms off the passage, towelling Plum's legs and tummy dry. He looked up and gave me a smile, which I returned, but didn't say anything. We already felt so easy together, even after such a short time.

I carried on up the stairs, thinking that Henry and I were, as usual on our assignments, quickly falling into a routine.

I could see a pattern forming in our relationships with our employer, too. My exchanges with her while delivering her breakfast appeared to be the extent of mine and I suspected that anything more I needed to know would be relayed via Henry, who seemed more in favour.

That suited me fine. I've always preferred keeping in the background when I can, whereas Henry is much more socially adept and good with people.

This morning I found Mrs Powys sitting up in bed reading a novel with a very retro cover, of the vintage murder mystery type, which she laid down when I wished her good morning and placed the tray over her knees.

'There is a scattering of snow, Mrs Powys, but Henry said the roads were clear.'

'Good – I need to go out later this morning, though I'll be back for lunch.'

She paused, contemplating her tray and presumably finding no fault with it, for she added instead, 'I must speak to Henry about the Christmas decorations, which are stored in one of the attics, though they don't go up until late next week. The evergreen garlands, too . . . and the gifts for the guests. I'm recording an early session with Xan after breakfast and then I'll ring for Henry to come to the library after that.'

'I'll let him know,' I said.

On my way back, I looked into the morning room and

found Lucy there, eating toast and marmalade. She said dear, kind Henry had brought her a pot of tea and how nice it was not to have to worry about going out into the snow this morning.

I left her to it and went along the passage to the kitchen, where I was met by the delicious smell of bacon.

Henry was trying to persuade Xan to try the strange pink tea in his glass pot, where a drowned Ophelia of a hibiscus flower floated.

'I don't really think it goes with bacon,' Xan objected dubiously. 'Maybe I'll stick to coffee. Shall I make you one too, Dido?'

Plum, who had looked up at my entrance, a long bacon rind dangling from one corner of his mouth, swallowed it in a gulp and came to greet me, tail flapping as if it had a separate life of its own.

'Please,' I said, sitting down as Henry fetched a plate and set it in front of me.

'I only just managed to stop Xan eating yours too,' he said, and I saw Xan grin.

'I suspect it was the other way round. I popped in just now to see if Lucy was OK, and she said dear, kind Henry had made her tea with his own fair hands.'

'I did and you'd have thought I'd brought her the Elixir of Life,' he said.

'I don't know what she does with herself when she isn't in the village with her friend Daphne,' Xan said. 'She's not called on to be any kind of companion to Sabine, who seems to like her space better than her presence. I feel quite sorry for her.'

'Oh, I think she's happy enough left to her own devices,' Henry said cheerfully. 'I've found two large empty chocolate boxes in her bedroom wastepaper basket already, when making her bed and tidying up. And there's stacks of steamy historical novels in her room, too. The covers are all very similar – pictures of muscular men – though I'm sure the one on top of the pile yesterday had too many ribs.'

'Each to their own form of escapism,' I said, then told him that Mrs Powys wanted to see him in the library after she'd recorded another session with Xan.

'There was something about telling you where the decorations were stored – though I don't know why she couldn't tell me that – but mainly I think she wants your input on what Christmas gifts to get for her guests.'

Henry fished out a battered sheet of paper from his tunic pocket and unfolded it.

'Luckily, I've been thinking about that and made a copy of the guest list. Xan helped me get a rough idea of everyone's ages.'

He read out: 'Lucy, of course, who is around fifty . . .'

'I think she's always been around fifty,' Xan put in dispassionately. 'I've only occasionally met her in the past, but she looked much the same as she does now. It was a surprise when Sabine told me she'd been her boss's mistress for years.'

'Really? Perhaps she was quite cute when she was younger,' I said charitably. 'Go on, Henry – I take it you've added Xan?'

'Yes, he's thirty-seven, the poor old thing.'

'Well aged, like a good wine,' Xan said.

Henry ignored this. 'Mrs Powys always buys her friend Nancy a bottle of Penhaligon's Bluebell perfume, I know that. There's Lucy's brother, Nigel, who is a year or two older than she is; Mr and Mrs Melling, who are sixty-ish; and their son, Dominic, who's in his early thirties . . .'

His finger moved down the list. 'Oh, yes, there's the solicitor, Mr Makepeace, too – I think he's ancient. And his granddaughter, Mrs Martin, who's probably about our age.'

He counted, using all his fingers. This is what a public school education does for you.

'There are four women, and five men, including Xan.'

'Or you could put him in a category under "Other",' I suggested, and Xan gave me a look.

'I decided to confine myself to Liberty's website for *everyone*, with variations on a theme – silk scarves for the women, for a start. But men are the most difficult – the usual socks, ties or ballpoint pens are *so* boring – but I think I've cracked it.'

'Should I put my fingers in my ears and hum, so as not to spoil the surprise?' asked Xan.

'Do!'

Henry turned to me and whispered: 'The most gorgeous pewter paperknives, very Arts and Crafts – a thing of beauty as well as useful.'

'Great idea,' I agreed, then gestured to Xan to unstop his ears.

'You could do with your present now,' I said, thinking he could use his to prise off withered rubber bands.

'If you're giving all the men pasting tables, then you'll need to order a lot of wrapping paper.'

'Don't be daft,' I told him, getting up. 'Well, duty calls. I've got a Christmas pudding to steam.'

'Yes, I'd better go, too. Sabine will be down soon to do her recording.'

'Followed by my grilling in the library, so I'd better whisk through my morning round like the fastest house fairy in Northumberland,' Henry said.

Mrs Powys had apparently been delighted with Henry's gift suggestions and they had ordered them online, then and there, including a long and vibrant silk scarf for Nancy, to go with the perfume.

'And while we were at it, we added gift-wrap, bows, ribbon and silver tissue paper . . .' he told me. 'And tags, for Mrs Powys to sign, but I'll do all the wrapping and make everything look wonderful.'

'Good, that's sorted then. What about the decorations?'

'First attic at the top of the stairs in the servants' wing, all the boxes labelled. We can sort them out in one of the disused bedrooms opposite ours, but they don't go up until after the cleaners have been in next Wednesday.'

'That makes sense,' I said.

'And she's going out in ten minutes, but will be back for lunch,' he said. 'I have her car keys and I'm just off to bring it round to the front for her.'

'It's a pity you haven't got a chauffeur's outfit as well as a butler's, Henry!'

'Don't tempt me!' he said with a grin, and went out jangling the car keys.

By the time the delivery from the wine merchant had arrived and been put away by Henry, the Christmas pudding in its spherical mould had been steaming on top of the stove for quite some time, and the first batch of mince pies was cooling on the rack. Two apple pies were baking in the oven, too, the largest destined for the freezer.

I took Xan a mug of coffee and a mince pie for his elevenses, and when I came back I told Henry I was popping out for a bit.

'I'm going for a walk with Xan and Plum shortly – do you want to come?'

'No, I think I'll make some of my famous Parmesan puffs for tonight's starter. And anyway,' he added with a wicked smile, 'three's a crowd!'

'Don't be silly! And Plum already makes three, doesn't he?'

'I'm not sure he counts. I must say, for two normally reserved people – I mean, Xan must have his guard up against women most of the time and you're the original ice princess – you seem to be getting on together very well.'

'I think that's just because I find him easy to talk to, and then I fell into the habit almost from the start of treating him just like one of your friends.'

'That's probably a novelty,' he said. 'And a bit different from the last time you met!'

I shuddered. 'Don't remind me! But if he had recognized me, I expect he'd still be keeping me at arm's length, in case I went all silly again!'

'No, I expect he'd just think it was highly amusing now,' Henry suggested.

'I think that might be even worse. I'd *die* of shame!'

Sabine

I enjoyed this morning's recording session, remembering those early days of my marriage when I was, as they say now, living the dream, even if I hadn't known this particular dream existed until Asa came into my life.

I soon settled down on Corfu and thrived in a bohemian atmosphere that was entirely new to me. Almost immediately, I felt myself turn into a happier, more sociable creature, like a flower opening in the sun, and the artists, writers, archaeologists and other academics who visited the house provided a rich mixture to grow new ideas in.

I was already a strong swimmer and quickly learned to dive, using an aqualung, as we called it then.

The sea was so clear and revealed a whole new underwater world to explore.

Asa taught me how to distinguish natural formations from man-made ones – the remains of old statues, walls and steps . . . the traces of ancient wrecks.

Tommy was usually with us, but his wife, Rose, was an artist with a large studio behind their small cottage where she worked long hours when inspired.

It was the start of such adventures, especially when the producer of the upcoming documentary series decided that including me in it would increase audience interest!

And so, it soon transpired, it had . . .

'The late fifties and early sixties were the best of times for us to work and flourish in – but, of course, we thought our happy existence would go on for ever,' I finished, and it was only then that I remembered where I was and that Xan was recording every word I said.

He smiled at me, turning the machine off. 'That was great, Sabine, but I think we should stop there. I'm afraid in the next session we must briefly touch on the loss of your father and stepmother in that car accident, since it led to you and Asa spending more time at Mitras Castle.'

The hint of a dark shadow seemed to creep across my golden memories.

'If you really think it necessary,' I said.

Henry joined me in the library when I rang, and I found our subsequent discussion about the ordering of Christmas presents for my guests surprisingly pleasant and soothing. He has such good ideas and is really a delightful and helpful young man.

Then I drove off to my appointment with the aptly named Pain Nurse, who *was* a pain, since she doled out my pills in such meagre quantities.

18

Thyme Out

Xan and I both donned wellies for our walk, and it was a pity Plum didn't have any, because his little legs sank into even the light covering of snow outside.

We climbed the hill and took the path up through the trees to the wicket gate that led to the Roman site.

I'd put on my anorak of many colours, and this time Xan had remembered to wear a hat – a black beanie one, which reminded me of the Phrygian cap Mithras was wearing in the mosaic. It suited him, though, and the rainbow silk scarf, the fringed ends blowing in the slight breeze, brightened up his long, dark, military-style greatcoat.

If instead he'd been wearing a cravat and Hessian boots, he'd have been a dead ringer for most people's idea of Mr Darcy.

He saw me looking at his green wellies.

'I wanted the kind with frog eyes on the top,' he said gravely, 'but they don't come in my size.'

'That's the trouble with having big feet. I take an eight and all the nicest shoes stop at size seven. Still, I wear moccasins and moccasin boots most of the time, anyway.'

'I like your moccasins,' he said.

'You should see my party ones – they've got beaded thunderbirds on the toes.'

'I look forward to it.'

He'd picked Plum up when he flagged halfway up the steep path, but once we were through the wicket gate, put him down again. Most of the snow had blown off the exposed parts of the site, so the ruins just looked artistically frosted. There was no sign of Simon that morning, unless you counted a thin swirl of gunpowder-grey smoke in the far distance, where his cottage lay hidden by the visitor centre.

'I bumped into Simon the first time I came up here and he told me lots of interesting things about the site,' I said. 'Apparently, it was more of a garrison, with living quarters for families, too, hence the Mithras temple and the extensive remains of heated baths. All mod cons.'

'I know they discovered a few clay tablets incised with invitations and messages, so there was some kind of social life going on,' Xan said. 'They found a lot more of them at another site a bit further along, though.'

'Oh, yes, I remember visiting that one,' I said without thinking, then quickly went on: 'I was taken to visit various sites along the Wall when I was a child, though I don't remember ever coming here.'

'Visitors tend to flock to the important sites with more facilities. The visitor centre and café here were only a couple of wooden huts until the new one was built about fifteen years ago. I came for the opening. Asa cut the ribbon and then downed most of the bottle of bubbly,' he said with a reminiscent grin. 'Though, of course, he'd supplied it in the first place.'

We circled round what a large sign proclaimed to be a communal loo – and yes, Simon had already imparted the information that the Roman idea of loo paper was to keep a sponge on a stick in a jar of vinegar next to each toilet seat – when Plum fell into a shallow trench and had to be fished out again.

Xan tucked him under his arm, where he hung limply, his pink tongue lolling tiredly out of his moth.

'Plum hasn't got a lot of energy,' I commented.

'No, but he's almost seven, which I think for a dog is sort of middle-aged – and he's only got little legs.'

'How did you come to choose a King Charles spaniel?'

'I didn't! I was visiting Nancy, who lives near me just outside Oxford, and she was looking for a new home for him because his elderly owner had passed away. Nancy decided I needed a dog for company.'

'You've known Mrs Kane a long time?'

'All my life. She and Sabine were students at Oxford together and were at each other's weddings, too – best friends for ever! So the Kanes were always welcome visitors here, or on Corfu. Nancy lost her husband about ten years before Asa died. He was a nice man – a vicar. I expect that's what influenced Nancy to move from academic work to being ordained herself.'

We skirted a wall and came out near the visitor centre, before turning to walk back along the lower part of the site.

To our right, the land fell away steeply, with outcrops of rocks, and I hoped Henry would check it out before any more snow arrived and he tried snowboarding down it.

There was still no sign of Simon, but I thought he'd be hunkered down in front of the fire, if he had any sense.

'So, if you visited the area as a child, did you come from around here?' Xan asked suddenly.

'No, it was just a holiday,' I said quickly.

'Oh, right. I was sure Henry said you live near each other in Cheshire.'

'We do – we have a pair of grace-and-favour lodges at the

gate of one of his relative's country houses,' I said. 'But I come from west Lancashire originally – a very small market town called Great Mumming. I imagine being brought up on Corfu was a lot more interesting, though!'

'My parents were living and working in Athens when I was born, though I still had wonderful holidays at the old house on Corfu,' he said. 'And then, when I came over here to school, Mitras Castle became a bit of a home-from-home.'

'Great Mumming wasn't exciting, but a nice place to grow up in,' I said. 'My granny lives there, with her friend Dora. They're both widows and share a passion for travelling, but when I came along and she became my guardian, I put a bit of a crimp in that for a while!'

And I don't know how it came about, but I found myself explaining the tangled history that had led to Granny first adopting my father, and then taking on me – the result of Dad's brief liaison with another university student – at a time when she and her friend were looking forward to a retirement spent globetrotting.

'So Granny isn't *really* my granny, but she has a great sense of duty.'

'Poor little girl!' Xan said gently. 'Duty doesn't sound much fun.'

'Oh, we love each other, in our own way, and she soon managed to arrange things so she and Dora could travel again. My childminder lived on a farm and her son was my best friend, so I often stayed there in the holidays . . .'

I tailed off, because Liam's betrayal was still a painful spot deep in my heart.

'Later, I went to a small boarding school and often spent the summer holidays with a friend,' I added, before realizing that might take me into difficult waters. I certainly didn't want to

216

mention Charlotte! 'Once I was old enough, I visited Dad in California. He's the curator of a large private art collection.'

'You know, Dido, I think your upbringing sounds a lot more interesting than mine!' he said. 'Are you ever called Di, by the way? I keep meaning to ask.'

'No, *never*!' I lied, darting a suspicious look at him, but just then I slid on a patch of snow and had to grab him to save myself.

He tucked a hand through my arm companionably and said, 'It's a bit slippery just here. Hang on to me till we get back through the gate.'

'You've already got Plum to carry,' I pointed out, but didn't release myself.

'I expect your experience of Christmas was a lot more traditional than mine in Greece,' he said, as we picked our way around the icy patches. 'The first one I spent with my parents at the Castle was quite an eye-opener!'

'Not really, Granny and Dora weren't that big on Christmas. I think the novelty had worn off and it was all too much work and fuss. As soon as I turned five, we used to spend the break at a small country house hotel near Bath. Then, much later, I spent a Christmas with some of Henry's family in a huge, cold mansion in Norfolk. I learned so much from their wonderful cook, and about all the Rudge family Christmas traditions, too, though they seemed to do things in their own slightly peculiar way.'

'I assume that was after you'd come back from your road trip abroad with Henry? He told me you met at university and then the summer after you graduated, a group of you set off around Europe in an old car.'

'Yes, but the others dropped out after a while. Henry and I kept going and we were away a lot longer than we'd originally intended.'

Henry, I thought, seemed to have told Xan a lot. But then, so had I . . . he was too easy to talk to!

'We both came back with lots of ideas – and in my case, recipes too – not to mention the inspiration for Heavenly Houseparties. Henry also started his blog and I began to turn all the material I'd collected abroad into a series of little books of recipes and reminiscences, and was lucky enough to find a publisher.'

'Those sound fun!'

'They come out annually, just before Christmas and they're all called *A Tiny Taste of* . . . This year's is *A Tiny Taste of Andalusia*. I've brought my box of author's copies with me, because they're always handy to give as gifts, so you could have one, if you like?'

'I'd love it. Wrap it up and give it to me for Christmas!'

I looked doubtfully at him, but he seemed to be serious. 'OK. And *you've* written quite a lot of books too, haven't you?'

Naturally, I'd already checked him out on Amazon . . .

'I turned my post-graduate dissertation into a biography, which sold well enough for the publisher to take another . . . and I just kept on going after that.'

He suddenly smiled and added: 'Chilling out in front of that film with you and Henry took me right back to my student days again. It was fun.'

'I don't think we've ever grown out of that phase,' I said ruefully.

When we were back on the sheltered path down to the house again, he put Plum down.

'It's time I was back and making lunch,' I said.

'And I should be working, though Sabine does keep telling me this is a holiday, too. But there's so much more paperwork in the study than I envisaged. I need to crack on with it before her other guests get here.'

'Yes, I suppose you'll have to stop and be sociable for a bit, after that,' I agreed.

Henry had gritted the stone slab bridge over the stream and

the paving in front of the door to the Garden Hall . . . and I hoped he'd remembered to top up the water in the steamer my Christmas pudding was cooking in.

When I left Xan towelling dry Plum's wet tummy and went into the warm and slightly steamy kitchen, I saw he *had* remembered and all was well.

I told him about the rocky slope below the Roman site.

'Maybe I'll take a look at the terrain after lunch, then, because with a bit of luck we might get more snow.'

'As long as the guests can still get through, I don't mind,' I said, as Xan came in to make himself a mug of coffee to take back to the study.

'I'm going to take the Land Rover down the track through the woods to look at the Christmas tree plantation later this afternoon,' Henry said. 'Why don't you both come with me?'

Xan paused, coffee mug in hand and said, 'I was hoping Dido would help me in the study for a bit, really.'

'I will, but then I've got a lot of food prepping to do, because Simon's coming for dinner.'

'You'll still have time to take a quick look at the Christmas trees, though, especially if I make the afternoon tea, and I know you want to,' Henry said persuasively.

'All right,' I said, giving in. 'Xan, what about you?'

'OK, and maybe we should take something to tie around the tree we choose? I wouldn't put it past Henry to bring back one twenty feet high, if left to himself.'

'True – you've got his measure. And Mrs Powys says we can have a tree for our staff sitting room, too. I've got some red gift ribbon in one of the boxes – I'll cut a couple of pieces.'

'There we are, then: the great tree expedition *will* take place,' said Henry, and went to lay the table, ready for lunch.

*

And not only did the Christmas tree expedition take place, but it was fun, rattling and jolting down the steep track through the woods, having to stop occasionally to move fallen branches out of the way.

Right at the bottom of the estate, where the track turned before beginning to ascend the other side of the valley, we found the small plantation of fir trees, in all sizes from tiny to enormous.

We selected a huge one for the Great Hall – but not as enormous as Henry would have chosen – and a modest five-footer for ourselves, and tied our ribbons round them.

Henry, of course, started singing about tying a red ribbon round the old fir tree, until I found enough snow on the nearby boundary wall to pelt him with.

The ensuing snowball fight was a little limited by the amount of ammunition . . .

Damp and glowing pinkly, we all returned to the Castle. Duty called and, anyway, I was looking forward to cooking up a complete roast chicken dinner, which would be like a mini dress rehearsal for Christmas dinner.

'Stuffing balls,' I murmured to myself, as the three of us wedged ourselves on to the front bench seat of the Land Rover, and Xan looked startled.

'It's all right, she's just dreaming about tonight's dinner,' Henry explained.

'I'll make stuffing balls – sage, thyme and finely minced onion,' I said, 'and an extra tray of them for the freezer, ready for Christmas Day. I could make extra bread sauce, too . . .'

And as my mind wandered off again down familiar, but no less exciting, culinary tracks I vaguely registered Henry, saying, 'We've lost her again.'

19

Old Chestnuts

The Christmas pudding was finally cooked, cooled and then rewrapped and stored in a bowl on a cold larder shelf.

I gave the dried fruit soaking in rum for the cake a good stir while I was in there, and it gave off such a rich aroma that I felt quite light-headed . . .

Henry took his Parmesan puffs starter through to the sitting room before dinner and was away some time.

'Has Simon arrived?' I asked when he finally returned. Henry had met him earlier, when he'd popped up to the site to look at the snowboarding possibilities, and they seemed to have got on surprisingly well. Apparently, Simon used to be a rock climber before his accident. I suppose even academics can be addicted to extreme sports.

'Yes, he arrived just as I was crossing the Great Hall to the sitting room, so I let him in. We were having a little chat while he changed his wellies for shoes – they're never a good look with a suit – when Mrs Powys called out, wanting to know what was holding him up. So then I threw open the sitting-room door and announced him in my best Jeeves manner.'

'I can imagine!' I said.

'I followed him in with the dish of Parmesan puffs and, at Mrs Powys's request, poured some drinks.'

He paused, then added, 'I think Lucy had already helped herself to more than one sweet sherry, because her cheeks were quite pink and she giggled when I refilled her glass and thanked me as effusively as if I'd handed her the Crown Jewels.'

'Oh, well, I expect dinner will sober her up,' I suggested, and Henry went off to check on the fire in the dining room and switch on the warming plates on the side table.

I put the finishing touches to the roast chicken dinner, which was perfection, of course . . . as would also be my lovely, deep apple pie, to follow. The chicken, a fat, free-range one, was golden brown, and I'd stuffed the loose skin above the neck with my own mix – breadcrumbs, sage, thyme and finely minced onion – and laid rashers of streaky bacon over the breast.

The kitchen smelled totally delicious. I'd kept the baize door closed to try and prevent the aromas from pervading the whole house, but it seemed a pity not to share it. Still, I expect mouthwatering wafts escaped whenever Henry went to and fro.

He beat the gong with his usual brio and then, when he carried out the chicken on a lordly dish, I followed with the vegetables, gravy and bread sauce, setting the covered dishes down on the hotplate.

Turning to go, I caught Simon's eye and he gave me that strangely heart-breaking smile, which I returned.

Xan, seated opposite Sabine, who was at the head of the table, turned his head in time to catch this exchange and regarded me with a rather curious, frowning expression, though I could think of no reason why he should, so perhaps he was just thinking of something else . . .

Henry took some time to follow me back to the kitchen,

having stayed to carve the chicken after Xan said he was useless at it and always ended up hacking it into lumps, and Simon, fearing Mrs Powys would ask him next, had hastily said he was even worse.

'But they're all tucking in now and Xan poured the wine while I was doing it. Mrs Powys told Xan not to give any to Lucy because she'd had quite enough to drink already, and the poor thing looked totally crushed.'

'I'm sure she did, especially in front of Simon!'

'Xan was kind, though, and said he thought they'd *all* over-indulged in the pre-dinner drinks.'

When the main course was cleared and they were consuming apple pie and cream, we sat down to our own dinner, which I'd kept warm in the oven, just adding a little leftover chicken and stuffing.

Henry is rather like Plum, in that he eats his own dinner amazingly fast and then sits staring longingly at mine.

Coming back from the sitting room after the coffee run, Henry relayed some compliments on my cooking, which always made me feel appreciated.

Simon had said it was a great treat to eat good home cooking, since it didn't really seem worth the bother to make dinner when he was on his own.

'And then Mrs Powys took pity on him, and said that, in that case, he must come to dinner on Christmas Day.'

'That makes it eleven, then,' I said. 'Not that it would matter if there were several extra guests, because the turkey's a *monster*.'

'Simon's in his thirties, so it'll make more of a balance between the ages and probably help me get a bit of a party atmosphere going,' Henry said. 'And my special Christmas Cocktail will oil the wheels.'

'You'd better be careful not to oil Lucy too much, or one

of her wheels might come off altogether,' I warned him, and he grinned.

There was a diversion at this point.

Earlier, Plum, rendered insanely greedy by the smell of the cooking chicken, had had to be bodily removed from the kitchen by Xan. But evidently he'd now escaped from the sitting room, for the baize door swung suddenly open and he did a backwards somersault into the kitchen. He looked so surprised that I wasn't sure whether it was intentional, or if he was simply sitting leaning against the door.

He got to his feet, tail wagging gently, and I said, 'Call me a soft touch, Henry, but I think that deserves a morsel of chicken!'

After a while, Henry said he'd take Plum back to the sitting room, but since he hadn't returned by the time I'd finished all my tasks for the night, I assumed Mrs Powys had graciously given him permission to hang out with Xan and Simon, probably in the billiard room.

I had a leisurely shower and washed my hair again; earlier, in the study, I'd been sitting on the floor sorting out the magazines in the boxes under the table and it *felt* dusty even if it didn't look it.

By the time I'd untangled and dried it, and gone downstairs again, I could hear male voices, so it wasn't a total surprise to find Henry, Xan and Simon in our sitting room.

'Hi, Dido,' Xan said, picking up Plum to make room for me on the sofa next to him. 'We were playing billiards, but now the ladies have retired for the night.'

'Yeah,' Henry said. 'Mrs Powys said we should carry on for as long as we wanted, though, so we thought we'd come and carry on here, instead.'

'I suspect that isn't what she meant,' I said.

'I hope you don't mind us invading your sitting room?' asked Simon. 'Henry said you wouldn't.'

'It's fine,' I said politely, and then leaned over and took the big tin of chocolates from Henry, before he ate all the best ones, and offered it to Simon.

'Oh, no, thank you. I haven't really got a sweet tooth, apart from desserts – that apple pie was wonderful! In fact, the whole dinner was!'

'Thank you, I'm glad you enjoyed it and I hear you're coming for Christmas dinner, too?'

'Mrs Powys did kindly invite me.' He gave me that sweet smile again. 'I only really came in to say goodnight. I ought to be getting home again.'

'Not if you don't really have to,' Henry said. 'I told you we were going to hang out and watch a Christmas film and you're welcome to join us.'

'Yes, do, if you don't mind watching purest seasonal cheese,' I said, turning to hand the chocs to Xan and finding him wearing that odd expression again.

'I'm going to roast some chestnuts halfway through,' Henry said.

'Now, that *is* irresistible,' Simon said.

'What shall we watch tonight, then?' I asked. '*Miracle on 34th Street*? *White Christmas*? We can sing along to that one.'

'How about the first of the *Home Alone* films?' Henry suggested.

Neither Xan nor Simon had seen that one, so we settled down with beer, nuts, crisps and the depleted tin of chocs – I'd have to order another one, possibly even two, at this rate.

I'd seen the film so often that I found I got just as much

entertainment from watching the expressions of horrified amazement on Xan and Simon's faces. They were riveted.

When it had finished, Henry was all for following it with the sequel, but Simon said he really *did* have to go home.

'And I need to go to bed, or I won't be fit to work in the morning,' Xan said. 'I've got to take Plum out first, though, so I'll walk partway with you, Simon.'

'In that case, I'll come too,' Henry said.

'I'm afraid I'll have to go to bed, or I won't be awake enough in the morning,' I said, going over to look out of the window and finding the world had turned white. 'Henry, you were right about the snow. It looks quite thick out there!'

'Great!' said Henry, but Xan said it would probably mean he'd have to carry Plum most of the way there and back.

'If you can prise him off the sofa in the first place,' I said. But I picked him up and carried him into the Garden Hall, while they put their outdoor things on, before handing him to Xan.

'Thank you for a lovely evening,' Simon said. 'I've really enjoyed it.'

'Well, we'll be watching films every evening until the guests arrive and we're too tired, or busy,' I said. 'So do come over and join us any time you feel like it.'

'Mrs Powys . . . ?' he began uncertainly.

'Oh, just come in by way of the Garden Hall, though I don't really see why she'd mind, anyway,' Xan told him.

I wasn't too sure about that where Xan was concerned. It was only OK for him to hang out with the help when it was Henry. But then, what she didn't know wouldn't hurt her.

'That's very tempting,' Simon said. 'Especially because my central heating boiler keeps playing up, though the cottage never feels that warm even when it's working.'

I opened the door on to a changed, white world. 'I certainly hope it's working when you get back because this is no night for a dodgy boiler!'

I was in bed when I heard Henry come back. Either that, or a burglar with the same taste in old films. I don't know how he can manage on so little sleep because I knew I'd still be tired in the morning.

But it had been a really enjoyable evening, I thought drowsily. How nice Simon was, with that diffident manner and strangely sweet smile . . .

But as I drifted off, it wasn't Simon I was thinking of, but Xan and the serious, almost questioning expression I'd twice glimpsed on his face when he'd looked at me.

I found it unfathomable . . . and then I was sinking fathoms deep into sleep.

It was still dark when I got up, but when I looked out, I could see the pale gleam of snow.

I'd assume Henry would wait till later before braving the roads to fetch the newspapers, but no, just as I got down to the kitchen, I heard the Land Rover scrunch past. I hoped he'd remembered the chains for the wheels, and also that he'd be careful. Still, he does seem to thrive on challenges.

When I took up Mrs Powys's breakfast, I found her uncommunicative and wondered if perhaps the previous evening had tired her.

I told her that it had been snowing, but had now stopped, so Henry had gone for the papers.

'Tell him I want to see him in the library again this morning, after my recording session with Xan. I'll ring when I'm ready,' she said. 'We can discuss the swags and garlands of greenery. He said he'd found some new ideas in one of the magazines.'

'I'll tell him,' I promised, though I had visions of him stuck in a snowdrift somewhere. However, he was already in the kitchen, pink-cheeked from the cold and looking even more cherubic than usual.

'The snow looked quite deep – I was worried about you!'

'It was quite easy really,' he said, sounding disappointed. 'The top road had already been cleared and gritted and I followed a tractor with a snowplough all the way down to the village.'

'Spoilsports,' I said, and he grinned.

'The cold has made me ravenous so I'm doing sausages, mushrooms and scrambled eggs – do you want some? Xan does – he's just taken Plum out and is drying him off in the scullery.'

'Just scrambled egg and mushrooms for me.'

'OK, and Lucy's already down, so I've taken her a pot of tea. She says it tastes so much nicer when I make it.'

'I bet she wouldn't say that if you tried her with one of your hellish herbal brews!' I told him.

Plum polished off his breakfast in record time and then sat and watched us eat ours.

I described to Xan how Plum had performed a backwards somersault through the baize door the previous evening.

'I would have liked to have seen that,' he said regretfully, 'but I expect it was totally unintentional and he'll never do it again.'

'Oh, I think it's something he's perfected,' I said, and a little later, when I was simmering the chicken carcass to make good, rich stock for the freezer, he did it again.

'Who's a gorgeous, clever boy, then?' I asked, stroking his little domed head.

'Me?' suggested Xan's deep voice from behind me.

20

Thin Ice

I looked up, startled – I hadn't heard him come in.

'Of course,' I agreed, recovering. 'That goes without saying! But actually, I meant Plum. He's just done his trick with the door again.'

'He obviously has hidden depths I'd previously never suspected.' Xan scooped Plum up and held him, nose to nose. 'You've been holding out on me, haven't you?'

Plum tried to lick his face and Xan tucked him under his arm. 'It's amazing what greed will do. I've only just noticed he'd gone, but it's about time for a break and a bit of a walk, anyway. Would you like to come too, or are you too busy?'

'No, I've finished for the moment and the stock has to cool before I can freeze it. Give me ten minutes to clear up and I'll meet you in the Garden Hall,' I suggested. 'Henry's taken his snowboard up to the field in the hope there's enough snow.'

'He might be in luck, because I think quite a lot more fell during the night. I'll just go and close down my laptop. I've been making some notes from a bundle of letters Tommy wrote to Asa. It's lucky Asa was such a packrat with his papers, really, even if sorting them is such a huge task,' he said. 'See you in a few minutes.' And he went out again, carrying Plum.

I stacked everything into the dishwasher except the large pan, which I left to soak, and then gave the dried fruit and rum in the larder another stir. There would be all the old favourite Christmas desserts: the cake, pudding, trifles and fruit jellies ... and speaking of jellies, I'd spotted a big pottery mould in the shape of a turreted castle, in one of the glazed kitchen cupboards ...

I realized I was daydreaming again, changed quickly and was putting on my coat when I reached the Garden Hall.

Xan was already there, pulling on his wellies, and looked up. 'We'll have to stop meeting like this,' he joked.

I felt myself go faintly pink, but replied sedately, 'All roads seem to lead to – or through – the Garden Hall.'

'True. Come on, let's see if the lake has frozen solid yet.'

There was certainly a thicker covering of snow, which, although it looked soft and fluffy, scrunched underfoot in a crystalline kind of way. The sky was a clear, pale and icy azure that reminded me of Mrs Powys's eyes, and our breath hung before us in white clouds. The temperature had definitely dropped.

We decided to walk down the track through the woods on the side further away from the Roman site, the one we'd driven down to select the Christmas trees, and it was sheltered under the canopy of branches.

Plum scampered ahead, plumed tail waving, turning from time to time, to check we were still there.

'I enjoyed yesterday evening, and so, I think, did Simon,' Xan said. 'I don't think he gets out much.'

'No, I suspect the tragedy of losing his wife at such a young age has turned him into a bit of a recluse. He's such a nice man, but his smile is quite heart-breaking, so I don't think he's ever got over it.'

For some strange reason, this seemed to cheer Xan up. 'He *is* nice, isn't he? Interesting, too, when you get him on to his own subject.'

'I suspect *Home Alone* came as a bit of a shock to his academic soul,' I said, smiling.

'It was a bit of a shock to mine, too, but I enjoyed it. I can see you and Henry are going to radically re-educate my taste in films.'

'It would be even more radical if you stayed on for his late-night horror film sessions.'

'I don't think I could take late nights and horror – I need my sleep.'

'Me too, and I'm still haunted by a couple of really old ones he showed me ages ago, after assuring me they weren't scary. One was called *The Beast with Five Fingers*, all about a severed hand that crawled about strangling people . . .' I shuddered.

'No, not my cup of tea either. But I hope Sabine will enjoy watching that old home movie I brought with me – Nancy, too. She must have been out there with her husband about then because they're in it.'

'I hope Henry and I can see it, too, at some point, because the more I hear about those times, the more fascinating they sound.'

'"The Golden Years", Sabine calls them, and Tommy felt much the same . . . though even golden years can't be entirely free of some tragedy.'

I looked at him curiously, but he didn't say any more and I didn't like to ask.

By then, we'd taken a path from the track that came out by the lake and there, in the open, it seemed even colder.

'The lake has iced over and it looks quite thick here, at the edge,' I said, pulling my hood up to stop my ears freezing.

'It'll still be too thin in the middle for skating, though,' Xan said, and then gave a wry smile. 'It's what I'm doing in the recording sessions with Sabine – skating over the thin ice, as best I can.'

'Is there a lot of thin ice?' I enquired tentatively.

'Patches, though luckily Tommy told me so much about the past that I can be tactful. The first one, of course, was losing her mother at such a young age and then her father almost immediately marrying the nurse who'd been looking after Sabine's mother up till her death.'

'Did he? That seems very insensitive and must have added to the trauma of losing her mother!' I said, shocked.

'Yes, and she was only seven at the time.'

'No wonder Mrs Powys wants this Christmas to be as like those of her early childhood as we can make it,' I said.

'She resented and loathed her stepmother and I don't think ever forgave her father,' Xan said. 'I don't think it helped that he doted on her half-sister, either.'

'I hadn't realized she'd had a sister.'

'She died very young,' he said shortly. 'And that's another bit of thin ice to skate over later . . .'

He fell silent again, staring out over the frozen lake. Plum, who had been investigating some reeds at the edge of the lake, now plodded back and gave an imperative bark.

'I think that means he wants his trusty bearer to carry him home,' I suggested.

'I think you're right. We'll go back through the terraces, shall we?'

'Yes, I want to see if anything else is magically flowering in the Winter Garden.'

As we set off up the first stone steps I said, 'I downloaded one of your biographies, Xan, the one about a Victorian female archaeologist.'

'I was lucky enough to know one of her descendants and he still had some of her papers. I started off with historical biographies but I've since digressed into writing about anyone who interests me – and Asa's was certainly one I've wanted to write for a long time.'

'You've written such a lot of books, it was hard to choose one. I think I'll have to buy the paperback too, later, just for the photographs.'

'No, don't. I'll give you a copy for Christmas in return for your recipes and reminiscences.'

'But I don't suppose you carry spares of your books about with you, so you'd have to buy it,' I objected.

'Well, yes, but it will boost my own royalties,' he said. 'I'm giving Sabine a copy of my last book for Christmas, because it was difficult to know what else to give her.'

'I suppose it must have been, especially in view of her health issues,' I agreed. 'I'm planning a little pre-Christmas surprise for her, which I hope she'll like.'

'What is it?' he asked.

'If I told you, it wouldn't be a surprise, would it?'

'You're very mysterious, Dido! I suppose you're going to serve up some fabulous feast?'

'All the meals I cook are fabulous feasts,' I said firmly.

'True, but I can't think what else it could be.'

'You'll just have to wait and see.'

'Call me greedy, but what *is* for dinner tonight?' he asked, as we zigzagged up the steep paths.

'Medallions of pork tenderloin with apple sauce, followed by treacle tart.'

He groaned. 'I can't resist your cooking, and at this rate, I'll be twice the man I was by New Year. I ought to get more exercise to burn it all off, though it's not really the weather for long hikes.'

'Perhaps Henry could teach you to snowboard?'

'I don't think that's my kind of thing, but there are some sledges in one of the outbuildings. We could take those out sometime.'

'And if the lake freezes solidly enough, you can skate,' I suggested.

'So could you. Sabine won't mind if you borrow some of the old skates from the cupboard in the Garden Hall. I learned to skate on this lake and Asa's old boots fit me.'

'I can't skate,' I said dubiously. 'I went to a rink with friends once and I had the bruises on my bum for a fortnight.'

'I'll teach you, if we get a hard enough freeze,' he promised.

For the first time, I noticed that leaden clouds had sneaked in while we were talking and now fat flakes of snow were falling.

'I hope it's a bit milder next week,' I said. 'We need the cleaners to come in on Wednesday, and Mrs Kane's arriving on Thursday. Do you know how she's getting here?'

'She's driving herself – she's quite intrepid. I think she's stopping overnight with friends near Blackpool on the way up, though.'

'She must be into her eighties, like Mrs Powys. It's a long drive, even with a break.'

'Well, Sabine still belts around in her sports car,' he pointed out. 'Nancy's bright as a button and very active. She often fills in as locum vicar, when needed.'

'She must be clever if she was a student at Oxford with Mrs Powys.'

'She is, and became a lecturer before she made the leap to the clergy.'

We'd now arrived at the level of the Winter Garden and came out from a path bordered with witch hazel bushes covered in yellow and orange flowers, to find Mrs Powys, standing, deep in thought, by the stream.

That part of the garden might be protected from the worst of the elements, but there was still a scattering of snow. She had the deep shawl collar of her long fur coat pulled up around her ears and was wearing a fur Cossack-style hat.

I'd have thought our voices would have carried on the cold clear air and alerted her to our presence, but she seemed entirely unaware of us until Xan spoke.

'Sabine! I didn't think you'd be out in this weather. It's bitterly cold and slippery underfoot on the steps, too.'

She seemed to pull her thoughts back from a long distance away and slowly focused on him.

'I'm not a hothouse flower, Xan, and I needed to spend a little time here. But yes, I'll go back now.'

'We'll go up together and you can take my arm so you don't slip,' he suggested.

'Yes, do, and I'll go ahead with Plum,' I said, removing the dog from under Xan's arm. 'Perhaps you'd like a nice pot of tea to thaw you out when you get back, Mrs Powys.'

'That would be . . . very acceptable,' she agreed, so I left them to their slower ascent and hurried off.

After lunch was cleared, I went on the internet and ordered the solar lights for the fir tree on the lawn. There was quite a variety of the outdoor type, but I chose ones shaped like stars. They were, allegedly, arriving on Monday.

After that, I left Henry in the kitchen, baking traditional

caraway seed cake for tea, and went to spend a bit of time in the study helping Xan.

He'd been doing a little internet shopping himself and had ordered some of those magazine file boxes, for the journals I'd started to sort out. I suspected he had ordered that copy of his book for me, too, but he didn't say.

'I noticed there were some empty shelves in the library and thought the journals could go in there,' he said. 'There's a lot of good reading in them and it's not like they're the sort of thing that goes out of date.'

'Good idea,' I said, settling down on the floor again and pulling the nearest unsorted box of them towards me.

'I'm just going to finish typing up my notes from these letters between Tommy and Asa, then I thought I'd go through the desk drawers. I meant to do it before, but when I pulled one of the top drawers out, it was just as crammed to bursting point as the cupboards, so I shoved it back again.'

'The rest might not be like that, though,' I suggested, weeding out copies of *Popular Archaeology* from a stack of more learned periodicals. 'Why not empty them into heaps along the other pasting table, like we did with the cupboards?'

'Might as well,' he agreed, and gave me a running commentary while he did so.

'The top ones on either side are packed with letters and newspaper cuttings . . . The next are for stationery and books of stamps . . . packets of rubber bands and paperclips . . . pens, probably dried out . . . highlighters, ditto . . .'

He paused. 'There's a stack of old desk diaries in this one, though Asa only seems to have used them to make brief notes of appointments. But they go back a long way, so might be useful. Can you pass me up one of the smaller cartons?'

I passed him up a tall, narrow box that had held wine. 'Is that big enough?'

'Just right. I'll label it, before I forget what's in it.'

When he'd done that, he emptied the next two drawers on to the table with a slithery sort of noise. 'Old packets of photos and several loose ones. I'll need to go through those carefully and I expect Sabine will like to look at them too.'

'Were those the last drawers?'

'No, there are two more.'

From my cross-legged seat on the floor I watched his feet return to the desk.

'The bottom left drawer is full of bits of pottery in zip-lock bags, all carefully labelled . . . but the one on the right appears to be locked.'

'Probably just well and truly jammed?' I suggested.

'No,' he said after a few moments. 'I'm *sure* it's locked, and none of the keys on Asa's ring fit it.'

'Perhaps he hid it somewhere because he kept a secret stash of whisky in there,' I joked.

'Actually, that's a possibility, because Sabine was very strict about his diet in the last few years. His doctor had told him to eat more healthily and cut down on alcohol.'

'It might be full of chocolate as well as whisky, then, but if he hid the key in here, it's bound to turn up while I'm cleaning.'

'Yes, I expect so, and I don't want to force the drawer, since it's a nice old desk. I'll go through the stuff out of the others and that one can wait.'

We settled down to our respective tasks, exchanging desultory remarks from time to time, while Plum snored loudly and incessantly.

It felt so cosy and companionable that I really had to tear

myself away eventually, in order to get tea ready and make a start on prepping dinner.

The kitchen smelled deliciously of seed cake and also, since Henry had got carried away, of sticky ginger cake, too.

Outside, as the early dusk drew in, the temperature dropped even further and snow began to fall more heavily, whispering on the windowpanes.

'Is this what you wished for when we were stirring the Christmas pudding?' I asked Henry suspiciously, but he just smiled cherubically and tapped the side of his nose in a highly irritating manner.

'Let's watch *Miracle on 34th Street* tonight, the original one,' he said, changing the subject. 'I bet Xan hasn't seen that, either.'

'OK, but if you're going to hammer the tin of chocs again, you'd better add another one to this week's shopping list!'

'And more caraway seeds,' he said.

It was some time till he returned from taking the tea trolley to the sitting room.

'Sabine told me her mother loved seed cake and the smell of it took her right back to her childhood, and Lucy wolfed down a slice so fast she choked and I had to pat her on the back. Or maybe,' he added thoughtfully, 'she choked in the hope I'd perform the Heimlich manoeuvre, but if so, she was out of luck.'

Sabine

'As I said at the end of our last recording session, Sabine,' Xan reminded me as I seated myself opposite him, 'I feel we must just touch on the accident in which your father and stepmother were killed, which occurred not long after your marriage.'

'If you feel it's *really* necessary,' I said reluctantly.

'I'll barely mention it in the book, of course, but it's relevant because after it, you and Asa divided your time between your house on Corfu and Mitras Castle.'

'Most of our time was spent on Corfu until after—' I broke off, then continued, 'until a few years later, when Asa gave up diving and began his land-based excavations.'

'I know you began spending Christmas here then, and my grandparents usually came over for that – and any friends or colleagues who could make it. It sounded as if it was a continuation of the parties you had in Greece!'

'They were, really. We often had a houseful, but it was all great fun,' I agreed. 'Asa was so gregarious and drew people to him like a magnet. And, of course, you could get the staff then, to cope with it all.'

'Mrs Hill and her husband? They were here from my first visit as a small child.'

'It was another married couple at first, but Mrs Hill stayed until they retired after Asa . . .'

I tailed off and sighed. 'Maria has been with me many years, too, as you know – so lucky she fell for the handsome gardener when she came over here that time with her parents.'

'It was, but we're wandering off the point a bit,' Xan said. 'Though of course, you wouldn't have spent Christmases at the Castle had that car accident not happened, would you?'

'No. The breach with my father remained until his death and I felt the Castle was tainted by my stepmother's presence. But after they were both killed, I could reclaim my home again.'

Xan hesitated and I knew he was about to broach a subject that was usually taboo.

'Your half-sister, Faye, was then about fourteen, wasn't she?'

I nodded, deciding to get this part over with as quickly as possible. 'And at boarding school. She wasn't left on my hands, but to the guardianship of the family solicitor – the uncle of my present one – and a relative of her mother's. They thought it best that she didn't attend the funeral. I hadn't seen her for several years . . . and it was to be a few more before our paths crossed again.'

'She didn't spend any of the school holidays at the Castle?'

'No, I made it clear the Castle was no longer her home and her guardians made other arrangements for her,' I said indifferently.

'Had Asa ever met her?'

'No . . . he only did so when she was seventeen and had been expelled from boarding school for the second time.'

'Expelled?' Xan said in surprise. He obviously didn't know that part.

'Yes, she'd already had to leave one school before my father died and the second time was for the same reason: sneaking out to meet men. She was always precocious – a born slut.'

I felt the old, bitter tide of hatred for my half-sister sweep through me.

Xan looked rather taken aback. 'Isn't that a bit harsh?'

'I don't think so. She was man-mad and we hadn't then arrived at the hippy era, when it could be prettied up as Free Love.'

'I suppose not,' he agreed, though he was still looking troubled.

'I don't see the need to go any further into all that,' I said firmly. 'Once I'd returned to Corfu after the funeral, the car accident barely impinged on our happy life together, except that I could reclaim my home.'

I smiled, letting happier memories push back the darkness.

'The late fifties and early sixties were the perfect time to be living in Greece and pushing the boundaries of underwater archaeology.'

'I think on that note we'll stop for today, Sabine,' Xan said, reaching forward to switch off the microphone. 'In the next few sessions we'll go into those years in more depth – the discoveries and the documentary making.'

'I'll look forward to it,' I said, but I knew that eventually another dark cloud would appear on the horizon . . .

21

Completely Chilled

Henry, intrepid as always, had been out early for the papers when I came downstairs next morning.

He said, when Xan had arrived and the three of us sat down at the table to eat breakfast – four, if you counted Plum, who was under it – that the roads were a little icy, but well gritted and he'd had no real problems negotiating them.

He sounded regretful, but added more cheerfully, 'The snow's lying just as thickly on the fields, though I don't think it's going to last much longer, according to the forecast, so we should make the most of it. Why don't we all go out to the slope below the Roman site later? I'm sure I saw some sledges hanging on pegs in the garage.'

'Yes, there are some out there,' Xan agreed. 'A big old wooden one and a couple of smaller ones.'

'There you are, then – and you can have a go on my snow-board, too, if you want to.'

We both declined this handsome offer.

'I think our centres of gravity are too high,' I told him.

'Are you saying I'm short?' demanded Henry indignantly.

'No, just a different build,' I said hastily.

Xan said he hadn't been on a sledge for years and he looked tempted. 'But I should really be working.'

'It's Sunday, so you could take some time off,' I suggested. 'I could come out for a bit too, but since dinner is at two today, I'll be cooking all morning. I'm making beef Wellington followed by a blackberry and apple crumble with custard.'

Xan groaned. 'I'm not going to be able to resist second helpings.'

'You'll need some exercise to work it off, then. Why don't you two head out right after dinner and I'll follow, once I've cleared up?' I suggested.

'I suspect Mrs Powys will still want tea at the usual time, even after a big dinner, but I could come back and make that,' offered Henry.

'Thanks, Henry,' I said. 'And after that, there's only cold supper to lay out in the dining room.'

'It seems a shame that one of you will have to dash back, just to make tea,' Xan said.

'Well, we're here to work, you know,' I said.

'That's *my* main purpose in being here too,' Xan said, 'but I'll skive off for the afternoon, if you will, Dido.'

'OK,' I said, then got up. 'I'd better see if Lucy's still in the morning room, though she never seems to want anything more than toast.'

'And *I'd* better get on with my house fairy chores,' Henry said, 'because I've offered to drive Lucy to church later. She wants to go, but is afraid of the icy roads.'

'That was kind,' I said.

'It's no problem, and her friend Daphne will bring her back, if the roads are OK then.'

Xan said he'd better put in some work now if he was taking the afternoon off, and he made himself a cup of coffee to take with him – and one for me, too.

'Seeing as it's your coffee machine and pods I keep using,' he said.

'It's OK, I'll give you a bill for the hire of the coffee machine and the pods at the end of our stay,' I told him, and he went off, grinning.

When I had the beef Wellington well in hand and the vegetables prepped, I baked a couple of quiches to use up various odds and ends in the fridge.

Time had slipped past quickly, as it always does when I'm cooking, and it was quite late in the morning when Xan came back in search of Plum.

'He somersaulted in ages ago,' I said, pushing a strand of hair off my hot forehead. 'The smell must have been too much for him to resist.'

'I'd left the door to the passage slightly ajar and he must have nosed his way out,' Xan said. 'I didn't notice for ages – you think I'd have missed the snoring.'

'You were probably too engrossed in what you were doing. It was only the door swinging open that made me look up and realize he was there.'

'I wanted to tell you I'd spoken to Sabine, anyway. I told her we were all going sledging after lunch, but Henry would dash back to make the tea and she said there was no need, since Lucy could get it for once.'

'Oh, that was kind of her!' I said, though I wondered if she'd have said the same thing if Xan had told her it was *me* who would dash back.

'Since there'll be cold supper at six, she said they wouldn't want anything to eat with it, so it shouldn't prove beyond Lucy's capabilities.'

'Poor Lucy! But I'm sure she can manage to make a pot of tea for two,' I said.

Xan and Henry set out for the field right after lunch, leaving Plum to enjoy a postprandial snooze in the sitting room with Mrs Powys and Lucy.

I soon had everything cleared away and then was free to change into a warm jumper and jeans, before heading outdoors.

I followed the trail of footsteps and the marks left by the runners of the sledge up to the wicket gate and across the field to the top of the slope, where two male figures were standing. The shorter one, wearing a bright green octopus beanie, slid out of sight as I neared, and when I looked cautiously over the edge he was swooping around a large, rocky outcrop at some speed.

'There's a nice, clear run down the hill a bit further along,' Xan told me. 'Come on!'

He'd brought the old wooden sledge, which was big enough for two, and soon we were hurtling downwards, Xan steering and me hanging on to him for dear life.

I think I was probably shrieking as we went, for after a while Simon came out, bringing a big Thermos of hot coffee and was persuaded to have a go on the sledge, too.

It was all such fun that the sky had started to darken before we finally went back to the Castle, damp, weary and glowing.

Simon, before returning to his cottage, agreed to come over later, to watch another film. The Heavenly Houseparties Film Festival continued.

'But I still feel a bit sneaky, since Sabine won't know I'll be there,' he said.

But to my surprise, Xan told us he'd mentioned to Sabine

that he'd been joining us late in the evening to watch old Christmas films and that Simon sometimes came over, too.

'She said, "I suppose you must amuse yourself somehow, Xan, until my other guests arrive."'

I smiled appreciatively and said, 'After which, you can stop fraternizing with the help.'

'Only *officially*,' he said, and smiled at me.

After we'd seen to supper, Henry and I had lots of time to ourselves and decided to go up to the attic in search of the Christmas decorations.

The stairs to it were next to my bedroom and led into the first of several attic rooms that opened out of each other.

They were dimly illuminated by dusty light bulbs hanging from the beams.

Henry had brought his big torch with him, in any case, and it came in handy for peering into dark corners and reading labels.

He went through to see how far the attic went, which was the whole extent of the older part of the house, though there wasn't much in the other rooms, apart from the usual broken furniture and bits of brass bedstead.

But Mrs Powys had told him that the decorations were all stored in this first attic and I'd already found some of the boxes by the time he got back from his explorations.

They were all labelled, which made it easier, and we dragged them out into the middle of the floor, under the light bulb.

Two very large, sturdy and heavy cartons were the last to emerge from the shadows, both bearing the words: 'Carved wooden Nativity set from Oberammergau'.

'Must be a big one, going by the size of the boxes,' I commented. 'Perhaps we should unpack them here and carry the figures down separately?'

'No, I can slide the boxes down the stairs after me, they're not that heavy,' Henry said.

'As long as they don't gain enough momentum to bowl you over, Henry, because "killed by a Nativity set" wouldn't look too good in your obituary.'

'It would certainly be novel,' he agreed, flashing his torch around into the darkest corners to make sure we hadn't missed anything – which we hadn't, unless they decorated their Christmas trees with huge spiders around here.

'Come on, let's start moving everything down to that empty bedroom opposite yours, so we can sort them out in comfort,' I said. 'I'm looking forward to seeing what's here. I do love baubles, especially old ones!'

'Me too,' he agreed.

'I'm dying to know why the Angel Gabriel has a whole large box to himself.'

'His wings may not fold,' Henry said seriously.

But I didn't get as far as opening any of the boxes, because by the time we'd transported everything down the narrow stairs, time had galloped past and I was hot, tired and very dusty.

I left Henry ripping the tape off the tops of cartons and went to shower, wash my hair and change into a pair of my soft and comfortable velour jogging trousers and a sweatshirt. And no, my joggers aren't the kind with cuffs at the ankles, because those make you look like a clipped poodle.

I plaited my still damp hair loosely over one shoulder. I was starting to feel that the days of wearing my hair up in a braided coronet were coming to an end. Maybe it was because Henry and I were thinking about winding up the business and I wouldn't need the protection of a slightly aloof professional persona any more.

*

Simon arrived, bringing a tin of shortbread biscuits, closely followed by Xan, who brought only Plum, and we all chilled out together in front of one of Henry's favourite films, *Chalet Girl*, which is not, strictly speaking, a Christmas one, but has lots of snow.

We seemed already to have our own seats – mine on one end of the sofa, with Xan at the other and Plum asleep between us – or on my lap – Henry, in a big chintzy armchair and Simon choosing a button-back wing chair.

The fake log effect of the electric fire lent a cosy air to the room, but it was already warmed by the clanking radiators anyway.

Henry went into the kitchen and popped corn halfway through the film and then, when it finished, I made us all hot chocolate.

While we drank it, Henry told the others about our quest for the Christmas decorations and the huge boxes containing the Oberammergau Nativity set.

'I opened the top of one and the carved wooden figures are almost as big as I am!'

'I think that might be a slight exaggeration, Henry,' I said mildly.

Xan remarked that he remembered the set from earlier Christmas visits. 'I think it dates back at least to Sabine's parents' day, if not before.'

'Where did they put it, can you remember?' Henry asked.

'Yes, in the back right-hand corner of the Great Hall. There's a wall lamp there, which lights it up a bit.'

'Then that's where it will go this time. We're trying to make things as close as possible to how Sabine remembers them from her early childhood, and I expect if it's old it was always set out in the same place.'

A thought suddenly occurred to me and I lowered my mug of hot chocolate. 'Do you realize it's only just over two weeks until Christmas Day?'

'Santa had better bring me something good, because I haven't had the chance to be naughty since we got here,' Henry said. 'Only nice.'

I gave a shiver of anticipation, feeling as excited as a child. I might have been a late developer in the traditional Christmas magic stakes, due to my rather austere experiences with Granny Celia and Dora, but I'd more than made up for it since.

It had been another relaxed and enjoyable evening, much like the gatherings at Henry's lodge, when I was the only woman in a room full of nice, if somewhat zany, youngish men.

Only . . . it wasn't *quite* the same, for I was always strangely conscious of Xan sitting near me, with only the width of a small dog between us.

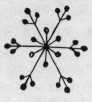

22

On the Shelf

The solar lights arrived first thing on Monday morning and looked very sturdy, as they would need to be, out there on the lawn, exposed to the elements.

The sun had appeared in a clear, pale azure sky again and I thought perhaps we were in for a spell of sunny, cold days and freezing nights. I hoped so, anyway, so the solar panel would charge up quickly, once the lights were up. There was a sturdy stepladder in one of the storerooms I could use to reach the top of the tree . . . but I'd wait till Wednesday, when Mrs Powys would be out, so sparkling stars would welcome her on her return just before tea.

Once the morning chores were done, Henry vanished upstairs to carry on sorting out the Christmas decorations, popping down to the kitchen from time to time, where I was baking up a storm, to show me special finds.

'Baubles, bangles, bright shiny things . . .' he warbled, appearing yet again, this time carrying an open box of glass birds with white, glass fibre tails. Then he stopped singing and sniffed. 'Something smells good!'

I was laying out wire cooling racks along the table, ready to receive the first offerings, fresh from the oven.

'I'm making Cornish pasties, cheese and onion pies, two more quiches and a big batch of mince pies, mostly destined for the freezer. I'm saving some pastry to top the Lancashire hot-pots for dinner one day this week, because I'll make those later.'

I had to keep reminding myself to leave a big enough hole in one of the freezers for the giant turkey.

'What are you giving them for lunch today?'

'The leftover beef Wellington, very thinly sliced, with warm potato salad.'

'Waste not, want not! You're so organized, Dido, darling,' he said, as I removed a tray of golden Cornish pasties from the oven and replaced it with one bearing the two quiches.

'Well, that's something I seem to have in common with Mrs Hill, the old housekeeper, *and* Mrs Powys, but it will be such a help to have ready-made things I can whip out of the freezer when the house party are here.'

'I hope you've left a corner in one of them for me,' he reminded me. 'I'll snowboard this afternoon if the snow's still right after all this sun, but if not, I thought I'd have a little baking session of my own and make a big fruit cake to cut at, and maybe a batch or two of savouries, like cheese straws.'

'I've left you a whole deep wire basket in the biggest freezer.' I glanced at the clock. 'Everything should be out of the oven in half an hour, then I only need to clear up and peel the potatoes for the warm salad, so I think I'll be able to squeeze in a short walk . . .'

'I expect Xan will come and drag you out by the hair, if you don't,' Henry said with a grin.

'Really, Henry, he's not some kind of caveman!' I exclaimed, but he simply grinned and vanished upstairs again.

Mrs Powys seemed to have settled for a regular recording session right after her breakfast now. Xan had said, while we were eating ours, that they were about to embark on the first years of Asa and Sabine's marriage, when they'd made all their major underwater discoveries and their TV documentary series.

Xan must have shut Plum in the study with him while he worked this morning, because he didn't make an appearance until he arrived with Xan, to see if I had time to go for a walk with them. Remembering Henry's joking remark, I felt myself going pink, though anyone less like a caveman than the elegant, willowy and scholarly Xan would be hard to imagine!

The idea of it made me smile and he returned it warmly.

'I was just about to go for a walk anyway,' I told him.

'Get your coat and put your wellies on, then,' he said, and soon I was trudging through the snow at his side, Plum running along ahead.

I realized I was starting to look forward to these walks and would miss them when the other guests arrived and Xan didn't need my company any more. We'd chat about everything and anything and he also told me about his holidays spent here as a schoolboy and how much fun Asa and Sabine had made them.

Asa sounded a charismatic and outgoing character, and a picture also emerged of a more sociable and unbuttoned Sabine, too. I think they must have complemented each other, the perfect partnership, and I remembered again the golden, glowing couple in that YouTube film clip.

In the study that afternoon, since I'd finished sorting the magazines, I decided to make a start on the bookshelves that covered two walls, from floor to ceiling.

They certainly needed a thorough spring clean, since it

quickly became clear that they hadn't had more than a feather duster run along them for years.

I decided I'd tackle them methodically, starting from the top of the first stack, and working downwards, before beginning the next. It would take me quite some time . . .

I commandeered the nearest pasting table to put the books on while the shelf was cleaned, then pulled over the mahogany library steps so I could reach the very top shelf.

Xan was still sorting letters. Asa seemed to have been a prolific correspondent and his habit of pinning copies of his replies to the originals made for even more work, though I'm sure they would be helpful to Xan for the biography.

At the sound of the library steps sliding over the floor, he looked up, watching as I climbed right to the top and reached up for the first books.

His eyes, which had been somewhat abstracted, sharpened and he said, 'Are you sure you're safe, teetering about up there?'

'I'm not teetering, I'm perfectly safe,' I told him, but after a few minutes during which I carried the first books down and laid them on the table, he got up and came over.

'I can't concentrate with you up there. Come down and I'll pass the books to you.'

I gave in without a struggle, because his help would speed things up no end. But when the first shelf was empty, I insisted on cleaning it myself, even if he did hold the steps steady.

I let him put back the books, once they'd been clapped together to remove any dust . . . which also dislodged the occasional bookmark, one in the form of a dried bay leaf, and another, a small newspaper cutting about one of Asa and Sabine's underwater discoveries – or at least, that's what Xan said it was about. I'd have to take his word for that because it was in Greek. He kept it, anyway.

The time passes too quickly when you're enjoying yourself and I was surprised when Henry came in to remind me it was almost tea time.

'You might both want to have a wash before then,' he said cheekily. 'You look grimy.'

'You'd be grimy if you'd been cleaning these shelves. I don't think the books have been taken down within living memory,' I told him. 'But yes, I'd better dash off to wash and change. Did you bake, or snowboard?'

'Snowboard, but I've cut sandwiches and sliced seed cake and a bit of the ginger, ready for tea. I'll bake tomorrow, because the way the snow's going, this will be the last day I can take out the board. The forecast isn't for snow again for the next few days, at least.'

'Good, because I want the cleaners to come on Wednesday and then Mrs Kane to arrive safely on Thursday – not to mention the supermarket delivery.'

'Never mind, Henry, if the temperature keeps dropping at night, then the lake will freeze solid enough for skating,' Xan said, and although, as far as Henry was concerned, that was hardly a substitute for snowboarding, he embraced the idea with his usual enthusiasm.

I could see I'd soon find myself dragged out there, whether I wanted to skate or not, an ungainly Bambi on ice.

Luckily for me, when Xan and I walked down to check on the state of the lake late next morning, he thought that we should give it another night or two of freezing to make sure of the middle.

I heartily agreed. I certainly didn't fancy plummeting through the ice into freezing water. Even the thought made me shiver.

Henry, after his promised baking session in the early

afternoon, popped up to Maria's cottage with some warm savoury scones and, on his return, came into the library, where we were at work on the bookshelves again, to report that Andy seemed much stronger and he and Maria were thinking of going to spend a couple of weeks over Christmas with their daughter and her family in York.

'They've got a small granny annexe, with a downstairs bath-room and bedroom, so it's ideal really, though Andy says he can now climb stairs. I think Maria's a bit overprotective.'

'That's natural, but I'm sure he needs to build his strength up again. It would do them both good to get away and be looked after, though,' I said. 'Didn't she tell us that both her daughter and son-in-law were doctors? Perfect to keep an eye on him!'

'They are and, what's more, they want Maria and Andy to go and live with them permanently. They've already had plans sub-mitted to extend the granny annexe, to give them more room.'

'Sounds perfect, and they really do need to retire. Coping with the work at the Castle on her own has been too much for Maria.'

'I think she wants to go but still feels a bit torn about leaving Mrs Powys, especially now she's ill.'

'That's understandable,' said Xan, 'but I think now they'll have to put what's best for them first.'

'Just what I told them,' agreed Henry. 'And that we'd see if we could arrange for some help before we leave in the New Year. There has to be someone local who could come in by the day, at least.'

'Perhaps Lucy's friend Daphne might know of someone,' I suggested. 'And if we ask around the agencies, we might even manage to find someone to live in.'

'That would certainly soften the blow when Maria tells Mrs

Powys she and Andy are moving to York,' Henry agreed. 'She's asked me to tell Mrs Powys that they're going away over Christmas and then, when they get back, perhaps Maria will break the news that they are leaving permanently. So let's get Christmas over and then put our minds to the problem,' he added cheerfully.

I sent a long catch-up email to Charlotte later, but reading it through before sending, realized that every other sentence seemed to have Xan's name in it and so I had to do a bit of editing first.

I'd heard nothing from Granny Celia and Dora, although I wasn't expecting to. Mrs Frant was making sure everything was OK at the cottage and she had my mobile number if she needed me. As to Dad, he forgot my existence unless I reminded him.

Charlotte replied almost instantly and said business was booming in her little needlework shop, so she probably wouldn't be able to get up to her parents' house to join the children until Christmas Eve.

It didn't look as if we'd be able to meet up, because by then, of course, the house party would be in full swing and I'd be too busy to get away.

And when I came to think of it, I hadn't left the Castle since I'd arrived – I hadn't even wanted to. It was a little world all of its own with the Winter Garden magically blooming at its heart.

23

Shooting Stars

Another cold, sunny day dawned and when I glanced out of the morning room window as I was clearing after breakfast, the snow on the lawn seemed to be stealthily deflating, like an undercooked meringue, the crisp coating probably covering nothing more substantial than air.

I couldn't see down into the steeply terraced garden from there, of course, but the distant view of hills and fields was still white and rather like a Christmas card.

As the cleaners took over the house, the other occupants slowly departed: Lucy to do her stint in the library-cum-folk museum and Mrs Powys to her beauty salon and usual haunts in Hexham. They'd both lunch out and, since Henry had decided to go and pick up a few odds and ends that the super-market couldn't supply, as well as buy fresh flowers for the house, that left only me and Xan for lunch again.

I decided to make a couple of batches of soup this morning – carrot and coriander, and leek and potato – and thought we could have a little of that and a cheese toastie apiece, if I could lure Xan out of the library into the kitchen later.

He'd found another run of interesting letters and intended

making lots of notes, but soup isn't something that goes well with laptops and precious paperwork.

I made the soup first, before the cleaning service invaded the kitchen, then stirred up the fruit and rum mixture in the larder: I'd be able to bake the cake in the next day or two.

Magic Mops would make up the bed in the Bluebell Room, ready for Mrs Kane's arrival the next day, but Henry would add the finishing touches when he got back.

'I'm going to get a bowl of flowering bulbs for Mrs Kane's room,' he'd announced before departing. 'And a pot of something pretty for Mrs Powys's boudoir, as she calls that little sitting room next to her bedroom.'

'Nice idea,' I'd said, thinking that that would make *two* surprises for our employer in one day, for I intended putting the outside solar lights on the fir tree as soon as I had a minute, in the hopes they'd have charged up and be twinkling brightly by the time she came home in the late afternoon.

Henry had offered to help me with the lights before he left, but I'd told him there was no need: the tree wasn't much taller than I was and, anyway, how difficult could it be to drape a string of oversized fairy lights on the branches?

When I could hear the zooming noise of vacuum cleaners approaching, I put my outdoor things on and then collected the box of solar lights and the stepladder I'd put ready in the Garden Hall.

I'd meant to tell Xan I was going out for a short time, but when I looked into the study, he was so totally absorbed in what he was reading that it seemed a shame to disturb him – and Plum, snoring on the hearth rug, didn't even wake up.

Burdened with the box and ladder, I trudged round to the front of the house and across the lawn, but as soon as I'd stepped off the path, I found the snow more substantial under its crispy coating than I'd thought, and once I was standing right next to the fir tree I realized it was a bit higher than I'd estimated.

It was fat and bushy, too, so I'd only be able to reach to loop the lights around it for the first couple of feet, after which I'd have to keep moving the ladder.

I untangled the long string of stars and opened the ladder, standing on the bottom rung to press it firmly through the snow.

It felt solid enough when I climbed to the top, trailing stars. I'd had to take my gloves off and the icy air was soon nipping at my face and fingers.

I fixed one end to the topmost spike of the tree and then began to wind the string around the branches, reaching round the back to pass them from hand to hand, so it must have looked as if I was hugging the tree!

It felt a long way up and a bit precarious, but after two turns I went down a step . . . and felt the ladder shift a little under me.

I stopped dead, but it seemed to have steadied again, and in any case, I thought, stretching out to loop the lights right round the tree one more time before I'd have to start moving the stepladder, I wouldn't have far to fall and a soft landing, if it did topple!

But this time I must have leaned out just a little *too* far, for the ladder suddenly slid backwards, unbalancing me, and then, as I teetered at the top, lurched sideways.

The steps went one way and I plummeted downwards in the other – though I didn't land with the soggy thump I was expecting, but instead was caught and held in a pair of strong arms.

'My hero!' I gasped, looking up into startled lilac-grey eyes, as Xan staggered slightly under my weight, though his grip remained firm.

I'd never been this close to him and I found myself staring into his eyes, unable to break the contact. They were strangely beautiful, like crystal, and framed in the longest of black lashes . . .

He blinked first – and once the connection was broken, I came to my senses with a rush of embarrassment.

'Oh, thanks, Xan! But you can put me down now.'

He set me on my feet, then said, scowling, 'Are you *mad*, teetering about on ladders in the snow on your own? You could have broken your neck! What on earth were you thinking of?'

'I wasn't teetering,' I said with dignity. 'Or at least, I wasn't until I tried to reach round a wider bit of tree. I should have moved the ladder round instead – it was a loop too far. These solar lights are the surprise for Mrs Powys I mentioned.'

'She'd be even more surprised to find you lying unconscious under them! Why on earth didn't you ask me to help you?'

'I did look into the study, but you were hard at work and I didn't want to disturb you.'

'You constantly disturb me,' he said obscurely, but at least appeared not to be angry any more. 'Plum asked to go out and then I spotted you – in the nick of time, as it happens.'

'Where is Plum?' I asked, but just then spotted something like a small, hairy snowplough heading in our direction.

Emerging on to the trodden-down patch by our feet, Plum sneezed and then shook himself, scattering icy crystals.

'Hello, Plum – your master's cross with me.'

'Only because it was stupid of you to try doing this alone when I could have helped.'

'Well, now you're here, you can help me finish it,' I suggested, and of course, with the two of us, it took no time at all.

This was just as well because it was perishing cold out there and the bright sun didn't seem to have any warmth in it, though I hoped it would at least charge the solar lights up a bit.

We needed the hot soup and toasted sandwiches to thaw us out, and luckily, the cleaners had finished in the kitchen by then.

Henry returned with two lovely pots of narcissi and enough flowers for a wedding, and vanished into the cloakroom off the Garden Hall to arrange them.

Xan had asked him to get some snacks, soft drinks and beer, as his contribution to our film evenings, and a packet of Jaffa Cakes for me. He must have remembered my not-so-secret vice.

Still, at least Xan and I seemed to be friends again even if, when I went to the study after lunch to do a bit more shelf-sorting, he didn't even trust me with the short library steps any more.

Instead, he abandoned his letters and helped me again, as I slowly worked my way down the next stack.

Outside, the skies began to darken as the afternoon drew on, and we went to look out of the dining-room window to see if anything was happening with the solar lights. There, like magic, the stars on the tree had begun to glow.

Mrs Powys only arrived back just before tea and Henry, who was placing one of his flower arrangements on the table under the Great Hall window, let her in.

'And she was absolutely astonished by the lights on the tree, and thought it was my doing,' he reported. 'But I told her no, it was a little Christmas surprise from you, and she would find *my* seasonal gesture in her boudoir when she went up.'

'I'm so glad she liked them,' I said, pleased.

'She said to thank you very much – and she *adored* my flower arrangements in the Hall.'

'Tea's nearly ready. Is there any sign of Lucy?'

'I know she's back because her car was in the garage when I took Mrs Powys's round. She must have gone straight up to her room, but she won't miss her tea.'

'She's just like a little mouse, creeping about the place and squeaking from time to time,' I said.

'Well, she eats more than mere crumbs – I don't know where she puts it all,' Henry said. 'Speaking of which, what's that lovely smell?'

'Lancashire hotpot. I'm making individual ones with short-crust pastry lids for dinner.'

'And for us, too, I hope!' he said.

There was quite a delay before Henry came back after taking the after-dinner coffee to the sitting room, which, it turned out, was due to Mrs Powys having traced a distant connection by marriage to Henry's branch of the Rudges.

'There's that big, framed family tree in the Great Hall.'

I sang 'I'm in with the in crowd!' at him until he threw an oven mitt at me, but it would appear that, as far as he was concerned, the lines between the help and the rest of the household had blurred just a little more.

That evening, watching the latest offering in our Christmas film fest, I was more conscious than ever of Xan, sitting so close to me on the sofa. Plum was snoring on my lap and only an opened packet of Jaffa Cakes lay between us.

Sabine

I went up to rest before dinner, though mainly because I felt I needed some time alone with my thoughts.

Recently, I've quite often found myself forgetting who Dido is and the reason I wanted her here in the first place . . . and she's so unobtrusive when she does venture out of the staff wing. Her cooking, too, is excellent and she and Henry have already made such a difference to life at the Castle. Everything runs smoothly, like it did in the old days, when staff were easy to get and to keep.

There have, I confess, been one or two moments when I've felt almost ashamed of the impulse that led me to employ Faye's granddaughter in a menial capacity in her former home. Looking back now, what satisfaction did I think it would give me? You can't revenge yourself on the dead by humiliating their descendants.

This was brought home to me even more when I emerged from the dark drive this afternoon and saw the fir tree on the lawn lit up with big, golden stars, and then learned from Henry that it had been Dido's idea, a Christmas surprise for me.

I asked Henry to give her my thanks, but must say something to her in the morning, when she brings my breakfast . . .

Henry, very sweetly, has placed a pot of spring bulbs in Nancy's room, as well as one here, in my boudoir, and they smell like the spring I may not live to see . . .

I'd brought my letters up with me but found nothing more interesting than a few Christmas cards, until I came to a strong manila envelope of the type used by my private detective, Mr Jarrold.

Until that moment, I'd almost forgotten that I'd asked him to investigate Dido's birth mother, but when I pulled out the printed report, there were three photographs folded inside it.

I'd been so sure that Dido must have got her striking appearance and golden hair from her mother that I had to check the enclosure to be sure this really *was* her.

She'd been snapped both full face and in profile, showing a narrow, aesthetic face and a nose that, though straight, was most certainly not Grecian. Her hair, according to the letter, was sandy, her eyes hazel and she was of medium height and slight build.

Briefly, I wondered if he could possibly have got the wrong person. But his firm had always in the past been both thorough and reliable.

I read the report again, more slowly. The woman was a research chemist in Switzerland, which explained why she was wearing a white lab coat in the third picture.

I unlocked the flap of my small desk and laid the photos out on it and then, from the small inner drawer, I took the snaps of Dido's father, Thomas, and placed them in a row above the others, like a strange game of patience.

Thomas Sedley Jones was tall, but that was the only resemblance to his daughter. He was thin, brown-haired and had a slightly beaky nose. He'd looked such a very nondescript and commonplace child in that first photograph I'd had sent to me, after I'd become aware of his existence.

Of course, in the most recent photo I'd realized he had a slight look of my father . . . who, of course, was Faye's father, too. But there was no Archbold blood to pass down to Dido and explain her height and golden fairness.

And as I sat there, a suspicion I'd hardly acknowledged to myself rose like some unspeakable flotsam from the depths of the past and a fresh tide of hatred, stronger than any I'd ever felt before, swept over me, entirely obliterating any softening of my feelings towards Dido.

24

Force of Nature

When I knocked and entered Mrs Powys's bedroom next morning, bearing her breakfast tray, I wasn't expecting that my Christmas surprise would have *entirely* thawed out her chilly manner towards me, but I had thought it might have melted just slightly around the edges.

But no, she glanced up on my bidding her a cheerful good morning and gave me such a look of what I could only describe as *loathing*, that I was quite taken aback.

Yet she'd sent me her thanks by way of Henry, who'd said she'd been delighted with my gesture, and I couldn't for the life of me think what I might have done since then to blot my copybook!

While I'd come to believe that she simply felt a natural antipathy towards me – we do sometimes take instant and unreasoning dislikes to people – that morning it seemed to have increased to a whole new level.

'There you are,' she said coldly, as I approached and laid the tray over her knees, just as if I was late – which I wasn't, but on time to the second. She cast a critical look over the tray, too, as if wanting to find fault with it, but there was nothing she could quibble at: the egg was perfectly cooked, the toast the exact shade of brown she preferred, the butter in little curls in its dish next to the miniature pot of honey and the coffee hot and strong. Underneath it all, the embroidered tray cloth was spotless.

Finding no fault, she said, in the same cold voice: 'I will not require a tray tomorrow, because once Mrs Kane is here, I'll breakfast with everyone else in the morning room.'

'Of course,' I said. 'Shall I put out a full cooked breakfast from tomorrow?'

'Do. Mrs Kane likes a substantial breakfast and I assume you've already been cooking one for Xan, even if Lucy won't touch anything other than toast.'

'That's so,' I agreed, though of course I didn't mention that Xan always ate his in the kitchen with Henry and me. I was sure she didn't know about that, but from tomorrow, he'd have to join the rest of the party in the morning room.

I took out my notepad and pen. 'Bacon, fried and scrambled eggs, grilled tomatoes, mushrooms, sausages . . . ? I queried.

'All of those, though I think only scrambled eggs – and then, once the other guests arrive, you can put out a plate of cold sliced ham, too.'

'Got that,' I said, making a note. Henry always helped me cook the breakfast when it was a large party, even though he was happy to do it solo when it was just us . . . the *us* having recently stretched to include Xan, of course.

In turn, I'd be helping more with the serving of meals and the bed-making. We were used to working as a team, fast and efficient.

I stowed the little notebook and pencil away in my tunic pocket and said, 'Henry says he'll cut the Christmas tree for the Great Hall today and then put it up tomorrow, ready for decorating.'

'Tell him to come and discuss it with me in the library after my recordings session with Xan this morning,' she said shortly and, since the audience was clearly over, I made my escape.

The supermarket shopping arrived, bearing a lordly whole fresh salmon for that evening's dinner. I wanted it to be extra special, in honour of the arrival of Mrs Powys's friend. And perhaps dauphinoise potatoes and a *macédoine* of vegetables to go with it . . .

Henry had charmed the recipe for the *macédoine* of vegetables out of the proprietor of a small family restaurant near Autun in France, where we'd stopped for lunch after a detour to see an outcrop of rock that was supposed to resemble President de Gaulle, though I can't say I could see it.

Salmon is so easy to cook, baked in a sealed aromatic parcel of tinfoil, yet always looks impressive.

I decided to make a lemon meringue pie for dessert and got on with that as soon as I'd finished putting the shopping away.

Henry went off for his little interview with Mrs Powys when the library bell rang – it seemed to be becoming a regular fixture – and on his return told me they had been discussing the Christmas tree.

'It's OK for me to cut it today and then put it up in the Great Hall tomorrow, after which, we'll have the tree decorating ceremony.'

'Tree decorating ceremony?' I echoed.

'Apparently, when Mrs Powys's mother was alive, they made quite a thing of it. I jotted down all the details she could remember, so we could recreate it, as far as possible. Mulled wine and mince pies are served while the decorations are put on the tree and carols playing.'

'Sounds lovely,' I said.

'I'm going to need you and Xan to help me cut the trees – we'll get the one for our sitting room while we're at it.'

'You tell Xan, then,' I told him. 'I want to put the meringue on my pie.'

Xan was agreeable so, instead of taking Plum out for our usual late-morning walk – another quickly formed habit! – we were to go down through the woods in the Land Rover with Henry.

When he was ready, Xan came into the kitchen to find us and admired the lemon meringue pie sitting on a wire rack, which would be nothing compared to how he felt after he'd actually tasted the perfect combination of crispy sweet topping and tart lemon base.

'I'm not surprised Henry's cousin Hector wanted to marry you,' Xan said. 'I'm starting to think the way to a man's heart really is through his stomach.'

His lilac-grey eyes were teasing, but held a warm glint and I felt myself blushing, though I said calmly, 'With Hector, the cooking *was* the clincher, I have to admit.'

'Yeah, but he wanted to get his hands on more than your lemon meringue pies,' Henry said, coming in just then, wearing his padded jacket and squid hat.

'Really, Henry!' I protested. 'And he hardly seemed heart-broken when I turned him down.'

'Passion had made him rash, but he's a confirmed bachelor really, so it was probably a relief when you said no. Come on,' he added, 'I've put everything we need in the Land Rover and brought it round to the side door. Xan, are you bringing Plum?'

'Yes, but I'll shut him in the cab so he's not underfoot while the actual tree felling is going on.'

We crammed on to the bench seat of the cab and Plum sat on my lap like a little furry hot-water bottle.

We jolted down the track to the bottom of the estate, where the bright red ribbons still fluttered from the tops of the two trees we'd chosen.

Plum objected vociferously to being left alone in the cab, so I stood with him in my arms and watched the other two cut down the smaller tree first, loading it into the canvas-covered back of the Land Rover, before turning to tackle the big one.

Xan firmly took the axe from Henry at that point and made a surprisingly good job of cutting down the tree. A notch at one side, then a chop from the other, and down it came with a soft flumping noise, just where he said it would.

It looked so much bigger on the ground and took a bit of manoeuvring before it joined its smaller sibling in the back of the Land Rover, though the tip stuck out from under the canvas.

'I only hope it fits,' I said dubiously.

'Of course it will,' Henry assured me. 'And a smaller tree would look ridiculous in such a big, high-ceilinged hall.'

We let Henry drive back on his own, so we could give Plum his walk and cut through the trees to the lake, which was now thickly encrusted with opaque ice.

Xan skimmed a large pebble across it and it made a strange humming, zinging noise and Plum attempted to follow it, only for his little legs to slide from under him, so that he landed on his bottom, looking surprised.

Luckily he was just within reach, so Xan could haul him back.

'The ice looks perfect for skating, now,' he suggested.

'As far as I'm concerned, I think that will have to wait for a bit because, with Mrs Kane arriving this afternoon, I'll be busy. In fact, I won't be able to help you in the study today either, because I'm going to bake the Christmas cake. And tomorrow, we've got the Christmas tree to put up in the Great Hall and decorate. I have a feeling Henry and I will be doing most of that, with Sabine directing us.'

'And me – I'll enjoy helping,' he said as we began to make our way up the terraces, pausing in the Winter Garden. What snow there had been on this level was almost vanished and a few narrow green spears were bravely pushing up through the earth. I thought they might be hardy daffodils, and now, under the witch hazels, I spotted a white scattering of snowdrops, too.

'This has to be the most surprising and enchanting garden ever,' I said.

'Well, that's an opinion you certainly share with Sabine,' Xan said, though I thought it was possibly the *only* thing we had in common . . . except, I supposed, I'd grown to love the Castle, too, especially the older, original part of it. I'd had that strange, instant feeling of connection with it the moment I'd arrived. Perhaps I'd lived there in a past life? If so, I was probably a scullery maid, or something like that. Maybe the cook . . .

Henry was already in the kitchen when we got back, sitting at the table with his notebook and the magazine with the article on Christmas garlands open before him.

He said he'd managed to drag the trees into one of the outbuildings until wanted.

'And I went back to the attic, because I was sure I'd seen a couple of those old-style metal stands for them. You know, the kind you clamp the trunks into. One of them is huge.'

'Good. For that monster tree you chose, you'll need it.'

'Mrs Powys told me there was a round green mat that always went under the tree to protect the mosaic, but I remembered that was in one of the boxes of baubles.'

'Haven't the moths got at it?' I asked.

'No, it was layered with lavender. It's made of hairy green material, like the baize on the kitchen door.'

'Probably the same thing,' I suggested. 'Now, can you move that magazine and your notebook up to the other end of the table? I want to make a start on lunch.'

'OK,' he said obligingly, shifting them. 'I've borrowed this magazine and the article has some really original ideas for making wreaths, swags and garlands on the grand scale, which is what we need.'

'Yes, you're right. But I suppose you shouldn't put them up *too* soon, or they'll dry out.'

'They'll take me a while to make anyway, though I've got everything I need now, except the actual foliage. I'll probably make them at the weekend. It'll be fun.'

'We should be able to find enough greenery on the estate for them, though probably not mistletoe.'

'There's some quite realistic fake mistletoe in one of the boxes that'll do,' he said. 'Safer than the real thing, when there's a greedy little dog about, too.'

'Good thinking, because he'd eat anything,' I agreed.

I began making the Christmas cake right after lunch. The dried fruit that had been soaking up the dark rum was shiny and plump.

I turned the oven on to warm up, then greased a very large cake tin, before also lining it with greaseproof paper. It was the kind of tin with a loose base, which makes it so much easier later to get the cake out.

After that I hauled out a mixing bowl big enough to take a bath in, and assembled all the other ingredients around it: flour, spices, butter, eggs, treacle, slivered almonds and halved, jewel-bright glacé cherries.

Then I lightly beat the eggs and then the butter. There's a lot of beating and mixing involved in a fruit cake and it can be rather tiring on the arms, even when it isn't the size of this one.

I'd got to the stage of adding the dried fruit, which made the mix much heavier, and was beginning to flag a little when Xan wandered into the kitchen, empty coffee mug in hand, with Plum hard on his heels.

'I used to come in here when I was a schoolboy, if Mrs Hill was baking a cake, and steal raisins,' he said. 'She always let me scrape out the mixing bowl afterwards, too.'

'I'll let you scrape out this one, if you give me a hand with the mixing,' I cunningly offered.

'It's a deal!' He took the big wooden spoon from my hand and began to turn the mixture over. 'This is going to be a monster of a cake!'

'I know, but there'll be quite a lot of people to eat it,' I pointed out. 'It keeps very well too, so there's always something to slice at.'

When it was ready, he held the bowl so I could spoon the mixture into the tin and smooth the top.

Then I held the oven door open, while he slid it on to the baking tray on the middle rack.

'There, that's it for a couple of hours,' I said, 'though I'll check it halfway, to make sure the edges aren't catching, and put a tinfoil cap over the tin if they look as if they might.'

'How will you know when it's cooked all the way through?'

'Well, I just . . . will,' I said, starting to clear away all the bowls and utensils I'd used. 'But you can stick a skewer in the middle and if it comes out clean, then that means it's baked.'

When I looked up, he really was sitting at the table with a dessertspoon, scraping out the last of the cake mix and eating it.

'You're such a child!' I told him. 'And Henry's another – he'd have beaten you to it, if he'd been here.'

Plum looked as though he'd have liked some too, but of course dried fruit isn't at all good for dogs.

I opened a packet of mini bone-shaped biscuits instead and gave him one.

'Where did those come from?' Xan asked.

'I put them on the supermarket order. I thought they'd be nice for little treats. I find him hard to resist when he looks at me so endearingly. You don't mind, do you?'

'No, but I think Plum might be falling for you just as hard as Henry's cousin Hector did – and me!' he teased.

Mrs Kane was due to arrive before tea and I was just starting to get it ready when the bell for the front door jangled, but I knew Henry was in the dining room and would hear it.

'Was that Mrs Kane?' I asked, when he came back to the kitchen.

'Yes, and as soon as Mrs Powys heard her voice she practically ran out of the sitting room and they hugged each other. It was very touching.'

'Xan says they've been best friends since their student days and I know Mrs Powys has been looking forward to seeing her,' I said.

'I've taken her luggage up and put her car in the garage. I moved the Land Rover into the log store to make room for it. She has a pale green Volkswagen Beetle.'

He sounded approving.

I added Xan's cafetière of coffee to the trolley, next to the big Minton teapot, and then it was all ready to go: we'd made an extra special tea, with slices of the fruit cake as well as warm savoury scones.

'What's Mrs Kane like?' I asked curiously, as he prepared to wheel it off.

He paused. 'Small, wiry, flyaway white hair . . . friendly,' he said, which wasn't really *that* illuminating. Then he rattled off down the passage, singing, 'Half a pound of tuppenny rice, half a pound of treacle . . .' though I hoped he'd remember to stop long before he got within earshot of Mrs Powys.

I thought I'd have to wait till breakfast to meet Mrs Kane, but a little later, while Henry was lighting the fire and laying the table in the dining room, she came in, pushing the depleted tea trolley.

I looked up from slicing cucumber into wafer-thin discs to lay over the salmon, thinking Henry must have decided to fetch it on his way back, but instead saw a wiry elderly woman, with a bony, beaming, eager face, pink patches on her high cheekbones and blue-grey eyes shining with intelligence, interest and warmth.

Henry can look like that in his more cherubic moments, but in his case it's misleading.

'Mrs Kane! You should have left that for Henry to bring back.'

'Oh, I thought I might as well save him a journey since I wanted to meet you, and Sabine has already gone up to rest,' she explained. 'Xan went back to the study ages ago, so Lucy and I have had such a nice chat.'

'Really?' I said, my knife poised over the cucumber. Lucy seemed to spout endless streams of slightly incoherent speech, but I hadn't yet heard her say anything interesting.

'Yes, indeed! I saw almost immediately that the poor girl was just dying to join in all the Christmas activities in the village with her friends, so I told her that now I was here to keep Sabine company, she wouldn't mind Lucy absenting herself as much as she pleased. Not that she would have objected in any case to *anything* that took Lucy out for hours,' she added candidly, 'because clearly having her here hasn't worked out. They're chalk and cheese, and Sabine has never suffered fools gladly.'

'No,' I said, slightly stunned by this candid assessment. 'I mean, yes!'

She beamed up at me. 'No one mentioned what a tall, beautiful girl you are! And Henry seemed a most delightful young man – *and* he's a former schoolfellow of Xan's, too, I understand. So nice for him to have young people here, as well as us oldies.'

'He and Henry have been catching up,' I agreed cautiously, since I was sure Mrs Powys had no idea how much time we'd all been spending together. 'But two of the guests arriving later are around his own age, so he'll have lots of company then.'

'Oh, yes, Sabine told me Dominic Melling is coming. His mother is some sort of cousin of Asa's and I met the family one Christmas when my late husband and I were staying here. And Sabine's solicitor has his granddaughter staying with him, so she's invited her, too.'

'The Director of Archaeology from the Roman site is also joining us for Christmas dinner,' I told her.

'How lovely!' she said, with a very Henry-like beam. 'I'm sure this Christmas will be such fun! I do adore everything about Christmas, don't you?'

'I do – and so does Henry. And we're determined to make sure this one includes as many of the traditions Mrs Powys remembers from her childhood, as possible.'

Mrs Kane looked sober. 'We must all help to make it a very special Christmas, for I'm afraid it will be her last one. Or not *afraid,* precisely, since of course I strongly believe in Eternal Life,' she added, and I remembered she was a vicar.

I wasn't quite sure what to say to this, but she'd spotted the giant cake sitting on its substantial cooling rack.

'What a beauty!' she exclaimed. 'You know, when I arrived, I thought I could smell something spicy and seasonal!'

'I baked it this afternoon,' I said. 'The pudding is already made and in the larder.'

'Sabine told me you were a wonderful cook and that although she couldn't eat as much as she used to, she still enjoyed her food.'

'I'm so glad, Mrs Kane,' I said, feeling that at least I could please Mrs Powys in one thing!

'Oh, do call me Nancy! No one ever calls me Mrs Kane and I'm sure we're going to be good friends! And I'm afraid I'll tend to be trotting in and out of the kitchen a lot, making tea – I'm a great tea lover – but I'll try not to get under your feet.' She caught sight of the kitchen clock. 'Must go and change. I'm sure Sabine still does for dinner, even if no one else bothers these days.'

She smiled warmly at me and then walked rapidly out, the upper part of her torso slightly inclined forward, as if eager to get to where she was going.

I suspected this was characteristic of her, and I'd liked her very much.

She must have gone up the Garden Hall stairs and missed Henry by moments.

'I thought I heard you going past the dining room with the tea trolley – but you didn't have to. I was about to fetch it.'

'I didn't. It was brought back by a small whirlwind called

Mrs Kane – though we're to call her Nancy and we're all going to be good friends! I don't think she understands the difference between paid staff and guests!'

'Tell that to Mrs Powys,' he said. 'If even I, with my posh pedigree and slight family connection, am somewhat below the salt, *you* have entirely dropped off the end of the table, darling.'

Sabine

Of course, once we'd gone upstairs that evening and bade goodnight to Lucy, as she headed up the next flight to escape into the arms of whatever fictional lover awaited her, Nancy and I settled down in my boudoir for a good catch-up.

I got out my bottle of whisky and two glasses from the wall cupboard and she contributed a box of slightly crumbled home-made pecan biscuits, fetched from her room.

We sat with our drinks and the years seemed to roll back to our student days at Oxford . . . There had still been a lot of petty restrictions on female students at that time – Oxford was very behind in those things – but Nancy and I had found ingenious ways to circumvent them.

We reminisced about that for a bit, then Nancy, offering me the box of biscuits, said, as if it had reminded her: 'I popped into the kitchen earlier, while you were resting after tea, to say hello to your cook. What a beautiful young woman she is! Very striking, especially with her hair up in that old-fashioned way – though it suits her very much.'

'I don't know about *beautiful*, with that nose . . . and her manner is rather cold and reserved,' I said. 'But she's certainly an excellent cook, and she and Henry make a very efficient team. They should do, for what I'm paying them!'

'I think Dido's perfect Grecian profile *is* beautiful – and with that golden hair and creamy pale skin, not to mention the almost turquoise blue of her eyes, she's certainly striking. As to her seeming reserved, I only had to talk to her for a few minutes in order to realize it's just a front to hide her shyness.'

I smiled affectionately at her. 'You always think the best of everyone, Nancy.'

'I do, until they prove themselves otherwise,' Nancy said. 'But you know, I had the strangest feeling I'd seen Dido before somewhere, though of course I can't have done, because I wouldn't have forgotten her.'

'Really?' I said, staring at her curiously. 'But then, they do say everyone has a double, don't they?'

'I think Dido's might be holding up the portico of a Greek temple,' Nancy said, grinning. 'Statuesque describes her perfectly.'

'I suppose so. I haven't really seen much of her since they got here,' I said offhandedly. 'She's been bringing my breakfast up, but otherwise has tended to keep to the staff wing, though I expect she'll have to help serve meals and do the bedrooms with Henry, once the rest of my guests arrive.'

'Henry's a delightful young man,' Nancy said, 'and so nice for Xan to be able to catch up with his old friend.'

'He is very pleasant and one of *the* Rudges, of course – *and* we have discovered our families are slightly related by marriage.'

'You're such a snob, Sabine! If you go back far enough, we're *all* related,' she said unanswerably.

'Xan has been very busy sorting out Asa's papers and taking notes for his biography.'

'Yes, you mentioned on the phone that you've begun record-ing your memories for him. How is that going? Is it good to revisit the old days, or difficult?'

Trust Nancy to go straight to the point!

'There *were* a few difficult moments,' I admitted. 'He wanted to touch on my early life and the death of my father and stepmother – and you know how I feel about my father's remarriage . . . not to mention my half-sister.'

'That must have been painful,' she said sympathetically, 'even though it was so long ago, but I'm glad he made you talk about it because I expect it was a boil that needed lancing.'

'Nancy! What an expression!'

'Well, you can't let all that bitterness and anger fester for ever,' she pointed out. 'And they are all dead now, even Faye, so I think it's time to let those feelings go.'

'I'll *never* forgive Faye for what she did to Asa!'

'Oh, my dear!' she said. 'After all this time?'

We were silent for a moment, sipping our whisky.

Then she said, 'As we get older, the events of the past, good or bad, often seem clearer than the recent ones. But those of your early childhood were very happy ones to reflect on.'

'True, and I've found myself thinking more and more about those days, when Mummy was here, organizing everything and especially our Christmases, with all the old traditions . . . And I want this one, which will be my last at the Castle, to be special, too.'

'Do you know how long you've got?' she asked, without any hesitancy or embarrassment.

'Oh, apparently I could whimper on into spring . . . or I might suddenly go earlier. It remains to be seen,' I said ambig-uously, and then I told her more about my diagnosis and refusal of more radical, but probably pointless, treatment.

'I mean to stay here and die in my own home, not go into a hospice,' I said.

'You can afford to have home nursing if you want that,' Nancy said, then added, 'Is there much pain?'

'It's slowly increasing and will carry on doing so, but it's not yet unbearable. And I have painkillers doled out to me as needed. But they fog my brain – I only take them when I must, at night.'

'I hope you aren't hoarding them out of stoicism . . . or for any other reason,' she said astutely, with one of her clear, searching looks.

She knows me only too well.

'Of course not! I'll take them when I really need them.'

'Good, and you know that if you say the word, I'll shut up my house after Christmas and come and stay with you to the end.'

'Thank you, Nancy,' I said gratefully. 'I've had a good innings and I'm not at all afraid of dying, just of the manner of it.'

Then I went on, more briskly, 'Meanwhile, I need to keep a clear head until I've worked out how to settle the estate. It wasn't until my diagnosis that I seriously began to think about a will. Asa and I never made them, because it always seemed to feel like tempting fate, somehow . . .'

'That explains why you've invited your solicitor for Christmas. I did wonder.'

'He's an old friend, as well, but not only have I invited him, but also all the remaining dregs of the family.'

'But I thought Lucy and her brother, Nigel, were the only relatives you had left,' she said, surprised. 'Your father's cousins.'

'They are, though of course that means they aren't descended from my mother's side, the Archbolds, who were the original Castle family. I expect Nigel would inherit if I died intestate.

His sister certainly seems to think he's been counting on it for years!'

'I expect he has, if there were no other near relations.'

'I've invited the Mellings, too, though of course they're related to Asa and only by marriage to me, but they do have a son, Dominic. He was an engaging scamp when he was young, but I haven't seen him for years. Apparently, he's now some kind of private dentist!'

'I thought the Mellings had taken a huff after Asa died and they found he hadn't left them anything?'

'They did, but of course, since he never made a will, it all came to me.'

'I suppose it was natural they should feel miffed, since they were Asa's nearest surviving relatives. Dear me!' she added, looking startled. 'Old families do seem to dwindle away over the generations.'

'While they're all here, I thought I'd like to have a little talk with both Nigel and Olive Melling, before I finally make my mind up about how to leave the estate, though my chief concern is for Mitras Castle – that it should go on and be cherished.'

'I know how you love it,' Nancy agreed.

'I do, and a body such as the National Trust would do that. Of course, it wouldn't be a family home any more, but it *would* go on.'

'I'm sure when you've considered it carefully over Christmas, you'll do what is right – for *everyone* concerned,' she said, with gentle certainty.

'I hope so. And, by the way, the Archbold line is not *totally* extinct: do you remember my telling you once that Xan's grandmother Rose Fellowes and Asa and I discovered a family connection way back?'

Nancy gazed at me. 'I do, now you come to mention it, by way of some long-forgotten ancestor who emigrated to America?'

'That's right. You know what these old American families are like for lineage – there were family bibles and documents tracing the link.'

'Not so much a link as the very finest, almost invisible thread!' she said.

'So is silk, but strong for all that.'

'Well . . .' she murmured pensively after a long moment, 'you have given me a lot to think about! But I suspect you're already well on your way to making up your mind. I'll pray for you to make the right decisions.'

'Thank you,' I said, and reached for the decanter. 'A last snifter before bed?'

'Why not?' She held out her glass. 'I don't often get the chance to let my hair down these days.'

Then she sat back and cast another of her searching, bright glances at me. 'Why do I still get the feeling you're holding out on me about something?'

'I have absolutely no idea,' I said firmly, and turned the conversation back to our student days again.

25

Gingered Up

Yesterday evening, once our work was finished, Henry dragged in our modest Christmas tree from the outbuilding, smelling deliciously of cold pine needles, and set it up in one corner of the staff sitting room.

We had brought a box of baubles for our own artificial tree and, since we'd packed that one away again, we could use those.

Henry put on the DVD of that old favourite, *White Christmas*, because although you can't watch anything while trimming a tree, we liked to have it playing in the background.

I'd just begun by fixing the fairy to the top of the tree, when Simon called in on his way home from an evening event at the university. He came in diffidently, as if unsure of his welcome, but was easily persuaded to stay and help – and so was Xan, when he and Plum came in a few minutes afterwards.

'Hi, Simon,' he said. 'It looks like I've just made it in time to join in the fun!'

'Has everyone else gone to bed?' Henry asked. 'I wondered if they might stay up later, now Mrs Kane is here.'

'Oh, Nancy said she doesn't keep late nights either and hoped I wouldn't mind amusing myself. But Sabine told her I sometimes play billiards with Henry, or occasionally, we watch a film.'

'Occasionally being every night,' I pointed out.

'Yes, but she doesn't know that,' he said. 'Nancy said that sounded like fun and made sure Lucy didn't linger behind when they went up to bed. She has a nice firm but kind way with her.'

'I know. She's already told Lucy that while she herself is staying here to keep Mrs Powys company, Lucy can take a holiday and do what she wants, which seems to be joining in the village activities as much as possible.'

'I can see Mrs Kane will be a force for the good,' Henry said with a grin.

'She insists we call her Nancy and told me she hadn't answered to anything other than her first name, or "Rev Nancy", for years.'

'Perhaps Sabine will unbutton a bit under her influence,' Xan said. 'I'd be surprised if the pair of them weren't upstairs in her boudoir right now, swapping old memories and generally catching up.'

Henry fetched some beer from the fridge and we restarted *White Christmas* before getting on with decorating the tree.

Our collection of baubles, mostly found by me in junk and charity shops, varied from antique glass fruit to sixties trumpets, bells and birds. Our plastic fairy was attired in a crêpe-paper dress, fanned out and up behind her head and had been tarted up with glitter glue by Henry, who loved a bit of sparkle.

I couldn't resist buying them when I came across them, so luckily there were a lot more than would have fitted on our little artificial tree.

With the addition of a long string of twinkling LED lights and a lot of lurid tinsel, the tree looked lovely when we'd finished, even if a little sparsely decorated in places.

'We've forgotten the candy canes!' I said, rummaging about in our boxes at the back of the room. 'Here they are.'

Those made all the difference, though there was still room to add a few more things.

'I thought I'd bake some of my spiced ginger Christmas tree biscuits for the tree in the Great Hall tomorrow morning, so I'll make a few extra for ours,' I said.

'They sound delicious. I love a bit of gingerbread!' Xan said.

'These are extra thin, so they stay crispy on the tree and pierced for hanging up. But I'll make you some proper gingerbread too, Xan, when I bake them,' I promised.

It wasn't all that late, so we watched *The Grinch*, accompanied by buttered crumpets and hot chocolate. Plum, since he was looking left out, got one of the little bone biscuits I'd bought him.

With huge restraint, I limited myself to two crumpets, because a few more nights like this one and my figure would be permanently overlaid with more blubber than a minke whale.

'I'll miss these evenings, once the other guests arrive and you're not free to join us any more,' I said, settling back down on the sofa next to Xan, with Plum crunching another biscuit between us. 'Still, by then we'll probably be too busy to do anything except slump when we've a moment to ourselves. Things are usually non-stop over Christmas itself.'

'You must have *some* time off, though,' Simon said.

'Oh, catering for Christmas is what we're paid for, so we just throw ourselves into it – and we enjoy it too, don't we, Henry?'

He agreed and said, 'But you're always welcome to drop in, Simon, however busy we are.'

'Yes, of course, Simon. Come in by the door to the Garden Hall whenever you like.'

'There are still several days left before the rest of the guests arrive,' Henry pointed out. 'Plenty of time for more nights like this.'

'Though of course, when everyone else has arrived, I'll expect you and Henry to treat me with all due deference and respect,' Xan said in a lofty voice. 'Not Simon, of course, because he's my social equal.'

I threw a cushion at him, but he fielded it neatly.

'Only in public,' said Henry, with a grin.

But there were already some changes to the household routine. Next morning, everyone, including Mrs Powys and Xan, breakfasted in the morning room.

Henry, having fetched the newspapers early, helped me cook breakfast – all as Mrs Powys had ordered. I added some small poppy-seed rolls I'd taken from the freezer first thing, too.

While I cleared up the pots and pans, Henry went to and fro between the kitchen and the morning room, filling up the jug of juice and getting more milk.

'Lucy, who insisted she only ever ate toast for breakfast, is tucking into the biggest plateful of bacon and eggs you ever saw,' he reported.

'Just as well we made a generous amount, then. It doesn't sound as if there'll be much in the way of leftovers for you to polish off, though, Henry!'

'I made enough extra bacon for a roll anyway,' he said. 'I like it just as much cold, with lots of tomato sauce.'

He took it from a covered dish on top of the stove and had just taken an enormous and greedy bite, when he exclaimed thickly, 'I forgot – Nancy asked for Marmite.'

'I'll do it. You look like a hamster with your cheeks bulging so much,' I said, getting out the little brown jar.

When I went into the morning room, Xan was sitting opposite the door and gave me a smile of such warmth, though I'm sure he was just being friendly. I felt my expression slip from its usual one of professional cool into an answering smile, though, until I set down the Marmite and found Nancy looking from me to Xan in a brightly interested way . . . and my employer staring at me in slight surprise.

'Is there anything else you need?' I asked hastily.

'No, we have everything we want – you may go,' Mrs Powys said dismissively, and I hurried out.

I was thinking one of her ancestors might have been a Gorgon.

Henry said he could still whip around the bedrooms and bathrooms on his own, seeing as there was only one extra guest, so once breakfast was cleared, I set to and started making my Christmas tree biscuits.

It felt as if I'd barely got going before Henry was back! Nancy had appeared and insisted on helping him, while Sabine was recording her session with Xan.

Nancy herself pushed open the baize door and asked, 'May I come in? I don't want to disturb you, if you're busy.'

'Of course – you're welcome in the kitchen any time,' I said, and she came in eagerly, as if not wanting to waste a moment of precious time.

'Sabine has an appointment in Hexham this morning and I'll drive her. That sports car of hers would be perishing cold, even with the hood up! But we'll be back for lunch – I thought I'd better tell you. And now Lucy's officially on holiday and a free agent, she's going to spend the day in Wallstone with her friend Daphne, helping put up the church Nativity scene.'

'That's fine – thank you for letting me know.'

'And thank you for helping *me* with my morning chores,' Henry said.

'I do love to be busy!' She beamed impartially at us both, pink cheeks glowing and misty, blue-grey eyes shining, then turned and trotted off again.

'I'll get my coat and then bring her car round to the front,' Henry said, though I thought he just wanted an excuse to drive it, because he seemed really taken with it.

'You couldn't put snowboards on top of a Beetle,' I warned him. 'It wouldn't be practical for you.'

'I've *definitely* seen one with a rack of surfboards on top,' he protested. 'And how did you know I was thinking of getting one?'

'To me, you are entirely transparent.'

'Not entirely, I sincerely hope – like a jellyfish with all my insides on display.'

'What a horrid thought,' I said as he went out, shrugging into his anorak.

But I expected he'd get one – and once we'd wound the business down, we wouldn't need the big van any more. The end of an era.

I still wasn't sure what I'd do with myself after that . . . but something new.

The star-shaped biscuits were cooling on racks, and I'd just taken out a tray of thick gingerbread pigs when Xan came in as if the smell of baking had summoned him, Plum at his heels.

'Gingerbread!' he said, heading for the biscuits like a homing pigeon, but I fended him off.

'Those are for the tree, hands off! These gingerbread pigs are for you, though, so you can have one of those, if you want to.'

'You made them specially for me? And are you insinuating I'm a pig?' he said, but took one all the same.

'I found the cutter and thought it was fun,' I said. 'I made them for you, really, but I thought perhaps they might amuse Mrs Powys and Nancy if I send some in with their afternoon tea tomorrow. There won't be any tea today, because you're having mulled wine and mince pies in the Great Hall, while the tree decorating is going on.'

'I think they'd love the gingerbread pigs, which will take them right back to their childhoods,' he said, then demonstrated that he hadn't entirely left his yet, by taking a great bite of the one he was holding.

'Oh, scrumptious!' he said, when he could speak again. 'I don't suppose you'd entertain my proposal of marriage, any more than you did Hector's?'

'No,' I said sedately. 'Not when it's cupboard love.'

Plum stared at the open box of bone biscuits on the counter and barked imperatively.

'You, too,' I told him.

'If you've finished baking, there's time to go and skate on the lake, if you fancy it?' he suggested. 'Unless you're doing something really complicated for lunch?'

'No, just eggs Benedict. Apparently it's one of Nancy's favourite dishes.'

'Then why not come and try skating with me?'

I looked at him dubiously, remembering the one and only occasion on which I'd gone to an ice rink with friends and spent most of my time lying on my back, like a dying beetle.

'*You* could skate and I'll watch and admire,' I suggested. 'And Henry has already had the same idea. He found some skates in the Garden Hall cupboard that more or less fitted, once he'd put on two pairs of thick socks, and has already gone down.'

'Come on, then. Sabine's boots will probably fit you and I know Asa's are the right size for me.'

'Oh, I don't think I could borrow Mrs Powys's boots!' I said hastily.

'She won't mind. All the skates in the cupboard are free for anyone to borrow.'

I was still a bit dubious, but they did fit and before I knew it, we were heading down to the frozen lake, where Henry circled, hands clasped behind his back, like someone from one of those old Dutch scenes of frozen canals.

The sky was clear and coldly blue, but it had turned much colder again. Any snow left was just a thin, crispy layer.

Henry waved as we drew near and sat on a bench to put on our skates with cold fingers.

I stood up shakily and nearly fell straight down again, before I'd even stepped on to the ice.

Xan took my arm in a firm grip. 'Come on, I'll teach you and I'll try not to let you fall.'

He helped me on to the ice and Henry zoomed over and took my other arm.

'Easy does it!' he said, as I felt my legs sliding off in two different directions.

'It's not easy at all!' I snapped, trying to jam my knees together and stay upright.

'Bambi on ice!' Xan said, laughing, but after a while I got a little better and Henry resumed his circling again.

Xan propelled me forward and I tried to move my feet in the way he'd told me to, though I did have a couple of falls. My legs soon started to ache, though, and the boots seemed to weigh a ton.

'Now you've straightened up and got your balance, you're moving much better,' he said encouragingly, and we went right round the pond.

'That's it,' I said, when we got back to the bank near the bench. 'I'm afraid I'm finished. My legs have gone trembly.'

'You've done very well,' he said.

'Well, I did improve . . .' I said dubiously. Maybe, with a bit of practice, it might even be fun!

'If you could just help me back to the bench, Xan, then you can go and have a good skate and warm up and I'll go back to start lunch.'

'OK,' he agreed, and while I changed the boots for my wellies, he went back on to the ice.

Unencumbered by my ungainly presence, his tall, slender figure moved elegantly across the frozen lake and I watched him for a few minutes before getting up and heading back.

I was almost halfway up the terraces when I looked up and saw that Mrs Powys and Nancy must have returned, for they were leaning over the balustrade that bordered the lawn, watching the skating figures below.

I didn't think they'd spotted me, so I took a side path into the woodland and followed the track up to the herb garden, where I could cut across into the Garden Hall.

After all, I was carrying Mrs Powys's white skating boots and, despite what Xan had said, I still had a sneaking suspicion she might not like my borrowing them.

26

Boxed In

Early that afternoon, I began making my preparations for the Christmas tree decorating ceremony. I threaded thin green cord loops through the holes in my Christmas biscuits, ready for hanging, and put some aside for our own little tree.

The mince pies were already defrosted – the special ones, like tarts with star-shaped lids – which I now frosted with a little water icing.

Meanwhile, Henry had found a big glass punch bowl, the kind with small cups that hooked all around the rim and a matching ladle.

He washed and dried these carefully – they didn't seem to have been used for years – and then assembled the ingredients he'd need to make his mulled wine.

'I forgot to tell you, I found an amazing epergne in the same cupboard as the punch bowl,' he said.

'Well, don't shout about it, or everyone will want one,' I replied absently, knotting a green cord loop.

'You know what I mean,' he protested. 'One of those big table centrepieces, with several little dishes to hold bonbons, nuts and that kind of thing.'

'No, I can't say I do. Is it nice?'

'Yes, this one's porcelain, decorated with Christmas motifs. It'll look lovely on the sideboard in the dining room.'

'I'll take your word for it, but if it's antique and valuable, you're in charge of cleaning it.'

'OK, and we'll fill the little dishes with nuts . . . though marrons glacés and crystallized fruit would look pretty, too. Fortnum and Mason do *the* most wonderful crystallized fruit.'

'You could always ask Mrs Powys if you could order some?' I suggested. 'And shouldn't those gifts she bought from Liberty be arriving soon?'

'I checked and they're on their way.'

'You'll have hours of harmless fun, then, helping Mrs Powys to wrap all those.'

'Speaking of fun, Xan said he'd help me bring the tree in and set it up in the Great Hall, so I ought to go and spread out that rug over the mosaic to protect it. I could bring down the boxes of decorations and take the stepladders through, when we've done that.'

'And you need that metal stand to keep the tree steady,' I reminded him.

He looked at me a little quizzically. 'While I'm doing all that, you've got time to closet yourself away in the study with Xan for a bit more dusting . . . or whatever it is you get up to in there.'

'Just dusting,' I said firmly, and then checked the clock. 'I suppose I *would* have time to clean another shelf or two, before we have to get the mulled wine and mince pies ready to go.'

'You do, especially if I have everything else ready: music, lights, cameras – action!'

'Music!' I exclaimed. 'Mrs Powys said there should be carols playing.'

'There will be. I've borrowed a double CD from Nancy; she was playing them in her car on the journey here.'

I relaxed a bit. 'Oh, good, that's sorted. And, Henry, I forbid you to wear your cyclops headband camera.'

He looked hurt. 'Would I, when it would spoil my impeccable professional image?'

'It might if you *had* one,' I said, but he just laughed and went off to winkle Xan out to help bring in the monster tree. I heard the swishing noise as they dragged it past the kitchen window a few minutes later.

I was already in the study when Xan came back. He told me they'd had quite a struggle getting the tree up and firmly clamped into its cast-iron stand, but now it looked magnificent.

'Before that, I recorded some of Nancy's memories of Asa and Sabine,' he said. 'She and her husband stayed with them on Corfu quite a bit, especially in later years when Stephen, Nancy's husband, suffered from ill health and had to take early retirement.'

'I suppose it gives you a different perspective,' I said.

'Yes, the onlooker always sees things differently, even when they're as old a friend as Nancy.'

He dunked the rear end of the gingerbread pig I'd brought him into his mug of coffee and then ate it before it crumbled.

I had one, too, though I just nibbled mine . . . and somehow, instead of getting on with the shelf clearing, we ended up simply sitting on the sofa, Plum between us as usual, while Xan told me about his boyhood in Greece and how his father and Tommy had taught him to dive.

'As he got older, Tommy liked to talk about the early days with Asa and the first expeditions, and *I* love to listen to his stories,' he said. 'It's useful, too, because it's given me a different slant on the things Sabine's telling me.'

'It must be useful,' I agreed, and then suddenly realized time had flown and we hadn't done a thing except talk!

'I must go and wash my hands and put a clean tunic on,' I said, springing up. 'Still, at least I'm not dusty and dishevelled today, that's something! I'll see you in the Great Hall in thirty minutes, with mulled wine and mince pies.'

'Life has become a moveable feast,' he said, and Plum snorted himself awake for the first time since I'd arrived and stared at us through his slightly prominent eyes, as if suspecting us of plotting to hide some treat from him.

'We must remember not to hang any of the biscuits within dog reach,' I said.

'*There* you are,' said Henry when I went into the kitchen. 'Everything's ready in the Hall and Nancy brought me the CDs – the Choir of King's College, Cambridge. There's an old stereo system in the billiard room, so we can play them on that and leave the door to the Hall open.'

'Perfect,' I said. 'So we only need the mulled wine and the mince pies on the trolley and we're good to go?'

'Got it in one,' he said, stirring a pan on the stove, from which emanated a spicy aroma.

When all was ready, he took charge of the trolley, while I followed with the box of gingerbread biscuits.

Plum, who had wandered in a few minutes before, brought up the rear of our little procession.

The daylight was fading fast, but the cavernous Great Hall looked warm and inviting, not least because, on his own initiative, Henry had lit a log fire in the baronial-sized hearth and the bright flames leaped and reflected off the copper and brass diving helmets.

There was a huge wooden cartwheel of a ceiling fitting, too, suspended from the centre of the ceiling, but since its rim was only studded with candle bulbs, it didn't give out a huge amount of light.

A little extra illumination was provided by several wall brackets shaped like naked, muscular arms, each holding out a frosted glass ice-cream cone that gave off a dim amber glow.

The Christmas tree was placed slight off centre, nearer the stairs, its circular green felt mat obscuring the mosaic of Mithras, all but one heel emerging from the cleft in a rock.

Scattered on the floor around it, as if washed there by a high tide, were the opened boxes of decorations, lights, tinsel and the Nativity scene. The stepladders stood open and ready for action, though after my mishap in the snow I felt no desire this time to offer to go up them.

Nancy and Sabine emerged from the billiard room, borne along on a loud waft of 'Once in Royal David's City'.

'That's loud enough from here, isn't it?' Nancy said. 'How lovely and inviting the Hall looks. This is going to be fun! Let's get cracking!'

Sabine smiled fondly at her. 'You're such a child at heart!'

'We're all children at heart, but not all of us admit to it,' she said, twinkling.

'Henry, let Dido serve the wine, while you and Xan help Nancy find the Nativity set, because I know she wants to put that up first of all,' Sabine directed, moving to sit on a suitably regal high-backed wooden chair, with padded velvet seat and armrests.

'I do – it's the most important element and should go up first,' Nancy said. 'And if they're helping, Dido and Henry must have some mulled wine too, mustn't they?'

'Well, I—' began Sabine.

'Good, because it's literally the very Spirit of Christmas!' said Nancy, and gave a little, excited giggle.

While I ladled the mulled wine into the little cups, Xan and Henry unpacked the Nativity figures from their wrappings and set them on the floor, where they looked like guests who'd arrived too early for a party.

'I'd forgotten how enormous they are,' Sabine said.

'You need something substantial in this size of a room,' Xan said. 'Anything smaller would be totally lost.'

The Nativity was set up in its usual corner, in front of one of the strange wall lights, the figures positioned under a sort of flat-pack pergola, which represented the stable.

It was an extensive – and must have been an *expensive* – set, including not only the Holy Family and manger, but an ox, a donkey and two sheep, all lying down, as if the excitement had been too much for them.

'I could do with some straw for the manger,' Nancy said, when it was all arranged out to her satisfaction. 'I'll borrow a cushion from the sitting room for now, but it won't quite strike the right note.'

'I think there's some in a packing case in the cellar,' Henry said. 'I'll have a look later.'

Sabine had drunk most of her hot wine and some colour had come into her pale face. I'd only had a token sip and then passed the plate of mince pies round before she began directing me to look among the boxes for two large, porcelain-faced figures – a Father Christmas, whose place was apparently at the foot of the stairs, and a very beautiful Angel Gabriel, about eighteen inches tall, with gilded metal wings and stiffened gold ribbons of gauze seeming to float around it.

This went on the table under the window, where the magazines and newspapers were placed in the mornings. The effect was as if it had just alighted there and was quite surprised about it.

Once I'd found these, I was allowed to top up the glasses and circulate the last of the mince pies while the others were unpacking the baubles, but we all helped to hang them up. Even Mrs Powys was unable to resist delving into the boxes in search of favourites.

Xan and Henry were in charge of hanging the highest decorations up, using the stepladders, though Xan managed to fit the huge golden star-shaped tree-topper over the very topmost spike by going up the stairs and leaning right out over the banisters.

There were still the strings of fairy lights and tinsel to wind through the branches and my biscuits to loop within reach of people, but not Plum.

Mrs Powys began to flag and retired to her chair, while everyone started to clear up. I gathered the used cups, plates and napkins and took them back to the kitchen, followed by Plum. He'd fallen asleep in front of the fire, but the sound of the tea trolley wheels seemed to wake him like a clarion call. I put a couple of dog biscuits in his bowl, before going back to the Hall to help with the tidying, but when I got there it was mostly done.

Nancy was standing back to admire the tree. 'It's perfect, isn't it, Sabine? I don't think we could have got another thing on it!'

'Lovely,' agreed Mrs Powys, her eyes seemingly transfixed by the dancing fairy lights, 'and the carols and mulled wine – it was all just as I remembered.'

'I'm so glad,' Henry told her warmly. 'It's been fun, too!'

'It's all starting to look like Christmas now,' Nancy said.

'It'll look even more so when I've made the swags and

garlands,' Henry told her. 'Mrs Powys and I have decided on quite extravagant and baroque arrangements – lush!'

Sabine smiled indulgently at him, but then, as she cast another look around the room, a frown creased her brow.

'You know, there's something missing . . .'

'I can't imagine what,' said Xan, then grinned. 'Maybe a bunch of mistletoe or two?'

'That's it!' exclaimed Mrs Powys. 'It's the Mistletoe Bough!'

'What do you mean?' asked Nancy, puzzled.

'It was a circular, light wicker framework that hung from the central light fitting – there are small hooks underneath it all the way round. It was like a horizontal wreath, I suppose, threaded through with holly, ivy and other evergreens. And bunches of mistletoe were attached to it, too.'

'I don't remember it,' said Xan.

'No, I don't think it was used after Mummy died and the framework may be long gone.'

'I don't know . . . I think I might have seen something like that in the attic,' Henry told her. 'But if not, I'm sure I can make one when I do the swags.'

Nancy was now looking anxiously at her friend. 'Sabine, you're tired. Come on, let's go up and have a little rest before dinner, shall we? Lucy should be back soon, too. What a pity she's missed all the fun!'

'I expect she's been having her own kind of fun down in the village,' Xan said.

He and Henry began to remove more of the empty boxes to the Garden Hall once Mrs Powys and Nancy had gone upstairs, and I tidied up the bits of tinsel and then went to draw the curtains behind the Angel Gabriel – but my hand was arrested by the brightly shining solar stars outside.

As the other two came back for the stepladder and a last box or two, I called them over.

'Come and look. The solar stars are lit up and with the lights on the tree in here reflected on to the window, it looks as if the two trees are signalling to each other.'

'Perhaps they are,' said Xan, coming to stand behind me. 'I think the one outside is saying, "Where are *my* gingerbread biscuits?"'

'They'd go soggy, if you put them out there – or the birds would get them,' Henry said seriously.

'He was joking,' I said patiently. 'Come on, I've got to start prepping dinner and you need to move all those empty cartons that are blocking the Garden Hall, Henry.'

'I'll help you; I don't feel in the mood for any more work before dinner,' Xan offered. 'We'd better get on with it, before anyone falls over them.'

But we were too late, for Lucy had elected to put her own car away and come in by the side door, and we found her floundering about among the boxes. She was somewhat impeded by a large armful of holly, insecurely wrapped in newspaper. Just as we got there, a tower of cartons fell on her head.

She staggered, then sat down rather suddenly, flattening a Nativity box.

I was so glad the Holy Family weren't still in it.

27

The Mistletoe Bough

Henry helped her up and she thanked him agitatedly, before thrusting the holly at him.

'From my friend Daphne's garden. Her holly bushes have lots of berries, and I wasn't sure whether ours did, or not.'

'How splendid!' cried Henry, receiving this prickly bouquet with every evidence of delight. 'You *angel*!'

She blushed hotly, but declined when he offered to make her some tea, saying she'd had tea with Daphne. Then she made off up the stairs to her room, still twittering gently like a slightly flustered canary.

'I think you've made her day, Henry,' Xan said.

Soon after we'd arrived, I'd drawn up my rolling seven-day menu plans, with built-in flexibility for any off-piste ideas I might have, which made catering so much easier.

Of course, since I've been doing this so long, I have a core list of tried-and-tested recipes, but this time I'd adapted it to include all of the favourite dishes Mrs Powys had mentioned, as well as a few she hadn't, but which I was sure she would love.

For tonight's dinner, I was making proper Anglo-Indian-style kedgeree, to be served in individual bowls, topped with a sliced soft-boiled egg.

There would be baked apples to follow, their sides slit around and bursting with dried fruit, brown sugar and treacle, served with custard.

When Henry returned from energetically beating the gong to announce dinner was ready, I helped him carry the trays of individual dishes into the dining room and when I put one down before Nancy, she exclaimed in delight.

'How delicious that smells! I can see already, Dido, that your food will be so scrumptious, I'll have to buy my clothes a size larger by the time I leave.'

'Nonsense,' Mrs Powys said, though she smiled. 'You burn the calories off by never being still, so you won't put on an ounce!'

'I've already been *Hectored* into eating too much,' Xan said wickedly, winking at me, and I heard Henry give a muffled snort of laughter behind me.

'What *can* you mean?' demanded Mrs Powys. 'No one is forcing you to eat more than you want to.'

'No, but as Nancy said, Dido's such a wonderful cook, I can't resist it.'

I gave Xan a quelling look as I went out, which he met with bland innocence. I'd pay him back for that one later – perhaps by hiding the last of the gingerbread pigs before he joined us in the staff sitting room to watch a film . . .

The parcel from Liberty arrived next morning while everyone was still eating breakfast.

I was checking the lidded dishes on the hotplate when Henry informed Mrs Powys of this and she told him to bring the parcel to the library after she'd recorded her session with Xan.

'I'll ring, as usual, when I'm ready – but, Nancy, you'll have to make yourself scarce, because there is something in there for you and it would spoil the surprise if you saw it,' she said. 'Come along, Xan, let's take our coffee through with us and get on with it.'

Once they'd gone, Lucy wandered out of the room, too, murmuring something indistinguishable, though I thought I caught the name 'Daphne' in there somewhere.

Nancy insisted on helping us clear the table and then went off with Henry to do the rooms, so I soon had the kitchen in good order again, and could turn my attention to the Christmas cake.

I'd been looking forward to this stage.

I fetched it from the larder, where it had been reposing under a giant glass dome that was almost big enough to use to force rhubarb, and put it on to the silver-foil-covered cake board I had ready on the kitchen table.

Humming happily, I warmed some apricot jam and brushed it over the cake, ready for the marzipan to go on.

Henry came back while I was unwrapping the big, almond-scented block and turning it out on to a board dusted with icing sugar.

'Nancy is *so* energetic, I can barely keep up with her!' he said, then saw what I was doing and added, 'If you keep any leftover bits of marzipan for me, I'll turn them into *petits fours* later.'

'OK, good idea.'

The library bell jangled vigorously on its metal spring. 'No rest for the wicked,' Henry said. 'That's Mrs Powys waiting to look at the box of presents from Liberty, so she can decide who gets what.'

He picked up the box from the top of the dresser and went out. A few minutes later, while I was sprinkling more icing sugar over the board and the rolling pin, the banished Nancy wandered in and sat down at the table to watch me.

'If you don't mind having an audience,' she said.

'Not at all.' I began to roll out a huge disc of pale marzipan and, when it was big enough and of even thickness, I dexterously folded it in half over my rolling pin and flipped it on top of the cake.

'I suspect you've done that before,' she said with a twinkle, as I smoothed the top and then pressed down the sides, before cutting off the excess round the base with a butter knife.

'Just a few times!' I admitted. 'I enjoy this part, especially the icing and decorating.'

'Royal or fondant, for this one?'

'Oh, royal. Just a simple whipped-up snowy effect and then a selection of old cake decorations on top. I've found a tin of them in a drawer and since some of them look very old, I'm hoping they date from Mrs Powys's childhood.'

'It's very kind of you and Henry to take such pains to try and give her the Christmas she wants.'

'It's what we do best,' I said. 'And, given the circumstances, we want it to be as close to the old celebrations she remembers as possible.'

'I can see you're terribly organized – as is Sabine herself. She likes everything worked out in advance . . . even the course of her illness . . .'

She sighed, looking pensive for a moment, then brightened and added, 'I suspect you know what we are all going to eat for every single meal until after the other guests leave!'

'Pretty much,' I admitted. 'I make a habit of cooking extra batches of anything that will freeze, so that makes things easier when I'm busier later. But of course, Christmas dinner itself *has* to be worked out in advance like a plan of campaign, with defrosting, preparation and cooking times, all leading to everything being ready to go on the table at the same time.'

'And of course, *you* are too professional to forget to defrost the turkey, as I most memorably did one year!'

'Definitely! It's a gigantic one, too, so it needs to go into the oven early on the day.'

I put the cake back on its stand under the glass dome, while I cleared away the bits of marzipan and the used utensils. Icing sugar does seem to drift everywhere, like fine snow . . .

'As soon as Sabine's free, I'm going to take her out for a run in my car,' Nancy told me. 'I thought we'd go to the big garden centre over near Hexham and have lunch there – and Lucy also said she'd be out gallivanting with her friend Daphne again, though I sincerely hope *not* at the same garden centre. Sabine tolerates Lucy's fussy little ways so much better when she sees much less of her.'

'I think you're right, but I'm sure Lucy is kind-hearted and means well. I don't think she's terribly interested in gardening, though.'

'In a way that's a pity, because it has become Sabine's main interest, especially the Winter Garden.'

Henry came in, carrying the Liberty box with the flaps firmly folded down, and said they were all done with the mysteries and Mrs Powys had gone to get her bag and coat, so Nancy hurried out.

'They're going to lunch out and so is Lucy, so there'll only be us and Xan for lunch today,' I said. 'Did you manage to decide which guest gets what?'

'Oh, easy-peasy,' he said airily. 'And Mrs Powys has written the tags, so now I only have to make pretty parcels of them and pop them under the tree.'

'I thought the presents were to go by the place settings on the table at Christmas dinner?'

'Change of plan, darling.'

'Won't those few small parcels look a bit lonely under that giant tree?'

'I expect there'll be more presents later. For a start, when I carried Nancy's luggage upstairs, I noticed an open holdall that seemed to be crammed full with cellophane cones of home-made fudge. I suspect she's going to dole those out to everyone as presents.'

'Home-made gifts always seem nicer than bought ones, somehow.'

'If she's going to put those under the tree, they'd better go up on a little table, so Plum can't get at them,' he suggested.

'Good idea! He's so greedy.'

'Do you want to look at the silk scarves before I wrap them?' he offered. 'They're absolutely beautiful, a mix of old style and modern.'

'Better not, in case I start to long for one myself,' I said. 'They're out of my price range.'

'OK, I'll take them into our sitting room to wrap, out of your way. After that I think I'll go and collect all the greenery for the garlands and swags. Do you and Xan want to come? We won't have to hurry back, if everyone else is out to lunch.'

'I don't know about Xan – you'd better pop and ask him – but I can if you give me an hour, because now I know I don't have to make a proper lunch, I think I might as well carry on and ice the cake.'

'All right. I want to go up to the attics and see if I can find the frame for that Mistletoe Bough thing first, anyway.'

Before I began icing the cake, I chose my decorations from the tin – cute, tiny china snowbabies in hooded white all-in-one suits. Some were sitting down, others lying propped up on one elbow, and two in the act of throwing snowballs.

Then I added an old-fashioned bright red postbox with a robin on top, completely out of scale.

I needn't have bothered clearing away the first icing sugar snowstorm, because I whipped up another one while making the royal icing.

I spread it on thickly, smoothed the sides, then whipped up the top with a fork, before decorating it.

When I stood back to admire it, I was startled to hear the sound of applause.

Turning, I saw that Henry and Xan had sneaked quietly in and were watching me.

'I had no idea you were there!'

'We didn't want to interrupt the artist at work,' Xan said.

'Well, it's all done now, other than wrapping a paper band around it – and all the washing up.'

'You can do that later and I'll help,' said Henry. 'And look, I did find the Mistletoe Bough frame.'

He showed me a sort of circular wooden hoop, wound around with thin, brittle branches.

'Great, now you won't have to make one,' I said. 'Look, if one of you could carefully carry the cake into the larder, and then stack everything in the sink, I'll go and put my jeans on and be down in five minutes.'

'All right, and then I'll bring the Land Rover round, because we'll need too much greenery to carry,' said Henry. 'I noticed something with berries on up near the front gates, and I'm sure there's a variegated ivy somewhere near the lake, so we'll be up and down the drive anyway.'

'Plum can come with us, then. I didn't fancy carrying him back when he's tired, as well as an armload of holly.'

Plum had flopped down on to the floor by his dinner bowl and closed his eyes and didn't open them at the mention of his name.

'He never looks anything else but tired,' Henry said.

We gathered red-berried branches of what we thought might be rowan from a bush near the lodge. We were none of us gardeners enough to be sure. There was an abundance of dark ivy growing around one gatepost, too, so we cut a lot of that and piled it all in the back, under the canvas hood, before taking the track down through the woods on that side of the valley.

Henry drove slowly and we stopped whenever we spotted something we could use, like holly and the variegated ivy, with its golden-hearted leaves, which Henry had mentioned earlier. It was growing round a dead tree trunk near the bottom of the hill, not far from the Christmas tree plantation.

The ivy jogged my memory and I said, 'You know, I'm sure I've seen a variated holly, too, somewhere.' Then it came to me. 'I know, it was near the lake, just behind the little temple.'

We added a few fir boughs to our collection and then drove on up the other side of the valley, stopping to get out and search for the holly.

Plum had entirely lost interest in the proceedings by now and stayed in the cab, grumbling when I moved him off my lap on to the seat.

The heap in the back of the Land Rover grew ever higher and we all had cold, prickled hands, before Henry was finally satisfied.

'Now I only need a load of branches from the bay tree by the herb garden and that should do.'

'I should think so, too!' I said. 'I'm sure you can't possibly use all this!'

'You'd be surprised. I'll probably need to add some of the fake greenery and gilded fir cones I found in the attic to pad them out, too. There were coils of thick, silky green rope in the same box, which I imagine they used to pin the garlands to, when they looped it down the stair banisters.'

Our garden gleanings filled most of the downstairs cloakroom, where Henry usually did the flower arrangements. Luckily, it was a very large room and he borrowed a pasting table from Xan, which just fitted up the middle, with enough room to move around it.

'I'll bring it back as soon as I've finished,' he promised.

'No rush, though having a spare one is handy, now Dido's piling the books from the shelves on to one as she cleans them,' Xan said.

'Speaking of which, I *might* have time to do a bit more of that before tea,' I said. 'But come on, let's go in the kitchen and have a bit of late lunch, first. Welsh rarebit, anyone?'

They both agreed that that sounded good. Afterwards, Xan and Plum returned to the study, while Henry vanished into his green bower.

I put everything I'd used for the icing away and then made a few preparations for later, before joining Xan in the study. I passed the open cloakroom door on the way, but Henry was so engrossed in what he was doing that he didn't notice me.

Entirely appropriately, he was quietly whistling 'The Holly and the Ivy'.

Xan was absorbed in his work, too, sorting out yet more letters he'd found in one of the desk drawers, but he looked up and smiled at me when I went in.

'These are from Tommy, with carbons of Asa's answers attached.'

'That makes more to read through,' I said, 'though at least you get both sides of the story, as it were.'

I left him to it and set to work on another shelf . . . and the room fell silent, apart from the rustle of papers, the click of Xan's fingers on the keyboard and Plum's soft, snuffling snores from the small sofa.

I thought how much I enjoyed these quiet times together, when we often barely spoke for an hour, yet the silence between us was so comfortable.

I'd just replaced all the books on the newly polished shelf when the door to the library swung open.

Nancy's voice said, 'There you are, Xan! You were so quiet, I wasn't sure anyone was in here. And Dido, too,' she added, beaming at me. 'You both look very busy and I don't want to disturb you, just let you know that we're home and Lucy's back, too.'

But I'd caught sight of the clock and exclaimed, 'Look at the time! It's lucky you did come in, Nancy, or tea would be late.'

'There's nearly half an hour before it,' she said, 'and what does it matter if it's a little later?'

But I knew it mattered to Mrs Powys, and I hurried off to wash and change into a clean tunic.

Henry hadn't noticed the time either and was still wrestling with his greenery in the cloakroom.

He'd already wrought miraculous garlands, which were looped around the room on the coat hooks, and was now threading ivy through the frame of the Mistletoe Bough.

'You carry on and finish what you're doing,' I told him. 'I can take tea through, for once.'

'Well, thank you, darling,' he said gratefully. 'I really don't want to stop now that my creative juices are fully flowing.'

'Sap,' I said, hurrying off.

'And the same to you!' he called after me.

28

Upside Down

When I pushed the tea trolley into the sitting room, Mrs Powys looked up.

'Where is Henry?' she demanded.

'He's in the middle of creating all the swags and garlands and the Mistletoe Bough, Mrs Powys. It seemed silly for him to stop when I could bring tea in just as easily.'

'Hmmph!' she said.

'He found the frame for the Mistletoe Bough in the attic, Sabine,' Xan told her.

'I thought it seemed a pity to disturb you and Xan in the library earlier, too, just to remind you we were back for tea,' Nancy said, twinkling. 'Such a cosy, quietly domestic scene, with both of you working away in perfect harmony, and old Plum snoring away in the corner, as usual! You two young people are obviously kindred spirits.'

'Oh – but . . .' I began to stammer, going pink with embarrassment, though I noticed that Xan, pouring himself some coffee, merely looked amused at Nancy's assumptions.

My employer, on the other hand, did not. She was wearing

an arrested expression and her glacial blue eyes looked me over assessingly.

'Nothing of the sort, Nancy!' she said shortly. 'Dido is merely helping with the cleaning in the study, that's all. You forget that she already has a young man of her own – Henry.'

'*Henry?*' I exclaimed in astonishment. 'But – we're only business partners and best friends, nothing more.'

'Well, of course not, because Henry's gay, isn't he?' Nancy said comfortably. 'I can't imagine how you came to think anything otherwise, Sabine.'

Lucy choked on her scone and Nancy turned and patted her on the back.

'He's *gay?*' demanded Sabine. 'Are you sure?'

'Well, *he* is,' I replied.

'I don't believe it,' choked Lucy, pink in the face and with watering eyes, once she could speak after Nancy's hearty ministrations, but no one took any notice.

'It's of no great moment to anyone other than Henry, in any case, is it?' Nancy pointed out. 'I know you and Asa never had any silly prejudices, Sabine, even back in the day when it was illegal – and how odd that seems now, doesn't it? The Dark Ages!'

She beamed generally around at us and then took up her cup and half a buttered scone.

Sabine shot another of those coldly assessing looks from me to Xan, as if someone had shaken her kaleidoscope and all the glittery bits had reformed into an entirely different and unwelcome pattern.

'Did *you* know Henry was gay, Xan?' she asked.

'I gathered so. I knew he and Dido were only friends.'

Lucy suddenly found her voice. 'Mr Graves, our vicar, feels very opposed to gay marriage.'

'Then I expect his gay parishioners look elsewhere for someone who can bless their union with a loving heart,' Nancy said. 'I think any two people who want to dedicate their lives to each other should be able to do so.'

'Of course they should, and naturally, it doesn't matter to me in the least. It was just a surprise, that's all,' said Mrs Powys, then snapped at her cousin, 'Lucy, don't be more of a fool than you can help.'

But poor Lucy was already looking crushed and miserable . . . though I wondered if she'd switch her attentions back to Xan!

I felt a strong desire to escape from the room at this point, which Xan must have noticed, for he said, 'Dido, you left a couple of books from that last shelf lying on the table. Perhaps you could put them back in the right place, on your way back to the kitchen?'

'Of course, I'll do that,' I agreed gratefully, heading out of the door, although we both knew I'd done no such thing.

I looked in at the cloakroom door on my way back. Henry was winding some thin fronds of fir into the Mistletoe Bough, now, which looked almost finished.

'Henry,' I said, 'Nancy's just outed you as gay in front of Xan, Lucy and Mrs Powys.'

'Oh, did she?' he said absently, then looked up. 'I was never in, in the first place, was I?'

'Well, we knew Lucy was in the dark and the poor thing looked absolutely devastated. But I was surprised that Mrs Powys assumed we were rather more than business partners!'

'Oh, well, it doesn't matter, does it?' He looked at me and grinned, before saying acutely, 'Or *does* it? Did she think that because we were a couple, it didn't matter if you were spending so much time with Xan . . . though luckily, she doesn't know the half of it!'

I felt myself go faintly pink. 'We do seem to spend a lot of time together, but . . . well, the three of us have become good friends, haven't we?'

'There's friends and friends,' he pointed out. 'I've seen how Xan looks at you and I can tell you now, he's well on the way to falling for you – and paint me green with yellow stripes if *you* don't feel the same way about *him*!'

I stared at him. 'I'm sure you're wrong about Xan, and as for me . . .' I pressed my hands against my hot cheeks. 'I hadn't even thought about it, except that I enjoy spending time in his company.'

'Xan's probably afraid of making a move too soon,' Henry said. 'Do you want me to give him a hint?'

'No, absolutely *not*!' I exclaimed, horrified. 'Don't you dare! And anyway, even if he *was* starting to think of me that way – which I'm certain he isn't – he'd back off pronto if he realized I was once the lovesick teenager who made his life a misery.'

'Of course he wouldn't! In fact, he'd probably just think it was funny. I mean, you're two entirely different people now, and this time, you've really got to know each other.'

He gave me his naughty-cherub grin. 'Admit you're falling for him, Dido.'

'Certainly not! Falling for one of the guests would be entirely unprofessional,' I said with dignity. 'And what's more, it wouldn't go down at all well with Mrs Powys! So, in the interests of giving her what she's hired us for – a wonderful, traditional Christmas – let's just put it out of our heads for the moment, shall we?'

'We can but *try*, darling, though of course, I can't answer for what's going on in Xan's head!'

Somewhat shaken by this conversation, I retired to the kitchen to make a start on tonight's main course.

But for once, I found it hard to concentrate on my cooking, because the conversation with Henry had disturbed me so much – not to mention forcing me to admit to myself that, at some point and without realizing it, I'd slipped from friendship into love with Xan . . .

I suppose it was hardly surprising that I should fall in love with him, but I couldn't believe that he felt the same way about me . . .

With an effort, I finally managed to focus my mind back on the job in hand: you can't make a *roux* without giving it your full attention.

Luckily, Henry had finished his green-fingered magic well before dinner and called me in to admire his creations.

The cloakroom was festooned with long ropes of greenery, looped over the coat hooks or laid out along the pasting table, while the Mistletoe Bough leaned against one wall, like an overgrown and bushy wreath.

'Good, aren't they?' he said with immodest – but perfectly justified – pride. 'And I've had a *lovely* idea: why don't we put them up later, when the ladies have retired to bed? Xan can help us.'

'That's a really nice idea,' I agreed. 'I'll ask Xan in a bit, when he comes in to feed Plum – but meanwhile, you'd better close the door, hadn't you?'

'True,' he said, coming out and shutting the door behind him. 'I don't want Plum cocking his leg against my Mistletoe Bough!'

And so it was that very late that evening, when the house had sunk into quietness, we emerged from the staff sitting room, where we'd been whiling away the time by watching a dark Christmas movie called *Krampus*, and sneaked into the Great Hall.

The two men held the ends of long ropes of foliage between

them, like hairy green sea serpents, while I had the Mistletoe Bough hung around my neck and carried a box of smaller swags and garlands.

We had to make a couple of trips before everything was assembled on the tiled floor, including the stepladders.

Plum pattered to and fro with us, in an interested but puzzled manner, before finally flopping on to the end of a rug and watching from there.

Fortunately, despite Henry's fears, he'd showed no signs of cocking his leg against anything, even when I leaned the Bough against the table.

Creeping upstairs like burglars, carrying their rustling burden, Henry and Xan attached the long garlanded ropes to the banisters up the first two flights of stairs, though I could only see the lower end of the top one, where it turned.

When they came down, Henry handed me a box of red velvet bows on wire picks.

'Here, you pin one of those at the bottom of each swag, all the way up the stairs, while we start on the rest.'

I'm not very artistic, but even I could manage that, and then I watched Henry as he added a few more finishing touches to his arrangements along the mantelpieces before, finally, adorning the copper and brass diving helmets with small wreaths of gilded bay leaves.

'I wondered what those were for,' I whispered, though the tower was so solidly built that I don't suppose Mrs Powys or Nancy would have been woken if we'd shouted.

'Just the Mistletoe Bough to attach now, and we're done,' Xan said, looking up at the cartwheel-sized wooden light fitting that hung from the centre of the ceiling.

'There are hooks underneath it – Mrs Powys was right. I've

put cord loops all the way round the top of the Bough, so it's just a question of looping them on.'

I thought it would probably be a lot trickier than he made it sound! And there were a few heart-stopping moments when Henry held the ladder, while Xan struggled to attach the wreath, but at last it was done and the bunces of mistletoe hung down from it, like strange herbs drying on a rack.

'It looks *so* baronial and medieval in here now, doesn't it?' said Henry. 'I expect the Lord of Misrule to prance in at any moment with a bladder on a stick, and smite us all.'

'Perhaps one of the guests might oblige,' I suggested with a grin.

'It's some time since I've seen the Mellings, or Lucy's brother, Nigel, but I can't quite see any of them in the role,' Xan said gravely. 'I seem to remember Dominic Melling was a bit of a joker when he was a boy, but he's a dentist now, so I should think he's put all that behind him.'

'I don't think we want any misrule anyway,' I said, looking up at the circle of greenery above me. 'Just peace and harmony.'

'I am the Christmas Fairy, and your wish shall be granted!' said Henry, striking a pose, then kissed me under the Bough.

'There, we've christened it – happy Christmas, darling!'

'Happy Christmas, Henry,' I said.

He picked up the ladder and carried it off through the arch to the old wing and I turned with a smile to wish Xan happy Christmas, too . . . and found him standing very close and looking down at me with a light dancing in his lilac-grey eyes.

'My turn,' he said and, pulling me close, kissed me.

It was not at all like Henry's brotherly salute, but full on the lips . . . and seemed to last a very long time . . . though actually I wasn't counting.

It was only when he finally let me go that I realized I had my eyes shut and opened them, bemusedly.

'It's gone midnight, but you've turned into a witch, instead of a pumpkin,' he said lightly. 'You'd better go and get some sleep; I know how early you have to get up tomorrow. I'll just let Plum out of the front door for a moment and then turn off all the lights in here.'

I was still staring at him, feeling rather dazed, but pulled myself together. 'I am tired, so I'll leave you to it. Goodnight, Xan.'

'Goodnight, Dido,' he said softly, but he was already turning away and snapping his fingers to summon Plum.

After a night of confused dreams, I woke up next morning feeling it would be wrong to read too much into Xan's kiss last night – *or* let Henry, romantic soul that he was, persuade me that Xan had any warmer feeling for me than friendship, even though that had been a *very* friendly kiss.

But clearly I was right, because when Xan came into the kitchen early next morning to give Plum his breakfast, his manner was just as casually friendly as usual.

He didn't linger, though, because Henry and I were both busy with the grill, hotplates and frying pan by then.

Henry took the hot dishes through to the morning room a few minutes later and when he returned, said that Lucy was already down.

'And she looked at me as if I'd killed her pet rabbit and said, "Oh, *Henry*!" I couldn't really think of a reply to that, so I said I'd fetch her some tea.'

'I've just made it, if you want to take the pot through, and I'll be along with the coffee in a minute,' I told him and when I did, found everyone was now down and the hot topic of conversation was the overnight appearance of the swags and garlands.

Lucy, who had come down by way of the Garden Hall stairs and so entirely missed seeing them, actually got up and went to look.

They were a definite hit with Mrs Powys. Henry got most of the praise, as was only right, since it was his magical flair that had created it all.

'You're so clever!' Lucy said, staring at him rather dolefully, then she got up and began loading her plate as if she'd had a ten-minute starvation warning.

I left Henry in the morning room watching the somewhat explosive toaster and went to fetch the reserve dish of bacon, which I was sure Henry had hoped wouldn't be needed. The conversation had moved on in my absence and Xan was just telling everyone about the old home movie he'd found among his grandfather's films.

'Not one of his – it must have got mixed up with them at some point and never given back. But there's old footage of parties at your villa, Sabine, and a picnic on a beach. I thought you might enjoy watching it, so I've brought it with me, as well as the old projector and screen.'

Henry was so interested he forgot the toast, but I just caught it as it shot out, slightly singed, and gave him a severe look.

'Oh, yes, that would be fun,' Nancy said. 'Wouldn't it, Sabine?'

'It might be amusing,' she agreed. 'I expect the film was taken by that poet, Georgio someone-or-other. He was always appearing under one's nose with his little cine camera.'

'How about we watch it right after dinner this afternoon? I can set the screen up in the drawing room,' said Xan, and then added, to my surprise, 'and I'm sure Henry and Dido would enjoy watching it, too.'

'I don't see why they should be interested,' said Mrs Powys, turning to look at us, as if wondering why we were still there.

I hastily put down the metal lid I'd just lifted from one of the dishes on the hotplate and started for the door, but Henry said in his most cajoling voice: 'But we'd *love* to see it, Mrs Powys! We've watched all the clips of you and your husband diving that are on the internet, of course, but I adore home movies – they're so spontaneous – and I expect you had a very interesting circle of friends on Corfu!'

I thought this was rather over-egging the pudding, but Mrs Powys said indulgently, 'Interesting was certainly the word for *some* of them! Still, if you really think you'd like to watch it, Henry, I suppose there isn't any reason why not.'

'Oh, super! We'll just slip in, quiet as mice and sit at the back.'

I don't know how he gets away with it, but this little mouse took herself off to the kitchen, where she belonged.

'I can't imagine how you manage to get round Mrs Powys,' I said, when he followed me.

'She likes me,' he said simply. 'And I don't suppose my having a pedigree that stretches back before the Norman Conquest does me any harm, either.'

'Snob value,' I told him.

'Admit you're dying to see the film, too.'

'OK – yes, I am,' I agreed. 'The younger Sabine Powys, letting her hair down with her friends, should be interesting! A glimpse into the past.'

Lucy went to church after breakfast, but apparently Nancy had decided the vicar was not on her wavelength. Instead, while Mrs Powys recorded her usual session with Xan, she helped Henry whip round the bedrooms again.

Then she and Mrs Powys wrapped themselves up warmly and went for a walk in the garden.

'Nancy now knows my entire life history *and* some of yours, too, darling,' Henry announced, coming into the kitchen where I was, as usual, whipping up a culinary storm. 'I'm afraid she just eases it out of me, without even seeming to ask questions.'

I looked at him. 'So, which of my secrets did you blab?'

'Oh, all about your being brought up by an elderly relative . . . your childhood sweetheart, Liam . . . his being one of the group of friends we travelled around Europe with after graduation and his dumping you in Avignon . . .'

'That was fairly comprehensive,' I said drily. 'Did you also tell her about Kieran, your long-term boyfriend, jumping ship for that waiter at the same time?'

'Oh, yes, and that Avignon was a doomed place for us both.'

'You certainly did spill your soul,' I said, carrying on making the little suet dumplings that I'd pop into the beef bourguignon.

'Very cathartic, though, darling. I even whipped through our further adventures, when it was just us two roaming round the continent, and how we found ourselves catering, at five minutes' notice, for a super-smart house party on the Riviera. And so,' he finished, 'our Heavenly Houseparties business was born.'

'You managed all that, in the short time it took you both to make the beds and tweak the bathrooms?' I said incredulously.

'Pretty much, though she'd already had one instalment.'

I finished the dumplings and my mind turned back to what I was doing. 'I think something very simple for dessert – chocolate custards in ramekins, perhaps . . .'

'I've lost you again,' he said.

'No, I'm still here . . .' I said vaguely. 'You know, I think I'll make a pineapple upside-down cake for tomorrow's dessert, while I'm at it.'

29

Old Haunts

Nancy wandered in soon after, her high cheekbones flushed even pinker than usual, perhaps from the cold.

'When we got back from our walk, Sabine sat down by the sitting-room fire with the newspapers and immediately fell asleep, so I thought I'd come and make a cup of tea – and one for you, too, perhaps?'

'Yes, please – but coffee for me.'

'Ah, a coffee drinker, like Xan!' she said, and when she'd put the mug by my elbow, sat down to watch me work.

'Something smells delicious!'

'It's slow-cooked beef bourguignon,' I said.

'Sabine told me Sunday dinner is at two, as it will be on Christmas Day.'

'Yes, I'll aim to have it on the table by then,' I agreed.

'That will be quite a feat, with so many more to cook for,' Nancy said, and added, 'I'm so glad Sabine's illness hasn't prevented her from enjoying all the lovely meals you produce, even if she can't eat as much as she used to.'

'Perhaps the cold walk will have given her a good appetite for lunch,' I suggested.

'The Winter Garden was looking especially lovely today. There are already so many daffodils and snowdrops out, and I'm sure I could see crocuses coming through! It's so amazing the way things flourish here in winter, when we're so far north!'

'I know. That sheltered terrace feels as if it's under some sort of enchantment,' I agreed, then smiled. 'But then, the Castle itself feels a bit like that, too – under a magical spell!'

She looked at me keenly. 'Interesting that you feel that, too. Sabine, of course, has a powerful connection to it – I think it's in her blood.'

'Generations of her family have lived here, haven't they? So I'm sure it is,' I said.

'We enjoyed our walk, but Sabine was glad to get back to the fire in the sitting room – so lovely that she now has Henry to attend to things like that.'

'He's having lots of fun pretending he's a lumberjack and chopping enough wood to keep the fires going for about ten years,' I said. 'He *was* cleaning up the cloakroom after his garland-making session yesterday, but I think he's just gone out to the woodshed yet again.'

'I expect the exercise is good for him,' she said, watching with interest as I poured the mixture for the chocolate custard into a pan and put it on the stove.

'He's been telling me all about your travels abroad, after you left university – so fascinating! And he said you'd collected so many notes and recipes that you've been able to turn them into books!'

'Yes, luckily I found a niche publisher who releases one every year, for the Christmas market: small, fat hardbacks in retro covers.'

She was quiet while I brought the custard to simmering point, stirring till it thickened, before carrying the pan back to the table.

I had a tray of small ramekins on a baking tray ready, and poured a little into each one.

'There, they'll soon cool and then can go in the fridge, but I'll grate the dark chocolate now, for the tops.'

'I loved the sound of your little books when Henry described them to me – that mixture of recipes and reminiscences is always irresistible.'

'*I* can't resist those by other authors, either,' I agreed, and, while I grated the dark chocolate finely into a little bowl, we compared our favourites.

But somehow, by the time I'd begun assembling the ingredients for my pineapple upside-down cake, I was telling her that my books didn't make a lot of money and that when Henry and I wound up our business the following year, as we intended, I'd have to find something else to make ends meet.

And that wasn't *all* I told her, by any means! Henry was quite right: Nancy can effortlessly abstract information by a kind of osmosis.

She certainly didn't pump me, yet by the time I'd finished making my cake, I'd also expanded a bit on what Henry had told her about my rather dysfunctional upbringing, too.

'Granny and her husband didn't have any children, so they adopted Dad, who was the illegitimate child of a distant relative. Then along *I* came, the result of a very out-of-character liaison Dad had with another student at university and poor Granny felt compelled to take me on, too!'

'Poor child, rather,' Nancy said.

'Oh, no, I think it was definitely poor Granny! She and a friend had hoped to travel extensively, once they'd both retired, but after a while they managed to arrange things so they still could.'

'Ah, yes, Henry told me about your best friend. Liam, the

son of your childminder, who used to look after you when they were away. But first love doesn't always endure and it was so sad that relationships came unstuck for both you and Henry in Avignon. Though, of course, these things often work out for the best, however little you think so at the time.'

By now, I felt that our lives were an open book to Nancy, but somehow I didn't mind. Her interest in us was what I could only describe as benevolent.

'God meant you and Henry to be free to come and help Sabine, in her hour of need,' she said, with one of her beaming smiles, then got up. 'I'd better go and see if Sabine is stirring yet – and is that pineapple sponge for today's dessert? So delicious, served in moist slices, with cream.'

'It is dessert, but for tomorrow, and there will definitely be cream,' I said.

When she'd gone, I made another mug of coffee and sat looking through my Christmas and Boxing Day dinner menus and timing planner while the cake was baking.

Xan managed to persuade me out for a short walk with Plum – just half an hour – and the icy touch of the air did freshen me up after all that cooking. We went down to the Winter Garden, pausing to admire the daffodils and the deceptively frail blossom of the witch hazel, then on to the lake.

We were both quiet, though it was a comfortable, friendly silence, only broken when we stopped by the temple folly.

'It's a pity we haven't got time to skate again today,' Xan said. 'We might have done, after dinner, but we'll be watching that home movie instead.'

'Probably just as well, because I still have bruises from last time,' I told him. 'But maybe the ice will stay firm for a few days yet.'

'When the sun's out, it does melt the surface a little, but then it seems to freeze again even more overnight,' he said. 'It's certainly very thick.'

I looked at my watch. 'I'd better get back and check on my dumplings.'

'That's something no other girl has ever said to me,' he told me with a grin, bending to scoop up Plum, who was about to wander out on to the ice, and tucking him under his arm.

We took the path that led behind the little temple and joined the wider track up to the house.

It was sheltered by the trees and very peaceful. A wood pigeon was making its soft, repetitive cooing, but it was not the call of the wild that was drawing me on, now, but the call of the kitchen.

After everyone had had time to recover from their hearty Sunday dinner, Xan set up the projector and screen in the drawing room and arranged the sofa and chairs in front of it.

When all was ready, he came to tell us, and Henry and I slipped in and took discreet chairs at the back of the room. Sabine and Nancy sat together on a small buttoned velvet sofa and Lucy in a large armchair, which gave the impression of having swallowed her up whole, since all that could be seen of her was her dangling feet.

When everyone was comfortably settled, Henry turned the lights off at a nod from Xan and the film began to unroll, in the slightly flickering manner of its kind.

'Oh, it's a picnic at our favourite cove!' Sabine cried. 'Do you remember it, Nancy? We took you and Stephen there more than once, when you were holidaying with us. You could only reach it from the sea, so we sailed there in a flotilla of small boats.'

'I do remember. It had a perfect little half-moon beach and

the cliffs surrounding it made it seem very private,' Nancy agreed. 'See, some of the men are lighting a fire to make tea for the picnic, just as we did.'

There was quite a large group of people, but it was easy to spot the tall, broad and golden-haired Asa Powys and a young, bronzed and glowing Sabine having fun among their friends.

Mrs Powys murmured a few of their names – some of them those of artist and writers I'd heard of.

'And there's Tommy and Rose,' Xan said, pointing his grand-parents out. He'd clearly inherited his dark good looks from his grandfather.

The film paused and then began again on a different scene, though some of the people in it were the same. This time, they were wearing more clothes and wandering around in some ruins. A few of them were seated on fallen masonry, near open picnic baskets.

'You'd think our lives had been one long picnic!' Sabine said, amused, then leaned forward for a better look. 'That's the ruins of a small temple in the hills, just above the spot offshore where we discovered the remains of a drowned town. Asa was con-vinced that the temple must be part of a larger complex, linked to the vanished port.'

'And as soon as he began to excavate there later, he was proved quite right, wasn't he?' said Nancy.

'Yes, of course, it was a great discovery,' Sabine agreed, though the brightness had gone out of her voice a little. 'Naturally, it never quite compensated for having to give up underwater archaeology – his first passion – but he devoted himself to his work there.'

'I'm looking forward to hearing more about those years and the fantastic discoveries he made at the site,' said Xan. 'I've already read his book and articles about it.'

More of the figures on the screen were gathering round the picnic baskets now and seemed to be unpacking wine bottles and food on to rugs laid down nearby. A young boy drove a herd of goats past them, glancing curiously at the group as he went.

Then the picture flickered once more and the scene vanished into whiteness.

'That's as far as I got when I checked it and seems to be the end,' Xan began, then broke off as a new scene unfolded. 'No, wait, I think there might be a little more I missed.'

'Not another picnic, I hope,' said Sabine.

'It doesn't look like it. In fact, isn't that the garden of your villa, Sabine?' asked Nancy. 'There seems to be a party going on!'

'You're right,' said Mrs Powys, 'and since everyone is in fancy dress, it must be one of Asa's birthday celebrations.'

By now, I recognized many of the guests, though there were several new faces among the groups of people standing in the shade of what I thought might be olive trees. Most wore some kind of fancy dress, mainly the sort of toga that anyone can produce from a white bedsheet.

When the camera panned right around, though, it showed the unmistakably tall and elegant figure of Sabine, attired in an Ancient Egyptian-style robe of gauzy fabric, with a tall headdress. She was laughing and talking to the friends around her, but her gaze seemed to be fixed on something – or someone – beyond them. Then the camera moved on and there was Asa, bronzed, bare-chested and splendid, wearing a short white kilted garment and a striped and folded headdress, so that he looked as if he'd stepped straight out of an Egyptian tomb painting.

He was – as I suspected he always had been – the centre of a large group . . . and standing very close to him, with her back to the camera, her hand on his arm and her head tilted back so she could look up into his face, was the small, slender figure of a woman.

Asa Powys bent his head down to speak to her and Sabine suddenly cried, with shocking harshness: 'Turn it off! Turn it off *now!*'

Xan did so instantly and Henry got up and put on the lights.

Nancy said calmly, 'That was your half-sister, Faye, wasn't it, Sabine? The only time she came out to stay with you on Corfu.'

'And look how *that* ended,' Sabine said with extreme bitterness. 'She destroyed everything we'd worked to achieve.'

'Not *everything*, darling, don't exaggerate,' Nancy said. 'You rebuilt your lives a little differently afterwards, that's all.'

I'd forgotten Lucy was there until her small face, with its inquisitive, pink-tipped nose, appeared around the side of the chair. She seemed oblivious to any underlying tensions.

'Which one was Faye? I've never seen even a photograph of her before!'

No one replied, but Xan said, 'I'm so sorry, Sabine. I'd no idea that was on the end of the film. I should have let it run on when I checked it.'

'You weren't to know,' Sabine said, sounding more like herself again. 'It was just . . . a shock to suddenly see her like that.'

Henry and I exchanged glances and slipped quietly out of the room.

As we made our way back to the staff wing, I said, 'Xan told me the other day that Mrs Powys had a half-sister, but she'd died young, so it was better never to mention her. It sounds as if there was no love lost between them, doesn't it?'

'It does, and it seems to be connected with something that happened on Corfu, years ago,' Henry agreed. 'Perhaps I could pump Xan about it after—'

'Henry, don't you dare! Whatever it is, knowing about it isn't going to help us do our job better, is it?'

'It might, if it's something we need to avoid bringing up,' he suggested.

'Yeah, and my pineapple upside-down cake is the universal panacea that cures all ills, past and present,' I said sarcastically.

'What's a universal panacea?' asked Nancy, coming into the kitchen, followed by Xan and Plum.

'Pineapple upside-down cake,' Henry explained. 'But it's just a theory.'

'I think hot chocolate works as well as anything,' Nancy said. 'Sabine has gone to lie down and I'm going to take her some. There's nothing quite as comforting when you've had a shock – and suddenly seeing Faye in that film, when she wasn't expecting it, *was* a shock.'

'I'd never have brought it if I'd known that party was at the end of it,' Xan said remorsefully. 'Tommy told me all about the accident, of course, which must have happened only a few days after the party.'

'I think I'd better explain a little to Dido and Henry, so they don't inadvertently say the wrong thing to Sabine,' Nancy suggested.

'Just what I was saying to Dido! And I, at least, am entirely consumed by curiosity, too,' confessed Henry.

'I still don't think it's any of our business,' I told him.

'Ignore her, Nancy,' Henry said. 'Tell all!'

'It's not a very edifying story, dear, and poor Faye is long dead now,' Nancy said. 'She was Sabine's half-sister by the stepmother she loathed and resented, and eight years Sabine's junior, which is quite an age difference. Sabine had little to do with her and after her parents were killed in a car crash, Faye was left to the guardianship of her mother's cousin and the family solicitor, the uncle of Sabine's present one, Mr Makepeace.'

While she was talking, Nancy began to get out mugs and milk for the hot chocolate.

'Anyone else for cocoa? No? Right,' she said, then carried on with her story. 'I'm afraid Faye was rather a wild child and had been expelled from one boarding school, even before her parents' death – sneaking out to meet boys in the village. Then, when she was just seventeen, she was expelled from another. A visiting music teacher this time, quite a scandal.'

'She sounds . . . an enterprising kind of girl,' I said.

'Her guardians didn't know quite what to do with her. Finding another school at that stage seemed pointless. Then some of the solicitor's friends, who were going out to Greece, offered to escort Faye to her half-sister's house and bring her back some weeks later, on their return. Her guardians leaped on the idea with loud cries of joy and relief, from what I gathered from Sabine at the time.'

'I'm surprised Mrs Powys agreed to have her to stay,' Henry said, interested.

'Oh, they didn't wait for a reply from Sabine; the girl was on her way there before she knew of it.'

'Difficult,' Henry said. 'I suppose she could hardly turn away her own half-sister!'

'No, and Asa, who was a kind and generous man, persuaded Sabine to make the best of it. So they taught the girl to dive and took her about with them. But it didn't take long before she showed her true colours, after falling in with a group of young people from a yacht that was moored in the harbour – the spoilt children of wealthy parents – and began sneaking out at night to go to parties on board. I think we called the idle rich "Beautiful People" at the time,' she added vaguely. 'Or maybe that was later?'

'We get the picture, anyway, and she sounds like a nightmare,' I said. 'Still, at least it was only for a few weeks.'

'Oh, she vanished before she was due to go home,' Nancy said. 'Xan, you tell them the rest, about the diving accident. It's all hearsay anyway, but at least you heard about it from your grandparents, who were there.'

'OK,' said Xan, who was sitting on the end of the table. 'Here goes. They were diving just off the coast, in fairly shallow water, but it was an overcast and choppy day, so you couldn't really see much below the surface from the boat. You pair up for safety when diving, so there was Asa and Tommy, and Sabine and Faye. When it was time to come back up, Asa saw that Faye had moved down a gully to look at a wartime wreck, instead of sticking near Sabine, as she was supposed to do. But Asa signalled to Sabine to go up with Tommy, while he fetched her.'

He paused and Henry said, 'Do go on, I'm all ears!'

'Sabine and Tommy swam to the boat, but there was no sign of the others, and then Faye came up on her own, without her mouthpiece in and half drowned. They hauled her on to the boat, but Tommy went straight back down and came up with Asa, who was semi-conscious and had had some kind of heart attack.'

'How horrible!' I said, staring at him. 'No wonder Mrs Powys hates to be reminded of that time!'

'But we know he was all right later, because he excavated the temple site,' Henry pointed out.

'Yes, he made a good recovery, but as you can imagine, it was all panic and pandemonium while they got him on board the boat and tried to bring him round.'

'You're putting it so well, dear, that I'll leave you to it and take up this cocoa. Don't forget the bit about murder.'

Nancy went out, carrying the mugs carefully, and Henry turned expectantly back to Xan, who shrugged.

'There wasn't any murder, though I'm sure Sabine might have tried to kill Faye later, if she hadn't run off that night. It's just that as soon as Faye had stopped coughing up seawater, she insisted Asa had tried to kill her – but she was hysterical, and it was so silly anyway, that no one took any notice.'

'But it was just an accident?' I asked.

'Yes, Faye had swum into the wreck and snagged her air pipes, and instead of remembering what she'd been taught, struggled so much she jerked off her mouthpiece. Asa got hold of her to calm her down and help – and that's when he had the seizure.'

'I can understand now why Mrs Powys blames her half-sister,' I said. 'If she'd done as she was told and stayed near Sabine, it would never have happened.'

'It might still have happened some time, because it turned out he had an undiagnosed heart condition,' Xan said. 'He always seemed so strong and healthy that no one ever suspected it.'

'And you said Faye ran off that night?' Henry asked.

'My grandmother, Rose, had been on the boat that day and took Faye back to the villa, while the others got Asa to the nearest hospital. But she vanished in the night, bag and baggage. They found out much later she'd sailed off on the floating gin palace with what Nancy called the Beautiful People, but of course, by the time they traced it to the South of France, the trail was cold.'

'It's like a mystery novel!' I said. 'Did she ever reappear?'

'Briefly, a few years later, to claim some money her father had left her. Then, not long after, she died. It appeared she'd got the sailing bug and the yacht she was on went down in a storm, with no survivors.'

'She sounded annoying enough to have got pushed overboard,' Henry said uncharitably.

'She was very young, so it was still a bit of a tragedy all round,' I said. 'I assume the heart condition put an end to Asa diving again, Xan?'

'He was advised against it, and Sabine wouldn't dive without him,' he agreed. 'Asa turned his attention to excavating that temple complex and life was still good, but I'm sure it was never quite the same as those first wonderful years of their marriage.'

We were all silent for a moment and then I said, 'Well, I'm glad now that you did tell us, after all, because I'll be very careful not to say anything that might remind Mrs Powys about it.'

'I can't really avoid touching on it when we're recording her memories,' Xan said. 'Some time soon we'll have to move on from the early years of their underwater explorations, to the land-based ones and I'll have to at least mention the reason for the change.'

He sighed and then looked at me. 'I suppose I can't persuade you to come and do a bit of therapeutic dusting? I could do with some company.'

'You go and enjoy yourself, in your own peculiar way,' said Henry kindly. 'There's a quiche for cold supper in the fridge, isn't there? And I'll cut some sandwiches.'

'My hero!' I said gratefully.

Sabine

Later, I tried to explain to Nancy why I'd been so very upset at seeing that film of the party.

'It wasn't just seeing Faye, or that the party took place only a few days before Asa was taken ill,' I said. 'We'd invited the usual crowd for Asa's birthday bash, and then Faye's new friends from the yacht turned up, with hangers-on, all more than half-drunk and making a nuisance of themselves. Faye had invited them without asking, but Asa was so easy-going, he didn't really mind . . .'

'I don't suppose he did,' Nancy agreed. 'And anyway, I expect he and his friends could have got rid of them easily enough, had they got really rowdy.'

'Yes, and that's what they had to do in the end. Faye sneaked off with them, though we didn't notice till much later. By then, we were counting down the days until the people who'd brought her out to us came back and collected her!'

'It was very bad of her guardians to dump her on you without notice, in the first place,' Nancy said. 'But I expect they were at their wits' end wondering what to do with her after that second school expelled her, and they thought a change of scene might do her good.'

'It didn't do *us* good,' I said bitterly, then confessed, 'But what *really* upset me in that film, Nancy, was the way Faye was standing so close to Asa, looking up at him and he—'

'Now, you know Asa could be silly with young women. It was his great weakness,' Nancy interrupted. 'And of course, they could rarely resist him, even though he was so much older. But despite that, it was never in question that he absolutely adored you and you were the centre of his life.'

'I know – and that these . . . *flirtations* meant nothing, but that didn't stop them hurting.'

Nancy reached across and patted my hand. 'Of course, but we all have our weaknesses, and you and Asa had a long and very happy marriage, despite these peccadillos.'

'We did,' I agreed, 'though, thanks to Faye, things were never quite the same again. Her name was never mentioned between us after she ran off.'

'Never?'

'Well, very rarely. I told Asa when she turned twenty-one and the solicitor informed me she'd turned up to claim her inheritance from my father, and then again, a few years later, when I was told she was dead.'

Nancy patted my hand again. 'Your lives took a new course after Asa's illness, but I think, once he'd recovered his health and thrown himself into the temple excavations with his usual enthusiasm, he found something that engrossed him almost as much as his marine archaeology.'

'He did always immerse himself whole-heartedly into everything he did.' I smiled wryly. 'And of course, *I* followed him wherever he led.'

'There, then,' she said. 'And as to that little vignette in the film, I dare say Faye was *trying* to flirt with him, but I saw nothing in his manner that wasn't avuncular – and since she was such a young girl and your half-sister, how could it be otherwise?'

'No . . . you're quite right, of course,' I said with a sigh.

'I expect she had a young man of her own in that party from the yacht, if she went off with them after the accident,' Nancy said.

'But she wasn't on it when they traced it to the South of France, was she?'

'No, and though her guardians tried to find her, the trail was dead. You know, despite her failings, hers is rather a sad story really, isn't it, Sabine? Her parents dying while she was still in her early teens, farmed out to guardians and then dumped with a half-sister who disliked and resented her . . .'

'I did my best with her, while she was staying with us,' I protested.

'I'm sure you did. And perhaps she found some happiness in her short life, wherever it was she settled,' Nancy said. 'But she's long gone now and it's time to forget old, bitter feelings and let go of the bad parts of the past. You'll feel so much better for it,' she assured me. 'Why don't you tell Xan in the morning that you'd like to record a brief description of the accident and how it led to a new and exciting turn in yours and Asa's careers? I'm sure you'd find it cathartic and then you could move on from that point.'

'I expect you're right,' I admitted, though I knew a spark of that hatred for Faye would continue to burn deep in my heart.

'Let's talk about something nicer,' Nancy said, filling our whisky glasses up. 'It's so pleasantly wicked, letting our hair down in the evenings, like this! I only allow myself one tot of whisky at home.'

'I promise not to tell on you,' I said, and she grinned.

'And we still have all the joy of celebrating Christmas with family and friends to come!' she said with a happy sigh. 'I've written a very special grace to read for before Christmas dinner.'

'It's not one of your long ones, is it?' I asked suspiciously.

'Oh, no,' she assured me innocently, but past experience made me hope the food was still hot by the time she'd finished.

30

Picture This

On Sunday night, without forewarning, the sky had inconveniently dumped a vast blanket of soft snow over the landscape, and though Henry, after the newspaper run, reported the lanes already snowploughed clear, he said it lay banked up high on the verges.

I thought Mrs Powys's manner towards me seemed to have turned even chillier, too, if that was possible, though Henry said I was imagining it.

Not that it mattered to me, really, for I was becoming increasingly engrossed in preparations for the arrival of the rest of the guests on Friday and focusing on the Christmas catering.

Not one, but two fine hams had been delivered and were now in the larder, with the Christmas cake and football-sized pudding.

I checked and rechecked lists, timetables and menus, and pinned them up on the big corkboard in the kitchen, made out the final supermarket shopping order for Henry and filled the freezers with pies, puddings, pasties, quiches, tarts and fruit crumbles, along with anything else that could be made in advance and pre-frozen.

Henry did a little baking on his own account – nibbles, cakes and starters – but he's much more laid-back about these things and, in any case, can whip up a batch of Parmesan puffs, or savoury vol-au-vents at the drop of a hat.

It wasn't *all* work over the next couple of days, though. Xan persuaded me back on to the ice again, and this time, I managed to stay upright and move of my own volition, even if I did still need to hang on to him.

And Henry took his snowboard out each day and then thawed out over coffee with Simon in his cottage, though he said, since his central heating boiler was still giving problems, it wasn't all that much warmer inside the house than out, unless you were sitting next to the small log burner in the sitting room.

It was no wonder the poor man liked to join our evening film sessions: it was probably the only time he felt really warm!

But I knew these cosy evenings must come to an end once the guests arrived – as must my enjoyable early-afternoon sessions in the study with Xan. At least I'd almost finished cleaning the long run of shelves along one wall, and I hoped that by Wednesday, I'd have arrived at the last stack, next to the door to the library. That would give me almost as much a sense of satisfaction as cooking up a very special dinner!

Nancy, Mrs Powys and Lucy went out after breakfast as usual on Wednesday, when the team of cleaners were to carry out their final visit before the Christmas break.

When they moved their activities downstairs, Henry and I made up the beds in the guest bedrooms and put out the clean towels and soap, ready.

The Melling family were still due to arrive on Friday, in time for tea, as was Lucy's brother, Nigel, but Mrs Powys had told Henry that the solicitor, Mr Makepeace and Mrs Martin, his granddaughter, would not now be here until after lunch on Saturday.

After the bed making, Henry decided to go out and do a little last-minute Christmas shopping, so I gave him a list of a few small extra presents to buy for me. I'd decided to give copies of my latest book to Mrs Powys, Nancy and Xan, so it seemed mean not to get something for Lucy. And Simon, too.

'A nice box of chocolates for Lucy . . . and perhaps a big pot of Gentleman's Relish for Simon, because I know he prefers savoury things. That should do it.'

'I'm going to get a little something for everyone, too,' Henry agreed, though goodness knows what, because his gift ideas tend to be a bit random.

Xan, emerging from the study just before Henry left, decided to go with him. Perhaps he felt the need to buy more presents, too, or just wanted a change of scene.

It was odd that I hadn't felt any desire to leave the estate since I got there, though I suppose I would have done if Charlotte had been able to meet me somewhere local. We'd have to make do with a long catch-up phone call, once she finally arrived to join her family near Hexham.

Xan left Plum with me, or rather, he left him fast asleep in the study, with the doors open, so if he woke he could come and find me.

It was an odd feeling when they'd gone and it was just me, other than the distant noises of the cleaners and the laundress's radio.

But I had lots to occupy myself with, so the time flew by. Plum, with impeccable timing, arrived to share my sandwich lunch and then, as the cleaners were approaching the staff wing, I told them I was taking Plum out for a walk in the garden and wouldn't be long.

The path across the lawn was snowy and Plum waded through it stoically, but once we'd gone down the first flight of steps, the garden was more sheltered by the rocky walls and overarching shrubs, so it was much easier going.

I stopped for a long time in the Winter Garden, lost in thought among the snowdrops, until Plum barked imperatively, waking me to the realization that my feet were frozen, my nose probably resembling an iced cherry and my fingers, even in their woolly gloves, entirely numb.

Plum wanted to be carried now and, small though he was, by the time we'd been down to the frozen lake and then all the way back up to the house again, he seemed to have doubled in weight.

I towelled him dry in the scullery as the cleaning team began to pack up their equipment and, soon after, departed.

Then, for the first time, I had the whole house entirely to myself.

Apart from Plum, of course.

Henry and Xan returned while I was still thawing out my fingers around a second mug of coffee, but vanished into the study for a mysterious wrapping session, from which I was banned, though Henry did show me the large box of pink champagne truffles for Lucy and Simon's pot of Gentleman's Relish, which he proposed we gave as joint presents.

I had a wrapping session of my own, with Henry's little painting I'd brought back from California and the three books. I'd ordered something for Plum, too, but that hadn't yet arrived.

I put our gifts under the tree in the staff sitting room and Henry, looking mysterious, came in and added one or two more.

'Right, now I'm going to light the fire in the sitting room so it's nice and cosy when Nancy and Mrs Powys get back.'

'With this central heating, it's always cosy.'

'I know, I think it's the warmest big house I've ever stayed in,' he agreed. 'There's something nice about a real fire, though. I might light the one in the Great Hall again, too. And then, when I get back, I'm going to whip up some vol-au-vents and curry puffs.'

'I love your curry puffs!' I said.

'I know, and I'll make enough for us, too,' he promised. 'And I'm sure you've been working yourself to the bone while we were out gallivanting, so why don't you treat yourself to an extra-long cleaning session in the study? Xan said he hoped you might finish the long run of bookshelves today.'

'I'd certainly like to,' I said, wavering. 'And I do have everything well in hand. Dinner is just steak and chips again, which apparently is a favourite of Nancy as well as Mrs Powys, so my cordon bleu skills are not exactly going to be challenged.'

'There you are, then. I'll make you both coffee while you change and then you can take it through with you – and remove this silly dog, too. I've fallen over him twice and I haven't even started baking yet!'

Xan and I drank our coffee and then began on the final run of bookshelves, which he insisted on helping me with.

'If we do it together, we can finish it today,' he said. 'I expect after that you'll be too busy to help me till after Christmas.'

'Probably – but once the guests have gone again, I'm looking forward to cleaning out the curio cabinets next! They can't be airtight, because everything in them is furry with dust.'

'You have a strange idea of fun,' he said, smiling at me. 'Come on, let's get going. We'll do things differently this time and remove *all* the books first, instead of one shelf at a time, and put them in stacks on the trestle tables for dusting.'

'I expect that will be faster,' I agreed and he started passing me books from the bottom shelf.

I don't think Maria had even run a feather duster along the top of the books in this section and there was enough dust to make both of us sneeze – not to mention Plum, who had inconveniently fallen asleep underfoot and now woke, making indignant wheezing noises, before removing himself to his favourite spot on the sofa.

Xan pulled up the mahogany library steps to reach the higher shelves, so I now got peppered with dust when he passed the books down to me.

'It's a funny mix of books up here,' he said, after a bit. 'Learned tomes and paperback thrillers, all mixed up with what looks like Asa's boyhood reading: hardbacks of *Treasure Island* and *Boy's Own* adventure stories!'

'It's nice that he kept his old books,' I said, clapping a copy of *The Coral Island* together and dislodging a small, semi-transparent paper packet of stamps, which seemed to have been used as a bookmark.

I showed it to Xan, who said he didn't think Asa would have used a Penny Black as a bookmark, even as a child.

'These are French, anyway, I think,' I said, opening the top and taking a closer look.

'Definitely not Penny Blacks, then,' he said, going up another step to reach the second shelf from the top. He handed down more of the same odd mix and then climbed down holding a large, leather-covered tome with faded golden cord and tassels hanging from the spines.

'It's an old photograph album,' he said, opening it carefully and turning a couple of pages. 'I think it must be Asa's family one – and it looks a bit fragile.'

'I'll dust it very carefully, then,' I promised. 'And if we leave it out, you might find some photos of Asa as a boy in there for the biography?'

'Yes, put it to one side so I can look at it properly later. Sabine might like to see it, too.'

I gently laid it down at one end of the table, while Xan climbed back up to the top of the steps.

'One more shelf,' he said, and I reached up to take the first of the books from it: large hardback children's books about history, archaeology, and ancient Egypt. Asa obviously had an early interest in the subject.

'I think I've found his boyhood stamp album up here in the corner,' he said. 'Yes – with all the stamps firmly stuck in place and, I'm sure, entirely worthless!'

I took it from him and flicked over the pages.

'I expect he had lots of fun filling it, though,' I said, then looked up. 'Is that it?'

'No, there's something right in the corner – another photograph album, I think, but a more recent one from the look of it.'

He climbed down, holding an album covered in what looked like padded white vinyl, that had yellowed on the spine. The front was embossed with lurid orange daisies.

'I have to say, compared to the other, that one looks a bit cheap and tacky.'

'Not quite up to the standard one expects in the dear old Castle?' he joked, and opened the cover.

'Ah, that explains it!' he said, enlightened. 'This seems to have belonged to Sabine's detested stepmother, so it's only surprising it's here at all, and hasn't long since been consigned to a bonfire!'

He flicked over a couple more of the pages and a large

photograph slid out and then fluttered down, as if it had a strange, moth-like life of its own, finally coming to rest face-down on the carpet at my feet.

I bent and picked it up, turning it over curiously. It was clearly of a family group – a thin, stooping, scholarly-looking man and a plump, but well-corseted woman, with a teenage girl standing between them.

I stared down uncomprehendingly at the girl's winsome face, with its tip-tilted nose and wide-apart eyes, framed in chestnut curls.

'What on earth's the matter, Dido?' Xan demanded. 'You've gone as white as a ghost!'

'It's not *me* that's the ghost,' I said incoherently, and pointed at the photograph. 'Who is that, in the middle?'

'It's Sabine's half-sister, Faye. I've seen her before in old photographs from when she was on Corfu.'

'Well, *I've* seen this photograph before – and she's also *my* grandmother!'

31

Relativity

Xan stared at me, a blank expression in his eyes and his dark brows drawn together in a frown.

'But . . . that's impossible! Faye didn't have any children and died quite young.'

'She must have had *one* child, at least – my father!' I told him. 'Xan, I know it seems incredible, but Granny Celia has an identical print of that picture in a box of old photographs and she told me the girl was a distant relative and also Dad's birth mother, but had turned out badly. She never would tell me any more about her, though.'

I remembered something else. 'You know, when you and Nancy were telling us about Faye last night, I did think that was the name of Dad's mother, too . . . but then I thought perhaps I'd misremembered and it was perhaps Gaye, instead.'

I looked down at the photo again and this time realized the family group were standing outside the door to the Great Hall. I could see the columns holding up the portico.

'You *are* absolutely certain?' Xan asked, but I think he already knew the answer from my stunned reaction.

I nodded. 'But I still can't believe this is happening! It's just too much of a coincidence that I should have been hired to come here, where Faye once lived!'

'Coincidences do happen . . . but you had no idea about the connection before this?' He looked at me searchingly and then answered his own question: 'No, of course you hadn't!'

He was silent for a few moments while he seemed to be turning it all over in his mind. Eventually, he said slowly, 'So . . . if we accept this is true, then Faye must have had an illegitimate child – your father.'

'If you remember, I did once tell you he was the illegitimate child of a distant relative of Granny Celia's, but I'm positive Dad has no idea about the connection with the family here at Mitras Castle, either. He doesn't even *remember* his real mother.'

'Let's try and piece this together,' Xan said. 'I know from Sabine that one of Faye's guardians after her parents died was her mother's cousin – so presumably that would have been your Granny Celia.'

'Celia Sedley Jones,' I agreed. 'And you told us that Faye came back at twenty-one to claim her inheritance, didn't you?'

'I did, but not that she had an illegitimate child in tow, as she must have done,' he pointed out. 'Still, if you accept that, then it does all seem to hang together, doesn't it?'

'It all fits . . .' I pressed a hand to my burning forehead. I'd been going hot and cold by turns, ever since I'd recognized the girl in the photograph.

'But I still find it hard to grasp the incredible coincidence of Mrs Powys employing me, without realizing that I was related to her, through the half-sister she obviously hated!'

'It *is* a *big* ask, isn't it?' Xan said, in an oddly dry voice, but I was now clutching his arm urgently.

'Xan, she must *never* find out! We'll have to keep this a secret from her, or it will ruin her last Christmas at the Castle!'

He gave me a wry, but affectionate smile. 'You always think of others before yourself, Dido. I don't believe you've given a thought to what this might mean to you.'

'Mean to me . . . ?' I echoed – and then the latch of the library door clicked loudly and we turned as one, to see Nancy, still in her outdoor coat and with her white hair even more flyaway than usual.

'Hello, you two, we're home,' she announced gaily, and then something about our expressions must have alerted her, for she came right into the room and closed the door behind her.

'What's the matter?' she asked.

I gripped Xan's arm again and whispered: 'No, please don't tell her!'

He put his warm hand over mine and said, reassuringly, 'It's the best thing we can do, Dido. We need Nancy's advice!'

'Yes, do tell me whatever is troubling you. I can see something is,' she invited.

Xan made a better job of explaining it all than I could ever have done, probably because he could fit my family history into Mrs Powys's more easily, and by the time he'd finished, it did seem like a jigsaw that fitted perfectly together.

Nancy listened with an air of surprised interest and seemed to agree. When Xan had finished, she said that it all made perfect sense.

'Sabine once told me that Faye had made her way to America after she'd run away and went back there after she claimed her inheritance, so she must have met someone out there and had the child – your father, Dido.'

'Dad vaguely remembers being in what he thinks was a hippy commune in California, but he was only about four when Granny Celia adopted him. I'm sure he doesn't know any more about Faye than I did. Granny never would talk about her.'

'Adoptive parents can be like that sometimes,' Nancy observed, sagely. 'And given Faye's past behaviour, it's hardly surprising that your granny wanted to forget about Faye, and about any connection to the family here at the Castle.'

'I suppose so,' I agreed. 'And I must say that nothing I've been hearing about Faye has made me happy to be related to her!'

'Oh, I don't think she was *bad*, just silly and very self-centred,' Nancy assured me. 'One of those people who think only of themselves and what *they* want.'

But those were hardly endearing qualities, either!

I realized Xan had been right to tell Nancy and get the benefit of her common sense advice about the situation we found ourselves in.

I'd started to feel less shaky and managed to smile at Nancy. 'It's been a shock and it'll take me some time before it all sinks in, but what's important right now is that we make sure Mrs Powys doesn't find out, so Henry and I can carry on doing the job we were hired to do – and make sure her Christmas is everything she longed for.'

'But my dear child,' began Nancy, 'you can't deny the relationship. Your grandmother was brought up in this very house!'

'I know, and perhaps that explains the odd feeling of connection with it that I've had from the moment I got here,' I admitted. 'But as to the relationship, I'm only the daughter of an illegitimate child of Mrs Powys's hated half-sister,' I pointed out. 'What's the point of dragging that out into the open? Can't we just quietly pretend we never discovered it at all?'

I saw her exchange a glance with Xan that puzzled me and then she said rather drily, 'I don't think there will be any need to tell Sabine, do you, Xan? And here *is* Sabine,' she added as the door opened once more. 'Have you come to find out where I've got to, Sabine?'

'Yes, you've been ages, Nancy!'

Her cool blue eyes took us all in and she raised one pencilled dark eyebrow.

'Why are you all standing around like a group of conspirators?'

'Because we've just worked out exactly who Dido is – Faye's granddaughter. But of course you already knew that,' Nancy said calmly. 'I was sure you were holding out on me about *something*, Sabine, but I have to say, this has all come as quite a surprise!'

'That's the understatement of the century,' I muttered involuntarily, and Xan made a small snorting noise as if he was trying not to laugh, though laughing was the last thing *I* felt like doing at that moment.

Mrs Powys looked perfectly composed as her glacial eyes briefly rested on me.

'Yes, I've known about Dido's father since that Sedley Jones woman adopted him, but I only found out about Dido fairly recently. I was sure she didn't know, and *I* had no intention of telling her or anyone else – even you, Nancy.'

'But – *how* did you know?' I asked blankly.

'The solicitor informed me when Faye came back to claim her inheritance – and that she'd had an illegitimate child, which her mother's cousin was to adopt. I had a private detective take a picture of the boy, out of curiosity, but he was totally nondescript and uninteresting . . . and I didn't give him another thought until recently, when I suddenly wondered how he'd turned out.'

'I see,' said Nancy. 'Dido says her father is the curator of an extensive private art collection in California, so he's done very well. I suppose he takes after your father in that way, Sabine?

He had an interest in an antique shop in London and used to buy stock at country house sales for it, didn't he?'

'Yes, and when I had a more recent photo sent to me, I realized he looked a little like my father, too.'

'I thought there was something familiar about *Dido* as soon as I saw her,' Nancy reminded her.

'I can't imagine what, since she's only related through my father, and she doesn't look anything like the Mordue side of the family.'

'So, when your private detective checked up on what Dido's father was doing now, he discovered there was another generation – Dido?' said Xan.

Sabine nodded. 'And when he told me that she and Henry were running this house party service, just when Maria had become unable to cope on her own and I needed help over Christmas – well, it seemed somehow meant to be.'

'But surely, knowing who I was, you couldn't want me in the same house?' I said, puzzled.

'I was curious, and since neither you nor your father had ever contacted me, I was sure you couldn't know about the relationship.' She shrugged her thin, elegant shoulders. 'Heavenly Houseparties sounded just what I needed and I could assuage my curiosity at the same time, without you ever discovering the truth.'

Nancy was eyeing her narrowly. 'I don't think that was entirely fair to Dido, Sabine.'

But at least now I understood why Mrs Powys had seemed to dislike me from the start, even if expediency and sheer curiosity had been enough to make my presence in the house bearable to her.

'So, where do we go from here?' asked Nancy.

Mrs Powys looked faintly surprised. 'We carry on as before,

of course. I expect Dido won't now assume she's here in any other capacity than her professional one, or presume on this unfortunate relationship.'

'Certainly not, Mrs Powys,' I assured her. 'I'm here to do a job and I'll continue to carry it out to the best of my ability. The relationship remains *purely* professional.'

'In that case, I don't think there's anything more to discuss,' she said coolly. 'And I see no need to inform Lucy – or indeed, anyone else – about any of this.'

Nancy opened and closed her mouth a couple of times as if struggling to get words out.

'But, Sabine, you can't possibly—' she finally began.

But Mrs Powys said to me, as if nothing of any moment had passed between us, 'I suppose we *are* to have tea at some point this afternoon?'

And then she turned and swept out.

'Oh, *honestly!*' exclaimed Nancy, and hurried after her.

Sabine

Nancy followed me back into the sitting room and closed the door to the hall behind her.

'Really, Sabine! I knew you were keeping something from me, but I never imagined it was anything like this! I assume Asa had no idea Faye had had a child, either?'

'No, I couldn't see any point in telling him. After Faye vanished we barely mentioned her again anyway, just got on with rebuilding our lives and settling down to the new order. Once Asa was well enough, he threw himself into the temple excavations and we were happy again, even if it wasn't quite the same.'

'I know you told him when Faye turned up again to collect her father's legacy,' Nancy said. 'You just left out the bit about the child she'd had!'

I shrugged and then sat down by the fire. 'I don't think even Timothy Makepeace, my present solicitor, knows about it, because it was his uncle who managed our affairs back then.'

Nancy planted herself in front of me.

'Still, you were curious enough at the time to obtain a picture of the child – Dido's father – and again, more recently, to find out what had become of him?'

'After my diagnosis, I suddenly felt I wanted to tie up all the loose ends in my life . . . and, yes, I wondered what had become of him.'

'And discovered he'd carved out a very successful career for himself?'

'He does appear to be an expert in his field,' I agreed. 'My detective found that Dido was the result of a brief liaison he had while at university and Celia Sedley Jones became her guardian and brought her up. Keeping it in the family, as it were.'

'And presumably the detective told you about Heavenly Houseparties, too?'

'He did and sent me the link to the website and, as I said, since Maria's husband had had the stroke and she was finding it hard to cope with her work here even before that, I thought I'd kill two birds with one stone and hire them.'

'If you expect me to believe that curiosity and the desire to have someone to cater for your guests were your main incentive, then you have vastly underrated my intelligence,' Nancy said acutely, though at least she now sat down.

I gave a wry smile. 'I knew you'd see right through me! So yes, I admit I had an ulterior motive and once I knew about Heavenly Houseparties, I went all out to obtain their services over Christmas. I even paid the woman who'd already booked them to cancel!'

'But *why*, Sabine?' she asked more gently.

'For what you'll think the worst of reasons. I wanted to revenge myself on Faye for what she did, through her grand-child. And employing Dido in a menial capacity in what had once been Faye's home seemed a good way to do it.'

'No, it was a *bad* way, but I'm sure, in your heart, you already knew that,' Nancy said. 'And it was in any case doomed to failure, since I'm certain neither Dido nor Henry thinks their work is menial. It's their profession and they are very good at it!'

'Dido was not at all what I expected,' I confessed. 'I could see nothing of Faye in her.'

'She is a dear girl and, even now, her only concern is to continue with her work as before, and give you the Christmas you really want.'

I leaned back with a sigh, feeling suddenly drained. 'I'm glad you know now, and I admit I've frequently felt rather shabby about why I hired her,' I confessed. 'I've also often entirely forgotten the relationship ... until something has reminded me of Faye, like a recording session with Xan, and I've found myself barely able to stand the sight of her.'

'Oh, Sabine!' Nancy said and, leaning forward, suddenly hugged me. 'The only person you're hurting is yourself. Try and let go, and don't blame Dido for her grandmother's actions.'

'I'll try,' I said dubiously.

'Forgive her with your head and then your heart will follow in due course,' she said practically.

'There speaks the vicar!' I said, and she grinned.

'I wonder where Dido gets her stunning looks from?' she said.

'It's a mystery. She must be a throwback – we have no idea who was the father of Faye's child.'

'Genes work in strange ways, their wonders to perform,' Nancy said vaguely. 'Rather like God.'

The sitting-room door was suddenly flung open and Lucy hurried in, her face pink with cold and excitement, still wearing her outdoor things.

'Oh, Cousin Sabine, such a catastrophe!' she exclaimed enjoyably. 'Mr Tarn, the publican at the Pelican, has badly broken his leg and of course, he's always Santa at the village Christmas fair, which is *this* Saturday!'

I felt quite underwhelmed by the revelation of this disaster, but Nancy was her usual kind self.

'How difficult! Can anyone else take the part?'

'I've already saved the day,' she cried dramatically. 'I rang Nigel, because *he* always plays Santa for his dramatic society Christmas party, and he said at once he'd be happy to do it. So he's coming over on Friday morning and I'll take him down to the village after lunch, to introduce him to the vicar and show him the venue.'

'That sounds a perfect solution,' Nancy said, smiling at her.

Lucy turned to me. 'I hope you don't mind if Nigel arrives a bit earlier on Friday?'

'Not at all, though you had better tell Henry, when he finally makes his appearance with the tea trolley, that there will be one more for lunch on Friday. But at least it means I'll be able to have a cosy little chat with Nigel, before the Mellings arrive. Tell him to come over after breakfast.'

'I . . . yes . . .' agreed Lucy doubtfully, and went out to hang up her coat, passing Henry with the heavily laden tea trolley on the way.

'Sorry if things are a *trifle* late, but my curry puffs are worth waiting for,' he said. 'And I've made more seed cake, because I know you enjoy it, Mrs Powys. I've been *such* a busy little bee in the kitchen.'

'We seem to have been gathering a bit of nectar ourselves,' Nancy said obliquely, and I gave her a quelling look and told Henry about Nigel, the substitute Santa.

'And he has his own costume and beard,' Lucy said, coming back in after divesting herself of her coat and many scarves.

There didn't seem to be an answer to that one.

32

Crushed

When I returned to the kitchen from the study, Xan hard on my heels, I found Henry putting the finishing touches to the tea trolley.

'Oh, ructions!' he said, looking up. 'I'm sorry, but I'm afraid I earwigged when you were talking to Nancy. I'd gone to remind you of the time, Dido, and the door to the passage was just a *teensy* bit ajar . . . You could have knocked me down with a feather, but I had to scarper when I spotted Mrs Powys heading in my direction.'

'That's all right. I was going to tell you in a bit anyway.'

'Then just let me whip this through and then you can fill me in on the finer details.'

I caught Xan's eye as Henry pushed the trolley out and said, 'I tell Henry *everything*. He'll keep it to himself.'

'I'm sure he will, and I suppose really he *needs* to know,' Xan agreed. Then he walked over and took me by the shoulders, looking searchingly into my eyes.

'Are you really all right? It was a huge shock even to me – and more so when I realized Sabine had to have known about it all along. It was one coincidence too many.'

'You and Nancy were way ahead of me there, and I still find it hard to believe that, knowing who I am, Sabine wanted me here.'

'I think she's turning into her mother, who by all accounts was a very autocratic and managing woman and who ran the estate and her husband with a firm hand. So *are* you all right?' he asked again.

'I'm fine, just a bit shaky, which I expect is shock. I think it was the way the two versions of Faye just dovetailed together. It's unbelievable, but I *have* to believe it.'

'I'm not sure I'm entirely convinced that Sabine's only reasons for hiring you were curiosity and expediency,' he said, frowning.

'Must have been – I can't think of any other reason,' I said. 'And when she suddenly realized this would be her last Christmas at the Castle and there *we* were able to provide what she wanted . . .'

'But if you hadn't found out by accident, it appears she'd simply have let you go in the New Year without telling you,' he pointed out.

'I expect Granny Celia would have told me, when she got back and found out where I'd been staying over Christmas,' I said. 'I can't see any point in disturbing her cruise now, though, because she only wants to be contacted in an emergency. I might give Dad a ring later, though, when it's lunchtime over there and I've got a good chance of catching him.'

'And meanwhile, you're just going to carry on as if you didn't know any of it?' he said, with a wry smile.

'Of course! I'm not *really* part of the family, just because Dad was the illegitimate son of her half-sister, am I? And the only connection I feel is with the house and the garden, especially the Winter Garden.'

'That's always been something you've shared with Sabine, from the start.'

'I suppose so – and we both like things to be planned and organized, too.'

'Henry will be back in a minute, ready to hear all the details . . .' He smiled at me in the way that seemed to particularly affect my knees and added, 'You and I have become good friends, haven't we, Dido? Do we still have any secrets from each other?'

I gave a shaky laugh. 'I expect so – or at least, things we haven't got round to talking about yet!'

'But it feels as if we've known each other for a lot longer than a couple of weeks, though perhaps that's being together so much in a short time.'

'I expect so,' I agreed, and then our eyes met again and held, and his arms slid around me . . .

We'd entirely forgotten Henry would be on his way back, until we heard his voice, right behind us, and broke apart.

'I hate to interrupt this touching scene, but if Xan doesn't get himself to the sitting room pronto, Sabine will start ringing that damned bell again, your coffee will be stone cold and Lucy will have snaffled all the curry puffs!'

Henry was amazed to learn that Mrs Powys had known exactly who I was before she even engaged our services, but agreed that we shouldn't let it make any difference to our work.

'It just explains her attitude to you a bit more . . . and it's going to add an interesting edge to our stay here,' he added. 'Are you going to tell Charlotte?'

'I hadn't thought about it. I mean, I know I can trust her, but . . . no,' I decided. 'I won't, but I'll give Dad a ring later, even though I'm pretty sure he'll forget what I've told him five minutes after I ring off!'

'And Granny Celia?'

'Xan asked me that, too, but there's no point in disturbing her.'

'I expect you're right,' he agreed. 'Now, why don't I make you a nice cup of coffee and you put your feet up for a bit – I'll warm you a curry puff to go with it.'

'That's tempting, but—'

'There's nothing urgent you need to do for a bit,' he interrupted firmly. 'I'll peel the potatoes, cut the chips for dinner and put them in cold water, ready.'

'Thank you, Henry, but leave tenderizing the steaks to me, because I think hammering them will release a lot of pent-up tension!'

I felt much calmer after a little time to myself and, of course, I wasn't about to let it all affect my professional competence.

Dinner was cooked to perfection, as usual, and I ran though my evening chores afterwards, though just before nine I left Henry finishing up and went upstairs to ring Dad.

Once I'd fully engaged his attention and he'd realized who I was, he seemed mildly pleased to hear from me.

'I'm working at a house called Mitras Castle, up near the Roman Wall,' I told him. 'And I've just discovered that there is a family link to your birth mother, Faye.'

'Oh, really?' he said vaguely before adding, 'Interesting part of the world you've got to.'

'Did you know anything about it – the family connection?' I said patiently. 'The current owner is called Sabine Powys.'

'No, your Granny Celia never wanted to talk about the past and I think there was some family rift.'

His voice kept fading in and out, though whether that was the connection, or because he was doing something else at the same time, I had no idea, but suspected the latter.

'I know all about the family rift now!'

'Do you? You must tell me all about it next time you come over,' he said kindly, and I could hear a buzzer in the background.

'Dear me! I'd quite forgotten there was a group from the university coming for a private tour of the gallery. I must go.'

And he rang off.

It had been an unsatisfactory and tenuous connection with my *very* tenuous father.

I unwound after that by taking a long, hot soak in the bath and then changing into my comfortable velvet joggers and a sweatshirt, before going downstairs again.

I found Henry there, with Xan, and Simon, whom he'd rung up and invited.

'Hi, Rapunzel,' Xan said. 'You always look about sixteen with your hair loose.'

Henry gave me a meaningful look, which I avoided. I really didn't want to look sixteen, in case it jogged Xan's memory!

Xan moved Plum, who was luxuriously spread out over my usual place on the sofa and then dumped him on my lap as I sat down.

'We're just debating what to watch,' Henry said. 'I vote for *Saving Santa*!'

Next morning, it was as if yesterday's cataclysmic revelations had been nothing but a very odd dream, for Mrs Powys's manner to me at breakfast was exactly the same as usual, although Nancy had already wandered into the kitchen early, apparently with the sole intention of giving me a warm hug.

After breakfast, Mrs Powys went off with Xan to record what would be the last session before the guests started to arrive, and

Nancy, as now seemed to be her habit, helped Henry with the bedrooms, while I cleared up in the kitchen and awaited the supermarket delivery.

Henry came back just after it had arrived and helped me put it away.

'Nancy's taking Mrs Powys to some appointment – medical, I expect,' he said, stowing vegetables in the rack. 'She said if you didn't mind, they would stay out for lunch, so I told her that would be OK. And Lucy mentioned at breakfast that she was going shopping with her friend, so *she* won't be here for it, either – I forgot to tell you.'

'So it's just you, me and Xan?' I said. 'That's easy, then, and gives me a little more time to do other things – like wrap those chipolata sausages in streaky bacon and then freeze them, ready for Christmas Day.'

'Lucy seems to be spending more time out than in now, but looking much better for it,' he said. 'I expect the effort of trying to please Mrs Powys, yet always getting it wrong, must have been very exhausting.'

'At least she seems to have got over the disappointment of finding you were gay, Henry.'

'I'm her new best friend, instead, darling,' he said. 'I'm going out shortly, by the way, to get fresh flowers. What are you going to do? No, don't tell me: cook something.'

'Make lots of soup . . . perhaps turn some of the minced beef that just came into meatballs and cottage pie for the freezer . . .' I said. 'Then this afternoon, I'm going to make stollen.'

'Yum!'

'For tomorrow's tea, when the Mellings will be here,' I said pointedly, then weakened. 'But perhaps I'll make two, one for us.'

*

Xan emerged from the study in the late morning and winkled me out to walk Plum. By then, Henry had returned with half the contents of a florist's shop and was busy arranging flowers in the cloakroom, so I gave him a kitchen timer and told him to take the cottage pie out of the oven when it pinged.

It was still very cold out, with a chill breeze, so we cut across the herb garden and then followed the track down through the woods on that side, where it was sheltered.

As we walked, Xan said, 'You look very pale this morning, Dido – didn't you sleep?'

'I'm always pale,' I told him. 'But I did have the weirdest dreams . . . and now everything that happened yesterday seems like one, too, and not at all real. Still, that's a good thing, because it makes it much easier for me to carry on as if nothing *had* happened,' I said cheerfully.

Plum was running on ahead, with his tail waving like a small flag, but stopped and turned, giving us a doggy grin.

Xan slipped his hand through my arm in a companionable way and said, with a regretful sigh, 'One more quiet evening tonight, when I might manage to slip off to join you and Henry again . . . and then I suppose Sabine will expect me to entertain the guests.'

'That makes it sound as if she's hired you to sing, or do conjuring tricks,' I told him, and he grinned.

'I suppose it's too much to hope for that they're all struck down with sleeping sickness and go to bed early.'

I laughed. 'Not unless one of Henry's special cocktails knocks them out! His Christmas one is *fairly* mild, but the Rudge Special can make strong men sag at the knees.'

'I'll bear it in mind,' he said, then added ruminatively, 'You know, I think I've enjoyed those evenings with you and Henry so much because it's been a bit like revisiting my student days. Simon probably feels the same.'

'It's always like that at Henry's place, with his friends dropping in, or showing up with sleeping bags and camping out all over the house. I'm not sure he's ever going to quite grow up.'

We were silent for a bit, then something he'd said yesterday, which had puzzled me at the time, rose to the surface of my mind.

'Xan, when you said yesterday afternoon that discovering my relationship with Mrs Powys was just one coincidence too many to swallow, what did you mean? There haven't *been* any others, have there?'

He stopped and turned to look at me, his lilac-grey eyes amused.

'Oh, yes, there have! I know you've been doing your best to pretend we've never met before, but we have – Di!'

I felt my face flood with scarlet as I stared at him, aghast. 'You *knew* I was the dreadful teenager with a crush on you, who made your life a misery that summer?'

'You weren't quite *that* bad!' he said, laughing. 'But of course I knew, though not at first, because you've changed quite a lot. That lovely Grecian nose of yours was a bit of a giveaway, though.'

'I hated it when I was younger, but I think my face sort of grew into it, and I suddenly shot up another few inches later that year, too.'

'You kept *almost* giving yourself away, you know, and I'm afraid I teased you once or twice,' he said. 'It was a bit irresistible, especially at first, when you were obviously trying to keep me at a distance. Ice Princess wasn't in it.'

'I was afraid you'd recognize me, and I still feel hideously embarrassed about the way I behaved.'

'But you were only – what? Fifteen or sixteen?'

'Sixteen, which should have been old enough to know better.'

'Although I remember you had a crush on me, I don't think it particularly bothered me at the time, because I was in the throes of a crush on one of those girls who used to come over to play tennis and swim in the pool – what was her name?'

'Sophie,' I said. 'And you did seem very keen on her – it made me wild with jealousy and probably even more of a pest!'

'I was a bit cut up after Gerry and I flew out to Greece and I never heard from her again, but I soon got over it. We'd changed our tickets to a day early, because my grandmother was ill, as I recall.'

I felt a fresh pang of guilt about that letter he'd left with me to give Sophie and was tempted to finally reveal the truth . . .

But did it *really* matter any more, especially since he seemed to have quickly forgotten her?

I smiled at him. 'It's a relief that it's out in the open now,' I said, and he tucked his hand back into my arm again as we walked on.

'I thought if you ever found out, you'd avoid me like the plague! Aren't you afraid I'll get another crush on you?' I teased.

He said, very seriously, 'No, I'm not afraid of that, at all!'

Sabine

Nancy told me last night that she was certain that, had the relationship with Dido not been revealed, my better nature would have asserted itself and I'd have told the girl myself, once I'd come to realize her true nature.

And I have to admit that knowing about our connection has not made the least difference to Dido's manner towards me.

I haven't discussed it with Xan. Really, there doesn't seem to be anything more to be said about it.

When we had our final recording session before breaking over Christmas, Xan suggested what Nancy already had: that we skate briefly over the accident that led to Asa being unable to dive any more and get it over with, before beginning on the start of Asa's important excavations at the temple site.

We are to carry on from there after Christmas, and I confess I'm glad to have moved beyond that terrible day when our lives changed.

Moving on with the *forgiveness* part, as Nancy urges me to do, will be a little more difficult . . .

Nancy drove me to my pain clinic appointment today, where

more pills were doled out: enough, the nurse said, to last me over the festive season.

I didn't tell her I still had quite a store of them, even though I'm now having to take them every night, in order to sleep.

But not, until I absolutely have to, during the day, for not only do I want to enjoy the festivities, but I need a clear head to make my final decision over the future of Mitras Castle . . .

33

Heirs and Graces

Overnight the weather had again sneaked in and dumped another substantial fall of snow, so that everything was hidden under a thick, white blanket.

However, when Henry fetched the papers he was disappointed to find that the local farmers had already snowploughed a narrow strip of road, so he'd hardly found the journey a challenge at all.

'And while I was putting the papers on the table in the Great Hall, I noticed the crown of gilded bay leaves had fallen off one of the diving helmets and Plum seems to have found it and ripped it to bits,' he said, displaying the sad remains. 'There are bits of debris all over that corner.'

'Naughty Plum! But never mind, I'll take the dustpan and brush through after breakfast and clean it up,' I offered.

Lucy was rather touchingly excited over breakfast about the imminent arrival of her brother, Nigel, but also worried he wouldn't be able to get through the snowy roads, even though Henry assured her that he would have no trouble.

And he was quite right, because he answered the door to

Nigel just before ten, while I was sweeping up the bits of leaves and twigs from the demolished wreath.

'Good morning, sir,' said Henry, in his best butler's manner. 'May I take your coat? And if you give me your keys, I will fetch in your luggage and garage the car.'

Nigel looked quite startled, though I'm sure Lucy must have told him about us, even if Mrs Powys hadn't.

Lucy's brother was a plump, rosy and cheerful version of her, and a very *shiny* person, too – his dark eyes, his rosy face and his large, white teeth all shone. His hair was pure white, though I knew he wasn't much older than Lucy, in his early fifties.

'Er . . . yes,' he said, handing Henry a whole side of smoked salmon and a giant bottle of champagne first.

'I'll see these are taken through to the kitchen, sir,' Henry said gravely, putting them on the table under the window.

Henry divested him of his overcoat and Nigel did another double take when he spotted me in the corner, dustpan and brush in hand.

Then the sitting-room door flew open and Lucy rushed out to embrace him. 'Oh, I thought I heard your voice, Nigel! I've been *so* worried about you, driving here in the snow!'

He thumped her on the back, in a kindly fashion. 'The roads were fine. The snow's only local.'

Mrs Powys followed Lucy out and greeted him with the words, 'Well, Nigel. Fatter than ever, I see.'

'Alas, the pounds do seem to pile on with the years,' he said ruefully, kissing her cheek and then that of Nancy, when she joined them, too. 'Haven't seen you for years, Nancy,' he said heartily.

'No, it must have been the last Christmas party Asa and Sabine held here, over six years ago,' she agreed.

'It's good you've arrived early, Nigel, because I want to have a nice, quiet chat with you before lunch,' Mrs Powys told him, and his expression turned wary.

'Perhaps you'd like to go to your room first, though?' Nancy suggested.

'I . . . yes, perhaps . . . just for a moment, to freshen up.'

'I'll take you up,' Lucy said eagerly. 'You're on the top floor, in the room next to me. Henry will bring your bags up in a bit.'

Nigel indicated the salmon and champagne with a hand like a fat, pink starfish. 'My contribution to the Christmas feast, Sabine. I feel you can never have too much smoked salmon and champagne!'

'Indeed,' Sabine said, slightly drily. 'When you come down, I'll be in the summer sitting room – the first door on the left through the arch to the old wing, if you recall.'

'Certainly,' he said, and went upstairs with Lucy, with the air of one granted a temporary reprieve.

Henry went to bring in the luggage and Mrs Powys's eyes seemed to fall on me for the first time.

'Dido, take the salmon and champagne to the kitchen and then, perhaps, you could bring tea for two to the small sitting room. I'll go there now.'

'Yes, Mrs Powys,' I said to her upright, retreating back.

I was already burdened with the long-handled dustpan and brush, but Nancy offered to carry the champagne.

'It looks terribly expensive, doesn't it?' she said. 'It must hold almost enough to take a bath in!'

Henry heaved two large suitcases into the hall and she added, surprised, 'What a lot of luggage for only a short stay! Still, I expect a complete Santa outfit would take up quite a bit of space.'

*

'It's just as well we're going to be a large party,' Nancy said, depositing the huge bottle on the kitchen dresser. 'Otherwise, by the time we'd finished this, we'd all be under the table!'

'I only hope Henry can find a wine cooler big enough for it, or it'll have to be a bucket,' I said, dubiously.

'Well, I'm off to the study now,' she said. 'Xan mentioned he'd found Asa's old family photograph album and I do love that kind of thing – all the funny hats and hobble skirts and so on. I thought he might let me borrow it.'

'I'm sure he will,' I told her, but my mind was already busy with ideas for using the unexpected glut of smoked salmon, though it had, I was pleased to see, been thinly sliced before being sealed in its packet.

It's so useful for sandwiches and all kinds of dishes. Perhaps scrambled egg cooked with snippets of smoked salmon would be perfect to serve to the house party for breakfast on Christmas morning?

I laid a tray with tea for two and took it to the summer sitting room, which I'd only previously glanced into. It was a pleasant, small room, with chairs and sofas covered in faded chintz. The window looked out across the lawn and beyond, to the distant hills.

Nigel had just come down and kindly held the door for me.

'Dido, isn't it? Lucy's told me all about you and Henry – and that we're all on first name terms here – no formality!' He gave a deep, rich chuckle.

I didn't look at Mrs Powys – I couldn't ever *imagine* calling her Sabine! – but as I put the tray down on the table in front of her, Nigel said heartily, 'Well, this is cosy! I can't remember ever being in this room before.'

'It is, as its name suggests, used mainly in the summer,' Sabine said, then added to me, dismissively, 'Thank you, Dido.'

But by then, I was already on my way out, though as I closed the door, I caught a glimpse of Nigel's face: he looked as if I'd just shut him in with a lioness.

In passing, I put my head into the study, to see if Xan wanted some coffee, and found him working at the big desk, while Nancy was sitting in one of the armchairs before the coffee table, carefully leafing through the old photograph album. Plum was asleep across her feet.

'Still here, as you see,' she said, looking up. 'This is so fascinating – but I'll take it away with me now and leave Xan in peace.'

'You aren't bothering me,' Xan said vaguely, then looked up and bestowed one of his singularly beautiful smiles on me.

'In fact, since you're here, Nancy, we might as well record a few more of your memories, if you have time.'

'OK,' she said amiably. 'But only if dear Dido brings me a cup of tea first.'

'One coffee and one tea coming up,' I said. 'Then I must get on with the preparations for lunch. You're having leek and potato soup, then eggs Benedict. Those are fiddly to cook for a lot of guests, so I thought I'd cook them today.'

'Wonderful!' Nancy said, beaming. 'You spoil us, my dear.'

At lunchtime, when I took the warm bread rolls through to the dining room, I saw that Nigel looked rather crushed and deflated, as if he had a slow puncture. Lucy was darting anxious glances at him.

'Well, that *was* an illuminating little chat we had, Nigel,'

Mrs Powys said, pouring herself a glass of water. 'I'm sure we understand each other so much better now.'

Nigel gave her rather a sickly smile and she continued, 'I'm looking forward to having a private talk with Olive Melling, too – not to mention reacquainting myself with her son. Of course, Dominic is the only representative of the next generation in the family.'

'The next generation of *Asa's* family,' Nigel corrected her, quickly. 'Not *ours*.'

'I *think* of them as family,' she said, and smiled blandly. I had a feeling she was enjoying winding Nigel up.

Henry, returning later after collecting used plates, said that Nigel had tried to ingratiate himself with Mrs Powys by employing a kind of playful badinage, but this hadn't gone down too well.

'Then he suggested that as the last male head of the family, he'd be glad to act as co-host with her, if she felt in need of his support.'

'I bet that went down like a lead balloon,' I said.

'Yes, she told him that if she had any need of male support, which she didn't, then she could rely on her dear godson, Xan, to provide it. Xan looked uncomfortable. I don't think he wants to be dragged into any family disputes.'

'No, I'm sure he doesn't. But he is genuinely fond of Mrs Powys and vice versa.'

'The fun has started already!' said Henry with a grin, and went out with a fine Stilton and a lordly bunch of grapes.

After lunch, without waiting for coffee, Nigel and Lucy set out for the village. Henry took the tray through to the sitting room for Nancy, Xan and Mrs Powys, and was away some time, returning with a mischievous expression on his cherubic face.

'We've hatched a plan for when the Mellings arrive,' he said. 'I'm going to open the door to them wearing my full Jeeves outfit! Mrs Powys says Frank Melling is a complete stuffed shirt and, since she hasn't told them she's got some help over Christmas, he'll be totally gobsmacked! They're probably expecting Maria's pot-luck for dinner, too.'

'Lamb and rice,' I corrected. 'Maria's meals seemed to lean heavily in that direction. So, yes, surprises all round!'

'Nancy thought it would be a great joke, too,' he said. 'But Xan told me he wasn't going to give me a tip, however much like Jeeves I looked.'

'Well, enjoy yourself,' I told him. 'I know you love dressing up.'

'It's only for an hour or so, then I'll resume the Henry the house elf look.'

'We'll do an extra lavish tea, shall we?' I suggested. 'Lucy and Nigel should be back for it, too. That will be almost all the guests, with only the solicitor and his granddaughter to come, and they aren't due till after lunch tomorrow.'

'Perhaps they'll help to dilute the family tensions that Mrs Powys seems to be determined to stir up,' he said optimistically. 'But I'll make my special Rudge Cocktail tonight, anyway. It's been known to oil the wheels of the stickiest parties.'

I'd taken the large container of chicken in white wine from the freezer to defrost overnight and was already scrubbing potatoes and prepping vegetables, so there would be little to do later.

A trifle in a cut-glass bowl reposed in the fridge, a thick layer of cold custard rich with sherry on top, ready for whipped cream to be added before serving.

Henry laid the dining-room table early, too. It's so much easier if we're ahead of the game.

'Eight for dinner,' he said, coming back, 'and the table looks like an illustration from *Country House Living*.'

'Then we've done everything in advance that we can, Henry.'

'Oh, we're *so* good at this!' he said. 'Now, just for fun, I'm going to go and move the cars around in the outbuildings, so I can fit in two more. I'll put our van in that open-sided barn thing round the back, with the Land Rover – there's plenty of room in there. I think the Mellings and their son are coming separately, and then, I suppose the solicitor and this Mrs Martin will come together, so one more car tomorrow.'

'Don't forget to leave space for Lucy's hatchback.'

'I'll see what I can do,' he said. 'It'll be like a giant metal jigsaw puzzle.'

'Have fun,' I told him.

He cut some more bay leaves on the way back, to make a new crown for the denuded diving helmet, but first went to check on the fires and see if anything was wanted.

He said he'd found Nancy in the library, wrapping Christmas presents – presumably all those packets of home-made fudge – and Xan was back in the study, with Plum.

'Mrs Powys has gone for a lie-down before tea – or to recharge her batteries, ready for the next onslaught of family members.'

'All quiet on the Western Front, then,' I commented.

'Probably only a temporary lull. Right,' he added briskly, 'I'm going to make that new wreath for the diving helmet. The poor thing looks very left out. Just as well it is quick-drying gold paint!'

'And, I hope, non-toxic? Though I don't think Plum actually *ate* any of the last one, he just pulled it to pieces.'

'Little stinker,' he said amiably, heading for the downstairs cloakroom with his bundle of bay.

*

Something I'd overheard Mrs Powys say to Nancy at breakfast had made me decide to change tomorrow's dinner menu to steak and kidney pie. She'd recalled her old cook making it and now she was missing it.

Fortunately, I had steak and kidney in the freezer and thought I'd make the pies with puff pastry, rather than the heavier, if more traditional, suet.

I was still contemplating my menu planner when Xan came in with Plum and insisted I go out for a walk with them.

'Come on, we both need some air and exercise, and I know you well enough now to realize that you can whip up a sumptuous afternoon tea in ten minutes!'

'Henry often does most of that, though. But it'll be easy today – more smoked salmon sandwiches, for a start,' I agreed, 'thanks to Nigel. OK, you're right, I do need a bit of air.'

Outside, the snow seemed to have receded from the middle of the paths, but now the temperature was dropping again and the slightly melted edges refreezing.

'The last guests should get here all right tomorrow, because there's no more snow forecast,' Xan said.

'This lot wasn't forecast in the first place,' I pointed out. 'But I hope the roads stay clear tomorrow, because Lucy's so looking forward to the Christmas fair in the village hall, and Nigel would probably be gutted if he'd brought his Santa suit for nothing.'

'I expect it'll be OK, Dido. And if this covering stays, we'll have a white Christmas.'

'There are still three more days to go, though, so it might all have thawed. But I don't really care even if we get snowed in, once all the guests are safely here, because I've got enough food for a month.'

'But it would matter to Sabine, because she's counting on

everyone leaving on the day after Boxing Day.' He grinned, and added, 'She said that visitors were like fish, and stank after three days.'

'She said that to me, too. They'd be pretty ripe by next Friday, then!'

'And probably ripe to murder each other – or Sabine,' he said. 'All these mysterious hints about gathering the last of her family together, and inheritance, are bound to wind them all up, especially since she's invited her solicitor to stay, too! It's getting more like the start of a vintage country house murder mystery every minute.'

'Well, we do have our own little Professor Plum here. He doesn't look very murderous, though.'

Plum, who was trotting just ahead, turned and looked back at the sound of his name.

'I suspect Nigel will try and be the life and soul of the party, in which case we'll probably all join together in strangling him with a length of tinsel,' Xan said darkly.

I slid on a patch of icy path and he grabbed me just in time and held me upright. My feet seemed to want to go in opposite directions, like when I tried ice skating.

'*Dido*,' he said, in such a changed voice that I looked up at him, startled to find him looking very seriously at me. 'There's so much I want to say to you, but whenever I think the moment's right, we get interrupted. But I've fallen in love with you and I think you feel the same way about me.' Then he looked at me uncertainly and added, 'At least, I *hope* you do!'

'Of course I do!' I said unguardedly, then held him off as his arms tightened around me.

'But we mustn't, Xan! It would make everything too complicated, now I know why Mrs Powys dislikes me so much.'

'She won't dislike you when she really knows you,' he said, which I thought was optimistic.

'Well, right now, I'm certain she'd hate it if she thought there was anything between us, and it would spoil her Christmas!'

'What about spoiling mine?' he demanded.

'But we could just stay as friends till after everyone's gone,' I said persuasively. 'We can get to know each other better, without rushing into things and see where it takes us.'

'I know where I'd *like* it to take us,' he muttered and then kissed me . . . and despite everything I'd said, I couldn't help responding.

We lost track of time and it was Plum who eventually brought us back down to earth.

He seemed to think Xan was attacking me and pranced around us, barking, till we drew apart.

'Oh, Mr Darcy, this is so sudden!' I said shakily.

'Look on that as something to be going on with,' said Xan.

34

Hampered

The Mellings were later than expected and Nancy brought a message to the kitchen from Mrs Powys to say that she wanted tea served at the usual time, whether her guests had arrived or not. Everyone else was already gathered in the sitting room.

I only needed to make the pots of tea and coffee and it would all be ready. The trolley was laden with smoked salmon sandwiches and some of Henry's little spiced fruit scones, halved and buttered.

Just as Henry, attired in pinstriped trousers and a black tailcoat, like an escapee from a P. G. Wodehouse novel, was poised to wheel it through, the bell for the front door finally jangled.

'Here they are at last. You dash off and let them in, Henry, and I'll bring tea.'

He was out of the room, coat-tails flying, before I'd even finished speaking and I followed him more slowly. Plum, who had somersaulted in earlier and had hung about in the hope of snippets of smoked salmon, was at my heels.

By the time I was wheeling the jingling trolley through the Gothic arch into the Great Hall, Henry had the door open and was standing back to let the visitors in, though at the moment they still seemed too transfixed by astonishment to move.

'Good afternoon, sir and madam,' intoned Henry magnificently. 'Please come in and I will attend to your luggage in a moment. The party are all assembled in the sitting room and tea is about to be served.'

They edged cautiously past him with sideways glances and I took my cue and pushed the trolley out on to the tiled floor – enter, stage right. Then I thought I'd better park it for a moment and assist.

'Do let me take your coat, Mrs Melling,' I said, and she turned and stared at me with almost as much astonishment as she'd regarded Henry.

I knew the Mellings to be in their sixties. Olive was a tall, bony, faded blonde, with greenish eyes set close together in a face like a well-made-up hatchet.

'Thank you,' she said, turning to allow me to slip off her coat. 'And you are . . . ?'

'Dido Jones, and this is Henry Rudge. Mrs Powys has engaged us to do the catering over Christmas.'

Divested by Henry of both his coat and his car keys, Mr Melling was revealed as not so much a stuffed shirt, as a stuffed suit – it was grey and perfectly cut to cater for a figure that had run to seed a little around the middle. Grey seemed to be his keynote colour, for the suit matched his sleek, thick hair and sharp eyes.

Now he'd recovered from his first astonishment, he had assumed an urbane, but colourless, professional manner that was probably second nature to him.

'I'm so glad Sabine has managed to get some help in, because I thought we'd be entirely at Maria's mercy over Christmas,' he drawled.

'Maria's husband has been ill, so they've gone to stay with their family for a couple of weeks,' Henry said. 'We hope to make your stay very comfortable.'

Since I knew Mr Melling was a semi-retired private cosmetic surgeon, that struck me as being probably much what he said to his wealthy patients.

The door to the sitting room opened and Lucy came out with a summons.

'Hello, Olive – Frank,' she said. 'Cousin Sabine says you're very late and are to come straight in.'

Her eyes fell on the parked tea trolley and she added, with relief, 'Oh, good. Cousin Sabine's been ringing the bell for tea for the last few minutes.'

'Dominic should be here at any moment,' said Mrs Melling. 'We stayed with him last night and he was right behind us, so I can't imagine where he's got to!'

Henry winked at me as I followed them into the sitting room. Plum must have sneaked in when Lucy opened the door, for he was sitting before the fire, looking like one of those antique pottery dogs.

In the flurry of greetings, no one noticed me, except Xan, who had politely got up when the Mellings went in. He gave me a very warm smile – hot, even – so it was just as well Mrs Powys's attention was otherwise engaged or the game would have been well and truly up.

Back in the hall, I found Henry had put the Mellings' luggage just inside the door and was now carrying in a Fortnum and Mason hamper.

'This must be their present to Mrs Powys. Coals to Newcastle really, darling, given the contents of the larder.'

He put it down by the table and turned to close the door, but before he could do so, we heard the loud tootling of a horn and then, with a scrunch of gravel, a long, dark car drew up behind the other. It was either the missing Melling or the Mafia.

'Master Dominic arrives,' Henry said, returning to his post and tweaking the front of his immaculate tailcoat.

Curious, I lingered to see what the new arrival was like and saw a small, slight young man get out of the car and run lightly up the steps.

'I'm terribly late – I had a puncture and—' He broke off and stopped dead halfway over the threshold, his dark, mobile face suddenly frozen as he gazed at Henry . . . and Henry, for once speechless, stared right back into his eyes, seemingly stunned.

They showed no sign of breaking eye contact any time soon, so I said, 'Do come in, Mr Melling, so I can close the door!'

He obeyed, but like a sleepwalker. Then they both suddenly seemed to become aware of their surroundings at once.

'You don't already know each other, do you?' I asked.

'Not *yet*,' said Dominic Melling, with a singularly impish grin. He had a boyish air about him, though he couldn't be much younger than Henry.

He held out a hand to shake Henry's. 'I *loove* the Jeeves outfit! I'm Dominic Melling, but call me Dom.'

'Henry – and this is my business partner, Dido. We're here to cater for the house party.'

Their hands remained clasped and I noticed that Dom's was somewhat grimy, presumably due to changing a tyre.

'You'd better show Mr Melling the cloakroom so he can wash his hands before joining everyone in the sitting room,' I suggested, then left them to it and returned to the kitchen, smiling to myself.

If ever I saw love at first sight – a total *coup de foudre* – I'd just seen it now. And Mrs Powys's attempts to keep a social divide between staff and guests, already undermined by Nancy, looked doomed to failure.

Henry didn't return for some time, having taken all the luggage up to the guest rooms, but when he did, he was singing 'I'm in Love with a Wonderful Guy'.

He caught my eye and grinned. 'Say nothing, or the spell might break!'

'OK, but only if *you* stop teasing me about Xan, because we've agreed to be just good friends until after Mrs Powys has had her lovely Christmas.'

'I'll try,' he promised. He put the two bottles of port he was carrying down on the table.

'These are Dom's present to Mrs Powys and I was told to bring the Fortnum and Mason hamper through, too. I'll fetch that now.'

'Odd how everyone's minds seem to have run to food or drink as presents.'

'Not really,' he said. 'I mean, Mrs Powys seems to have told them about her illness, so that must have limited the gift options a bit.'

'I suppose you're right, Henry. Did you go into the sitting room? I wondered how things were shaping up.'

'I followed Dom in, to see to the fire, and everyone was being very *polite* to each other, but my Rudge Cocktails before dinner will loosen them all up a bit.'

'As long as you don't make it so strong that they're loosened to the point where their wheels drop off,' I warned him. 'I'm going to have a little break in our sitting room now, with a cup of coffee and a sandwich, before I start to think about dinner.'

'Good idea. I'll get that hamper and then join you,' he said, and went out, bursting into song again.

This time it was 'Love Is the Sweetest Thing'.

I only hope he remembered to stop before he got within earshot of Mrs Powys.

The dining room looked rather splendid when I helped Henry carry the main course through.

He'd laid the table with a white cloth and then added a long festive scarlet runner down the centre. This, together with the rich red of the drawn velvet curtains and the firelight gleaming off the silver and cut glass, made it look like a scene from a Victorian novel, or it would have done except for the guests' modern dress.

This was mostly informal. Nigel and Frank Melling wore suits, but Xan had on an open-necked shirt and dark cords, while Dom sported a black T-shirt that proclaimed across it: 'Hogwarts Forever!'.

Nancy had made a token gesture by donning a long, rubbed-velvet skirt, while Mrs Powys was, as usual, attired in an evening dress that looked simple and inexpensive, but was probably the opposite.

As to Lucy, it was hard to tell one set of layered grey or beige garments from another.

Of course, Henry had long since resumed his black tunic and trousers, and I noticed that he and Dom seemed to be trying not to catch each other's eye, a ploy I was using with Xan after his giveaway smile at me in the sitting room earlier.

'How nice it is to have all the remaining members of my family gathered around this table with me tonight,' Mrs Powys said. 'I hadn't realized how few were left, until recently.'

The triangular smile appeared, as she spread a snowy napkin across her lap.

'Really, Sabine, as I said before, Lucy and I are the *only* family members you have left,' Nigel pointed out.

'Yes, descended from my father's side, the Mordues,' she agreed.

Xan had opened the wine and now began pouring it, but he paused at her next words, looking startled.

'Though, of course, dear Xan is related to my mother's family, the Archbolds, by way of his grandmother Rose.'

'That is such a *very* remote link, I don't really think it counts,' Xan said.

Nigel stared at him. 'I do remember hearing you say something about it, but I believe the link, *if* there really is one, is so far back as to mean nothing.'

'I wouldn't say *that*, precisely,' Sabine said.

I suddenly realized I was so interested in what they were saying, that I was still standing there, holding a hot dish.

I put it down hastily and headed for the door, as Olive Melling said plaintively, 'Of course, *we* aren't relatives of yours except through marriage, Sabine. As Asa's closest connections, I admit I was disappointed he didn't leave us some small memento, or remembered Dominic, who is the only representative of the next generation.'

'Don't drag me into it,' Dom said. 'I didn't expect anything!'

I closed the door, though not without a last glimpse of my employer's face; she seemed to be deriving some slightly malicious enjoyment from the conversation.

'This family seems almost as dysfunctional as yours,' commented Henry a few minutes later, joining me in the kitchen.

'Mine isn't so much dysfunctional, as very loosely connected,' I said.

'I think that might be the same thing.'

Plum had come in with him and was now polishing his empty dinner bowl, in case he'd missed a bit earlier, then gave up and came to give me a beseeching look from his dark eyes.

I weakened and gave him one of his little bone-shaped biscuits.

'I think I've got a handle on the situation now,' Henry said. 'Nigel, as Mrs Powys's father's cousin, considered himself her heir – along with Lucy, of course. Mrs Melling is only related to Asa and was obviously deeply miffed not to get anything when he died. I don't think there was a will, so it all went to Mrs Powys.'

'Yes, I'd gathered all that,' I agreed.

'After you'd gone out, Mrs Powys seemed to be hinting that she hasn't yet made her mind up who she intends leaving the Castle to – and it seems the Mellings aren't entirely left out of the reckoning.'

'She could be using them to wind Nigel up because he was taking it for granted that he was the heir and it annoyed her?' I suggested. 'And what about when she suddenly dragged in some very distant-sounding family connection with Xan?'

'I suspect that was just another red herring, like the Mellings.' Henry grinned. 'I get the feeling Mrs Powys is simply stirring them all up for fun, and in the end, she'll leave the Castle to the National Trust!'

'You may well be quite right,' I agreed.

The underlying tensions didn't seem to have affected anyone's appetite, but then, I always think that excellent food has a mellowing effect on people.

When Henry took in my beautiful sherry trifle and I followed with the jug of cream, Xan was refilling the wine glasses again, so that probably helped to account for the more relaxed atmosphere in the room, too.

Lucy was holding forth on the delights of tomorrow's Christmas fair in the village which, as well as the appearance of her brother as Father Christmas, would feature all kinds of handicraft stalls, raffles, bran tubs and such traditional games as Pin the Tail on the Donkey.

I'm not sure how interested her audience were, but at least it was an innocuous subject.

But Henry told me later that when I'd gone out of the room, Mrs Powys had suddenly decreed that *everyone* should go to the Christmas fair next morning, which was tantamount to a command.

'Us too, so long as we're back in time to prepare lunch. Then the last two guests arrive after that.'

'But is Mrs Powys going to the fair, too? I wouldn't really have thought it was her kind of thing.'

'No, she's staying here and so is Olive Melling. She's going to have a nice little catch-up with her, like she did with Nigel, when he arrived.'

'I'm not sure he's recovered from that yet,' I said. 'But it's kind of her to say we can go to the fair, too.'

'Oh, I asked her,' he said cheerfully. 'I love that kind of thing, don't you? All those naff hand-knitted things in lurid colours and raffle prizes you'd so much rather not win.'

'It does have a certain fascination,' I admitted. 'I haven't left the estate since I got here, so I suppose it's time I saw the village. I'd like a look at that Roman Janus stone on the Green you told me about, too.'

'There we are, then: a morning of unbridled fun and frivolity before the last of the guests arrive and we're run off our feet for the duration.'

'We're fairly busy now,' I pointed out. 'Hadn't you better take the cheeseboard through?'

'Just going,' he said with dignity.

*

Of course, now there were more guests, clearing up took a lot longer and the dishwasher was still chugging over its first load when I went to set the extended table in the morning room, ready for breakfast.

When Henry made a trip to fetch the coffee tray and any used glasses, he said that Mrs Powys, Nigel, and the Mellings were playing bridge, while Nancy was helping Lucy to thread silk tassels into bookmarks she'd made from old greeting cards, which she intended selling at tomorrow's fair.

'What about Xan and Dom?' I asked.

'Playing billiards. They suggested I join them, but I said duty called and I still had a lot of glassware to hand-wash, not to mention the cutlery to dry, polish and put away.'

'What heroic self-denial!'

'Not entirely. I thought Mrs Powys might consider my presence extraneous when Xan had someone else to play billiards with.'

He watched me haul out a large saucepan from the cupboard.

'You aren't going to start cooking now, Dido, are you?'

'Just mulligatawny soup for tomorrow's lunch. It won't take me long.'

'You're a glutton for punishment,' he said.

'I'm like the Boy Scouts: I always like to be prepared.'

'Well, so do I, if it comes to that. I really should whip up some more nibbles and starters tomorrow.'

Finally, the soup was gently simmering and the kitchen was immaculate.

Henry made another sortie to the sitting room, ostensibly to collect more glasses and see to the fire, but really, I suspected out of curiosity and a desire to see Dom. He returned saying that the bridge party was still ongoing, and it looked like Mrs Powys would make a much later night of it than usual.

'I think she might be a bit of a bridge fiend and enjoying having someone to play with.'

He washed up a few last things and I turned off the heat under the soup.

'Come on, Henry, let's go and put our feet up for a bit. I'm tired out, and this is only the beginning!'

Then a thought struck me and I crossed to look at today's to-do list. 'Take bacon and sausages out of freezer,' I read aloud. 'I knew I'd forgotten something!'

'That's *so* unlike you. You must be in love,' he said, then dodged through the door into our sitting room as I threw an oven glove at him.

I was slumped in a semi-stupor of tiredness in front of *Elf*, which we'd watched so many times we didn't need to concentrate on it, when Xan tapped at the door and put his head in.

'Hi! I didn't want to interrupt you,' he said apologetically. 'I just thought you'd like to know that everyone's gone to bed now, except me and Dom. We've collected the rest of the used glasses and brought them through with us.'

'That was kind,' I said. Plum had already insinuated himself through the gap in the doorway and was heading for his usual place on the sofa.

'Is Dom there with you? Why don't you both come in?' Henry said eagerly.

'I'm here,' Dom said, looking round Xan. 'We just didn't want to disturb you both in your off-duty time.'

'You're not disturbing us, we're glad to see you,' Henry said, and he and Dom exchanged smiles.

'I thought you might have already gone to bed, Dido,' Xan said to me.

'No, but I will as soon as the film's finished. It's only *Elf* again, because I was too tired to concentrate on anything else.'

'My most favourite film ever!' Dom declared.

'Then why don't you both join us?' suggested Henry. 'Here, you have my chair, Dom, and I'll pull up a pouffe.'

'Choose your words!' Dom said with a grin.

Plum had decided to curl up on my lap and Xan settled down in the vacated space and brazenly put his arm around me.

I gave him a look and he said, innocently, 'Just being friendly.'

'Can we go back to the revolving door bit? That's my favourite,' Dom asked.

'Mine too,' Henry agreed. 'Two minds with but a single thought!'

35

Forgotten

That night I gave up and went to bed as soon as the film finished, because I knew I'd be fit for nothing in the morning if I didn't.

Xan said he'd take Plum out and then go up then, too, but Dom seemed just as much of a night owl as Henry, so we left them deciding which of Henry's horror collection they'd watch.

It still took me a couple of strong coffees next morning, before I was ready to tackle the preparation of breakfast for eight, assisted by Henry when he got back with the papers.

He was annoyingly bright-eyed and bushy-tailed, despite so little sleep.

Xan came in to give Plum his breakfast, and stayed to turn the sausages over, before taking the first pot of coffee into the morning room. Plum remained, though, looking hopeful as he watched the bacon and sausages being transferred to the lidded dishes.

I helped Henry take them through, along with the teapot. By then, everyone was down, so I suspected Mrs Powys had already informed them that breakfast would be cleared away at nine, whether they'd arrived in time for it, or not.

This suited us, though, because it's very tiresome when the members of a house party keep trickling down till late morning, when you need to be thinking about cooking lunch.

Mrs Powys was dealing briskly with Frank Melling, who had declared he had no interest in Christmas fairs, and would prefer to stay at the Castle.

'Nonsense!' she snapped. 'If you don't want to go to the fair, then I suggest you look around the old church and visit the folk museum.'

'Oh, yes, do,' urged Lucy. 'It will be open, except for the library, and it's so interesting! I'd offer to show you round, but of course Nigel and I will be going down to the village hall right after breakfast, then be busy at the fair.'

'I'll change into my outfit here, before we go,' Nigel said jovially. 'Must get in character!'

I felt we should be grateful he hadn't appeared at breakfast in it, though it would have been hard to wolf down the bacon and eggs while wearing a cotton-wool beard.

'I'm sure the rest of you will fit into two cars,' Mrs Powys said, and Xan and Dom volunteered to drive.

I went back to the kitchen to make another pot of coffee at this point, but Henry told me that Xan had said he would bring me back early.

'Then you could make a start on lunch. The rest of us could squeeze into Dom's car. But I'll lay the table for lunch as soon as I've whipped round the bedrooms.'

'We could do that quickly now together, while they've got their feet in the trough,' I suggested. 'A lick and a promise!'

I didn't see Santa's departure, but Henry went off in Dom's car a little later, along with a huffy Frank Melling.

'Mr Melling really didn't want to go out, did he?' I said to

Nancy, who was helping clear away the last of the breakfast things in the kitchen. 'But they all do what Mrs Powys tells them!'

'You must call them Frank and Olive. I've told them we're an informal party and all on first-name terms,' Nancy told me.

'That's nice,' I said. 'But I think I'd rather stick to more formal terms with Mrs Powys and I'm sure she'd prefer that, too.'

'Such nonsense!' Nancy said, smiling, then took the tray of tea I'd prepared through to the sitting room, where Sabine and Olive were to have their little tête-à-tête, and told them we were off.

We left Plum in the kitchen, with a biscuit and the door to the staff sitting room open, so he could go to sleep on the sofa. I didn't think he'd miss us.

It actually felt odd to be leaving the Castle grounds, rather like a snail winkled out of its shell . . . but on the other hand, it was nice to be sitting next to Xan as he drove down the narrow lane to the village, the snow banked up on either side and Nancy happily chatting in the back seat.

We arrived to find there were cars parked all around the Green and up the side roads, but squeezed into a spot beyond the church.

We detoured across the grass for a quick look at the Janus stone, the weather-worn faces back to back, one grimacing horribly and the other wearing a complacent smile, then paid a pound each to go into the village hall.

I thought this was a bit steep till I discovered it included a cup of tea or coffee and a slice of cake.

There were stalls all around three sides of the large room and also up the middle, not to mention the refreshment table, with its steaming urns, piles of thick white china crockery and plates of cake.

There was a small stage at the further end of the hall, where Nigel, a very creditable Santa in a big white beard, hooded red coat and black boots, was being besieged by small children and their harassed-looking parents.

Every few minutes you could hear him roar: 'Ho, ho, ho!' as if he had an intermittently faulty battery.

When the proceeds of something like this are going to a good cause – this one apparently was the local hospice – I always decide how much I can afford to spend and then just enter any competitions, or buy odds and ends I don't want till I'm spent up.

When I emerged from the throng some twenty minutes later, I was carrying a large cotton shopping bag printed with a black and white image of the church. Inside was a random selection of the type of home-made goods so dear to the heart of workers for good causes: lurid knitted scarves, mittens and toilet roll covers shaped like hats, dolls or poodles, peg bags disguised as tiny dresses on coat hangers, pebbles painted with flowers by Lucy's friend Daphne, and, of course, Lucy's pinked and tasselled bookmarks.

I wasn't entirely sure what I'd got in the bag, though I *was* entirely certain that the packet of brightly coloured bath crystals I'd won in the tombola would give me a mega allergic reaction, should I be mad enough to use it.

Dom and Henry were standing by the refreshment table, eating chocolate fudge cake, when I got there and both had bulging tote bags, just like mine.

'I *love* those poodle toilet roll covers,' Henry said. 'And look, Dom's bought me a peg bag.'

This one was shaped like a black dinner jacket over a white shirt and tiny red bow tie.

'Lovely,' I said. 'I think I've spent up now, though. I wonder where Nancy and Xan have got to.'

'I don't know, but there's Simon,' Henry said, as his familiar figure approached us. He was carrying a large traybake in a foil container and had a pink and magenta scarf wrapped around his neck.

'Hi, Simon,' Henry said, and introduced him to Dom. 'Nice scarf.'

'I'd no intention of buying it, but before I knew where I was, it was draped around my neck and they were waiting for the money,' he said.

'You can put it into the next jumble sale,' I suggested, laughing. 'I wouldn't have thought this was your kind of thing, though, Simon.'

'It isn't, really, but my boiler's now totally bust and the plumber says he can't do anything with it until the day after Boxing Day, so I thought it would be warmer here, and then afterwards I could have lunch in the pub.'

'Oh, what a nuisance about the boiler!' I commiserated. 'You're going to be freezing over Christmas, though at least you're spending Christmas Day at the Castle, so you can thaw out a bit then.'

'Yes, and I'm looking forward to more of your wonderful cooking, too,' he said, with that sweet and strangely heart-breaking smile.

'I pull out all the stops for Christmas dinner,' I assured him. 'Here's Xan,' I added, as his tall and elegantly willowy figure emerged from a scrum of pensioners, like a giraffe from a herd of stampeding wildebeest.

We told him about Simon's boiler and then Xan handed me a large, emerald-green velvet beanbag frog.

'For you! I'm not sure what it would turn into if you kissed it, though – it's really hideous.'

'Thank you – I think,' I said dubiously, taking it.

'I thought you might be ready to go back to the Castle now,' he suggested.

'Yes, I'd better,' I agreed, checking my watch. 'Henry, you stay on. There's not much to prepare for lunch and I can manage.'

'We'll be back soon, anyway. I'll round everyone up shortly,' Dom said. 'I saw Dad just walk in, too, so the delights of the folk museum must already have palled.'

A little weak sunshine made the windows of the Castle sparkle like jewels as we came out of the dark maw of the drive.

The house looked serene and peaceful, and I wondered if Olive Melling was looking the same way after her talk with Mrs Powys.

We went in by way of the Garden Hall and dumped our purchases on the kitchen table.

Plum was so fast asleep, we had to wake him up to tell him we were home, though I don't think he'd even realized we'd been out.

'I'd better go and collect the tea tray from the sitting room before I start lunch,' I said. 'Mrs Powys and Olive must have long since finished their talk.'

'I'm sure they have,' Xan agreed. 'Shall I fetch the—'

He broke off as the big bell on its metal spring jangled to announce a visitor at the front door, and we looked at each other.

'Can that possibly be Mr Makepeace and his granddaughter already?' I said. 'They aren't supposed to be here till after lunch.'

The bell jangled again. 'We'd better answer it, whoever it is, because no one else seems to be,' Xan said, and we headed for the Great Hall, Plum pattering in our wake.

The door into the sitting room was open, but since there was no sound of voices, perhaps Olive and Mrs Powys had gone upstairs to their rooms until lunch.

'You get the tray and I'll answer the door,' Xan suggested as the bell jangled for the third time.

'OK,' I agreed, and heard him open it and say, 'Hello, Mr Makepeace! Sorry for keeping you waiting, but . . .'

I lost the rest, but when I went out again with the tray, an elderly man was ushering a dark-haired young woman into the hall.

'Ah, Xan,' he said, 'good to see you again.'

His voice was dry and so was he – a small, shrivelled husk of a man, like a spent chrysalis from which all life had long since flown.

'So sorry we're early, but my granddaughter drove us and she was worried the roads might be difficult because of the snow. This is my granddaughter, Sophie Martin. Sophie, Xan Fellowes.'

And as she turned towards Xan, who had been closing the door behind them, my heart gave a sudden, sickening lurch. It might have been almost twenty years since I'd last seen her, but the feathery dark hair framing an enchantingly pretty heart-shaped face, with a tip-tilted nose and huge, soft, pansy-brown eyes, did not seem to have changed in the least.

I heard Xan exclaim incredulously, 'Sophie!' And when I looked quickly at him I saw, bizarrely superimposed over his own dear face, the dazzled expression of a young man deep in the throes of first love.

'Xan! I can't believe it!' she exclaimed breathily. 'I never thought to find *you* here! *How* many years is it?'

'Too many,' he murmured, still looking dazedly at her.

The tray tilted in my hands and the crockery begun to slide towards the floor, but I righted it in the nick of time.

'What were you saying about there being too many

coincidences, Xan?' I said tartly, before bitter tears blinded my eyes and I fled to the haven of the kitchen.

Once there, I sank down on a chair, feeling quite sick when I remembered that expression on Xan's face.

He'd told me he'd soon forgotten all about her after that summer, but the sight of her had clearly brought it all back, and now it would probably all come out about the letter he'd asked me to give her on the day he'd left, and my sins would finally catch me out.

It took me a good ten minutes to pull myself together and begin on the preparations for lunch, but I was glad when Henry came back and I could pour it all out into his sympathetic ear.

'I suppose Charlotte and this girl's family are all local, so it's not *that* much of a huge coincidence that she should turn up,' he pointed out. 'It's lucky Xan had already recognized you, isn't it? I expect he's already told her you're here, too.'

'Yes, and then he'll ask her why she never replied to the letter he left for her. Which she couldn't, because instead of giving it to her I burned it in a fit of adolescent jealousy!'

'Ah!' he said. 'You never told me that bit.'

'I was too ashamed. And I couldn't bring myself to tell Xan, either.' I swallowed hard and then wailed, 'Henry, you should have seen his face just now, when he first set eyes on her! It was as if time had rolled right back and he is just as dazzled by her now as he was then!'

'I'm sure that was only momentary surprise and you've read too much into it,' he said soothingly. 'It's *you* he really loves; you must know that by now!'

'I thought I did,' I said miserably.

'Look, you get that soup on while I go and see what's happening. I should probably take their luggage up, anyway.'

'OK,' I agreed dully, and he hugged me comfortingly before going out.

He'd found Xan and Sophie alone in the sitting room, deep in conversation, he told me.

'But Xan was exactly like he always is. He introduced me to Sophie and then said she'd get a surprise when she met you later, too, Dido.'

'Nice of him to remember me,' I said sourly, and he gave me another of his slightly rib-cracking hugs.

'Don't be silly. It's you he *really* cares about; you can't mistake it.'

'But, Henry, *you* didn't see his face when she arrived – and I didn't imagine it! He looked bewitched.'

'If he did, it was only a momentary thing and he's over it now, you'll see.'

I summoned up a watery smile, even though I wasn't at all sure he was right.

'Is there any dessert after lunch, other than cheese and fruit?'

'No, let them eat cake,' I said, and he grinned.

'Nice to see the old Dido back again!'

Of course, with a party of ten, I was in and out of the dining room a couple of times, but I didn't linger, especially after I caught a glimpse of Xan and Sophie sitting next to each other, their dark heads close together.

Henry kept coming back with snippets of information, like a retriever displaying a dubious collection of bones.

'Lucy held forth about what a huge success Nigel had been as Father Christmas, and then, when he could get a word in,

Xan told them all that he and Sophie had met many years before, when they were still teenagers.'

'Like Romeo and Juliet,' I said sourly.

'Mrs Powys thought it was nice that they were old friends,' he continued, ignoring this interruption. 'And then Xan said that oddly enough, *you* had been there at the time, too, but you'd been very young and changed so much since that it had taken him a while to recognize you.'

'Not a problem he had with Sophie,' I said.

'Mrs Powys suggested the young people go skating on the lake this afternoon – by which, of course, she meant Dom, Xan and Sophie.'

I bet Sophie could skate like an Olympic champion!

The next time I went into the dining room, everyone was just getting up from the table.

'Ah – Dido,' Mrs Powys said. 'Xan has told me that the gas boiler in Simon's cottage has broken down completely, so I've told him to ring him up and invite him to come for lunch tomorrow and then stay with us over Christmas, till it can be repaired.'

'That's such a kind thought, Sabine,' Nancy said, beaming fondly at her friend.

'Which room shall I get ready for him, Mrs Powys?' I asked.

'The small bedroom opposite Xan's, in the old wing.'

'*I'll* see to that this afternoon,' Henry said, and she followed the others out, quelling a suggestion by Dom that he stay and help us clear the table.

Xan and Sophie lingered behind, though, and as soon as the others were out of earshot, Xan said to me, 'Dido, you remember that last day at your friend's house, when Gerry and I had to change our tickets and flew out to Greece early?'

I nodded, numbly, suspecting what was coming.

'It was all a bit of a mad rush, but I left you a note to give to Sophie when she came over, didn't I? Only she says she never got it.'

I opened and closed my mouth a couple of times, but Sophie spoke first.

'I told him my friend happened to be ill that day, so I'd popped in just to say goodbye, not knowing they'd already left. But I found the house empty, not a soul about.'

'But . . .' I stared blankly at her, then found my voice, 'I *did* see you that day. You were coming out of the side door of the house.'

'Your memory must be playing tricks,' she said, with a silvery laugh. 'I didn't go in the house, because there was no reply when I rang the bell . . . and it was too hot to trail down to the tennis courts to see if anyone was there, so I just went home.'

While I was still gazing blankly at her, wondering if I'd contracted False Memory Syndrome – though actually, that scene was burned on my subconscious for ever, because of the guilt – Xan said, 'So Dido never got the chance to deliver my letter? And then I suppose she forgot all about it.'

He smiled at me, but I avoided his eyes.

'What a shame you didn't get the chance to give me the letter, Dido,' Sophie said.

And into my mind slid the very clear image of seeing her slipping out of the side door of the house, a very strange, almost *furtive*, expression on her face.

'But, Sophie,' I began, 'I definitely saw—'

'What a long time ago it all was,' she said brightly, cutting across me.

Then she laid a red-taloned claw on Xan's arm and said,

looking winsomely up at him, 'But now, let's have our coffee and then go skating, as dear Mrs Powys suggested. It'll be such fun!'

Xan said uncertainly, 'What a pity you and Henry can't join us too, Dido.'

'Oh, I'm sure they must have way too much work to do,' she said, and again gave that tinkling laugh. If she was a bell, I'd be ramming paper round the clapper right at that moment.

'Yes, indeed – duty calls,' Henry said cheerfully from behind me and I started. I think we'd all forgotten he was still in the room.

Xan scooped up Plum. 'Would you mind having him till we get back, Dido?'

'Not at all,' I said, automatically, and Plum, passed across to me, tried to lick my nose.

'Henry, I *did* see Sophie coming out of the house that day and told her Xan had already left, even if I didn't give her the letter. Can she have possibly forgotten?'

'No, I think she was lying,' he said thoughtfully. 'I've no idea why she would do that, though.'

'Nor me . . . unless she felt awkward about having gone into the house, when no one answered the front doorbell? But that side door was always left open.'

I told him about the strange expression I'd remembered seeing on her face, too.

'Perhaps she was secretly a burglar, casing the joint?' he joked.

'Don't be daft!' I said, though his words rang a vague bell in my mind . . . but whatever it was proved elusive.

'It's a mystery – but for now, we must press on with the gay round,' Henry said. 'Let's clear in here and then I'll go and get

Simon's room ready. It'll be fun having him staying here, too. He can sneak off with Dom and Xan to slum with us when no one is watching.'

'I wouldn't count on Xan. I think as far as he's concerned, I've lost my charm.'

'But not for Plum,' Henry consoled me as the little dog tried to lick my nose again. I had forgotten I was still holding him.

36

Wicked

On automatic pilot, I consulted today's list and made crème brûlée and two batches of brandy butter, before taking a break in our sitting room, with a mug of hot chocolate and a plate of Jaffa Cakes for comfort.

Then I got Plum's lead and took him out for a little airing. I'd thought we might go down and see if anything new had flowered in the Winter Garden, but when I looked over the balustrade at the edge of the lawn, I saw Mrs Powys, Olive and Nancy making their way down to it and, far below, small figures moved on the icy surface of the pond.

Dom's slight figure was unmistakable, and he didn't seem much better at skating than me, though he did stay upright and moved about more.

I didn't need binoculars to know that the other two, arms linked as they circled gracefully around the lake, were Xan and Sophie.

I turned away quickly and took Plum up the drive instead, under the sheltering intertwined branches.

When we reached the top, I found the road was still a narrow, snowploughed lane between banks of snow, though the exposed tarmac surface was oddly dry.

Maria and Andy's cottage had that shut-up and empty look, though Henry, to whom they had given the keys, had popped in a couple of times to make sure the pipes hadn't frozen, or any other calamity happened.

The other cottage, which I knew was occupied by an elderly shepherd, showed a faint haze of blue-grey smoke from the chimney and hens were running in and out of a tumbledown outbuilding next to it.

I stood in a reverie by the crumbling gatepost for a few minutes, until Plum barked to let me know it was time to go back to the Castle.

'Where did you get to?' I asked Henry when I found him in the Garden Hall, taking off his boots and padded jacket. 'You went to make Simon's room ready and never came back!'

'I thought I'd just hike over to Simon's for half an hour to see if he'd turned into an icicle yet.'

'And had he?'

'Not quite, though the room with that small log burner is the only vaguely warm one in the house. He's really looking forward to coming over here in the morning.'

Henry went to put a bit of laundry in one of the washing machines and I fetched the Christmas cake from the larder and put it in pride of place on the tea trolley: it had to be cut some time, and why not now? It looked absolutely splendid, if I said it myself.

I added plates, napkins and a pearl-handled cake knife, and then it was all ready to go through, apart from making the tea and coffee.

It had been bitterly cold outdoors, so those who had ventured out would probably be glad of a hot drink and the glowing fire in the sitting room.

They seemed to appreciate the cake, too, for when Henry fetched the trolley later, the bright red paper band had been peeled back and it was minus a generous segment. Two of the little snowbabies had been dislodged from the top and were now sitting on the cake board, so I washed and dried those carefully and put them away, before glancing at the clock: Xan usually came in to feed Plum around this time.

And as if on cue, I heard his deep, mellow voice outside in the passage – and also the unmistakable higher-pitched one of Sophie.

I was out of that kitchen and up to my room in less time than it took to say 'unwelcome ingredient'.

I applied a little make-up to my angrily flushed face and then re-did my hair into a style Henry always refers to as 'Warrior Princess': gathered high on the back of my head and wound about with one braided strand, so the long ponytail projected out and swung heavily when I moved.

Thus fortified, I went down again, cautiously checking the coast was clear before fully opening the door to the kitchen.

'The coast is clear,' Henry said, spotting me. 'Sophie wanted to see where the dear little doggy ate his dinner, though really I think she's just superglued herself to Xan – and he wasn't looking too pleased about it, if you ask me.'

I shrugged. 'He must have had a lot of practice in discouraging overeager women in the past, so I'm sure he could deal with Sophie if he wanted to.'

'He has beautiful manners, though, Dido, and it's probably a little difficult, since she's a fellow guest.'

I wasn't impressed by this argument and changed the subject. 'Have you laid the dining table?' I asked pointedly. 'And I hope you've decided on a starter?'

'Triangles of French toast with pâté – easy-peasy,' he said. 'If that's crème brûlée in those ramekins in the fridge, are you going to let me caramelize the sugar on top, with that special little blowtorch thing?'

'I suppose so, if you're careful. I think Dom might prefer you with eyebrows.'

He grinned and, then, taking a very sharp knife, began to slice thick rounds of bread each into two very thin ones, ready for his French toast.

He still had all his fingers when he'd finished, though, which was something.

When Henry had beaten the gong for dinner, and carried through the huge and wonderfully golden steak and kidney pie, I followed with a jug of thick gravy.

Perhaps the delicious aroma had permeated the house, for everyone was already seated at the table.

Sophie was admiring Mrs Powys's necklace of huge, matched South Sea pearls.

'They're a family heirloom – and pearls need to be worn, to keep their lustre,' she told her.

'They're so beautiful!' Sophie enthused, and I caught a very strange expression cross Mr Makepeace's face as he looked across at his granddaughter: 'anxious' would be the only way to describe it.

Curious . . .

I put the jug of gravy down next to the pie, which Henry, at Mrs Powys's direction, began to slice and serve.

'That does looks delicious, Dido,' she said graciously. Then she looked around the table with that curiously puckish three-cornered smile of hers and said, 'Well, now we're all gathered together, friends and family, for what I hope will be a memorable Christmas – and I'm sure that spending this precious time with you will also help me make my mind up about the future of Mitras Castle.'

There was a small silence. Nigel looked as if he'd like to point out again that he and Lucy were the only *real* relatives she had, and Olive Melling exchanged a quick look with her husband, eyebrows raised.

'Lucy and Nigel represent my father's side, the Mordues, of course, and dear Xan the Archbolds.'

'Very, very remotely,' Nigel couldn't resist putting in.

I'd just brought over one of the dishes of vegetables from the hotplate when, out of the corner of my eye, I saw Sophie – who was wearing the kind of plunge-fronted dress that makes you question whether Newton got it right about gravity – look sharply from Mrs Powys to Xan.

'I hadn't realized you and Sabine were related, Xan,' she said.

'You can hardly call it *related*. My grandmother was distantly descended from a branch of the family who emigrated to America. Sabine's just winding you up, Nigel.'

'Am I?' she said, but smiled at him.

'You've always had a wicked sense of humour,' Nancy observed, holding out her plate for pie. 'But I know you'll do exactly what is right, in the end.'

Frank Melling seemed to suddenly realize that Henry and I were not actually part of the furniture.

'Really, you know, this is all quite private. *Pas devant les domestiques*,' he said.

'Oh, don't mind us,' said Henry, in perfect French. 'We're mum as oysters where our clients' confidentiality is concerned.'

'Yes, Frank, and actually, Henry and I have found our families are connected by marriage, too, though back in the eighteenth century,' Mrs Powys said, giving the pot an extra stir.

For a moment, I thought Nigel might be about to have a seizure because his face turned such a dark red, but Mr Makepeace lived up to his name, saying quickly, 'These distant connections link most of the old families, but of course, as far as inheritance goes, Nigel, you and Lucy are Sabine's closest relatives.'

Then he added, as if half to himself, 'Of course, if your half-sister had had issue, the situation would be entirely different.'

I saw Mrs Powys's eyes glance towards me as she said, 'There *were* no legitimate children, or I'd have long since made a will cutting them out.'

'As far as the legitimacy or otherwise of any issue is concerned, the law has changed and illegitimate children are not now debarred from inheriting,' said Mr Makepeace in his dry-as-dust voice.

'You know, I thought there'd been some change in the law like that,' Nancy said brightly. 'So much fairer, I think.'

For a moment, I saw that Mrs Powys looked quite as stunned as I felt, before she recovered her composure.

I quickly slipped from the room, but not before I heard her say sharply, 'Indeed? Well, luckily the point has never arisen, and in any case, I mean to sign a will right after Christmas. Timothy has drawn up two, according to my instruction, and when I've made my final decision, I'll sign one and burn the other.'

As I hurried off down the passage, it occurred to me that if Mrs Powys had died without making a will, Dad might have inherited everything! He'd have been totally nonplussed and, I expect, have unburdened himself of the Castle at the first opportunity. I'd take a bet on one of those two wills leaving it all to them. Perhaps the other was in Nigel's favour and she might still sign that one, once she'd had her fun teasing him?

I got the feeling she was deriving quite a bit of enjoyment from the situation – and Henry, coming back to crisp up the tops of the crème brûlée, agreed with me.

After that, I stayed out of the dining room until the bell rang to say the party were moving to the sitting room, and then I took a large tray and went to help Henry clear the table before I made the coffee.

I didn't quite get there, though, for as I passed the door to the study, it swung open and a long arm shot out and dragged me into the room. The door clicked shut behind me and I heard the key turn in the lock.

'What on earth are you doing, Xan?' I demanded, turning to face him.

He looked frowningly at me for a moment and ran his fingers through his dark hair, before saying, 'I just wanted to talk to you and this is the first chance I've had to shake off that bloody woman all day. She's like a human limpet!'

'Can you possibly mean the beautiful and charming Sophie?' I said sardonically, then realizing I was holding the large tray like a shield, lowered it.

Xan removed it from my hands and tossed it on to the nearest pasting table.

'Yes, Sophie! I just had to dive into the Garden Hall cloakroom to shake her off. Even she couldn't follow me in there. She's been driving me mad!'

'Going by your expression when she arrived, I think she's already driven you senseless – talk about *Love Awakened*! Or reawakened, I suppose,' I added sarcastically and he flushed.

413

'I'm so sorry, Dido, I don't know what came over me. When I first saw her, I suddenly felt exactly how I did when I was nineteen and thought I was in love with her.'

'Yes, so I saw. And she's just as pretty as she ever was. She hasn't changed in the least.'

'No, she hasn't, and I think she was probably always shallow, silly and self-obsessed, only I didn't see that at the time.'

I began to feel my heart starting to thaw out a little round the edges.

'How did *you* feel when you first saw me again that day when you arrived here?' he suddenly demanded, slightly defensively.

'Well, I wasn't immediately re-smitten with a mega adolescent crush on you,' I said tartly. 'In fact, to be truthful, I just felt stunned, embarrassed and horrified.'

'*Horrified?*'

'In case you recognized me. I just prayed you wouldn't . . . and of course, I had a guilty conscience about that letter you asked me to give to Sophie. And whatever she says, I *did* see her that day.'

'Then why does she insist she didn't see anyone at all?' he said, frowning.

'I've no idea, but I clearly remember seeing her coming out of the side door of the house . . . and, as I said to Henry, she looked a bit odd.'

'Odd? What kind of odd?'

I shrugged. 'I don't know, it was just an impression. Maybe she was disappointed she hadn't found you there.'

'Well, none of it matters now, anyway. In fact, now I'm really glad you never gave her the letter! She might have taken me up on my suggestion she come out to Greece and by then, I'd found another girl.'

'I don't want to know about all your past conquests,' I said coldly. 'Now, I'd better go, or Mrs Powys will wonder what's happened to her coffee.'

'She's probably wondering where *I've* got to, as well.'

Behind us, the handle of the door to the passage suddenly rattled, and we froze. Then he drew me away to the far side of the room.

'I bet that's Sophie,' he whispered, then took me by the shoulders and looked very searchingly at me, with those wonderful, lilac-grey eyes.

'Dido, I was just momentarily dazzled by seeing Sophie again, but in less than ten minutes I was not only entirely cured, but that high-pitched tinkling laugh of hers had started to drive me mad.'

'It has the same effect on me,' I agreed.

His hands left my shoulders and slid round my waist, pulling me closer.

'Dido, you know you're the only girl for me . . . even if you do look rather terrifying with your hair like that. You should have been wearing a breastplate, not using that tray as a shield.'

'Henry calls this my Warrior Princess look.'

'He's right.'

I looked up at him, serious again. 'Xan, that was a bit of a stunner for Mrs Powys about the legitimacy thing, wasn't it?'

'It was. She clearly had no idea the law had changed, though she recovered almost instantly.'

'Poor Dad! I had to laugh, because he would have been so horrified to find all the responsibility for the estate hung around his neck. Possessions mean absolutely nothing to him!'

'Just as well she's going to sign a will and make sure he doesn't get it all, then,' he said. 'I get the feeling, whatever she says, that she's already made up her mind how to leave it.'

'To the National Trust, I should think,' I agreed.

'That would be a good outcome. They'd look after the house and estate well.'

'You love Mitras Castle, don't you?'

'It has happy associations for me – and there's something welcoming about it that makes me feel at home here. You feel that too, don't you?'

'Yes, right from the moment I arrived. And I love the garden, too – there's a magic about it.'

He smiled at me. 'I suppose we'd better go, but first . . .'

The kiss lasted a long time . . . and might have gone on even longer had we not been disturbed by the sound of the door to the library opening behind us and Sophie's voice exclaiming furiously, 'Oh, don't let *me* disturb you!'

Then it closed behind her with an almighty slam.

'Damn,' said Xan.

Henry must have guessed where I was, because he'd already made the coffee and taken it through.

He came back just after I did, shutting the baize door behind him and saying, dramatically: 'Fly, all is discovered!'

'What do you mean?' I said defensively. 'And I'm sorry I left you alone to clear up.'

'I wasn't alone, because Dom helped, and don't change the subject,' he said. 'Sophie just burst into the sitting room, looking like a Fury and told everyone she'd just found Xan in the study, "snogging the help" – her words.'

'He was,' I said. 'I didn't really expect her to make an announcement of it, though!'

'Nancy put her in her place. She said: "I don't want to be unchristian, but you are a very ill-bred girl, Sophie!" And then Xan walked in and no one seemed to have any idea what to say, so I expect they're all pretending they never heard what Sophie said.'

'I wish they hadn't,' I said. 'It's going to make things awkward, and Mrs Powys isn't going to like it.'

'She's probably cutting him out of one of the wills already,' he said flippantly.

'I don't suppose he was in one in the first place. I'm sure she was only dragging him into the discussion earlier to get up Nigel's nose.'

'She succeeded, then. She's *totally* wicked!' he said, but in an admiring kind of way.

Sabine

When I excused myself and went up to bed early, Nancy followed me into the boudoir and said, brightly, 'Well, this has been an evening of interesting revelations, hasn't it?'

'You might say that,' I replied, taking the whisky decanter out of the cupboard. 'A quick snifter?'

She looked at me keenly. 'I think you'd be better letting me pop down to make us some cocoa and then taking one of those painkillers you're hoarding with it.'

'I do realize there's no point in stoicism just for the sake of it, so yes, I'll take one – but I'll wash it down with this.'

'All right – I'll join you, then,' she said, and when she'd taken her glass and sat down, watched while I fetched a tablet from the bedroom and took it. When she spoke again, though, it was on an entirely different subject.

'You know, Sabine, I had a feeling there had in the not too distant past been a new law, or act, or whatever they call it, about the legal rights of illegitimate children.'

'Did you? It was a complete surprise to me! If I'd had any idea that Faye's son would inherit everything if I died intestate, I'd certainly have made a will long before this.'

'I don't know why you haven't, anyway.'

'As I said, it seemed to be . . . tempting fate.' I felt my lips twist into a wry smile. 'Now there's not a lot of fate to tempt; my sand is running out.'

'Well, you'll feel easier in your mind when you've come to a decision and signed one of those wills – whichever it is,' Nancy added with a twinkle.

'I need to talk to Timothy in the morning. There are a few points I want to discuss with him, and of course, he still has no idea that Faye had a child, or that her granddaughter is actually in the house.'

'You'd better tell him!'

I shrugged. 'I suppose so, but the will, when I sign it, will take care of that particular problem.'

I stopped and took another good slug of whisky.

'Before I see Timothy, though, I need to have a word with Xan. After what Sophie said, I want to know what's going on between him and Dido.'

'You know, I find it hard to like Sophie Martin,' Nancy said. 'She seems very shallow and spiteful, and if she *has* any good qualities, she's hiding them well.'

I looked at her, surprised. 'This isn't like you, Nancy! You usually see the best in everybody.'

'I'm still hoping she'll prove me wrong, but something about her makes me feel uneasy. And have you noticed that her own grandfather looks at her as if she was a bomb about to go off?'

'He certainly looked horrified when she burst in at tea time and told us about Xan and Dido.'

'I don't think Timothy's very fond of her. He told me that she's only staying with him because she's fallen out with her parents, and her divorce has left her in a difficult position.'

'A difficult financial position, do you mean? She doesn't exactly look penniless, does she?'

'He said she'd signed some kind of pre-nuptial agreement, against his advice.'

'More fool her!'

'Yes indeed,' she agreed, then looked at me and beamed. 'You must feel relieved that Xan hasn't fallen for Sophie. He told me that seeing her again had knocked him for six – for all of ten minutes!'

'Everyone tells you everything!' I said, 'But no, it won't be a relief that he hasn't fallen for Sophie if he simply turns his attentions to Dido!'

'Oh, but it was *always* Dido. I realized how he felt about her the moment I first saw them together, though of course since Dido is very reserved, I wasn't at first sure how she felt about him. But now I'm quite sure they love each other.'

'I hope you're wrong,' I said grimly. 'This is not what I bargained for when I decided to employ her at the Castle.'

'But I'm sure you promised me that you'd strive not to blame Dido for her grandmother's actions,' Nancy pointed out gently. 'And you know, dear Sabine, that however complicated things seem, they have a way of working themselves out satisfactorily, in the end.'

She put her empty glass down and got up. 'I can see from your face that the pill is working and I think you should go to bed and get a good night, for once.'

When she hugged and kissed me, I felt the warmth of her love embrace me and thought, as I so often did, that I was not entirely worthy of it.

37

Clinched

Henry, returning earlier from a sortie to the sitting room to see to the fire and collect used glasses, said that the bridge party was in full swing again, but Frank had been so rude about his wife's playing that she'd refused to go on.

'So then Mr Makepeace took her place, but partnered Mrs Powys, and Nigel, Frank. It was a bit like musical chairs.'

'Isn't it odd that we quite happily call everyone by their first names, except Mr Makepeace and Mrs Powys?'

'I just can't *see* Mr Makepeace as a Timothy,' Henry said pensively. 'And unless Mrs Powys personally asks us to call her Sabine, we'd better not get overfamiliar!'

'What's everyone else doing?' I asked.

'Well, Lucy and Nancy were watching the TV and Sophie seemed to be permanently playing with her phone.'

'That all sounds fairly civilized.'

'Not if you'd listened to Sabine's comments on the bridge, she's even more critical than Frank,' he said. 'Dom and Xan were playing billiards again, but they came out to snaffle a bit of gingerbread from the tree in the Great Hall.'

'Good, it's there to be eaten, as well as look decorative.'

'Before I came away, I asked if I could freshen anyone's drink – I really don't know how Lucy can stomach that ghastly sweet sherry – and Mrs Powys wanted to know what was for dinner tomorrow. So I told her: roast beef and Yorkshire pudding. She said she hoped there would be horseradish sauce.'

'There will, and mustard, too.'

Because of Christmas, dinner would be in the evening tomorrow, instead of its usual Sunday time of two o'clock.

'I think I've done everything I need to, for tonight,' I said, and suddenly found myself yawning hugely. 'Sorry,' I apologized.

'You look tired out, though a whole lot happier now you've had things out with Xan!'

'I am, but it's been such a physically and emotionally exhausting day that I think I'll have a soak in the tub and an early night.'

'You do that, darling,' he said. 'If there are any gentlemen callers later, I'll tell them you're Not At Home.'

As usual, Xan came into the kitchen early next morning, to feed Plum, and then, sliding an arm around my waist, kissed me.

'Don't let my presence cramp your style,' Henry said, flipping bacon over.

'I won't,' Xan said. 'Do you want me to take anything to the morning room with me?'

'No, it's OK – most of it's already on the hotplates, and I'll bring the rest through now.'

'I'll go and see who's down, then,' he said, but Plum remained behind in the hope of scraps.

Henry, having delivered the last of the hot breakfast dishes, said everyone was now down and discussing plans for the morning.

'Or rather, Mrs Powys was telling them what she'd got planned, though Olive and Lucy are going to church. Frank told Mrs Powys he's going to spend Sunday morning reading the papers, just like he does every week. So, it's just as well I fetched them as usual first thing, isn't it?'

'Perhaps that's Mr Makepeace's idea of fun, too?'

'It might be, but Mrs Powys told him she expected him to join her in the library at ten, because they had a lot to discuss, but before that she'd just like a little private word with Xan.'

I stared at him. 'Do you think it's about last night and Sophie telling them all he was kissing me?'

'Maybe. Perhaps she's going to ask him if his intentions are honourable?'

'While sincerely hoping they're not, you mean?'

'Probably, though in that case, she's doomed to disappointment!'

'I don't know – I mean, Xan and I have only really just started to get to know each other, so it's early days yet. It's a pity Sophie had to blab about it, or Mrs Powys need never have known till after Christmas.'

'Speaking of Sophie, I was just coming out of the morning room, when Mrs Powys suggested the "young people" take the sledges out to the slope below the Roman site, while the snow's still deep enough. Then Dom said it would be great if I could go with them and take my snowboard, so he could have a go.'

'And did she agree to that?'

'Yes, she said very graciously: "Of course – if Henry has time to get his work done, first."'

But of course, he did have time, because both Dom and Nancy helped him.

First, they carried the empty breakfast dishes into the kitchen, while Mrs Powys was talking to Xan in the library. Then Nancy said that since Sabine would be occupied with Mr Makepeace after that, she'd got plenty of time to help, and she and Henry could whip through the rest of the chores together.

'Then you can take your snowboard and join the others on the slope,' she told him. 'Xan's going to ring Simon before he goes out, to suggest he comes back to the Castle with them afterwards. They can put his luggage on one of the sledges.'

'That's a good idea.'

'I realize it's no use trying to persuade you to go with them, Dido,' Nancy said. 'You're such a whirlwind of activity now we're counting down to Christmas and I'm sure you have your morning planned out to the very last second.'

'Almost, though if Xan wants to leave Plum with me, I'm sure I'll have time to give him a little run later in the morning.'

The snowboarding and sledging party returned just before lunch and Simon popped into the kitchen to say hello, before Henry showed him to his room.

I'd noticed when I took Plum out that the temperature had started to rise, and Henry said that a bit of a thaw was setting in, so it was just as well they'd gone out on the slope today.

While Henry changed into his black tunic and trousers, I poured the minestrone soup into a large blue and white tureen, then he carried it through and gave the gong a hammering. He seems to derive a lot of enjoyment out of these simple activities.

I followed him with a basket of warm bread rolls, before hurrying back to the kitchen to put my cheese and onion flan in the oven to warm. There was just coleslaw to go with that – though *my* coleslaw is extra special and delicious.

Afterwards, Dom and Xan helped clear the table.

'Sabine keeps telling us there's no need to help, but I'm not used to sitting about being waited on,' said Dom, 'and I'm sure Xan isn't, either.'

'I expect Simon would have helped, too, but he's otherwise engaged,' Xan said, grinning. 'Sophie has literally got a grip on him and I heard her tell him she's madly keen on Roman history and wants to know all about the site.'

'I expect he'll enjoy that a lot more than she does, because experts do love to talk about their subject,' I said, putting the lid on the coffee pot. 'There, that's ready now.'

Henry and Dom went off together with the coffee tray – the heavenly twins – but Xan lingered.

'Aren't you dying to know what Sabine asked me this morning when we had our little talk?'

'I think I can guess. She wanted to know how involved we are.'

'That's it in a nutshell. So I said I hoped we'd soon be even more involved, because I love you, but since you didn't think she'd like the idea, you'd suggested we just be friends until after you'd fulfilled your contract.'

'And then *she* said, "So why were you and Dido having a passionate clinch in the study last night?"' I suggested.

'More or less. I told her that was entirely my fault and it was unfortunate that Sophie saw us and decided to broadcast the news.'

'Yes, that was really spiteful of her,' I agreed. 'Was that it?'

'No, she said I'd probably think it none of her business, but she had my best interest at heart. Then she asked me if I meant to marry you.'

He came closer and pulled me into his arms, looking gravely down at me. 'So I said I would if you'd have me. *Will* you have me, Dido?'

'I might, if after Christmas you get down on one knee, holding a ring, in the traditional manner.'

'In that case, I hope I find one in my Christmas cracker.'

'You won't, because they're Marwood's Magical ones, so they'll be full of tricks and jokes, instead of the usual bits of unidentifiable plastic.'

'I might have to borrow a curtain ring, then,' he said, and we had a long and satisfactory kiss.

When I finally surfaced, I said, 'But still, Xan, let's keep it all low-key for now. I don't want anything to spoil Mrs Powys's last Christmas and the festivities *really* kick off tomorrow afternoon: there will be carols, mulled wine and mince pies round the tree, just as Mrs Powys remembered from her childhood.'

'You know, you really are a kind, unselfish, caring person,' he said. '*Are* you likely to accept my proposal after Christmas?'

'I think I'll have to, because Plum's stolen my heart and I really don't want to be parted from him.'

'I think you've already won his. He seems to spend more time with you than with me, now.'

'Cupboard love,' I said. 'And perhaps, like Henry's cousin Hector, *you* only want me for my treacle tart and suet dumplings, too?'

He spent quite some time proving to me that he didn't, before taking himself off to the sitting room for his coffee, passing Henry in the doorway.

'I'm *starving*,' he announced, 'and they scoffed all the cheese and onion flan, so how about I make us some cheese on toast? And then I might whip up some Parmesan puffs and a batch of cheese straws, if I'm not going to get in your way.'

'Feel free,' I told him. 'I'm about to put that monster of a frozen turkey in the larder to start defrosting, which will leave a satisfyingly huge hole in the freezer for me to fill up again.'

'You can cook up a storm after I've finished – it won't take me long – and then I'll leave you to it for a bit, because Dom and I are going to chop wood.'

'I hope he's safer with an axe than you are.'

'I haven't chopped anything off yet,' he said with dignity. 'And I think,' he added with a grin, 'Sophie's going to find

426

herself dragged down the garden to see the Roman mosaic, even though she looked less than thrilled about the idea of going out in the cold again!'

'Well, that's what comes of pretending you're passionate about Roman history to an expert!' I said.

Sabine

When we went upstairs before dinner, Nancy followed me into my boudoir and said she was curious to know how my interview with Xan had gone and this was the first chance she'd had to ask.

'Not that it's any of my business, really – just call me nosy!'

'It didn't go the way I'd hoped,' I admitted. 'And even my discussion with Timothy afterwards wasn't as straightforward as I'd originally intended it to be. I thought I'd come to a decision, but now, things have changed . . .'

'Well, you don't need to tell me what's worrying you if you don't want to, because how you leave your property really *is* your own affair.'

'But I don't seem able to keep any secrets from you anyway, Nancy. You home in on them like a human divining rod.'

'That makes me sound terrifying!'

'I expect it's because you know me so well – and I always did call you the voice of my conscience, didn't I? In fact, whenever I'm about to make a big decision, I always wonder what you'd think of it . . . as I did when I decided to employ Dido.'

'That turned out to be a good idea, even if it wasn't originally undertaken for the best of motives.'

'Nancy,' I said abruptly, 'Xan says he's in love with Dido and hopes she'll marry him. She wanted him to just keep things between them on a friendly footing, though, until after Christmas, because she knew I wouldn't be happy about it. But he said he got carried away – as Sophie so graphically described to us.'

'I said Dido was a good, kind girl! I expect she didn't want to upset you with an announcement of their engagement because she's determined to make this Christmas exactly what you told her you wanted it to be.'

'And so far, she has – she and Henry, between them,' I admitted. 'The tree decorating ceremony in the Great Hall, the Mistletoe Bough and the lovely wreaths and swags of greenery Henry created. And Dido put those solar lights on the fir tree outside as a special surprise for me.'

'That was a lovely thought – *and* she's cooking all the dishes you told her you missed most, isn't she?'

'She's done everything I've asked her to – and more,' I agreed.

'But you still need to accept in your heart that Dido is *not* her grandmother, don't you?' she said. 'She's never wronged you and, in fact, now she knows of the link, seems to be redoubling her efforts to please you.'

I moved about the room restlessly, picking things up, then putting them down again.

'I know, it's just . . . if I only *knew* for *sure*,' I burst out. 'But even if I did, would that make things better, or worse? I thought worse, but now . . .'

I tailed off and looked at Nancy, who was regarding me intently.

'Sorry, Nancy, you have no idea what I'm talking about! It turns out that I do have one last secret you haven't yet divined.'

'I wouldn't be too sure about that!' she said. 'One moment, I'll just fetch something from my room.'

She was back in a moment, carrying a large, leather-bound volume.

'Asa's family photo album. I borrowed it from Xan, though, apart from Asa, I didn't expect to recognize anyone in it.'

She opened the album where a slip of paper marked a page and held it out to me, so I could see a large photograph of Asa, with his arm around the shoulders of a tall, blonde, frail-looking young woman.

'Asa's younger sister, Ariadne. She was such an invalid, wasn't she, poor girl?' Nancy said gently. 'I only met her once, when Stephen and I came out to stay with you for our honeymoon and I believe she died soon after.'

I stared at the photograph speechlessly. Ariadne had half turned towards her brother and there was no mistaking that perfect, Grecian profile.

'The moment I saw it, I realized why Dido looked so familiar,' Nancy said.

'I hadn't made the connection with Ariadne, but it was such a shock when I first saw how very tall and fair Dido was . . . and her eyes are green, even if not the same shade as Asa's. And then, of course, I checked and discovered that she didn't take after either of her parents – nor Faye, of course.'

'And these suspicions made you feel even more bitterly towards Dido?'

'Yes. I knew Asa had had his little flings, but to think he and Faye . . .'

'Yes, it was very bad of him indeed, but I'm sure he must always have had it on his conscience.'

'The horrible suspicion first crossed my mind when I heard that Faye had come back with a child in tow . . . but then, when I saw a photograph of the boy, so small and nondescript, I felt ashamed that I'd even thought of it!'

I took another hasty pace or two around the room.

'And now Xan, who has always been more like a son to me than a godson, wants to marry Dido, and I feel totally confused about what I should do.'

'There is nothing you *can* do about Dido and Xan, because they love each other. But I do think, dearest Sabine, that it's time for you to be brave and let the old wounds finally heal, no matter how deep they run.'

'It's not that easy, Nancy!'

'It might be, if you could look at it in the right way: that Xan, whom you love like a son and who is a very distant family connection of your mother's, and Dido, who is both related to your father's family and, as I'm sure we're both now convinced, to your beloved husband, should unite and go on together into a happy future, would be a most wonderful outcome.'

I looked at her speechlessly, but she was smiling lovingly at me.

'I don't think I can do it, Nancy! I'm not that brave – or generous!'

'You can if I help you. And once you've readjusted your mindset and accepted it,' she went on, as if I was a faulty television, 'everything will become *much* simpler.'

She got up. 'Now I'll go and pray that your heart will be filled with love and forgiveness, and that, in the coming days, we'll all experience the true spirit of Christmas.'

'I think *you're* the true spirit of Christmas, Nancy!' I told her, and she kissed me and went out, taking the old photograph album with her.

38

Broken Ice

The rest of the afternoon had flown by as I cooked for the days ahead and then prepared the dinner, all accompanied by the steady dripping of water from the gutters as the snow melted. It was looking unlikely that we'd have any left for Christmas Day.

Henry and Dom, who now appeared to have become a double act, laid the tea trolley and wheeled it off at the usual time, but when Henry collected it later, he said the sitting room was now like the *Mary Celeste* and he thought everyone must have gone upstairs.

'To change, or sulk, or whatever takes their fancy. I've lit the dining-room fire and Dom and I got the table looking *lovely* before he went upstairs, too.'

'What's tonight's starter?' I asked.

'Some of the little savoury tartlets I whipped up earlier. They're light little morsels, which is all they'll need, before tackling the full Roast Beef Dinner Experience à la Dido.'

'Just right – and everything seems to be on track,' I said, glancing at the clock. 'Let's have a break and you can tell me all about love's young dream.'

'Dido, I think this is the real thing!' he said earnestly. 'It was instant, for both of us!'

'I noticed! And he's so nice, too. Just don't rush things!'

'You're a fine one to talk!'

'In my case, *I* wasn't the one rushing things!' I said with dignity.

Henry, when he'd plied the assembled party with his tasty morsels and Rudge Cocktail, reported that everyone was now well oiled and that this, together with the efforts of Nancy and Nigel, had created a more relaxed and mellow atmosphere among the guests.

'Mrs Powys is looking very *grande dame* tonight in black lace and *very* sparkly earrings, and Sophie's wearing a one-shouldered slinky jumpsuit that looks as if it's been painted on her. Quite indecent, really.'

'Is she going to wear a different outfit every evening, do you think?' I asked. 'How much luggage did she bring with her?'

'Two large suitcases and one of those professional-looking vanity boxes.'

'Obviously prepared for every eventuality!' I said.

The roast beef was quite perfect – brown on the outside and faintly pink within. The Yorkshire puddings were perfect too, though, of course, I'd cheated with those and they were ready-made frozen ones.

But my roast potatoes looked so golden they seemed caramelized, and the gravy was rich and thick, as I knew Mrs Powys preferred it.

When I helped Henry carry in the main course, Xan was pouring the wine, as usual, and Dom passing the filled glasses, and both looked up at our entrance and smiled. Simon, though, seemed unable to tear his eyes away from Sophie's cleavage, a crevasse down which you could have concealed several mountaineers and at least one Sherpa.

I thought Mrs Powys looked tired and a little remote, as if she was thinking deeply about something. But when Sophie remarked loudly and rudely that my cuisine was certainly not cordon bleu and on the stodgy side, she told her sharply that I was cooking the dishes *she* had chosen and if any of her guests didn't like it, they needn't eat it.

I left the room after that, but I'm sure Sophie must have done her best to backtrack, for the next time I went in, she was fulsomely admiring Mrs Powys's earrings. I noticed Mr Makepeace giving her another of those uneasy glances – and I supposed, for a cautious solicitor, not knowing what his granddaughter would do or say next would be worrying!

The earrings *were* very spectacular – a large South Sea pearl, to match her necklace, set in a rectangular border of sparkling diamonds.

'They were my mother's, but I rarely wear them, because they're quite heavy . . . and I think,' she added, touching one, 'that the catch has become loose on this one.'

She looked across the table. 'Lucy, you must take it to the jewellers in Hexham after Christmas and get it repaired.'

'Yes, Cousin Sabine,' said Lucy, who had arrayed herself in unbecoming grey again, as if in half-mourning for something.

The treacle tart went in – *more* stodge for Sophie, though I expect she kept her mouth shut about it this time – and I laid the coffee tray ready, before starting to stack the first lot of dirty crockery into the dishwasher, under Plum's melting and ever-hopeful dark gaze.

Henry, bringing back the cheeseboard and the remains of the

treacle tart – a scant sliver – opened his hand to show me some-thing that caught the kitchen light in a shower of sparkles.

'I just found one of Mrs Powys's earrings under the table.'

'She did say something about the catch on one of them being loose.'

'I'll give it to her when I take in the coffee,' he said, popping it into the pocket of his tunic and then adding a plate of mar-zipan *petits fours* to the tray. In his eyes, no drink should be unaccompanied by something to nibble, even if they'd just had a big roast beef blowout.

'You do,' I said absently, looking at the remains of the beef and thinking it would make good sandwiches to go with the soup for lunch tomorrow – but what *kind* of soup?

'Carrot and coriander,' I decided aloud, 'the old standby, but always good. I'd better take some stock out of the freezer.'

'Lost you again,' said Henry, picking up the tray and bear-ing it out.

When he came back, I remembered to ask, 'Did you give Mrs Powys her earring?'

'Yes, but she said she didn't trust the catch any more, so took the other one out, too, and dropped them into that china jar of potpourri on the mantelpiece for safekeeping.'

'What's everyone doing now?' I asked curiously.

'Oh, mostly just slumped into a postprandial stupor after that sumptuous dinner, though I expect Mrs Powys will insist on bridge again. Nancy was looking for the Monopoly set. She says it's her favourite game, but she always has to be the top hat, just as *you* always insist on being the dog.'

'And then I feel compelled to buy all the properties in my favourite colours, whether it's a good financial idea or not,' I laughed.

'We haven't had much chance to play board games since

we've been here,' Henry said. 'But maybe later tonight, if you aren't too tired. I bet you're only halfway through your list of things to do this evening!'

And he was right, because when Xan came in later to see where Plum had got to, I was just at the critical stage of rolling up a sheet of sponge cake, spread with chocolate butter icing, to make a Swiss roll.

'Nigel was suggesting we play charades, so I sneaked out,' he said. 'Where's Henry?'

'Talking to himself on camera upstairs, I think,' I said. 'He pre-set a load of film clips to go up on his vlog over Christmas, but he's been adding occasional live ones.'

I finished rolling the sponge up without it cracking and put it on a rectangular silver cake board, before pulling a bowl towards me and starting to beat the contents.

'What are you going to do with that Swiss roll?' he asked.

'It'll be a festive log, once I've spread this chocolate butter icing all over it: haven't you ever had one of those?

'No, but I know what you mean.'

'This one's for tea tomorrow, so you can try it then.'

He watched me as I took a butter knife and spread the icing over the cake in a rough bark-like effect, then added an over-sized plastic robin and a sprig of holly to the top.

'There,' I said, standing back to admire it.

'I can see I'm going to be vying with your cooking for your attention for the next few days,' he said wryly.

'Well, it is Christmas Eve tomorrow – and then Christmas Day dinner is always quite a challenge – so much to get on to the table at the same time!'

Xan, it appeared, loved scraping chocolate butter from mixing bowls, almost as much as he did cake batter . . .

*

After that late-afternoon thaw, the temperature must have plummeted dramatically overnight, because Henry only got as far as the top of the drive next morning on his way to collect the papers, before turning back: the melted snow had turned the road into an ice rink.

'Maybe later, though it's still freezing out there, so I suspect no one is going anywhere today.'

'The lake's probably OK for skating again, though,' I suggested.

'I'd better grit the path across the lawn and the first flight of steps later, then, in case anyone fancies it,' he said.

'If it's really that bitterly cold, it might not seem very tempting,' I suggested.

Xan said much the same when he came in with Plum, having only ventured out as far as the edge of the herb garden. Plum hadn't been too keen on the icy wind.

'Neither was I – it felt like blades of ice,' he said, filling Plum's bowl up with gourmet doggy dinner. 'It's made me ravenous, though.'

'Then it's just as well breakfast is nearly ready,' I said. 'And then I've *such* a lot to do afterwards!'

'She loves it all, really,' Henry told him. 'She's going to be a culinary tornado until after Boxing Day.'

'I create, rather than destroy,' I pointed out.

'Nancy's told Sabine that you and Henry must join us for dinner tonight, as well as on Christmas Day,' Xan said.

'That was a kind thought, but I'd much rather not, because it's easier for me just to cook and serve. I suppose we'll have to, on Christmas Day, though, since Sabine's already mentioned that to Henry.'

'I'll tell Nancy,' he said, 'or you can, because here she is!'

'Good morning, my dears!' said Nancy, her misty blue eyes

bright and her silver hair as flyaway as ever. 'I thought I'd come and tell you that everyone's now down, except you, of course, Xan, but I thought you'd be in here.'

Xan told her that we'd much rather *not* dine with everyone that evening, and she said she quite understood.

'But we must all eat together on Christmas Day!' she insisted, and then she and Xan took the coffee pot and milk jug, and followed Henry as he bore the last of the hot dishes to the morning room.

I made tea in the big, flowery pot and when I took it in, found Henry on toaster duty, catching the slices as they flew out of the slightly explosive machine.

'Can I get you something hot, Sabine?' asked Nigel, lifting the lids of the dishes on the hotplate and examining the contents.

'Just scrambled eggs and bacon, thank you, Nigel,' she said, and accepted a cup of coffee from Xan.

Then, looking round the table, she said, 'I find myself somewhat mystified this morning, for on my way down I went into the sitting room to retrieve my earrings. If you recall, I took them out because the catch on one was loose and I distinctly remember dropping them into that pot of potpourri on the mantelpiece.'

'Yes, you did, right after I'd given you the one I'd found in the dining room,' agreed Henry, putting more triangles of toast in the silver rack.

'Precisely. But they were not there this morning,' said Sabine. 'Lucy, did you remove them, meaning to put them by till you could take them to be mended?'

'No, Cousin Sabine, I haven't been in that room since yesterday evening.'

'Anyone?' asked Sabine, looking questioningly round the table.

Sophie, who was nibbling a slice of dry toast, just shook her head in a disinterested way, but there was a chorus of 'no' from the others.

Mr Makepeace looked worried. 'But they must be there somewhere, my dear Sabine! Perhaps they've slipped right under the potpourri?'

'I felt right around the jar, and they were not there,' Sabine said.

'You might have managed to miss the jar entirely and we'll find them mixed in with Henry's holly and ivy swags,' Xan suggested easily. 'They'll be there somewhere.'

'Yes, let's all play Hunt the Earrings after breakfast, the new Christmas party game!' Dom said with a grin.

'I expect you're right, Xan, and I wasn't concentrating on what I was doing,' Mrs Powys said.

'I could go and look now, if you like?' offered Simon, kindly. He'd loaded his plate high, like one starved of good food for a very long time, which he probably had been.

'Thank you, but no, after breakfast will do.'

'Is there any cream for my coffee?' asked Olive Melling plaintively. 'I do prefer it to milk in the mornings.'

'Of course – I'll fetch some now,' I said, and hurried out.

'That was very odd,' said Henry a little later, shutting the baize door behind him. 'I thought everyone had left the morning room, so went to start clearing – but there were Mr Makepeace and Sophie over by the window, having what looked like a furious argument in whispers.'

'I wouldn't have thought he was the argumentative type,' I said, surprised.

'No, he seems even more buttoned up than Frank Melling!'

'I expect he finds the way Sophie's been behaving – not to mention what she's been wearing! – very embarrassing, especially since he's here partly in his professional capacity,' I suggested. 'She does seem a bit of a loose cannon.'

'Maybe that's it,' he agreed. 'They stopped talking when they saw me and went out.'

He dumped his load of dishes on the work surface. 'I'll just stack these in the dishwasher and then go and see if they've found the earrings.'

'Oh, I expect they have by now . . .' I said absently, thinking I really ought to add a layer of custard to the fresh trifle, now that the jelly and sponge was firmly set. I'd made a fruit jelly in the antique pottery mould I'd found in the shape of a turreted castle. I hoped it would come out in one piece . . .

'The mystery thickens!' Henry announced, coming back with Nancy in tow.

I looked up. 'Haven't they found the earrings?' I asked, startled.

'Oh, yes – just now. But only after they'd all been searching for ages – and then in waltzed Sophie, stuck her hand into the matching jar of potpourri at the other end of the mantel-piece and—'

'Pulled out a plum!' finished Nancy. 'But not this one,' she added, stooping to pat Plum's head, as he looked up at the sound of his name. I hadn't even noticed he was there till then.

'So the earrings had been in the other pot all along?' I said.

'Well, that's the mystery,' said Henry, 'because Xan said he'd already looked in there and, in any case, I'd be prepared to swear that Mrs Powys put the earrings in the *other* jar last night.'

'I wasn't looking, but if you say so, Henry, then I believe you,' said Nancy. 'It's all very strange – but the main thing is that we have found them. Sabine's gone to lock them away in her jewel case.'

She turned to Henry. 'Now, let's get on and whisk around the bedrooms, Henry, dear – and I think Dom said he'd help, too, though he's not terribly domesticated.'

'You don't need a lot of skill to hang the towels neatly on the heated rails and wipe a washbasin,' Henry pointed out. 'It'll be good for him.'

'What's Xan up to?' I asked.

'He's taken Simon into the study to show him some of the artefacts you found in the cupboards,' Nancy said. 'Sophie tagged along, too, but if she's expecting to see treasure from shipwrecks, I feel she's going to be bitterly disappointed!'

I transferred a few things from the freezer to the fridge and then began to make stock with the turkey giblets, for tomorrow's gravy.

Advance preparation is the key to a successful Christmas dinner . . . but it was just as well that today's lunch would be a doddle, with roast beef sandwiches and the soup I'd already made.

The stock was simmering gently when the bell for the library suddenly jangled and, since there was no sign of Henry, I went to answer it.

'There you are,' said Nancy, who was standing next to Mrs Powys, by the window. 'And I'm *sure* we've dragged you away at an inconvenient moment, but Sabine wanted a quick word with you.'

She smiled encouragingly at my employer, who returned it with one pencilled eyebrow raised and then, as if she'd been given a silent command, turned to face me.

'Dido, since you got here, I haven't always spoken to you as I should have done. In fact,' she added, as if the words were being dragged out of her, 'I've let my knowledge of your link

441

to my half-sister colour my attitude towards you and I'm very sorry for it.'

I stared at her for a moment in complete astonishment and then stammered, 'Th-thank you! But once I knew . . . I mean, it was perfectly understandable, Mrs Powys.'

'There,' said Nancy comfortably, beaming from one to the other of us. 'And Sabine has come to appreciate everything you do to make us so comfortable – not to mention, well fed!'

'I – enjoy it,' I said lamely, then asked if I might be excused, since I had stock simmering on the stove.

'Yes, thank you, Dido, that will be all,' Mrs Powys said, more in her usual manner, and I left the room.

What an odd little scene that had been! I suspected Nancy had had her friend in a sort of virtual armlock, but for all that, she had held out an olive branch and I was not the one to refuse it.

After lunch Xan insisted I go for a short walk with him, and since several of the others had had the same idea, we took the track through the woods rather than head down the garden terraces.

'It'll be nice when the guests have all gone home again, apart from Nancy, and we can spend more time alone together,' he said, putting an arm around me. 'It's an odd situation, with you and Henry running yourselves ragged, doing all the work, and the rest of us swanning about, enjoying ourselves.'

'We don't mind. It's our job and what we're here for,' I pointed out. 'And anyway, you, Dom and Nancy are helping out, too, which makes it all much easier.'

'Dom and Henry seem practically joined at the hip, don't they?' he said with a grin.

'Yes, it's rather nice – and Mrs Powys doesn't seem to mind *that* little romance. She's stopped objecting when you and the others help us out with the chores, as well.'

'I think she's mellowing and she'll soon get used to the idea of you and me, too. I suspect Nancy's been talking her round and telling her you couldn't help having Faye as a grandmother.'

'And I'm sure you're right!' I said, and told him all about that very strange little scene in the library earlier.

'Well, it's certainly a step in the right direction,' he said. 'By the way, Sabine's told us all to be in the sitting room just before three this afternoon, ready for the next instalment of the Mitras Castle Christmas Experience.'

'I bet she didn't put it like that!' I said, laughing. 'But yes, you're to all gather around the radio at three, for the annual carol service by the Choir of King's College, Cambridge. There'll be mince pies and mulled wine. I usually listen to that in the kitchen,' I added. 'It's one of *my* annual traditions, too.'

'I think Nancy wants us *all* there together – and then afterwards, we're to gather round the upright piano in the billiard room and sing some carols of our own, with Nancy playing the music.'

'What, Henry and me, too?'

'I expect so – even if you do slip off at some point, lured by the call of the kitchen.'

Plum, who had run ahead, now came back and looked up hopefully.

'Time to turn back, I think,' I said. 'And there are Dom and Henry in a clinch in the shrubbery. Let's tiptoe tactfully off and leave them to have their moment.'

'I'd quite like a little moment of my own, first . . .' he said.

39

A Christmas Carol

We carried the mulled wine and warm mince pies through to the sitting room just before three, so we could serve them before the carol service started on the radio.

Then we took seats by the window, outside the group of guests gathered around the fire, and I closed my eyes and leaned back in my chair to enjoy the singing.

It was, as always, both beautiful and uplifting. For me, this service always heralded the true start of Christmas.

I think almost everyone present seemed to feel the same way . . . except Sophie, who continued to play with her phone. Mrs Powys, who was sitting on the sofa next to Nancy, continued to lean back with her eyes closed and I noticed, for the first time, that her face, under the mask of make-up, had gone from thin to haggard.

She had such a vibrant nature, I tended to forget that she was very ill, and also very old, although like Nancy, who was now talking quietly to Lucy and Nigel, you tended to forget that because their spirits were perpetually youthful.

Henry and I slipped quietly away, bearing the empty glasses and plates and the bowl that had held the mulled wine.

'Nearly time for tea. It's just one long round of food and drink till after Boxing Day now,' said Henry, pausing to switch on the fairy lights on the big tree in the Great Hall as we passed.

The pile of presents on the low table and around it seemed to have multiplied . . . and I'd noticed a couple more under our tree, too, that morning.

'You wouldn't think anyone would be interested in tea after the mulled wine and mince pies,' I observed, 'but I'm sure Mrs Powys would have something to say if it didn't appear at the usual time, Christmas Eve or not!'

I expected they'd make short work of my delicious-looking chocolate log, in any case!

Xan was quite right about Nancy insisting that the whole household should gather together in the billiard room after tea, to sing carols and other Christmas songs, while she played a vigorous accompaniment on the upright piano.

'Olive, you can turn the music for me and, Sabine, you sit here, in this comfortable chair,' she directed. 'The rest of you should stand, so you can fill your lungs properly and really sing out with a joyful heart!'

'Such a bossy boots!' murmured Sabine affectionately, but she did as she was told and Plum immediately lay across her feet in his best heraldic beast pose.

'Can we start with "O Little Town of Bethlehem"?' asked Lucy. 'That's my favourite!'

'Of course – it's mine, too,' agreed Nancy.

'*And* mine,' said Nigel cheerfully. 'This is fun, isn't it?' He seemed to have put aside any huffiness and was full of bonhomie and the desire to ensure that everyone enjoyed themselves . . . whether they liked it, or not.

Glancing round at the others, I wasn't sure the general level of appreciation matched his own, except for Lucy, who looked flushed and eager, and Olive, seated next to Nancy and ready to turn the music.

Mr Makepeace stood politely ready, but Frank had his hands in his pockets and wore a bored, but resigned, expression.

Dom and Xan came in last and joined us at the back of the group. I think Simon would have, too, except Sophie put a detaining hand on his arm and began whispering something in his ear.

Nancy struck up the first tune on the piano, and we were off. Olive sang in a surprisingly deep contralto, while Mr Makepeace produced a light tenor from somewhere in that wizened frame.

Xan had slipped an arm around my waist, which was distracting, as was his habit of humming along when he forgot the words.

It was all great fun, though. Carols and popular Christmas songs succeeded each other, and Dom and Henry tried to harmonize over 'Away in a Manger'.

In one of the pauses, Nigel, who had been singing along lustily, if untunefully, said it reminded him of when he and Lucy were little and their grandmother would play carols and hymns on the piano.

I thought Nigel was probably softer-centred and nicer than I had at first thought, even if he did have an inflated sense of his own importance in the family, which was doomed, I feared, to disappointment as regards Mitras Castle.

Eventually I had to creep out in order to make a start on preparations for dinner – and it was only then that I noticed Sophie and Simon were no longer there. They must have sneaked away at some point. If Mrs Powys had noticed, she wouldn't be pleased about it!

It was rather rude of them and I wouldn't have expected it

from Simon, who was not only a guest but also, to some extent, her employee, since she was the director of the trust that employed him and owned both the site and his cottage. But then, the poor man was, it seemed, entirely in thrall to Sophie, who I was sure was only amusing herself by flirting with him and not at all serious. I hoped he wouldn't get hurt – he struck me as very vulnerable.

Still, there was nothing I could do about it and I put it out of my head as I made my way back to the kitchen, still filled with the feeling of peace and goodwill to all men – and *almost* all women – engendered by the singing.

The members of the house party were finally beginning to come together and enjoy themselves, so now, if only Mrs Powys refrained from amusing herself by winding Nigel and the Mellings up, all would be well . . .

'You should see what Sophie's wearing tonight,' Henry said, having taken through to the sitting room tonight's starter, along with a shaker full of his renowned Christmas Cocktail. 'She's literally the Scarlet Woman – or rather, vermilion, with lipstick, talons and a whopping great ring to match.'

'What stone is vermilion?' I enquired, looking up from the pots and pans.

'Carnelian, I think. That seems to range from pinkish to bright red, doesn't it?'

'I'll see if I can get a quick look when we take the main course in,' I said. 'And see – my castle-shaped fruit jelly came out in one piece!'

'It looks as if it came out of a child's sandcastle mould! Do you want me to whip any cream up for the top of the trifle?'

'No, that's for tomorrow, for those who prefer it to Christmas pudding.'

'Since we'll be there for dinner too, albeit below the salt, *I* hope to eat both,' he said greedily.

'You have to ignite the brandy on the pudding and then carry it in, first,' I pointed out. 'I'll put heatproof mats down on that little table in the passage outside the dining-room door, and you can light it there. Preferably, without singeing your eyebrows.'

'I only did that *once*,' he said, hurt. 'But I always enjoy the bit where the lights go off and I carry the flaming pud in!'

'Me too . . . and this is all nearly ready,' I said, checking the oven.

'So is the dining room! Dom helped me make the table look uber-festive, with one of those tasselled and embroidered Christmas runners down the middle.'

'Lovely. In ten minutes you can beat the gong for dinner, because you can't hang about when it's fish.'

Tonight, I was giving them thick, melt-in-the-mouth fillets of smoked Scottish rainbow trout, which would look impressive, but was really very easy to cook. It would be accompanied by dauphinoise potatoes.

When the time came, I carried the dish of trout fillets through myself, and when I set it down in the middle of the table Mrs Powys looked at it appreciatively.

'Is that trout? How lovely!'

'Smoked rainbow trout,' I said. 'I thought it would make a nice change.'

'Indeed. I think you're an inspired cook, Dido,' agreed Mr Makepeace.

'I must say, one was rather dreading Maria's monotonous lamb and rice offerings,' drawled Frank.

Sophie, whose red dress left as little to the imagination as her previous ones, reached out a hand for her wine glass, which Dom had just filled and I spotted the ring Henry had mentioned. Given the size and colour of it, it would be a bit hard to miss.

It had a large, flat, oval stone, the same colour as her dress, surrounded by a twisted, rope-like gold setting, and had caught Simon's eye, too.

'That ring – isn't it a Roman intaglio stone?'

'How clever of you to spot it, but then, you *are* an expert,' she said.

'May I see?' he asked eagerly, and she slid it off and passed it over.

'The setting is more modern, of course – Victorian, I should think,' he said, 'but the stone *is* Roman.'

He examined it more closely, then said with interest, 'I think I've only seen that particular design once before. It looks like a mouse, driving a chariot pulled by a rooster!'

But I had now edged round a bit and was staring at the ring too, for there was something about it – and especially that description – that rang a bell in my memory. I, too, had seen one like it once before . . .

Sophie, looking up, must have caught my expression for her own suddenly changed and she said, very sharply, 'Could I have it back, please, Simon?'

He looked surprised, but immediately returned it and she put it back on to her finger.

I recovered myself with an effort, hoping everyone had been looking at the ring and not at me, then went quickly out of the room.

Alone in the kitchen, I felt both shaken and confused. Sophie's expression when she'd suddenly noticed my interest in the ring – both guarded and guilty – had been exactly the same as the one she'd worn on that day, so long ago, when I'd spotted her coming out of the side door of Charlotte's parents' house.

All at once, dizzyingly, a whole raft of fragmented memories from that time had clicked together in my head to form a pattern.

'Are you all right, Dido?' asked Henry a few minutes later. 'You suddenly went quite white and dashed off.'

'I . . . had a shock, but I hope no one else noticed,' I said. 'It was that Roman ring Sophie was wearing – Charlotte's mother had an identical one and, what's more, it went missing that last time I stayed with them! I was so miserable about Xan that it sort of got pushed to the back of my mind at the time, but later I thought Charlotte's mum might have suspected me of taking it, because they never invited me to stay again.'

'I'm not sure I've got the hang of this,' Henry said. 'Charlotte's mother lost a ring like Sophie's when you were staying with her that last time?'

'Yes, she said she'd left it in the downstairs cloakroom, but it wasn't there later and was never found. But I'm sure now it happened on the same day that I bumped into Sophie coming out of the side door of the house. I said she had a strange expression on her face then, didn't I? And I've just seen its twin now, when she noticed me staring at the ring!'

Henry was frowning. 'So . . . you suspect it's the same ring and she took it?'

'Well, it does all sort of fit together, and then Sophie denied ever going into the house, or seeing me that day, which puzzled me.'

'But surely, if she *had* taken it, she wouldn't wear it now, when you might see and recognize it?' he suggested reasonably.

'I think, after all this time, she might have forgotten exactly what it was she'd taken, until she saw me looking at it. I mean, she's not the brightest bunny in the box, is she? And I don't suppose she'd ever *seen* Charlotte's mum wearing it, because she and a friend only came over to play tennis, or swim in their pool, with Xan and Gerry.'

'I can see you're quite sure in your own mind that she took it.'

'Yes, I am,' I said, positively. 'It's the design of the stone, too, because I remember Charlotte's mum telling us all about it one evening, and how unusual it was. And she treasured it. It was a family piece and she thought it was lucky.'

Henry accepted this. 'I wonder if it was a one-off moment when she gave into temptation, or if Sophie's a habitual picker-upper of valuable trifles.'

'I don't know,' I said, startled. 'Why do you say that?'

'Because I was thinking about the way Mrs Powys's earrings went missing – and how Sophie suddenly came in and found them in a place both I and Xan had already searched.'

'That was . . . odd,' I agreed slowly. 'And you said her grand-father seemed to be arguing with her in the morning room only minutes before that, so perhaps he suspected she'd taken them.'

'If so, she might be a kleptomaniac and not able to help herself,' Henry said charitably. 'But if she is and he knows it, he really shouldn't have brought her with him!'

I sighed. 'I could be wrong – we might *both* be wrong – and there could be two rings with stones like that, though actually, it wasn't just the stone I remembered, but the gold setting, too, like twisted rope.'

'What are you going to do about it?' he asked.

'Nothing right now, till dinner's over. You'd better go and clear while I bring the dessert,' I said more briskly, though I still felt as wobbly as my castle jelly.

'I think after that, I'll email Charlotte, who'll be at her parents' house by now, and see if they still have a photograph and description of the ring she could scan and send back to me. I expect it was insured at the time, though I think old Roman rings aren't as valuable as you might imagine.'

'No, but it sounds as if it had great sentimental value to Charlotte's mum,' he said. 'Good idea – let's not say anything about it until you hear back.'

Charlotte had been wrapping presents and quickly pinged me back photos and a description of the ring, including hallmark and maker's mark. She wrote:

> They were still in Mum's insurance file in the cabinet. Why do you want to know? Have you spotted one that might be it somewhere? Mum would think it was the best Christmas present ever to have it back again! Stop being so mysterious!

I wrote back:

> I'll explain as soon as I can – don't say anything to your mum yet, in case I'm wrong.

But looking at the photographs and the description, I was very sure in my own mind I was right.

Nancy, Dom and Xan helped Henry clear away, then joined the others when he carried the coffee tray to the sitting room, though Nancy lingered a little.

'Are you all right, Dido?'

'Fine,' I said. 'Just preoccupied with everything I still need to do tonight to be ready for tomorrow.'

She seemed satisfied with this, but Henry knew me better

and when he came back he demanded to know what Charlotte had said.

He whistled when he saw what she'd sent me, then got me to forward them to him, so he could print them out in the library later.

'Nancy told Mrs Powys she would have liked us to join them all in the sitting room tonight, but she was sure we'd be much too busy – which of course, we will be. I think she hates leaving us out of the fun – though, of course, you have your own unique idea of fun.'

'Mm . . .' I said absently, unpinning the next to-do list from the corkboard and spreading it out on the table.

And after that, I managed to put the whole worry about the ring to the back of my mind, even if it was reawakened later, when Henry shoved under my nose the printouts of what Charlotte had sent me.

'All we have to do now is compare these – especially the hallmarks and maker's mark – with Sophie's ring to be sure one way or the other.'

'That *sounds* easy, but if either of us asks to borrow it she's going to smell an enormous rat!'

'There has to be a way round it,' he mused, just as the baize door swung open and Nancy and Xan came in, followed by Plum.

'We sneaked off on the excuse that Plum wanted to go out and we both needed a breath of air,' Xan said.

'But really we've come because I'm convinced, despite what you said earlier, that there's something troubling you, Dido – and Xan thinks the same.'

Henry and I exchanged glances. Then he said slowly, 'A trouble shared . . . ?'

I nodded and he spread the printouts across the kitchen

table. 'Take a look at these. Does anything strike you as familiar about that ring?'

When they'd pored over the photographs, we told them everything we knew – or suspected – and that I was quite certain in my own mind that it *was* the same ring.

'Well,' said Nancy finally, 'I expect you are right and, of course, it can easily be proved, one way or the other. But if it *is* the same, then the girl might simply say she bought it in an antique shop – and perhaps she did.'

'It's possible,' I agreed. 'But in that case, who stole it in the first place? And why did she insist that she never saw me on the day it went missing, when I met her coming out of the house?'

'There is that,' agreed Xan. 'And there's something else that has bothered me: that business with the earrings earlier. I suspected Sophie had taken them and then put them in the other jar, possibly from malice, because Sabine has slapped her down a couple of times.'

'*We* wondered about that, too!' Henry exclaimed. 'They definitely weren't in that jar a couple of minutes earlier.'

'Then there's the way Timothy keeps glancing at her, as if she's a bomb about to go off,' Nancy said, to my surprise.

'You noticed that, too?'

'You couldn't really miss it,' she said, then added practically, 'So, we can easily prove if it's the missing ring, though not how it came to be in Sophie's possession.'

'I don't think Charlotte's mum would be too concerned about that. She'd just be so delighted to have it back again,' I said.

'Then at some point, it must be compared to these print-outs and, if it is, as we think, the same ring, we must face Sophie with it.'

'At which point, she can say, "Oh, how very strange! I had

no idea when I bought it!" and offer to return it to its original owner,' supplied Xan.

'Yes, that would get over the matter easily,' Nancy agreed. 'But of course, this is Sabine's house, and Sophie and her grandfather are her guests, so the matter must be laid before her, and what happens then must be her decision.'

'Yes, you're right,' said Xan. 'We can't keep her in the dark about something like this. But must we tell her right away?'

'No. I think we should strive to put it out of our heads until after tomorrow, so we can embrace Christmas with love and joy towards each other.'

'As long as I don't actually have to embrace Sophie, I think I can manage that,' I said. I gathered the printed pages and held them out to her. 'You'd better take charge of these.'

'Of course. I'll keep them for the right moment, if you're happy to leave it to me?'

'More than happy!' I said with a sigh, feeling a huge sense of relief that any investigations or decisions would be taken out of my hands.

'We'd better get back,' Nancy said, and though Xan showed a desire to linger, I firmly shooed him – and Plum – out before metaphorically rolling up my sleeves.

'Come on, Henry. We've got a lot to get through tonight!'

When I finally fell into an exhausted sleep that night, I had a nightmare in which Sophie, wearing Minnie Mouse ears, was pursuing me in a chariot pulled by a plucked and headless turkey.

Sabine

'It's been such a lovely Christmas Eve,' Nancy said, as we reached our landing and paused outside my door. 'But it's so late, I won't come in, if you promise me you'll take one of your pills and get straight into bed.'

'I'm not stoical enough to do anything else tonight but obey,' I said, smiling at her.

'There's no need for stoicism – and you'll enjoy tomorrow all the more for a good night's sleep.'

'I know – but there's been something puzzling me all day and I want to talk to you about it. Do come in, before any of the others come up!'

'Just for a minute, then,' she agreed, closing the door behind her. 'What's troubling you?'

'Well, the way my earrings vanished from one jar and re-appeared in another, like some kind of conjuring trick! I mean, my illness has not affected either my memory or my mental faculties and I'm perfectly certain that last night, I put those earrings in the right-hand jar on the mantelpiece. Yet this morning, in waltzes that granddaughter of Timothy's and immediately finds them in the other one – which I'd just watched Xan sift through.' I looked at her questioningly. 'You don't think . . . ?'

'I don't think you've lost your marbles and, happily, you haven't lost your earrings either,' she said, smiling. 'I think you should just put the whole incident out of your mind and concentrate on what a wonderful day we'll have tomorrow.'

I eyed her narrowly, with the suspicion that she knew more than she was saying, but she returned my gaze blandly and then gave me one of her sudden, warm hugs and kissed my cheek.

'I was so proud of you earlier today, Sabine, for taking the first step of reconciliation towards Dido. You'll find the rest of the path easier from now on.'

'It couldn't be harder,' I said, but later, as I got into bed, I thought perhaps she had something, for I had an odd feeling of lightness, as if I'd let go of some of the heavy burden of bitterness and hate.

40

Bachelor's Button

Henry and I were both up and busy extremely early. But first, before we did anything else, we unwrapped our presents from under the tree.

There was a big box of chocolate mints from Simon, addressed to both of us, which while uninspired was a nice thought. Henry loved the little oil painting I'd brought him back from California, and his gift to me was a big, bright pink pen with a feathery flamingo fixed to the top on a spring, so it wobbled.

'Tell me you're not giving one of these to Mrs Powys?' I begged.

'I bought the whole box, so I had enough to give one to absolutely *everyone* in the house,' he said, smiling seraphically.

I almost missed the tiny package from Xan, which contained the loveliest pair of gold earrings with tiny dangly spaniels, just like Plum, which I put in straight away.

We cleared up the discarded wrappings and then Henry said, 'Right, let's brace ourselves for a busy day and get on with it!'

Xan must also have been up long before dawn, for he appeared in the kitchen only a few minutes after Henry had gone to lay the fires and tidy the sitting room.

'Happy Christmas, darling!' he said, kissing me, and I thanked him for his present.

'They're beautiful. I love them!'

'Just a token gesture – I'd really like to give you a ring, but we'll have to wait till after Christmas for that,' he said, sliding an arm around me and kissing me again. 'Preferably when I don't have to share your attention with a turkey the size of an ostrich! What are you doing with it?'

'Nothing at the moment, it's just resting. It needs to go in the oven by half past nine at the latest, though.'

'Resting?' he queried, then said, looking puzzled. 'No, never mind!'

Plum had been remarkably patient up till this point, but now vociferously demanded his breakfast.

Once he'd nosedived into it, I said apologetically to Xan, 'My present to you is only that copy of my latest book. It's under the tree in the Great Hall.'

'So is a copy of one of mine, for you – we can open them later.'

'There's a present for Plum there, too, which I hope he'll like,' I said.

'Is it edible?'

'No, though that might not stop him trying.'

Henry came back and said severely, 'Stop distracting the staff, Xan!'

Xan put mugs of coffee in front of us, then looked dubiously down at the jeans he was wearing. 'Perhaps I'd better change these for something a bit smarter. Sabine never expects anyone to dress up, even for dinner, but I feel I should make a bit of an effort on Christmas Day.'

'Yes, we feel the same way, now we're going to be eating our Christmas dinner with everyone else, but in our case it had better be a quick change just before we start serving it,' said Henry, who was energetically beating eggs in a large glass bowl.

'Since I see from her hairstyle that Dido's in Warrior Princess mode again, I'll be interested to see what she changes into!'

'Nothing exciting, and the only thing I'm going to do battle with is the turkey!'

When I suddenly remembered that Olive preferred cream in her morning coffee and took some into the morning room, I found everyone there, except Sophie, tucking in.

'Happy Christmas, everyone!' I said generally, and they all chorused greetings in return. Dom, I noticed, was wearing a particularly bright red Christmas jumper with a sparkly reindeer on the front, while Xan, in a soft, loose white open-necked shirt and with one dark lock of hair falling over his forehead, looked exactly like a romantic poet.

'We'll have the present opening at ten, in the Great Hall,' Mrs Powys was decreeing. 'And you and Henry must be there, too, Dido, even though I'm sure you'll be very busy this morning. You can slip away for ten minutes.'

'Of course you can,' Nancy said, beaming at me. 'I'll put on that lovely CD of carols again, Sabine, while we open our presents. But first, right after breakfast, Dom and I are going to help Henry to whip round the bedrooms – and you know I love to be busy, Sabine,' she added firmly, as Mrs Powys looked about to demur.

'I could help, too, if you liked?' Lucy surprisingly offered. Nancy thanked her, but said kindly that they could manage between them this morning and she should continue enjoying her holiday.

'Shall I put on my Santa suit and hand out the presents?' suggested Nigel eagerly.

'Thank you, Nigel, but I don't think we need trouble you,' Mrs Powys said, and he looked disappointed for a moment.

Then he brightened again and said gaily, 'Then Lucy and I will be two little elves and hand the presents out anyway, though of course *my* gifts – and yours too, Olive – were edible or drinkable, so went straight to the kitchen.'

'Everyone's eating part of *your* gift this morning, Nigel,' I pointed out. 'The smoked salmon you brought.'

'There are still loads of presents under the tree, many of them from me. I think I got carried away at the Christmas fair,' Nancy confessed, twinkling. 'So many *interesting* things.'

Lucy looked gratified and I suspected that her presents to the others would also be more of the same – possibly her own pinked and tasselled bookmarks, or Daphne's ghastly painted pebbles.

I left Henry in charge and hurried back to the kitchen to get the turkey into the oven.

First, I put a little stuffing under the loose skin of the breast and then laid fat, overlapping rashers of streaky bacon over it, before wrapping it in tinfoil.

When I'd slid it into the hot oven, I laid out a row of kitchen timers on the dresser, the first to be set being the chicken-shaped one for the turkey and then the last, shaped like a Christmas tree, would tell me when the pudding was reheated.

To get everything for each course to the table at once required meticulous planning and timing but I had a lot of experience to call on.

Henry, coming back with some empty serving dishes, said, 'Sophie has only just put in an appearance and then immediately complained that there was nothing left on the hotplate and suggested you could cook her something fresh, Dido.'

'In her dreams,' I said, ticking 'Put turkey in oven' off this morning's list.

'That's much what Mrs Powys told her,' he said with a grin. 'And that if she wanted hot food she should have been down earlier.'

'I've never seen Sophie eat anything other than a bit of dry toast anyway,' I said.

'Me neither. I think she was simply being awkward. Simon had a huge plateful of cooked breakfast and offered to share, but she declined.'

'Good, because he needs feeding up, poor man,' I said. 'I do like to see my food appreciated.'

'It was. Even Mr Makepeace had a plateful. He said scrambled egg with smoked salmon was his favourite thing, especially when the salmon had been cut into snippets and cooked with the egg, in the way you do it.'

Henry made us both a couple of rounds of cheese on toast and then sat down to have his, with a pot of one of his strange herbal brews.

'Step one is already accomplished,' I said, standing up to eat mine. 'Now I'll tackle the vegetable mountain!'

'We'll all have to assemble in the Great Hall at ten for the presents,' he reminded me. 'Though you can sneak off after a few minutes, if you need to. I think it might be a coffee and mince pie occasion, too, but I can see to that.'

By ten, the vegetables were sitting in cold water and the Christmas pudding had been removed from the larder, freshly wrapped in greaseproof paper and returned to its spherical mould. This was now sitting on a raised metal ring in a giant saucepan with a little water at the bottom, ready to be steamed for an hour.

I had the brandy for the top ready to be warmed before it was poured over it and lit, just before serving.

That was the trouble with being asked both to cook the dinner and sit down with everyone else to eat it: you were up and down to the kitchen like a yo-yo.

Nigel and Lucy distributed the presents, many of which consisted, as expected, of crafty items from the Christmas fair. Dom and Nancy had been particularly generous in this respect, but there were also conical packets of Nancy's fudge for us all.

Xan and I exchanged copies of our books – and discovered we'd written almost exactly the same messages inside . . .

Mrs Powys's gifts of Liberty scarves and paperknives were well received, even by Sophie, as were the pink champagne truffles Henry and I gave to Lucy. In fact, for a horrible moment, I thought she was going to cry, until luckily her attention became distracted by Xan, who had unwrapped my present to Plum and was now putting him into his new, bright tartan doggy coat.

Plum seemed to rather fancy himself in it, wading about in the discarded, crumpled wrapping paper, so I hoped it would keep him snug on his winter walks.

I think for me, the highlight of the occasion was seeing Mr Makepeace's face when he unwrapped his bright pink flamingo pen, though Mrs Powys seemed quite taken with hers.

Xan and I exchanged smiles before I quietly slipped out, carrying my booty, and left Henry to circulate the last of the mince pies and coffee.

When he brought in his loot ten minutes later, he told me I'd missed seeing Sophie throw a hissy fit.

'Something Nancy said made it suddenly dawn on Sophie that we'd be thirteen for dinner and since she's really superstitious and thinks that's unlucky, she went a bit overboard.'

'Well, we can't magic up another guest, just to please her!'

'It's all right, I told her I'd lay a place for Plum, even if he can only join us virtually. Xan says his table manners aren't up to the challenge.'

Finally, the turkey, roasted to perfection, was resting on one end of the kitchen table and the pudding gently steaming.

Henry had already done a quick change into a shirt and chinos and I left him in charge of the kitchen, while I dashed off to do the same – only in my case, into a sea-green silk tunic and narrow black velvet trousers, *and* my party moccasins, with the gold-beaded thunderbirds on the toes.

'Right!' I said, back down in the kitchen again and wrapping a big apron over my finery. 'I'll make the gravy and then we're good to go!'

'Everything's all ready in the dining room. Mrs Powys gave me place cards and we're sitting at one end, on either side of Xan. Dom helped me lay the table and put the crackers out, so it all looks *perfect*.'

Dom, Xan and Nancy came to help transport the feast to the table, but first Dom was dispatched to beat the gong, which he did with almost as much enthusiasm as Henry usually brought to the task.

'Dinner is served – or about to be,' Henry said, picking up the enormous oval plate bearing the turkey and leading the procession to the dining room.

I was glad I'd remembered to change, because the other women were all wearing what I mentally labelled 'cocktail dresses', though in Sophie's case, that was more of a cocktail tunic.

Of the men, only Frank and Mr Makepeace wore suits. Nigel had now, like Dom, donned a Christmas jumper, though his was adorned, appropriately enough, with the jolly, smiling face of Father Christmas.

Everyone found his or her place and Nigel said he'd take charge of the enormous bottle of champagne, which Henry had had to put in a galvanized pail in lieu of an ice bucket.

'Henry can carve the turkey,' directed Mrs Powys. 'I expect he'll do it better than anyone else.'

'I'm sure you're right, but first, everyone,' said Nancy, 'you must sit down while I say grace.'

'One of your shorter ones, I hope!' said Mrs Powys, but she bowed her head obediently and we all followed suit . . . or at least, since I also closed my eyes, I *assumed* we did – I wouldn't vouch for Sophie.

'Let us pray,' said Nancy, and then, in her soft voice, began:

> *On Christmas Day our hearts we raise*
> *In words of thanksgiving and praise*
> *For bringing us together here*
> *To feast, and share in festive cheer.*
> *But first let's pause, reflect awhile:*
> *Not everyone this day can smile.*
> *You see, dear Lord, we're well aware*
> *That we are in a castle fair;*
> *And many folk cannot afford*
> *Anything like this festive board.*
> *Whoe'er they are, both far and near,*
> *We pray they may be free from fear*
> *Of hunger, loneliness, despair;*
> *And all who have enough may care.*
> *Protect them, Lord, and may they know*
> *Thou cam'st from heaven to earth below*
> *For the whole world, to save us all.*
> *So hear us when to thee we call.*
> *We thank our kind and generous host*

And, gathered here, we're grateful most
To thee, our loving, gracious God,
Who through this human life once trod.
Dear Lord, we pray, leave nothing out:
Bless every parsnip, every sprout,
Bless all thy children, too, and then
We'll praise thee evermore. Amen.

'Amen,' everyone echoed and looked up, blinking back a sudden rush of tears: that had been both touching and funny – and typically Nancy!

'Who wants to pull a cracker with me?' said Nancy brightly.

Lubricated by copious amounts of good champagne, and perhaps influenced by Nancy's words, the party became a very merry one, even Mr Makepeace unbending enough to wear a golden paper crown on his grey head and read out the joke from his cracker.

Sophie, perhaps also due to the champagne, wore her crown like a tiara and throughout the meal, sparkled flirtatiously at Simon, who seemed quite dazzled.

Sophie wasn't, I noticed, wearing her Roman ring today . . . but then, it wouldn't really have gone with her purple dress.

Of course, I had to slip out a couple of times to check on the pudding, finally taking it from its mould to rest on the dish it was to be served in and pouring the brandy for the top into a little pan, ready to warm.

As we cleared the first course, I glowed with the compliments I'd received for my cooking. It's so good to be appreciated!

And then, after the trifle, the jugs of cream and the brandy butter had gone through, Henry carried the pudding to the table outside the dining-room door. Dom was standing ready by the light switch just inside the room and watched as I poured the warm brandy over the top of the pudding, and Henry lit it.

A blueish flame sprang up, Dom clicked off the lights, and Henry triumphantly bore in the pudding, to general applause.

I suppose it was inevitable that, of all the charms it contained, Nigel should get the bachelor's button.

Finally, Mrs Powys tapped her glass for silence and said it had been a wonderful meal – the best Christmas dinner she'd ever eaten – and then graciously thanked everyone for helping to make the day so truly special.

'I'm sure we've *all* been blessed with the true spirit of Christmas today, my dear,' Nancy assured her. 'We're full of goodwill, loving kindness . . . and turkey.'

I saw her eyes rest thoughtfully for a moment on Sophie, then she bestowed a charitable smile on her.

Mrs Powys raised her glass and, to my surprise, said, 'Now, a toast to Dido, for her wonderful cooking!'

'To Dido!' they all said, though Henry added, irreverently, 'And God bless Tiny Tim!'

Nancy organized a small army of helpers for the mammoth clear-up afterwards: Lucy, Dom, Xan and even Simon, temporarily detached from Sophie's grip.

Sophie, of course, had followed Mrs Powys and the others to the sitting room, but I hadn't really expected her to help.

Plum was eager to volunteer for scrap-clearing duty, though, and I slipped him a bit of turkey, before covering it up and putting it back on the stone shelf in the cold larder.

I'd kept a few slices back, though, and now made some turkey and ham sandwiches for cold supper later. By the time those were covered and in the fridge, the kitchen was magically cleared, cleaned and sparkling and the dishwasher busily chugging.

I thanked everyone and then Henry insisted they go and join the party in the sitting room and he'd follow with the coffee shortly.

'Only if you both join us, too,' Nancy said. 'I don't think there's much more you need to do here at the moment, is there?'

'I don't see why not,' agreed Henry.

'Goody – we'll play board games!' she said. 'How else would we spend the afternoon of Christmas Day? Monopoly and Scrabble!'

'*And* Snakes and Ladders,' Dom said. 'That's about my level.'

Henry, returning from taking the coffee, said that Mrs Powys, Olive, Nancy and Lucy were in the drawing room, watching one of the gardening DVDs Mrs Powys had been given for Christmas, and Frank and Mr Makepeace were in there too, but sleeping off the effects of dinner.

'Nigel and Simon are playing chess and Sophie's back to fiddling with her phone again, but perhaps she'll join in with the board games later, you never know.'

'Speaking of phones, I just rang Dad to wish him a quick happy Christmas – he's spending the day with his friends from the university, as usual. He said Granny Celia called earlier, too, and told him to pass her Christmas greeting to me, too, to save her the expense!'

He grinned. 'That sounds like her!'

He removed the bowl containing what was left of the trifle from the fridge and got a spoon.

'There's only a morsel left, so it's not worth putting away.'

'You seem to be putting it away, all right,' I said pointedly. 'You can wash and dry the bowl, when you've finished.'

'Of course, *and* I'll wash the silver pudding charms, too. I had to wrest the horseshoe from Dom, he wanted to keep it.'

'I'm amazed the whole pudding vanished!' I said. 'I now have a spare batch of brandy butter, though . . .'

I'd once made brandy butter ice cream – and now I remembered I'd seen one of those ice-cream makers in a cupboard, the sort where you freeze the container overnight. I fetched it while I remembered and put it in the turkey-sized hole in the biggest freezer, then removed the very large salmon that was to form the basis of tomorrow's dinner.

We sat down at the kitchen table with our own coffee after that. I texted a Christmas message to Charlotte while Henry sent out about a million to all his friends.

'Could you make a few of your thin, crispy almond biscuits to go with ice cream tomorrow?' I asked him.

'OK,' he said amiably, without looking up from his phone.

I stood and stretched. 'I don't think there's anything else urgent to do now, so I'll just go and tidy up, then we'd better join the others before Nancy comes to find us!'

Nigel joined in enthusiastically with all the board games and even Sophie drifted over, from sheer boredom, I think, since Simon was now playing chess with Mr Makepeace.

By then, too, Henry had made his Christmas Cocktail again, which might have mellowed her a little.

Later, we had the cold supper of sandwiches and the remains of the Christmas cake . . . and more drinks.

Then Henry suggested to Mrs Powys that he put on an old Christmas film and we all ended up watching the original version of *Miracle on 34th Street* . . . or dozing off in front of it, as the fancy took us.

And at some point, Sophie and Simon vanished into the next room, ostensibly to play billiards . . .

But, sitting next to Xan on one of the sofas with Plum, as usual, on my knees, I thought it really *had* been a lovely day.

It was late by the time the party began to break up and by then I was feeling bone-tired, but happy.

Henry and I wished everyone goodnight and went back to the staff wing, but it was no surprise that Dom and Xan followed us a few minutes later.

Henry and Dom, kindred spirits, didn't seem in the least sleepy, and said they were going to watch a spoof Christmas horror film, and did we want to join them?

'No, I'm way too tired and want to go to bed,' I said, but I let Xan persuade me to go out with him, when he took Plum for his bedtime walk.

We crunched around the gravel drive to the front of the house, where the solar stars still twinkled on the tree – and so did those set in the clear, ultramarine sky.

The air was still, but bitterly cold, though I breathed it in deeply anyway, feeling my head clear.

'The stars look so beautiful tonight,' I said. 'I'm glad you made me come out.'

'*I'm* glad you did – and *you* are my one true star now,' he said, slipping an arm around me, as Plum skittered off across the crisp grass, where only small patches of snow glimmered here and there.

I turned and kissed him and as his arms tightened around me, he said, 'Best Christmas ever!'

Sabine

'Here's one I prepared earlier,' Nancy quoted, like a TV chef on a cookery programme, brandishing a flask and two mugs as she came into the boudoir.

'Let me guess – cocoa?' I said.

'Got it in one. I could see you were tired but overstimulated – tears before bedtime! – and thought it would help you to sleep.'

'I did feel tired earlier, but got a sort of second wind and woke right up again.'

Nancy poured us both some cocoa and then sat down, saying, cosily, 'There, I do love a good cup of cocoa, and, goodness knows, we've both had enough alcohol today to float a battleship.'

'I never feel champagne really counts,' I said, and she grinned.

'I know what you mean,' she agreed, 'but those cocktails Henry produced were stronger than they tasted! But it's worth being tired tomorrow . . . and possibly a little hungover, because today was so much fun, wasn't it? And also, I felt everyone showed themselves in their true light and I found myself liking them much better than before.'

'True. Frank's still a pompous stuffed shirt, but I've warmed more to Nigel. And even Lucy, irritating though she is, *means* well and tries to be helpful.'

'Damned with faint praise,' said Nancy, with a twinkle. 'Still, today brought everyone together, thanks in no small part to Henry's efforts and Dido's delicious food.'

'And to you, too, Nancy. You're a people person.'

I sighed as the faint feeling of euphoria, which had been keeping me going, finally evaporated and tiredness invaded my body.

'Asa could bring the most disparate of people together – he had such charm and charisma, didn't he?' I said.

'He did indeed, and he would be very proud of you now, my dear,' she said gently. 'I'm also quite certain he'd approve of whatever decision you've come to, regarding your will, because I'm sure you'll have made fair provision for everyone.'

'*I* hope so, too, though some may not agree,' I said. 'But yes, I've made my mind up which will to sign and which to destroy.'

I finished my cocoa and then leaned forward towards her and said, 'And now, dear Nancy, you can tell me whatever it is you've been hiding from me, which I suspect is something to do with the lost and found earrings. And *you* accused *me* of keeping secrets!'

'There is something I haven't yet told you, but at the moment it's just suspicion and conjecture on Dido's part,' Nancy said. 'She had no idea what to do about it, but we agreed that I should lay the matter before you after Christmas, so as not to spoil the day.'

'Well, you've done that – so now, spill the beans!'

She did, carefully presenting the facts and not drawing any conclusions, though I drew a few of my own, especially after she pulled some folded printouts from her bag and showed them to me.

'I never got a good look at the ring,' I said regretfully. 'But it sounds as if Dido is sure in her own mind that it's the same one her friend's mother lost.'

'Yes, though of course that could easily be proved by comparing the photographs and the hallmarks with these,' Nancy said, indicating the papers. 'Of course, even if it *is* the same one, she may have a perfectly innocent explanation for how she came to have it.'

'Perhaps . . .' I said absently, thinking it all over. 'What has Dido told this friend of hers?'

'Only that she might know where the ring is now, but needed the details to be sure.'

'Then that's what we'll do tomorrow. And if, as seems likely, it is the same ring, then I'm inclined to think Sophie stole it – and even more sure than before that she also took my earrings, even if she did return them later.'

'Yes, I think you're right,' Nancy agreed. 'I also suspect that poor Timothy knows she takes things.'

'Poor Timothy nothing! If the girl is a kleptomaniac he should have at least warned us!'

'But if she is, then that's an illness, isn't it? And he might have hoped she'd stopped doing it,' Nancy said charitably. 'But anyway, you *will* be tactful tomorrow, won't you? And, if it's the same ring, proceed on the lines I suggested, so that she can say she bought it somewhere, and then it can be quietly returned to the rightful owner.'

'Tact is my middle name,' I assured her.

'Not that I've ever noticed,' Nancy said drily.

41

Exit, Pursued by a Bear

Xan took Plum up to the top of the drive first thing next morning and, when he came in to give him his breakfast, said that the road was still solid ice, ridged, rutted and refrozen, and nothing was moving along it.

'Not that much *would* at this time of the morning, anyway,' Henry pointed out, turning sausages to brown the other sides, while I took a tray of hash browns out of the oven.

'We're going down-market with breakfast today,' I said. 'Hash browns and baked beans are on the menu, but mushrooms off, since we've run out.'

'I like fried bread, too,' Xan said hopefully.

'I'll make you some after all the other guests have left,' I promised. 'But don't blame me if your arteries immediately fur up.'

'Plum loved wearing his new coat,' Xan said, 'though I still had to dry his tummy and legs.'

Plum looked up for a moment and then, as soon as his bowl hit the floor, nosedived into his breakfast.

Dom wandered in, yawning and with his dark, spiky hair standing on end, and sat on the table while I fried eggs. Then

Nancy came in, too – it was starting to feel like Grand Central Station.

'Sabine's on her way down,' she announced, '*and* she knows about Sophie and the you-know-what. She was suspicious about the earrings anyway and guessed I was keeping something from her, so she made me tell her last night.'

'What *do* you mean?' demanded Dom, intrigued. 'Tell her what? Henry, have *you* been keeping secrets from me?'

'Of course – I want to retain a little mystery,' Henry said. 'Nancy, what's she going to do? Did she say?'

'No, except that she'd deal with it . . . tactfully, I hope. And probably today.'

'Now I feel nervous!' I said, sliding the eggs into a stainless-steel dish. 'Xan, Dom – can you help Henry take these through? And Nancy, perhaps you could carry the plates of sliced ham and cheese?'

I followed them with pots of tea and coffee – and remembered the cream for Olive, this morning.

Today, Sophie was already there and it was Lucy and Mr Makepeace who were the stragglers, coming in together just after me. They were talking about morris dancing, in which they had discovered a bizarre and unlikely mutual passion.

'Oh, *please* don't get Grandpa started on the bells and ribbons stuff,' Sophie said rudely, casting up her eyes.

'Actually, I find the history of morris dancing and mumming fascinating, too,' said Xan mildly. 'You can trace elements of it right back to pagan times.'

'It *is* interesting how those pagan elements were also later absorbed into the Christian mystery plays, like St George and the Dragon,' put in Simon eagerly, before wistfully adding, 'If it hadn't been for my bad leg, I'd have joined the Wallstone Morris Men.'

'*Really?*' Sophie said, disbelievingly. She had put a fried egg on top of her usual slice of dry toast, but now seemed to be having second thoughts about it.

Henry slotted two more slices of toast in the silver rack and asked Mrs Powys if she wouldn't like to try a hash brown with her bacon this morning?

'Maybe just one,' she agreed. 'And perhaps someone could pour me another cup of coffee? I feel a little tired this morning.'

From Mrs Powys, this was quite an admission and she did look fine-drawn and haggard, even if those light blue eyes were as youthfully alive as ever.

I put her coffee in front of her, and she smiled directly at me for the first time *ever*. It wasn't quite the whole three-cornered puckish job, but it was getting there.

'Thank you, Dido – that's just how I like it.'

Nigel said, 'Could I trouble you for some brown sauce, Dido? I always have it on hash browns.'

'You have depraved tastes, Nigel,' joked Mrs Powys. 'Do we have any in the house?'

'Yes – *I* have depraved tastes too,' Henry said.

'I'll fetch it,' I told him. 'You keep an eye on that toaster. The bread does seem to hurtle out of it and hit the floor, if you don't catch it.'

When I got back, there was a certain air of tension in the room that hadn't been there before.

Mrs Powys was in the middle of saying something to Simon. '. . . and I was so interested in what you said about that Roman ring Sophie showed you the other evening that I've been reading up about it. It seems a very rare design.'

Simon was too interested in the subject to question when and how Mrs Powys had read up on the subject, but said eagerly,

'It *is* unusual and I think there's only one other like it, in a museum somewhere.'

'Almost unique, then,' she said as I stood, rooted to the spot and wondering what was coming next . . . until I remembered the bottle of sauce I was clutching and set it down in front of Nigel.

I thought Sophie seemed to have stiffened, but she was now making a big deal of stirring her coffee.

'I didn't get a chance to look at the ring properly, Sophie,' Mrs Powys continued, 'but I'd love to see it again and in a proper light. Why don't you pop upstairs and fetch it?'

'*Now?*' said Sophie, looking up, her brown eyes huge and startled.

'Yes, why not? It won't take you a moment and you appear to have abandoned your breakfast.'

'I – it's gone cold. I was about to have some fresh toast . . . so surely *afterwards* would do?' she suggested.

'Yes, won't later be better, Sabine?' Nancy urged, but when Mrs Powys shook her head, she and Xan looked at each other in a resigned kind of way.

'Timothy and I are going to the library right after breakfast, for a long talk, but I really am *most* interested to see the ring first, so do go and get it, Sophie.'

Mr Makepeace looked sharply across the table at his grand-daughter. 'There's no reason why you shouldn't bring it to show Sabine, is there?' he asked sharply.

'No, of course not!' she said, getting up very slowly. 'I . . . it's just that I'm not entirely sure where I put it when I took it off the other night!'

'Then if you can't find it, we'll all come and help you hunt for it, just as we did for my earrings,' Sabine said, with a smile that seemed to totally unnerve Sophie.

I saw her grandfather glance quickly at her again. 'I expect you can find it.'

Simon, who seemed impervious to any tensions in the room, said, 'I'd like a better look at it in good light, too.'

Without another word, Sophie scraped back her chair and left the room, though I noticed her dart a suspicious look at me as she passed.

'Pity I haven't got a magnifying glass with me,' Simon said regretfully.

'There's one in Asa's desk – I'll fetch it,' said Xan, suiting the action to the words, and I made to leave the room too until Mrs Powys's voice stopped me in my tracks.

'I think you should stay in the room for the present, Dido,' she said. 'We might need you.'

'Me too?' asked Henry eagerly, and I saw him wink at Dom, who was looking intrigued again.

Those of the party who had been stolidly continuing with their breakfast now appeared to get a faint inkling that something was happening and looked up as one, rather like a herd of cows disturbed from their grazing.

'I suppose you might as well stay, Henry. I expect you already know all about it,' said Mrs Powys.

'*I* don't,' said Dom.

'Well, you soon will,' said Mrs Powys, and I began to suspect she was going to bring it all out into the open in front of everyone, then and there.

I began to feel anxious. What if I'd been mistaken and it wasn't the same ring at all?

Sophie returned, wearing a guarded expression on her pretty face and held the ring out to Mrs Powys, who took it and examined it closely.

'A Roman stone in a Victorian setting, did you say, Simon?'

Xan handed her the magnifying glass and she peered through it, then passed both ring and glass to Simon.

'You're the expert,' she said.

Sophie had sunk back down in her chair next to him and he asked her if she had any provenance for the stone.

'Provenance?' she said blankly.

'I mean, do you have any idea where it was originally found?'

'No, I bought it from an antique shop and they didn't tell me anything,' she said, reaching out a red-clawed hand for her coffee cup.

'That's a shame,' he said regretfully, 'but so often the way with these small objects.'

'Oh, I think we might be able to give it a little more *recent* provenance,' Mrs Powys put in blandly. 'Nancy, pass Simon those photographs and the description, so he can compare them.'

I heard Sophie gasp and her coffee cup suddenly tilted, sending a brown stream over the white cloth. She put it down again and it rattled in the saucer.

Nancy gave her friend a rather reproachful look, but then silently pushed the papers across the table and Simon picked them up and examined them, curiously.

'This looks like the same ring! Where did these come from?'

'Dido remembered that a ring just like Sophie's had gone missing some years ago, from the house of a friend she was staying with. It belonged to the friend's mother and she still had these details in her insurance file, so Dido got her to email them across. Apparently,' she added, 'Sophie was a frequent visitor to the house at the time.'

She put no particular emphasis on this, but Sophie snapped, with a venomous glare at me: 'So what? Are you by any chance insinuating that I took it, just because I have a similar one?'

'Now, now, Sophie,' began Mr Makepeace. 'There's no need for that kind of wild talk. No one is accusing you of anything!'

'Actually,' said Simon, who had been quietly comparing the details on the printouts with Sophie's ring, 'the hallmark and maker's mark are identical. There's no doubt it *is* the same ring.'

'Really? Well, that's quite a coincidence, because as I told you, I bought it from an antique shop,' Sophie said defiantly. 'Dido probably stole it and sold it on,' she added spitefully.

'You've forgotten *I* was staying at the house at the same time too, Sophie. Dido was only sixteen at the time and, as I recall, only interested in ponies and tennis,' Xan said. 'So I doubt it.'

Of course, I'd also been very interested in *him*, but fortunately he didn't mention that . . .

'I'm sure Dido wouldn't have dreamed of taking it,' said Nancy. 'Sabine, wouldn't it be better to continue this discussion privately?'

'I don't think there's much left to discuss,' Mrs Powys said. 'The ring was lost . . . and now we've found it.'

'I don't think I quite understand,' said Lucy, brows knitted. 'Nigel . . . ?'

But her brother was staring at Sophie as if he hadn't seen her before – and so were Frank and Olive.

This seemed to unnerve Sophie, who lost her cool and said, slightly hysterically, 'I don't know why you're all looking at me like this, as if I've done something wrong! I bought the stupid ring, that's all!'

'But no one has accused you of anything else, dear,' pointed out Nancy. 'Though of course, now we know it's the same ring, perhaps you can give it to Dido so she can just quietly return it to its rightful owner – and then no more need be said about it.'

'Yes, that would be the best course of action,' put in Mr

Makepeace, a faint note of relief in his voice. 'And as Nancy says, it need go no further.'

'You just shut up!' Sophie screamed at him with shocking suddenness, standing up so abruptly that her chair went flying.

'Well, really!' murmured Olive, and Nigel tut-tutted.

'*I* believe you took the ring – *and* my earrings, too,' said Mrs Powys, 'but then, you returned those when the loss was quickly discovered.'

'You *told* them?' Sophie demanded, turning on her grandfather again. 'You said you wouldn't, if I put them back – and I did.'

She looked around wildly, as if seeking a sympathetic face, and finding none. 'I told you all to stop staring at me like that! I can't help taking things. It's kleptomania!'

'Thought as much,' said Henry. 'There's one in my family and he can't resist anything shiny – he's like a magpie.'

But Sophie was now beyond hearing him. She'd rocketed into peals of shockingly loud hysterical laughter, which only stopped when Nancy removed the flowers from a nearby vase and dashed the water from it into her face.

'There, that's better,' she said as the laughter dwindled into racking sobs. 'You sit down and try and calm yourself. We *all* understand that kleptomania is an illness.'

Simon, who had picked up the fallen chair and was now looking both horrified and embarrassed, patted one of her hands gingerly.

'Of course Sophie can't help it,' he agreed. 'I'm sure we all know she wouldn't do anything . . .' he petered out, uncertainly.

Despite this appeal, not everyone was looking sympathetic and although I had begun to feel sorry for her, I hadn't forgotten that she'd accused me of taking the ring!

Olive was now eyeing Sophie with extreme distaste, while

her hands closed over a big gold locket she was wearing, as if she expected Sophie to lean across the table and snatch it.

'A thief in our midst, Frank!' she said to her husband.

'Oh dear, how awful this all is!' said Lucy, wringing her thin hands like an attenuated Lady Macbeth. 'But I'm so glad Sophie didn't take Mummy's bog oak and Irish pearl brooch.'

'I wouldn't have touched your tatty little bit of bog oak with a barge pole,' snapped Sophie, emerging from the handkerchief that Nigel, with surprising practicality, had passed across to her.

The vase of water seemed to have restored some semblance of her former self, though there was still an edge of trembling hysteria in her voice.

Mrs Powys turned to Mr Makepeace, who seemed to have slid down in his chair, in the hope of becoming invisible.

'Well, Timothy, it's evident you know about your grand-daughter's little foible, so I really do think you should have warned me, before you brought her here.'

'With hindsight, yes, my dear Sabine, but she assured me . . .' He tailed off, flapping his hands in a helpless gesture. 'I never imagined she would do such a thing in the house of someone who is not only an old friend, but a client! When I realized she had taken your earrings, it was a great shock to me.'

'But I couldn't help myself. It's not my fault!' Sophie cried in a trembling voice and this time, Simon put an arm around her shoulders.

'Of course you couldn't, we understand,' he said soothingly.

'I don't. I think kleptomania is just another name for being a thief,' said Mrs Powys.

'Oh, no, dear, you're quite wrong – it's a recognized syn-drome,' said Nancy. 'Still, now everything is out in the open, all we have to do is, as I said earlier, let Dido return the ring to her friend's mother, who she thinks will be so happy to have it back that she won't take any further action.'

'Take it, then – *I* don't want it,' Sophie screamed, and, picking it up, threw it at me with some violence, though luckily she was a rotten shot and it merely fell into the butter dish.

'I'm sure that will be best, Nancy,' agreed Mrs Powys, ignoring this. Then she gave her puckish, three-cornered grin and added, 'So now, all we have to do is lock up our valuables until you leave, Sophie!'

'Leave? I'm leaving right now,' declared Sophie wildly. 'You don't think I'm going to spend another minute under this roof, do you?'

'My dear girl,' said Nigel, 'I don't think you have any choice. Xan told me the road is still quite frozen and impassable.'

'It is,' agreed Xan. 'Better wait until tomorrow.'

'I don't believe you. And anyway, I'd rather die trying than stay here! I must go – I *must*!' Her voice was beginning to rise ominously again and Simon gave her an anxious look.

'Then why not come and stay in my cottage, until the roads thaw out?' he suggested.

She stopped on a sob and stared at him with huge, wet, pansy-brown eyes.

'The central heating boiler's broken, so it's freezing cold, but I can light the log burner to warm the place up a bit . . .'

Sophie said quickly, 'Oh, *yes*! Do take me there right now, Simon. You are so kind – I think you're the only one who truly understands me.'

'In that case . . .' he said, and glanced enquiringly at the rest of us. 'Don't you think that would be for the best? I can fetch Sophie's car as soon as the roads are passable again.'

'I think rain is forecast for tomorrow,' Frank said suddenly.

He'd been so quiet, you would have thought he'd had no interest in what had been going on.

'Don't be silly, Sophie! I wouldn't throw you out into the cold, cold snow, like a Victorian heroine in a melodrama, even if there was any left,' snapped Mrs Powys. 'You had better stay here another night, where it's at least warm and comfortable.'

But Sophie flatly refused. 'I'm going with Simon. I'll pack now and then perhaps someone would be kind enough to carry my luggage down?'

'I will,' said Henry. 'But you aren't going to take it *all* with you, are you? It's a bit of a walk.'

'I'll need one suitcase; the other can go in the boot of my car,' she said. She seemed to be recovering now the prospect of escape had opened up. 'And my beauty box too, of course.'

'I'll walk across with you and Simon to help carry stuff,' Xan said kindly.

'Me too,' agreed Dom, and Nigel said he'd quite like a stroll and would accompany them.

'In that case, I'll stay and get on with being a busy little house elf,' said Henry.

When Sophie and Simon had gone upstairs to pack, Olive said, in her slightly plaintive voice, 'Well, what a turn-up for the books that was!'

'I can still hardly believe it,' agreed Lucy.

'I can only apologize to all of you for my granddaughter's behaviour,' said poor Mr Makepeace.

He looked at me. 'You *are* sure the rightful owner of the ring will not take the matter further?'

'Yes, she'll just be so happy to have it back,' I assured him.

'In that case, you'd better take charge of it straight away,' he said, and Henry, who had retrieved it from the butter dish and wiped it on a napkin, held it out to me: such a small thing to cause such a huge scene! But then, I suppose the same could be said of Sophie . . .

Mrs Powys, who was looking wonderfully revived, said bracingly, 'Well, cheer up, Timothy! Now we've sorted that little problem out, we'll go and deal with more pressing business! Come along, we'll go to the library. Dido, perhaps you could bring some fresh coffee there?'

'Of course, Mrs Powys,' I said automatically, and made for the kitchen, feeling slightly shattered.

Henry caught me up and said, 'Fun and games! Mrs Powys looked quite invigorated by it all, didn't she?'

'She did, though *I* feel quite the opposite – and I have to admit, I feel a bit sorry for Sophie. I mean, it's an *illness*; she can't help herself.'

'She can help being such a cow, though – and don't forget she tried to accuse you of stealing the ring.'

'I know, but . . .' I paused. 'Henry, don't let Xan leave until I've packed up some food for them. I shouldn't think Simon's got much in the house – and they're going to freeze tonight!'

'Perhaps love will keep them warm, who knows?' he suggested.

But somehow, I doubted that.

42

Strong Willed

After the party had set off and I'd taken the coffee tray to the library – though frankly, Mr Makepeace looked as if a strong brandy would have done him much more good – I firmly refocused my mind on my work.

Lunch would be at the usual time of one, and for tonight's dessert, I thought I'd create a kind of raspberry Eton Mess using frozen fruit, and save the brandy butter ice cream I was about to whip up for tomorrow.

Once I'd made meringue for the Eton Mess and the ice cream was safely stowed in the freezer, it was time to make a start on the soup and salad for lunch. Plum, who had stayed with me instead of accompanying Xan, had long since got bored and gone to snooze on the sofa in our sitting room. He has a loud snore for so small a dog.

'Happy in your work, darling?' asked Henry, as he and Nancy returned from their slightly belated bedroom tidying.

'Delirious,' I said. 'Pass me the timer shaped like a Brussels sprout!'

*

I left most of the serving of lunch to Henry, though when I did take the salad in, Mrs Powys graciously told me she was expecting me and Henry to join them again that evening for dinner.

'In fact, I insist upon it!' she added, and Nancy gave her an approving smile.

Henry told me the atmosphere at lunch had been more relaxed, probably at least in part due to Sophie's absence, but two fewer for meals did make a difference to the catering, too.

'And we won't be thirteen for dinner tonight, so no need to lay a place for Plum!'

He finished washing the cut-glass water jug and then carefully dried it.

'There we are, that's everything either washed up or in the dishwasher, so if you don't need me for an hour or two, then Dom and I are going to skate on the lake, while it's still frozen. The forecast *definitely* says warmer tomorrow and heavy rain.'

'How very unseasonal,' I said, 'though I'm sure Mrs Powys will be glad if the roads thaw out so her guests can leave tomorrow as planned!'

'I wonder if she'll have told them how she's left the estate by then?' he mused. 'I'm sure she's made her final decision, but will Mitras Castle go to Nigel, or the National Trust?'

'Oh, the National Trust, I should think, together with the bulk of the estate. Xan thinks so too, and Nigel probably suspects it by now, even if he hopes he's wrong.'

'Nigel's coming skating with us. Lucy doesn't skate, but she's going to watch.'

'I can't imagine Nigel skating!' I said.

'He says he's quite good, so I'll let you know – unless you can come and join in for a little while?'

'Oh, I've got so much to do, I really don't think I can,' I told him . . . but later, being by now putty in Xan's hands, I let him persuade me out on to the ice for half an hour.

I spent most of it upright and not always hanging on to Xan's arm, which was an improvement. Nigel was actually quite a good skater, and what with Dom and Henry too, the ice was quite crowded.

When I left them to it and walked up the terraces back to the house, I found Nancy, Olive and Mrs Powys in the Winter Garden.

'Hellebore, Dido,' said Nancy, by way of greeting. 'So pretty!'

'You do love this part of the garden, don't you, Dido?' Mrs Powys said, looking intently at me.

'Yes, it's so magical, the way things flower in the middle of winter.'

'There must be *something* about this spot, because even in my Hampstead garden there's practically nothing out at this time of year,' complained Olive. 'But I'll try those hardy daffodils, Sabine.'

I carried on up to the house, where we'd left Plum asleep on the sofa. I didn't wake him – he has a tendency to get underfoot when I'm busy.

I thought it might make a change if tonight's starter was prawns and crudités with a dip. It would sort of go with the fishy theme of the main course.

First, though, there were the remains of the turkey to deal with and I was still stripping the meat from it when Henry returned.

Most of it was destined for the freezer, and eventually would be used for risottos, paellas, casseroles, curries and pies.

'Have you finished for the moment?' asked Henry, as I put the turkey carcass in a big lidded container.

'Yes, I can turn this into stock tomorrow.'

'Good,' he said, and commandeered the other end of the long table, while I cleared up the utensils I'd used.

'Dom has never tasted proper seed cake, so I'll make some for tea. There's just time – *and* it's even nicer warm.'

After tea, Dom and Henry laid the table ready for dinner and Nancy came to ask if there was anything she could do to help. But really, there wasn't: I had everything well in hand.

'Xan told me about the food you sent over for Sophie and Simon. That was such a lovely, kind thought!'

'I do feel sorry for her, but more for poor Simon, who was enjoying being warm and well fed, for a change!'

'Perhaps he could come back for the New Year, because I suspect Sophie will get away at the first opportunity. I'll mention the idea to Sabine.'

And with another beaming smile, she went out, followed by Plum, who had given up hope of any further scraps being forthcoming.

I changed into my lovely green tunic again for dinner, though this time early, and then simply wrapped an enormous apron around my waist while I finished cooking.

The whole large salmon en croûte, with its creamy spinach topping under the golden pastry, looked magnificent, and when I took my place at the table everyone was very complimentary. We pulled the rest of the Marwood's crackers and, under the influence of a good white wine, even Frank began to look faintly merry, going so far as to loosen his tie.

Poor Mr Makepeace, though, looked even more as if what life force had been left in him had been entirely drained. Some of that might have been due to his discussion with Mrs Powys that morning, or the scene with Sophie, though perhaps it was a relief to have her kleptomania known about, because he must have felt as if he'd had a sword suspended above his head!

But as the meal progressed, I noticed he was beginning to cast much the same sort of worried glances at his hostess as he had at his granddaughter, rather as if she was a ticking time bomb that might go off at any minute.

We discovered why once the dessert had been removed and the cheese and fruit put on the table, for Mrs Powys tapped on the side of her glass for attention and said she had an announcement to make.

'Since for some of my guests, this is likely to be their last night here, it seems a good moment to tell you all about the decision I've made to ensure the future of Mitras Castle and the estate.'

There was a silence, into which Henry said, tactfully, 'Would you like me and Dido to leave you, Mrs Powys?'

'No need,' she said, then continued: 'As you know, I had Timothy draw up two wills, though the minor legacies, which righted one or two past wrongs, remained the same in both.'

I saw Olive and Frank Melling, who I'm sure had no real expectation of inheriting the estate, look at each other and away again.

'This morning,' continued Mrs Powys, 'I made my decision, and the will leaving the estate to the National Trust . . . was destroyed!'

I heard Nigel, who was staring intently at her, let out his breath in a long sigh.

'But then, that means . . .' Lucy began eagerly, but Nigel shook his head at her and she faltered into silence.

'My main concern was to ensure the continuity of the estate and the Castle as it is now, and though I knew the National Trust would look after it, I preferred it to remain a loved and cherished family home.'

She looked around the table and the puckish, three-cornered smile appeared.

'There seemed only one way of ensuring that – so, I'm leaving it to Xan.'

There was such a deep, stunned silence after this bombshell that the cracking of a log in the fire sounded like a whiplash and we all jumped.

I turned my head to look mutely at Xan and found him gazing down the table at Mrs Powys, a frown twitching his dark eyebrows together.

'*Me?*' he said incredulously. 'Is this some kind of joke, Sabine?'

'It must be, because it's quite preposterous!' cried Nigel, springing to his feet. 'To leave it to Xan, when you know that I, your nearest relative, would love and care for it?'

'I'm quite serious,' Mrs Powys said calmly.

'But . . . that's so *unfair!*' Lucy wailed, tears springing to her eyes. She appealed to Mr Makepeace: 'Timothy, surely you—'

'I advise, but the decision must, of course, rest with my client – and she has made it.'

Xan, still staring fixedly at Mrs Powys, said slowly, 'To *me*? You've really left it to me? But why?'

'Because, as I said, I want it to remain a much-loved family home – and I hope that you will marry and settle down here. For not only have you been as good as a son to me, but you are, no matter how distantly, related to my mother's family.'

'A ridiculously remote connection, at the most!' protested Nigel, sinking back into his chair as if his legs would no longer hold him.

Xan was still frowning. 'But, Sabine, you know I mean to marry Dido?'

'I do and, with Nancy's help' – she paused to exchange a smile with her friend, who nodded at her encouragingly – 'with

Nancy's help, I have come to accept and embrace that idea. And Dido has an affinity for the house and the Winter Garden.'

My brain seemed to be having trouble processing what she was saying, and now, Frank, Nigel, Olive and Lucy were all starting from me to Xan and back again, as if we'd turned into some kind of two-headed monster.

'There's something else most of you don't know about Dido,' said Mrs Powys, and my head jerked round so suddenly my neck cricked.

'Her father is my half-sister, Faye's, illegitimate son – so Dido is my great-niece.'

'A fact even *I* only learned this morning,' said Mr Makepeace drily. 'I admit, I was quite dumbfounded.'

'Not, I assure you, as much as *we* are!' faltered Nigel, his usually rosy face now looking pale and shell-shocked, which was much how I felt.

But Xan now laid his warm hand over mine and squeezed it, and I immediately felt heartened by the contact.

'It was your uncle who dealt with Faye when she came back from America to claim the money my father left her, Timothy, and although he told me of her return, and that she had had a child out of wedlock, at the time that was still the kind of thing that was hushed up.'

'Did you know about this?' Olive asked me curiously.

'Only in the last few days, and my father had no idea. He was adopted by a cousin of Faye's mother, but she wouldn't talk about her.'

'*I* suspect you knew before you got here and have been busily inveigling yourself into Sabine's good graces – not to mention getting yourself engaged to Xan,' began Nigel hotly.

'Really, Nigel!' reproved Nancy. 'You've had enough time to form a better estimate of Dido's character than that.'

Nigel looked a bit shamefaced at his outburst, but said sulkily, 'I find it hard to believe, Sabine, that you really want a grandchild of Faye's, who we all know you detested, to marry Xan and live here!'

'But I do,' Mrs Powys said firmly. 'Nancy has made me see that it would complete a pattern, by bringing the past and present together – that is, if she and Xan are willing to accept the inheritance and the responsibility?'

She looked questioningly at us.

'If that *is* what you truly want,' Xan said, and then smiled lovingly at me. 'What about it, Dido? Will you take me on – and all that comes with me?'

I looked doubtfully at Mrs Powys. 'I don't think this can have been a very easy decision, Mrs Powys! Are you *quite* sure . . . ?'

Her lips twisted slightly. 'Only the first step was hard and I know it is the right decision. And I think it's time you started to call me Sabine, don't you?'

'Very touching,' drawled Frank.

'Well, *I* think you've been quite unfair to Nigel,' exclaimed Lucy, tears rushing into her eyes again.

'I hope I've been fair to everyone,' Mrs Powys said. 'For although the bulk of the property will go to Xan, I hope I've made a fair and equitable division of the rest. I will speak to you, Nigel and Olive, in the morning before you leave – that is, if the roads are unfrozen enough to make that possible.'

As if on cue, heavy rain began to hammer the windows behind the drawn curtains.

'It sounds as if the thaw might be setting in early,' said Dom, grinning, and then said kindly to Mr Makepeace, 'I think Sophie drove you here, but if you like, I could easily drop you home tomorrow. It's not much out of my way.'

'Thank you, dear boy,' said the solicitor.

'Excellent, but not, of course, before the will has been signed,' said Mrs Powys. 'Henry, you will have to be one of the witnesses and we'll get Simon over to be the other.'

'All right, I can text him and let him know,' agreed Henry. 'Though I expect if it has thawed by then, he'll come over for Sophie's car anyway.'

'I could be the other witness,' suggested Dom.

'No, because you're in the will. But don't get your hopes up, it's just a little mention,' she told him.

'Cool!' said Dom.

'Well . . .' said Mrs Powys brightly, leaning back and surveying the variety of expressions on her guests' faces, 'now all that's satisfactorily settled, we can enjoy the rest of the evening, can't we? And, Dido, when you and Henry bring the coffee, you must stay and join in.'

We all rose when she did, but I heard Xan say, 'Can we just have a quick private word, Sabine?' before they went out together.

'Well, you could knock me down with a feather,' Henry murmured in my ear. 'Would you like a strong cup of coffee when we get back to the kitchen, or a stiff shot of the cooking brandy?'

'Both, I think,' I said. 'Then pinch me, because I think I'm having a seriously weird dream.'

Our willing helpers soon had everything cleared away, but I let Henry take the coffee through while I lingered in the kitchen, needing a few minutes to myself . . . and I must have been there longer than I thought, for Xan came to fetch me.

'You can't hide in here for ever!' he said, pulling me into his arms, and would have kissed me except I held him off so I could see his face.

'I know, but I simply wanted a bit of time to think it through. Xan, is this *really* what Sabine wants?'

'She says so. We're to go and talk to her in the library tomorrow, right after breakfast.'

'Professor Powys, in the library, with a double-headed Minoan axe?' I suggested, and he grinned.

'No, she seems to have entirely buried any hatchets.' He looked at me seriously. 'She's quite right about Mitras Castle: it's a special place, but it should be a family home, too . . . and we could make it *ours*.'

Then, as his arms tightened around me, the irresistible smile reappeared. 'The sooner we start, the better!'

Sabine

That evening, I was suddenly overwhelmed by a wave of exhaustion, which wasn't surprising, for it had been quite a day.

Nancy urged me to go up to bed and said and she'd follow shortly, so it was no surprise when she came into my boudoir ten minutes later, bearing the inevitable flask and two mugs.

'I'm so glad you've rediscovered the joy of cocoa,' she said, putting them down on the table and starting to unscrew the top of the Thermos.

'In conjunction with, rather than instead of, my usual whisky nightcap.'

'Of course! But cocoa really is the most comforting thing I know. The cup that cheers,' she said. 'We had a very late night yesterday and I know you were still tired this morning, even if the adrenalin rush of getting to the bottom of poor Sophie's problem revived you!'

'*Poor* Sophie?' I questioned.

'She can't help her kleptomania. Nor, I suppose, her stupidity, which evidently led her to forget exactly what it was she'd taken from the house of Dido's friend, until it was too late.'

'She strikes me as unpleasant as well as stupid,' I said. 'The only person I feel sorry for is Timothy, but I expect he'll revive, once she's not under his roof any more. He has written her a note, which will probably make for uncomfortable reading.'

'Before they accepted your invitation I expect she assured him that she was cured and he believed her,' Nancy said.

'Men seem capable of believing anything a pretty young woman tells them,' I said with a slight resurgence of the old bitterness . . . an acid reflux of the soul, as it were.

'Not *all* of them,' she said gently. Then she looked at me over the top of her mug and smiled, misty blue eyes shining: 'But, Sabine, I was so proud of you at dinner! It took real bravery to embrace both Xan and Dido, in the true spirit of forgiveness and love, knowing they would care for Mitras Castle in the way you would want and make it a family home again.'

'You were right about the first step being the hardest, but none of them since have been easy . . . and I'm not sure yet that I've *completely* won the struggle to forgive with my heart, as well as my head.'

'Oh, I think you're almost there, and I expect you're already experiencing such a wonderful lightness of spirit, aren't you?'

'Yes . . .' I admitted, 'though not quite enough for me to take wing and fly away.'

'It isn't time yet,' she said practically. 'I'll briefly return home in the New Year to close up my cottage and then I'll come back and stay with you to the end.'

'I'll be strong enough, if you're there, Nancy.'

'We will take this journey together, and when I finally have to let go of your hand, you'll see Asa reaching out from the other side to take it,' she assured me, with the complete and comforting conviction of her faith.

Then she poured us both another mug of cocoa and said, with a twinkle, 'Now before I go to bed, you might as well tell me how you've provided for Nigel, Lucy and Olive – which I'm sure you've done very generously.'

'I'm not sure any amount would be generous enough to assuage Nigel's disappointment, but for the rest, I hope so,' I said, and told her.

43

Unlocking the Past

I woke next morning to the unseasonal but strangely soothing drumming of heavy rain on the roof and lay for a few moments listening to it, before suddenly remembering all the events of the previous day.

I sat bolt upright, heart hammering almost as loudly as the rain. Had I imagined everything, especially the moment when Mrs Powys – even in my mind I was having trouble calling her Sabine – had told Xan that he was to inherit Mitras Castle?

And not only that, but she had accepted that Xan and I would marry, which seemed, given all that had gone before, the most improbable of fairy tales!

'Get up, Cinderella, and get down to the kitchen!' I told myself. 'There's still work to be done and a substantial breakfast to prepare, to speed the departing guests on their way.'

And it certainly sounded as if anyone who wanted to leave would be able to do so now, even if it might have to be in an ark.

I knew Frank and Olive hoped to set off by mid-morning, since they were driving straight down to London, and I didn't think Nigel would want to linger much longer than that.

Everything would soon be back to the way it was before Christmas . . . except, of course, that *nothing* would ever be quite the same again!

Xan came into the kitchen with his dark hair clinging damply to his head and a Plum who had been rough-dried around the edges.

'I'm so glad you chose a waterproof coat for Plum, because it's a deluge out there!' he said, ripping open a sachet of doggy dinner and spooning it into the bowl, while trying to fend Plum off as he did it.

Henry pushed a mug of coffee across the table in his direction. 'Here, you look as if you could do with it.'

'I could, thanks,' said Xan. 'To be honest, Sabine's announcement last night was such a bombshell that I hardly slept and I half thought I'd dreamed it this morning.'

'I felt as if I was in a fairy tale,' I confessed. 'Cinderella.'

'I see you more in the Rapunzel role, but I'll try and resist the temptation to shut you up in the tower,' he said.

'I'm going to give it a couple of hours for the roads to wash clear, then I'll go and see if I can get the newspapers,' Henry said. 'If you're out of anything, Dido, let me know.'

Yesterday evening, the party had tended to divide itself into three: Sabine, Nigel, Frank and Mr Makepeace playing bridge and bickering, while Nancy, Olive and Lucy watched another old Christmas film provided by Henry.

That left Henry, Dom, Xan and me to play Monopoly, before unearthing an old bar billiards board that Xan had spotted behind the piano in the billiard room.

'Asa picked it up somewhere but I'd forgotten all about it, until I noticed it when we were singing carols.'

On the whole, it had been a fun evening and as if by some

silent agreement, no one mentioned wills, relationships or engagements.

But today, when I went into the morning room, I discovered that Olive, Frank and Nigel all had a tendency to stare curiously at me and then look away quickly when I caught them at it.

'Good morning, Dido,' said Nancy brightly. 'What have you got there?'

'Soft-boiled eggs. I know Mrs . . . *Sabine* likes them and thought some of you might like a change. But if not, I'll use them up in something.'

'Thank you, Dido, that will be very pleasant,' said Sabine, who was looking tired but tranquil, as if she'd arrived at the end of some long and arduous journey.

'Toast soldiers coming up!' said Henry, catching two slices of bread as they shot out of the toaster, and cutting them into fingers.

Frank said, with somewhat forced humour, that it seemed odd to be waited on by a member of the family.

'Not to mention, the future wife of the Castle's heir!'

'Oh, I don't know,' I said, pouring out coffee for Sabine and adding just a dash of milk, the way she liked it. 'Mothers and wives do it all the time for their families, don't they? And no one thinks anything of that.'

'Very true, and I'm sure everyone will soon be used to the idea – and delighted to welcome Dido into the family,' Nancy said.

'*I'm* used to it already,' said Dom, 'and I think it's great!'

'Thanks, Dom,' said Xan, smiling at me. 'Consider yourself invited to the wedding!'

Xan came to the kitchen to fetch me when Sabine had finished her breakfast and summoned us to the library.

'And after that, she's going to see Olive and Frank together, then Nigel, and finally Lucy,' he said. 'The Mellings and Nigel hope to leave before lunch, but Dom and Mr Makepeace after it.'

'It's soup and then warm cheese-and-potato slice, with winter slaw,' I said, 'so it's extendable if necessary.'

'After today, you won't have to cater for the multitude. It'll just be the family and Nancy and Henry again.'

'It feels odd to be included in the family,' I confessed, hesitating as we reached the door to the library.

'Come on, Sabine won't bite!' he urged.

To my relief, Nancy was there too and Sabine didn't bite me – but instead formally welcomed me into the family. Then she added, slightly stiffly and prompted by a look from Nancy, that she felt a great sense of relief in knowing that Mitras Castle would be so well looked after in the future.

'We can safely promise you we'll do that,' Xan assured her.

'Of course. And I've been thinking,' I added diffidently, 'that if you will allow me to, I'll stay on after New Year to do the cooking and housekeeping, so you don't have to worry about that. Not as a contract,' I added hastily, 'just because I *want* to.'

'That is a very generous offer, Dido,' said Sabine, looking surprised and, for once, her pale blue eyes were not like chips of ice. 'But don't you have other bookings?'

'Henry and I were going to wind up our business this year, anyway, so we'll just have to do it sooner rather than later – and I have a feeling Henry won't mind.'

'No,' said Nancy, 'I don't think he and Dom will be able to bear being separated from each other for long, do you? So lovely, all this romance in the air.'

'Well, I expect you are as right about that as you have been about everything else, Nancy,' Sabine said in her more usual tart tones.

'I could write Asa's biography here as well as anywhere else, if you'd like me to stay on too, Sabine?' Xan offered.

She was silent for a moment and then she said, slowly, 'I think what I'd *really* like is for you both to get married and make your home here as soon as it can be arranged. There's a lot to learn about the running of the estate, not to mention the Rowenhead Fort Trust.'

Xan looked at me, one dark eyebrow raised in enquiry. 'I'd marry Dido tomorrow if she agreed!'

'Perhaps not *quite* that soon – and only when Nancy can conduct the ceremony!' I told him firmly.

Xan, following Sabine's instructions, sent Frank and Olive to see her next and then rang Simon to request he come over later so he could witness the will, along with Henry.

'And the roads should be fine by then, so you could collect Sophie's car,' he suggested and Simon agreed.

Henry and Dom had driven down for the newspapers and Henry said the roads were rivers and it had been an interesting drive, but he didn't see why any of the guests who wanted to leave shouldn't be able to get away later.

Olive and Frank emerged from their interview with Sabine looking both pleased and surprised, and even Nigel, after his, was less huffy and almost back to his usual cheerful and hearty self.

Simon walked over, arriving looking as if he'd had a shower with all his clothes on, though he wouldn't even stay for a cup of coffee after he and Henry witnessed the will.

'I need to get back, because the plumber's coming about the boiler and Sophie wants to leave as soon as she has her car,' he explained. 'The cottage was freezing last night and she hardly slept, so she just wants to get away.'

Xan gave him the note for her that Mr Makepeace had written and Simon added, rather miserably, 'Sophie's been offered a flat-share by a friend in London.'

I thought, for his sake, that was probably a very good idea.

We all waved goodbye to Olive, Frank and Nigel, though not before Lucy had flung her arms around her brother's neck and wept copiously. You'd have thought he was leaving for Australia, not just up the road to Alnwick.

Sabine gave the departing cars one final, royal-style wave, with her arm bent from the elbow, and then we all followed her back into the warmth of the Great Hall . . . which Plum, very sensibly, had never left.

'*You'll* have to wait to find out what I've left you in my will, Dom,' she told him, with that triangular grin. 'You might call it a dowry!'

'Do you think I need one, before anyone will marry me?' he asked, then smiled at Henry.

'A little nest egg is always useful, dear,' Nancy told him.

'Lucy,' said Sabine, 'let's have our little private moment together before lunch, shall we?'

It was a command rather than a suggestion, and poor Lucy looked faintly terrified.

'Timothy, you had better join us, too – come along,' said Sabine, and led the way briskly out of the hall.

During lunch, which Nancy had told us we were expected to join, Lucy was in floods of tears – but of happiness and gratitude.

'Dear Cousin Sabine is buying me a little cottage of my own in Wallstone – *and* giving me an income from the estate, too,' she explained.

'That's a very excellent idea,' approved Nancy without surprise, so that I was sure she'd already known about it.

'Of course, I wouldn't be far away and could come and help you whenever you wished, Cousin Sabine,' Lucy said earnestly.

Since she was as much use as a chocolate teapot, Sabine was unlikely to take her up on this offer, but she thanked her gravely and said she knew she could *always* rely on her.

'There's the sweetest little end-terraced cottage right on the Green,' Lucy said, and the moment lunch was over, she excitedly rang her friend Daphne and then drove down to see her.

Before Dom set out with Mr Makepeace, I left him and Henry alone in the kitchen, to have a private moment.

But they were not to be parted long, for before they left, Sabine kindly told Dom that, if he liked, he could come over for Sunday dinner and spend the day with us . . .

'We're going to have sausages with mustard mash for dinner tonight – simple but comforting. And the brandy butter ice cream to follow,' I told Henry when he followed me back to the kitchen, looking rather downcast, even if he was to see Dom again on Sunday. Then: 'Put the kettle on and sit down, Henry. I need to talk to you.'

And when I'd made us both coffee, I told him about my talk with Sabine and Nancy earlier.

'Nancy is going to shut her house up and come and stay with Sabine until . . . well, the end. And *I'm* not going back to Cheshire in the New Year. In fact, Xan and I are going to get married as soon as we can and make our home here!'

'Well, that's lovely,' he said, his cherubic smile appearing. 'And in any case, *I* was about to suggest that we wind the business up straight away and return any deposits to our irate clients – because I intend moving in with Dom!'

'Oh, Henry!' I cried. 'How wonderful! I thought it was serious.'

'Mutual hugs and congratulations, darling,' Henry agreed, getting up and suiting the action to the words. 'And if it all works out, we might be following you and Xan down the aisle before long!'

At dinner that night, Sabine regarded the depleted group at the table – me, Henry, Xan, Nancy and Lucy – and said, 'It's been a most enjoyable, not to mention *interesting* Christmas, but I have to say, it's very nice to be just us again.'

'It certainly is, and I'll be happy to get back to work tomorrow,' Xan said. 'Dido, are you going to help me again?'

'Of course – and *I* can hardly wait to clean out those curio cabinets!'

'I can see that's your idea of fun,' Sabine said, looking amused.

'I think before you start work again, Xan, you really should take Dido to buy a ring,' Nancy suggested, twinkling.

'Good idea,' Sabine agreed. 'I know an excellent jeweller in Hexham, and you can take those earrings of mine to be mended at the same time!'

It was after lunch next day when I entered the study, armed with cleaning materials, and found Xan on his hands and knees by the desk.

'Dropped something?' I asked.

He looked up, now running one hand under the bottom drawer on the side nearest to me.

'No, it's just that I suddenly remembered an old murder mystery novel I'd read, where the key to a locked drawer had been taped to the underneath of it . . .' His eyes suddenly widened. 'It would appear that Asa read the same book!'

'It's there?' I said eagerly, dumping my feather duster and going over, just as he sat up, holding a piece of brown tape with a key stuck to it, like a bluebottle on flypaper.

'This stuff has gone horribly tacky over the years,' he said, unpeeling the key, before inserting it into the lock of the bottom drawer and turning it, with some difficulty.

'Bluebeard's Drawer!' I said. 'I wonder what's going to be in there? A secret bottle of brandy, or a stash of forbidden chocolate . . . ?'

'Wrong on both counts. It's just more letters,' he said, sitting back with a thin bundle in his hands. 'And if I'm not mistaken, they're yet another exchange between Asa and my grandfather, Tommy.'

He got up and put them on the desk and the inevitable shrivelled remains of a rubber band crumbled away.

'Definitely Tommy,' he said, flicking through them. 'And Asa's pinned carbons of his replies to them, as usual.'

He frowned. 'But I've already found loads of Tommy's letters, so why lock these away?'

'There must be something important in these particular ones, Xan. Look, why don't you read through them while I make us some coffee, and then you can tell me what they're about – unless it's something really private, of course.'

'I don't think there can be any family skeletons left in the cupboard,' he said. 'Not even a mouse-sized one!'

When I got back, he had the letters spread out and was still frowning over them.

'Any skeletons?' I asked, putting the mugs down.

'One small, unsavoury one I didn't know about . . .' he said slowly. 'Tommy talked to me quite a lot in his last few years and I knew that Asa, even though he adored Sabine, had a few flings with other women. He couldn't resist them and to him, they meant nothing.'

'They'd have meant a lot to Sabine, though, if she'd found out about them!' I exclaimed, my picture of the idyllic couple fracturing slightly.

'Asa was a kind and generous man, he just had this . . . weakness.'

'If that's what the letters are about, no wonder he locked them away from Sabine!' I said.

'There's a bit more to it than that. It seems that when Faye was staying with them on Corfu, he had a bit of a thing with *her*, too.'

'Oh, no!' I cried. 'Surely not? I mean, she was his wife's half-sister and also, in his care.'

'I said it was an unsavoury secret,' he reminded me. 'It's clear from the letters that it only happened the once and he was very guilty about it, but Tommy's telling him not to beat himself up, because the seizure he had that stopped him diving, right afterwards, was punishment enough.'

'He certainly did pay for his weak moment,' I agreed, thinking about it.

'He *did* see it as a punishment – for that, and also for another moment of madness: he says that on the day of the diving accident, when he went to help Faye, who'd managed to rip her mouthpiece out and was panicking, he took her by the shoulders – and for a brief instant wanted to hold her there till she drowned!'

'But he didn't!' I said quickly.

'Well, no, because sanity came back almost instantly. He says he let her go again and was just going to get her to the surface – they weren't deep, she would have been in no danger if she hadn't lost her head – when he had his heart attack, or seizure, or whatever it was. And we know the rest of the story – how they got him to hospital and Faye ran off.'

'But why on earth should he have wanted, even for a moment, to kill Faye?'

'Oh, that's clear enough in the letters, too. He had no secrets from old Tommy. Faye was threatening to tell Sabine about them, because she wanted to stay on Corfu and be part of the filming and the glamorous, bohemian life they had out there – and she didn't see why she couldn't take Sabine's place!'

'She must have been mad!'

'No, just young and silly, I think – and totally self-centred.'

'I can understand now why he'd want to keep it from Sabine at all costs! Well, *almost* all,' I amended.

'Which he did – though, actually, I don't think anything could have broken the marriage up, even that. The bond was too tight.'

I wondered if he was right, but then, he knew them much better than I did. It would certainly have increased the bitterness and hate Sabine felt for her half-sister, though . . .

'There's just one other thing, though,' Xan said, breaking into my reverie. 'Apparently Faye had told him she was pregnant, though he didn't believe her and in any case, she wasn't exactly exclusive with her favours.'

'It was just another threat to hold over him?'

'Perhaps,' he said, with an odd expression. 'Dido, what year was your father born?'

'What year?' I echoed blankly, then a horrible and incredible suspicion entered my mind.

'Xan, you surely don't think—' I began, and then we were interrupted by the opening of the door and Nancy came in, with the old photograph album under her arm.

'Hello, you two! I thought I'd better return this album—'

She broke off, looking at us curiously. 'Have I interrupted something? Shall I go away again?'

'I don't think so, do you, Dido?' said Xan, exchanging a look with me. 'You seem to be in on everything and you can tell us if we're imagining connections where none really exist.'

She listened carefully as he told her what he'd discovered in the letters – *and* what he'd started to conjecture.

'You don't look remotely surprised,' Xan said when he'd finished.

'Well, no, dear, I can't say I am,' she agreed. 'Asa adored Sabine, but I did know he had his little flings with other women, even though they seemed to mean nothing to him. In this case, though, well, it was very reprehensible of him, but he was punished for it, goodness knows.'

I looked at her rather wildly. 'Do you think we're mad to suspect that Asa – that my father was—' I broke off: it all seemed too incredible an idea to put into words.

'There's something I found,' she said, then opened the album and pointed to a girl in one of the photographs who looked unmistakably like me.

'I knew you reminded me of someone! This is Asa's sister, but I only met her briefly once, and she died very young, poor girl.'

'Then . . . you think Asa *was* my grandfather?'

'In my own mind, I'm certain of it, though of course, there's no actual proof.'

'No, none and, Nancy, Sabine has managed to put so much of the past behind her and accept me for who I am, not as Faye's grandchild, but *this* would break her heart! She must *never* find out about it!'

'Henceforth, my lips will be entirely sealed on the subject,' she promised.

I wished someone would put me in the recovery position.

Epilogue

Blooming

Summer 2019

Xan, Plum and I wandered down the terraces in the warm sunshine, carrying our rug and picnic basket, until we came to the Winter Garden.

Now, in summer, only a few low-growing shrubs were in flower, their white blossom reminding me of drifts of snow . . . and of Sabine, whose ashes we'd scattered, at her request, under the Christmas roses.

I shook out the rug I was carrying and Plum immediately lay down on it.

'You are so lazy, I think you might be a sloth and not a dog at all!' I told him. 'He seems blissfully happy here, Xan, doesn't he?'

'So am I. Everything seems to be working out so well that I constantly feel I should be touching wood!'

'I know: Henry and Dom setting their wedding date, Lucy happy in her little cottage and already a pillar of the community, and Maria and Andy loving their new annexe at their daughter's house.'

I'd already found a couple to live in their old cottage, to help with the house and garden, and I thought they'd turn out to be a real find . . .

Like Xan – he'd been a real find, too! I turned and gave him an impulsive hug, which he returned enthusiastically.

'I'm so glad Simon got over Sophie so quickly after she left,' I said. 'He did seem to hit it off with Charlotte, though, when she came over to collect her mum's ring,' I mused. 'And now she's decided to move her business up to Hexham or Corbridge, I think he's been helping her look for suitable premises.'

'You're an incorrigible matchmaker,' he told me. 'Those twins of hers would drive him distracted!'

'Oh, no – they'll *be* a distraction, and I was surprised how good he is with children. He made the Roman site come alive for them.'

'Let's hope they distract him from pressing me for the return of the original Mithras mosaic!' he said. 'I can see his point, but I can also imagine what Sabine would say if I did!'

'She'd be pleased with the new display about her and Asa's lives in the visitor centre, though,' I pointed out. 'And moving those big curio cabinets up there made room for all your books in the study, so you could make it more your own.'

'I still feel Asa's presence there sometimes, when I'm working,' he said, 'an approving one, just as Sabine always seems to be here, in the Winter Garden, doesn't she?'

I thought that was hardly surprising, given that she'd loved it so much.

'Then there are all our exciting plans for the Castle to look forward to next spring!' I said happily, for we'd decided to hold residential writers' and artists' weeks there, some just retreats and others with workshops.

'The old manor house will make a cosy family retreat, when the tower is full of visitors and we want to get away for a bit!' I said. 'A few "Private" signs on the study and small sitting-room doors . . .'

'I expect everyone will just naturally gravitate to the kitchen, where you will literally be whipping up a storm, as usual,' he teased.

'I hope both Sabine and Asa would be happy about the prospect of bringing new life into the Castle – in more ways than one.'

'It's good that Sabine lived long enough to know about the baby,' he said. 'And she was delighted!'

'The baby will be born around the time the Winter Garden starts to flower, which seems somehow right. And it will mean there'll be plenty of time afterwards for all the planning we need to do before we open for our first guests – but it will be such fun!'

He put his arms around me and then looked at me seriously. 'Are you *sure* it won't be too much for you, once you have the baby?'

'Of course not!' I said, looking at him in astonishment. 'No, my only worry is that most of the female guests will fall in love with you, because they'll think you look *so* romantic!'

'I'm not in the *least* romantic,' he said, looking revolted.

'You're romantic enough for me,' I said firmly. 'And don't worry about next year, because good organization is always the key to success.'

'I think perhaps we should have that carved over the front door, as the family motto,' he suggested with a grin. 'You've certainly got me organized since we got married!'

I looked at him anxiously. 'You don't mind, do you?'

His arms tightened and he kissed me. 'Dido, I *adore* being organized by you!'

Plum, who was now sitting pointedly next to the picnic basket, barked sharply.

'See,' Xan said, 'the family heraldic beast agrees!'

Acknowledgements

I would like to thank my son, Robin Ashley, for research, technical support and other invaluable assistance. Also, grateful thanks are due to the Reverend Joanna Yates, for so generously allowing me to adapt and use one of her lovely Christmas graces.

About the Author

Trisha Ashley's *Sunday Times* bestselling novels have sold over one million copies in the UK and have twice been shortlisted for the Melissa Nathan award for Romantic Comedy. *Every Woman for Herself* was nominated by magazine readers as one of the top three romantic novels in the last fifty years.

Trisha lives in North Wales. For more information about her please visit www.facebook.com/TrishaAshleyBooks or follow her on Twitter @trishaashley.

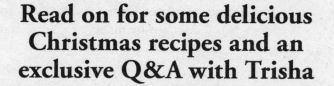

Read on for some delicious Christmas recipes and an exclusive Q&A with Trisha

Recipes

Cheese Puffs

Makes 12
Prep time: 15 minutes
Cooking time: 10 minutes

1 cup/128 g/4.5 oz grated strong cheddar cheese
1 cup/128 g/4.5 oz plain flour
2 tsp baking powder
1 tsp salt
1 tsp cayenne pepper
1 tsp ground black pepper
1 egg
1 cup/200 ml/7 fl oz milk
Butter for greasing and serving

- Preheat your oven to 200°C/180°C fan/gas mark 6. Grease 2 small muffin tins.
- Mix the dry ingredients (cheese, flour, baking powder and spices) in a large bowl.
- Lightly beat the egg and milk together. Add this mixture to the dry ingredients and combine with a fork until the dough has just combined and there are no lumps of flour.
- Fill the tins and bake for 10 minutes.
- Leave the tins to cool for 10 minutes before removing the cheese puffs.
- Serve hot with butter.

Smoked Salmon Blinis

Makes 24
Prep time: 10 minutes

24 ready-made blinis
1 cup/200 g/7 oz garlic and herb cream cheese
150 g/5 oz smoked salmon
30 g/1 oz chopped chives
Cracked black pepper

- Warm the blinis.
- Spread the cream cheese on the blinis, then add a slice of smoked salmon on top of each.
- Add the chopped chives and season generously with cracked black pepper.

Brie and Cranberry Filo Parcels

Makes 18
Prep time: 20 minutes
Cooking time: 10 minutes

12 sheets pre-made filo pastry
½ cup/100 g/3.5 oz melted butter
1¼ cup/250 g/9 oz brie, cut into 18 2cm thick slices
250 g jar of cranberry sauce
¼ cup/50 g/1.5 oz walnuts, roughly chopped
Poppy seeds

- Preheat your oven to 220°C/200°C fan/gas mark 7.
- Place 1 filo sheet on top of another. With a widest edge facing you, brush with some melted butter.
- Put 3 brie fingers at even intervals across the bottom of the filo. Top the brie with 1 tsp cranberry sauce, then sprinkle on some chopped walnuts.
- Roll up the filo from the bottom. Cut into 3 parcels and twist the ends.
- Brush with the rest of the melted butter and sprinkle with poppy seeds.
- Repeat with the remaining ingredients until you have 18 twists.
- Bake for 10 minutes. Serve immediately.
- Top tip: You can cover the unbaked twists with cling film and keep them in the fridge for up to 1 day and bake just before serving.

Christmas Cocktail

Spiced Cranberry Punch
Serves 8

1¼ cups/150 g/5 oz of cranberries (fresh or frozen)
1 litre/34 fl oz cranberry juice
500 ml/17 fl oz vodka
450 ml/15 fl oz grapefruit juice
3 limes

- First, fill each section of 2 ice cube trays with 2 cranberries.
  Fill with water and freeze. This can be done up to 1 week in
  advance.
- Slice the limes into circles.
- Half fill a large jug with the cranberry ice cubes. Do not use
  all of them – set some aside for decoration.
- Over the top, pour the cranberry juice, vodka and grape-
  fruit juice.
- Add the sliced limes to the jug.
- Add 2 cranberry ice cubes to each glass. Pour over the
  punch, serve and enjoy!

A festive Q&A with Trisha

1. There are lots of twists and turns and family secrets in One More Christmas at the Castle. *When you first started writing, did you have everything planned out or did you work out the story as you wrote?*

I am very much a character-driven author, so I don't set out to write a new novel until I understand what has shaped the character of my heroine to the point where the story opens. In this case two heroines, Dido and Sabine, share the centre stage and although I knew their stories would overlap, the details of how that would happen evolved as I went on. The first draft is very much a finding-out process.

2. Mitras Castle is such a fabulous setting – what was the inspiration behind such an enchanting house?

The house itself is completely imaginary, though I'm sure elements of many stately homes I've visited will be twisted into it somewhere. But the setting of the house, up near the Roman wall in Northumberland, *was* inspired by one of the many Roman sites along its length, Vindolanda. The countryside there is bleakly beautiful, but right next to it is a small house set at the top of a narrow and very sheltered valley – a little world of its own, quite magical.

3. For many people, putting up the Christmas tree and ornaments signals the beginning of the festive period, and it's lovely to see that characters decorate the castle together in the book. Do you have any favourite Christmas decorations?

I have all the old family ones, which go on the tree every year and my favourites include the little glass trumpets, bells and birds with fibreglass tails. There is also the Santa tree topper, which has appeared in more than one of my novels, not to mention in newsletters! He is over a hundred years old and made from *papier mâché* and was bought by my mother's eldest sister when she was four. It has faded into a soupy brown over the years, but at one point my mother spruced it up with glitter glue and a cotton wool beard . . .

4. What is your favourite Christmas activity?

I love it all, but perhaps the moment when I put on a CD of carols and decorate the Christmas tree is the best of all.

5. In the novel, Sabine wants to spend Christmas in her beloved home. How would you prefer to spend your Christmas – in your home, or taking a warm holiday to escape the cold British weather?

Oh, at home in the cold British winter weather, every time! I don't cope with hot weather very well and although on two occasions in the past I had to cook a full traditional Christmas dinner on a Caribbean island, I nearly expired from the heat in the process!

6. Aside from the delicious festive recipes you've written for this book, what is your favourite Christmas food or meal?

That is a difficult one! Our family tradition is that we have roast duck on Christmas Day, and although I haven't eaten meat for years, I still cook that. It is also the only time of year when I make a proper sherry trifle, so that's a great treat. And of course, it wouldn't be Christmas without the cake and the preparations for that and the pudding begin weeks earlier, on Stir-up Sunday! With my cake, I use the method I mention in more than one of my books, where you soak the dried fruit in dark rum for at least three days – this gives it a delicious moist texture and flavour.

7. You've written so many wonderful stories and have another coming soon. Can you tell us anything about your next novel?

Only that it is set in West Lancashire and based around a little wedding dress museum with a difference . . .

Look out for a brand-new delightfully
heart-warming read from

Trisha Ashley

Coming summer 2023

If you loved escaping into *One More Christmas at the Castle*, there are more of Trisha's wonderfully heart-warming and uplifting novels to read right now

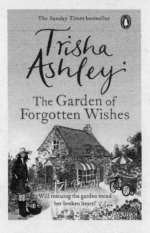

THE GARDEN OF FORGOTTEN WISHES

All Marnie wants is somewhere to call home.
Mourning lost years spent in a marriage that has finally come to an end, she needs a fresh start and time to heal. Things she hopes to find in the rural west Lancashire village her mother always told her about.

With nothing but her two green thumbs, Marnie takes a job as a gardener, which comes with a little cottage to make her own. The garden is beautiful – filled with roses, lavender and honeysuckle – and only a little rough around the edges. Which is more than can be said for her next-door neighbour, Ned Mars.

Marnie remembers Ned from her college days but he's far from the untroubled man she once knew. A recent relationship has left him with a heart as bruised as her own.

Can a summer spent gardening help them recapture the forgotten dreams they've let get away?

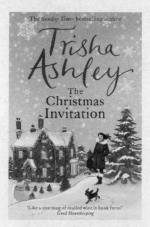

THE CHRISTMAS INVITATION

Meg is definitely not in the Christmas mood. She's never gone in for tinsel, baubles and mistletoe, and right now she's still getting over an illness. Yet when she's invited to spend the run-up to Christmas in the snowy countryside, rather than dreary London, she can't refuse.

Arriving at a warm and cosy family home in a small hilltop village, Meg soon begins to wonder what a proper Christmas might be like. But just as she's beginning to settle in, she spots a familiar face. *Lex.*

Despite the festive cheer, Meg suddenly wants nothing more than to get as far away from him, and their past secrets, as she can. **But if she stays, could this be the year she finally discovers the magic of Christmas . . .?**

THE HOUSE OF HOPES AND DREAMS

When Carey Revell unexpectedly becomes the heir to
Mossby, his family's ancestral home, it's rather a mixed
blessing. The house is large but rundown and comes with
a pair of resentful relatives who can't be asked to leave.

Still, newly dumped by his girlfriend and also from his job as
a TV interior designer, Carey needs somewhere to lick his
wounds. And Mossby would be perfect for a renovation show.
He already knows someone who could restore the stained-
glass windows in the older part of the house . . .

Angel Arrowsmith has spent the last ten years happily
working and living with her artist mentor and partner. But
suddenly bereaved, she finds herself heartbroken, without a
home or a livelihood. Life will never be the same again – until
old friend Carey Revell comes to the rescue.

**They move in to Mossby with high hopes. But the
house has a secret at its heart: an old legend concerning
one of the famous windows. Will all their dreams
for happiness be shattered? Or can Carey and Angel
find a way to make this house a home?**

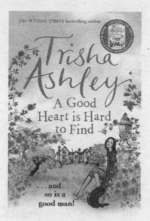

A GOOD HEART IS HARD TO FIND

It is a truth universally acknowledged that a single man of over forty is in possession of a major defect . . .

Cassandra Leigh has woken as if from a bad dream: desperate for a baby, and finally out of patience waiting for her 20 year affair with Max to end happily ever after. Maybe Max is not the only man for her?

Perhaps she could find love with her friend Jason – though he's perhaps a little *too* rugged, and there's something strange about the way his wife disappeared . . . Or there's Dante, the mysterious stranger she meets on a dark night in his haunted manor house . . .

Cass must throw caution to the wind and claim the life she's always wanted. Suddenly, it's a choice between Mr Right, Mr Wrong or Mr Right Now . . .

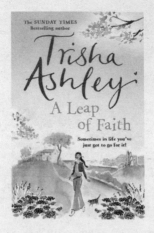

A LEAP OF FAITH

Sappho Jones stopped counting birthdays when she reached
thirty but, even with her hazy grip on mathematics, she
realises that she's on the slippery slope to the big four-oh!
With the thought suddenly lodged in her mind that she's a
mere cat's whisker away from becoming a single eccentric
female living in a country cottage in Wales, she has the urge
to do something dramatic before it's too late.

The trouble is, as an adventurous woman of a certain age,
Sappho's pretty much been there, done that, got the T-shirt.
In fact, the only thing she hasn't tried is motherhood. And
with sexy potter Nye on hand as a potential daddy – or at
least donor – is it time for her to consider the biggest leap of
all? It's either that or buy a cat . . .

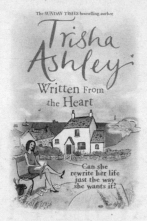

WRITTEN FROM THE HEART

Tina Devino makes more money teaching people to write than writing herself. A middling romance novelist who dreams of penning a bestseller, she's increasingly forced to compete with younger, blonder debut authors for her publisher and agent's attention.

Feeling forgotten, Tina realizes the only way up is to take her career and destiny in hand and build her own happy ending; which is perfect because, for a romance writer, Tina isn't the most traditional of women . . . Although she does see her long term partner lover *friend,* Sergei, once a week which is 'quite enough, thank you very much'. But her uncomplicated love life might soon need some unravelling when a mysterious Tube Man, unwelcome ex-husband and a shadowy figure in a butterfly mask waltz into the picture.

Only Tina can work through the drama and claim the life she's always wanted . . . but will she succeed?

Are you signed up to the

Trisha Ashley
NEWSLETTER?

Trisha's newsletters are full of exclusive
content and the first place to find out about
book deals and competitions.

You will discover recipes and craft ideas
inspired by your favourite characters
and sneak-peeks into new books.

To sign up to the newsletter, search
for Trisha Ashley on **penguin.co.uk**

All year round, you will always
find a warm welcome in a book by

Trisha Ashley

Page
TURNERS

Great stories.
Unforgettable characters.
Unbeatable deals.

WELCOME TO PAGE TURNERS.
A PLACE FOR PEOPLE WHO LOVE TO READ.

In bed, in the bath, on your lunch break.
Wherever you are, you love to lose yourself in a brilliant story.

And because we know how that feels, every month we choose
books you'll love, and send you an ebook at an amazingly low price.

From tear-jerkers to love stories, family dramas and gripping
crime, we're here to help you find your next must-read.

Don't miss our book-inspired prizes and sneak peeks into
the most exciting releases.

Sign up to our FREE newsletter at
penguin.co.uk/newsletters/page-turners

SPREAD THE BOOK LOVE AT